'What previous experience have you had as a footman?' she asked.

'I worked for the Duchesse de la Croix-Blanche and the Comtesse de Dreux,' he replied.

She completed the brief note and looked up, surprising him with the quiet intensity of her scrutiny. Her mood had seemed so impatient he'd not thought she'd taken the time to study him closely. The man Pierce was pretending to be might well have shuffled uncomfortably beneath her gaze, but he wasn't inclined to give her that advantage, so he fixed his eyes on a point just past her shoulder and waited her out.

Nevertheless, he was aware of the way her eyes measured the breadth of his shoulders and the fit of his coat. She looked at his hands. Then her gaze shifted to his thighs, hesitated—and stayed there.

Good God! The lady wasn't trying to hire a footman—she was measuring his ability to fulfil her requirements in a lover! For an instant Pierce was shocked by her boldness. Then he was coldly amused. It seemed he was not the only one who had seduction in mind.

Author Note

I had the original idea for a story featuring a hero who takes a position as the heroine's footman while I was reading *Memoirs of Madame de la Tour du Pin*. Henrietta-Lucy was a young, fashionable lady in French noble society who witnessed at first hand all the upheavals and dangers of the Revolution. Within the space of a few years she was presented to Queen Marie-Antoinette, had to hide from zealous Revolutionaries, and then fled to safety in America.

Her footman, Zamore, was with her throughout these adventures. He is mentioned briefly but frequently in her memoirs. He was so talented at dressing Henrietta-Lucy's hair that when Henrietta-Lucy was staying with her husband at the Court in The Hague the Princess of Orange wanted Zamore to dress *her* hair. But Zamore was also loyal and brave. Even when she no longer trusted her other servants, he played an important part in helping Henrietta-Lucy and her children remain safe during hazardous episodes in her life.

I loved the idea of writing about a hero in a role which not only made it possible for him to become part of the heroine's household within hours of meeting her, but actually *required* him to stay close to her.

Mélusine, the heroine of MY LORD FOOTMAN, notices immediately that her new footman has a natural air of authority he can't quite conceal— and he's also disturbingly attractive…

MY LORD FOOTMAN

Claire Thornton

MILLS & BOON

Pure reading pleasure

First published in Great Britain 2007
Large Print edition 2008
Harlequin Mills & Boon Limited,
Eton House, 18-24 Paradise Road, Richmond, Surrey TW9 1SR

© Claire Thornton 2007

ISBN: 978 0 263 20153 6

Set in Times Roman 14½ on 16 pt.
42-0408-88246

Printed and bound in Great Britain
by Antony Rowe Ltd, Chippenham, Wiltshire

MY LORD FOOTMAN

Claire Thornton grew up in the Sussex countryside. Her love of history began as a child, when she imagined Roman soldiers marching along the route of the old Roman Road which runs straight through her village high street. It is also a family legend that her ancestors were involved in smuggling, which further stimulated her interest in how people lived in the past. She loves immersing herself in the historical background for her books, and recently taught herself bobbin lace-making as part of her research. She enjoys handicrafts of all kinds, and regularly has her best ideas when she is working on a piece of cross stitch. Claire has also written under the name of Alice Thornton. She can be contacted via her website at www.clairethornton.com

Recent novels by the same author:

RAVEN'S HONOUR
GIFFORD'S LADY

and in the *City of Flames* series:

THE DEFIANT MISTRESS
THE ABDUCTED HEIRESS
THE VAGABOND DUCHESS

Chapter One

Morning, Wednesday, 8 July 1789

A woman depended on the men in her life for comfort and security; it was a man's duty to provide for those who depended on him. Pierce had learnt that lesson at the age of seventeen when his father's debts had left his mother and his siblings facing destitution. Eleven years later, he had not forgotten his mother's distress after his father's death, nor the desperate measures a man or woman might be forced to take to survive.

But despite his natural sympathy for a widow in straitened circumstances, blackmail could not be tolerated. If long-kept secrets were exposed to the world, the result would not only be scandalous, but possibly fatal to at least one of the individuals involved.

The Comtesse de Gilocourt had been widowed eight months ago. Until her husband's death she had been mistress of a magnificent town house in the most exclusive part of Paris. Now she'd apparently leased an apartment in a house in the place Vendôme on the other side of the Seine. The place Vendôme was a respectable, prosperous square, but it was the home of bankers, not members of the elite, fashionable society the Comtesse had been part of during her marriage.

Pierce stood in the empty hallway outside the first-floor apartment, waiting to be summoned. The staircase that led down to the ground floor and up to the apartments above was elegant and well proportioned. The French often made the staircase an important architectural feature of their houses, because it was usually the first thing visitors saw, but the Comtesse had done nothing to make the hall outside her apartment more comfortable or inviting.

The door opened and the previous candidate emerged. Pierce threw him a quick, appraising look. The man had been smugly confident when he'd entered the room. Now there was a slight jerkiness to his movements, which suggested the interview had not gone according to his plan. He avoided Pierce's gaze as he went past. Pierce heard footsteps within the room approaching the half-open door and turned fully towards it.

A lady in a dove-grey muslin gown, with a mass of auburn curls tumbling around her shoulders, suddenly appeared before him. Despite himself, Pierce almost blinked at the unexpected sight of so much fiery disorder. Curls were in vogue, but so was hair powder— white was generally considered the most flattering colour. Pierce had known Bertier's second wife was over twenty years his junior, so he'd expected the Comtesse to be young. But he hadn't expected her to be so vividly colourful. She had moss-green eyes, clear, pale skin and freckles across her nose and cheeks that she hadn't concealed with cosmetics. Nor had he expected her to look the epitome of fresh innocence. He wondered if she'd known her husband was a master smuggler while he was still alive—or if she'd only discovered that after his death when she'd found the evidence she'd used in her blackmail scheme.

Despite his initial surprise, he stood submissively as she looked him up and down, his expression revealing none of his thoughts. Over the years he'd learned to let others see only what he wanted them to see, and it suited him that the Comtesse should see only a servant in need of employment.

Her cheeks were pink with heightened emotion and there was a stormy expression in her eyes. Pierce wondered what the previous candidate had done to rouse her temper. Her eyes lingered briefly on the neatly mended pocket of the coat he'd bought from a second-hand shop. Its original owner had been a member of the prosperous bourgeoisie and a slightly larger man than Pierce. He knew he looked like many other servants wearing the hand-me-down clothes of their betters.

The Comtesse glanced round the hallway. 'Are you the last one?'

'Yes, *madame*.' He hadn't been, but it had only

required a few well-chosen comments to discourage the lad who'd been waiting with him.

'Hmm.' She frowned and turned with an impatient swish of her skirts. 'Enter,' she said.

He followed her into the room, appreciating the curve of her hips before his gaze was once more drawn to her hair. Several long, thick tresses cascaded down her back. Many ladies adopted such a style, but frequently they needed hairpieces to achieve such abundance. Its distinctive colour and lack of powder made it clear the lady needed no artificial assistance. Pierce felt an inexplicable urge to touch the shimmering curls. A brief, ironic smile twitched his lips and vanished before the lady could turn and see it. Since Rosalie's death, he had been unmoved by feminine attractions. It struck him as somewhat perverse that the first woman who'd stirred his interest was a blackmailer. He'd not planned on seducing the information he needed from his quarry, but he was adaptable. And the lady was…surprisingly alluring.

She wore a soft green sash around her waist, which matched her eyes, but was very definitely not mourning attire. Her husband had died eight months ago—she should still be wearing black silk and black jewellery. But she wore no jewellery, not even, Pierce noticed with sharpened interest, her wedding ring. What did that omission signify?

The lady's full skirts lengthened to a short train at the back and slightly muffled her footsteps, but Pierce's heels echoed loudly on the bare floorboards. It was a large salon, which seemed even larger because it was almost entirely unfurnished. There were no pictures on the walls—though Pierce could see patches where they had once been—and no curtains at the tall, multi-paned windows that overlooked the square below. The only furniture consisted of a table and one upright chair. Pierce noted these signs of the Comtesse's reduced circumstances with dispassionate interest.

She sat down at the table. Several pieces of paper were scattered over the surface, most of which had been written on. She pulled a clean sheet towards her and picked up the pen.

'What is your name?' she asked briskly.

'Pierre Dumont,' said Pierce, and watched as she wrote it down.

'What previous experience have you had as a footman?' she asked, still focusing on the paper.

'I worked for the Duchesse de la Croix-Blanche and the Comtesse de Dreux,' he replied.

She completed the brief note and looked up at him, surprising him with the quiet intensity of her scrutiny. Her mood had seemed so impatient he'd not thought she'd taken the time to study him closely. The man Pierce was pretending to be might well have shuffled uncomfortably beneath her gaze, but he wasn't inclined to give her that advantage, so he fixed his eyes on a point just past her shoulder and waited her out.

Nevertheless, he was aware of the way her eyes

measured the breadth of his shoulders and the fit of his coat. She looked at his hands. Then her gaze shifted to his thighs, hesitated—and stayed there.

Good God! The lady wasn't trying to hire a footman—she was measuring his ability to fulfil her requirements in a lover! For an instant Pierce was shocked by her boldness. Then he was coldly amused. It seemed he was not the only one who had seduction in mind.

He'd stood in the bare hallway, steeling himself not to feel sorry for a poor widow who'd made an error of judgement. But a woman who boldly recruited her lovers from unemployed servants didn't need his sympathy. He lowered his gaze to look into the lady's eyes.

The morning had not gone well. Mélusine had never hired a servant before. She didn't want to do so now. She'd left the responsibility for selecting the household staff to her lawyer, Monsieur Barrière, but she wasn't willing to delegate the choice of footman to anyone else. Her experiences had prejudiced her against the tribe. If she could have done without a footman she would—but a lady needed a liveried servant to escort her about town, run her errands and stand behind her chair to serve her when she dined as a guest in other people's houses. Since the man would be by her side every time she appeared in public, she wanted one whose presence she could at least tolerate.

She stared at Pierre Dumont, trying to see past his impassive expression to the man beneath. The last candidate had sensed her lack of experience in such interviews and tried to take over the direction of the conversation. Mélusine had arrived in Paris resolved never to let a man make her decisions again. She hadn't appreciated a prospective servant trying to dictate her actions and her response had been curt. She didn't know which of them had been more ruffled by the encounter. She'd been glad to see him go.

Dumont hadn't tried to dominate the conversation. He hadn't done anything except obey her orders and wait patiently for her next question. Despite his wooden expression, she didn't think he was dim-witted. She'd seen his eyes flick to her unpowdered hair and then to her gown. He was wondering why she wasn't wearing mourning. She had in Bordeaux. For eight months she'd worn black twill gowns, a black crepe belt, black crepe hats, black gloves, black shoes…

She was sick of black.

It would be another four months before she could wear colours in public. But for the first time in her life she was the undisputed mistress in her own home—and here she could wear what she liked.

No black. No powder—and she'd have preferred no footman. But that wasn't a reasonable option.

Dumont was staring at a point past her shoulder. She didn't believe he was slow-witted. He clearly wasn't nervous of her, and his demeanour revealed none of his thoughts. All of which made her wary. She'd been in his position too many times—standing impassively in the presence of a more powerful person—to believe he *had* no thoughts. What was he thinking?

She took her time looking at him. It was disconcerting, but very satisfactory to be the one in the position of power. She judged him to be five feet nine or ten inches. His plain wig was mouse brown. No doubt he'd worn something far grander when he'd served the Duchesse de la Croix-Blanche. His eyebrows were much darker, which made her wonder why he'd adopted the wig even when he was unemployed. Perhaps he was going bald and vain about his hair?

His coat didn't quite fit, but it was carefully mended. It was the wrong choice of colour for him and at first glance gave a false impression of his figure. He was straight and lean, but she suspected there was power in his compact body. He'd done no more than stand still and walk across the room, yet she'd seen men who had that unquestioned confidence in their physical prowess before.

Mélusine was fascinated by that masculine quality, though she'd come to the conclusion it gave more pleasure depicted in marble than experienced in the flesh. She looked at Dumont's hands. Hands could tell important stories. Dumont's hung relaxed and empty by his thighs. She looked at his legs, remembering the classical statues she'd seen in the Louvre and elsewhere. If he removed his breeches, would his thigh muscles be as clearly delineated as those in the statues she'd seen? Excitement quickened within her as she realised there might be unanticipated compensations to hiring a footman. She would have to word her request very carefully—and it wasn't his thighs that particularly interested her—but maybe…

It belatedly occurred to her that she'd been staring at his legs for far too long. She looked up and her gaze clashed shockingly with his. She caught her breath as she realised he'd noticed the direction of her gaze. There was an ironic, slightly cynical gleam in his grey eyes that made her face flame with embarrassment.

'Do you have testimonials?' she demanded curtly.

He raised one eyebrow. 'In what capacity?'

'As a footman.' She resisted the urge to grit her teeth. 'You're no use to me if you've spent the past ten years as a schoolmaster.'

A faint crease appeared briefly between his brows. He was either offended or confused by her comment. She didn't know what had put the idea into her mind either, except that he was dressed all in dull brown and his reserved demeanour gave him a certain austerity.

'I am not a schoolmaster.' He drew some folded sheets from an inner pocket, and presented them with a graceful bow that reminded Mélusine uncomfortably of her own lack of grace. The merchant's daughter had been educated in a convent alongside the daughters of noblemen, and even married a comte—

but her deportment had never quite reached the pinnacle of languid elegance.

She tried to read the flowing writing, but she was distracted by the knowledge he was watching her. His position, standing before her while she sat, was entirely appropriate to their stations, but she disliked the way he was now looking down at her with self-controlled, ironical scrutiny.

'Sit down at once!' she ordered.

Both his eyebrows elevated, then he glanced around the bare chamber.

'Do you want me to sit on the floor?'

'Oh, for Heaven's sake!' Mélusine exclaimed, taking refuge in exasperation. 'I'm not surprised you're seeking new employment if you're always so insufferably supercilious!' She jumped up and planted her own chair in the middle of the room. 'Sit there. Now!'

Part of her thought she would be wiser to terminate this interview, but Dumont was the last candidate for the post. He was unsettling her, but he didn't make her skin creep. After two years of enduring Jean-Baptiste's services, that was a very important qualification for any footman she employed in future. Besides, there was an element of pride involved. She'd come to Paris determined to take charge of her own life. At the very least she should be able to hire a footman.

She took several brisk paces away from Dumont, then turned to face him. This was better. He was sitting, looking up at her, and she was free to move about the room as she pleased.

'Why are you looking for a new position?' she asked, feeling in control again.

'I travelled to America with my previous mistress. She decided to stay in America longer, but I wanted to come back to France.' He shrugged slightly. 'So, here I am.'

'America?' Bertier had been one of the French officers who'd fought beside the Americans in the War of Independence. There had been many American visitors to Paris over the past few years and Mélusine had been fascinated by the stories she'd heard about the new republic.

She opened her mouth to ask Pierre about his experiences in the new world, and then thought better of it. Instead she stood by the empty hearth and read the testimonials he'd given her.

'The Duchesse de la Croix-Blanche writes very highly of you,' she said at last. Madame de la Croix-Blanche's comments were verging on fulsome.

'She was graciously willing to give me a reference when I left her service,' Dumont replied.

'Hmm.' Mélusine tapped the papers against the palm of her hand as she stared at him through narrowed eyes. 'If I employ you—and I am in grave doubt as to your suitability at present—I expect you to be loyal, discreet and obedient in all things.'

'Would you be better able to assess my suitability if I remove my breeches?' Dumont asked.

'*What?*' Mélusine thought she must have surely have misheard him, but to her shock he stood up.

'These are the attributes in which you are most interested, are they not?' he said, and began to unfasten his breeches.

'*Stop!*' She thrust out her hands towards him, the papers she still held rustling wildly. 'Do not move a muscle!'

He obeyed her shrieked command except for one arched eyebrow.

She took a deep breath and fanned his testimonials in front of her overheated face.

'You are a rogue. A scoundrel. A…a…' Words failed her. 'Sit down again at once. And do not, on any account, allow any particle of your clothing to come undone or come off. Good God!'

To her relief he obeyed. She was trembling, her heart racing. She looked at him warily, wondering if she should scream for Paul the porter—or simply order him from the house. He blandly returned her gaze, which was almost as unsettling as his previous action. She glanced away and caught sight of the fire irons from the corner of her eye. Acting on instinct, she bent down and seized the poker. Then she looked swiftly back at Dumont, alarmed she might have provoked him to anger.

He grinned. 'By all means arm yourself, madame. I have never yet bedded an unwilling woman.'

'Bedded…?' His obvious amusement reduced her fear, though not her shock or embarrassment.

'That is the discreet service you require from me, is it not?' he said.

'*No.*' Mélusine shuddered. 'Never.' An idea suddenly occurred to her. She retreated to one of the windows, as far from Dumont as it was possible to get. 'Do not move,' she ordered, then reread his references with new insight.

'Is *that* why the Duchesse is so fulsome about your abilities?' she exclaimed, staring at him in a completely new way when she'd finished. 'How long were you her lover?' Despite her fascination, Mélusine kept a good grip on the poker. She was under no illusions that, servant though he was, the only reason Dumont was still sitting in the chair, answering her questions, was because he chose to do so.

'I wasn't her lover.'

'I see you remain discreet and loyal even though she is no longer your mistress.'

'My employer,' Dumont corrected.

'If the Duchesse was not your lover, what on earth made you think *I* would require such a…a service?' Mélusine asked sceptically. 'Something must have put the idea into your head.'

'You did,' Dumont retorted.

'*I…*' He must be referring to the way she'd looked at him at the beginning of the interview. 'My footman will be required to escort me when I leave the house, take messages for me, dress my hair—but those are the *only* services I require from him,' she said, with emphasis.

'Your hair?'

'Mmm.' It was common for the roles of footman and hairdresser to be combined. No one as fashionably elegant as the Duchesse would ever have employed someone who couldn't fill both capacities. Mélusine was about to move on to her next question when it occurred to her that, if the Duchesse had employed Pierre for his other talents in the boudoir, his hairdressing skills might be lacking.

'You can dress hair, can't you?' she said, frowning at him.

'Assuredly,' he said.

'You said you left the Duchesse's service because you wanted to return to France. Why was that?' she asked. She couldn't employ him. Of course she couldn't. A man so boorish he threatened to remove his breeches in front of her! But she wanted to terminate the interview with dignity—not order him to leave with all the authority of a frightened deer.

When she was in command of the conversation—and when she was sure he *knew* she was in command of the conversation—she would dismiss him.

He paused. 'For the sake of my mother and sister,' he said, when she was beginning to wonder if he would answer her question.

'Your *mother*?' That was the last thing she'd expected him to say. 'I suppose your father is dead and you must provide for them.'

'Yes.'

Mélusine stared at him. There was such an air of cool independence about him that she would never have guessed he was motivated by a sense of family obligation.

'Do they live in Paris?'

'No.'

'Where, then? Why are you not with them?'

'Brittany,' he said curtly. 'There are more opportunities for me in Paris.'

'But it is easier and quicker to send money to them from here than from America,' Mélusine said. 'I dare say you must find them a tiresome obligation.'

It was his turn to frown. 'No.' He looked at her so disapprovingly that Mélusine had to resist the urge to take a step backwards.

'I'm sure they would be shocked if they'd seen your behaviour just now,' she said. He had no business judging *her* when he was the one with no sense of propriety.

His expression lightened in a brief smile. 'Probably. What happened to your last footman?'

Mélusine had been thinking his smile was unexpectedly attractive and the question took her completely by surprise.

Her last memories of Jean-Baptiste flashed into her mind. She didn't want to think about him and she certainly didn't want to talk about him.

'He's gone,' she said brusquely. 'You need not concern yourself with him.'

'Is he coming back?' Dumont's voice was mild but his eyes were sharp.

'I haven't even decided you will be my footman yet,' said Mélusine coldly, determined not to let him interrogate her. 'It is presumptuous of you to speculate on how long your employment with me will last.'

He inclined his head, but there was nothing submissive about his posture.

She ought to send him away. A footman who acted as if he were her equal was the last thing she needed. From what she'd seen of him, if she wasn't careful, Dumont would be taking charge of her household and challenging every order she gave him from the moment she appointed him. But he was a servant, who would be dependent upon her for his wages, which meant the ultimate power lay with her. And he wasn't sly or snide. He'd threatened to remove his breeches, but he'd stopped the moment she told him to, and he'd remained in the chair throughout the rest of their conversation. Could she tolerate his hands in her hair every day? She looked down at them, still resting palm down on his thighs.

He held them out, turning them over for her inspection. She bit back a startled exclamation. She wasn't used to having her thoughts read. His hands were clean, well shaped, with neatly trimmed nails. She imagined them in her hair, and a small, not unpleasant shiver rippled along her spine. She would not take him, or any other man, as her lover, but it might be acceptable to have her hair done by him.

'Thank you,' she said coolly. 'I am sure you are as

adept with comb and pomade as you are with words. I will give you a trial,' she continued briskly. 'If, at the end of the week, you have proved satisfactory, I will employ you permanently. If you displease me before then, I will dismiss you instantly.'

'Thank you, *madame*.' He gave her a seated bow.

'Good. Stand up and wait while I write a note to Monsieur Barrière. You must take it to him when I have finished.'

'Monsieur Barrière?' Dumont stood and set the chair before the table for her.

'My lawyer. You must look elegant and imposing—and your coat must fit properly! And you need a better wig. Since you're only on trial, I won't have a complete livery made for you yet. I have some braid in my trunk,' she added as an afterthought. 'Once you have a suitable coat, I'll sew it on.'

Mélusine followed Pierre Dumont to the door and watched him walk down the stairs. Paul, the porter, opened the door for Dumont and he went out. Paul went back into the servants' quarters on the ground floor and the house suddenly seemed very empty. Mélusine realised she was trembling and sank down on to the stairs. She was afraid she'd made a terrible mistake, but she reminded herself it wasn't too late to change her mind. If she didn't like having Pierre Dumont as her footman, she would simply dismiss him. After so many years of having little say in who

served her, it was going to take a while before she took
her new freedom for granted.

Despite that, she couldn't help replaying her conversation with Dumont. She was still shocked by his
apparent willingness to remove his breeches—if he did
anything like that again, she would dismiss him instantly. But perhaps it had only been a misunderstand-
ing caused by the way she'd looked at his legs,
especially since he might have been the Duchesse's
lover. He'd denied the charge very firmly, but he could
have done that out of loyalty to his former mistress.

She twitched her shoulders. It was odd to think she
was employing another woman's lover to dress her hair
and run her errands. On the other hand, she'd been
married to a man who'd spent most of their marriage
in another woman's bed. Paris was full of infidelity. No
doubt all the male servants she'd previously known
had been someone's lover. The only difference with
Dumont was that she knew the lady's name.

She smiled wryly. It was very unlikely any of the
other servants she'd known had had such a distinguished lover. No wonder Dumont was so arrogant. But
he'd left the Duchesse to be nearer to his mother and
sister, and he'd seemed offended at the suggestion he
found them a burden. And when he'd spoken of them
his expression had briefly softened into genuine affection. It was that single fact, more than any other, which
had swayed her decision in his favour. She wondered
what he was like when he was in their company. He'd

admitted they would have been shocked by his brazen behaviour. She was sure he gave them orders and believed he knew what was best for them, but she imagined him giving his orders in a kind voice with consideration for their feelings…

What on earth was she thinking! She was building his entire family history on a couple of brief remarks and a half-smile. She stood up and deliberately turned her attention to the house. It belonged to her now.

Her husband had been found dead in the Bois de Boulogne on the outskirts of Paris, at the beginning of the previous November. No one knew exactly who'd killed him, but the police inspector who'd brought his body to the house had said he'd been the victim of brigands. The harvest had failed, the winter had already turned harsh and there had been an increasing number of robberies and attacks on carriages.

Mélusine had been deeply shocked by Bertier's death, and almost as surprised when she'd discovered he'd left her this house and two others in Paris. For the first time in her life she had an independent income. Until a month ago the house in the place Vendôme had still been leased to the Champiers, who'd sublet the first-floor apartment to their cousins. When the Champiers' lease had expired and they moved out, it had been a Heaven-sent opportunity for Mélusine. For once in his life, her father had been too busy to inter-fere in her affairs, and she had quietly made plans to leave his home in Bordeaux and return to Paris. The empty house had given her a safe destination. All she'd had to do was write to Monsieur Barrière and ask him to hire reliable staff and furnish the house with what she considered the most basic necessities. She was going to start a new life.

She walked slowly up the stairs. One of the first decisions she must make was whether she would lease the first-floor apartment. But she didn't need the rent, so perhaps for the time being she would limit the number of strangers who entered her house.

Someone knocked on the front door. She didn't pay any attention at first, but when the knocking grew more insistent she decided Paul must be out of earshot and went back downstairs.

She opened the door and found herself face to face with Daniel Blanc. She felt a brief spurt of pleasure at his familiar face, then her stomach twisted with apprehension and she looked past him to see if her father was waiting in a carriage. She'd known Daniel since she was a child. He was one of her father's most trusted servants. She'd not sent her father a message to say she was coming to Paris. She'd asked the servants not to send one either, but one of them must have done so as soon as she'd left Bordeaux.

Daniel's eyes widened at the sight of her opening the door, but he quickly recovered his poise. 'A message from your father, *madame.*'

'Where is he?'

'Versailles, *madame.*'

Mélusine's tension eased at the discovery Raoul Fournier was still twelve miles distant from her, though the sight of his handwriting on the letter still made her slightly nauseous. She'd hoped his duties as one of the representatives at the Estates-General would occupy all his thoughts and time. But he hadn't become one of the wealthiest men in Bordeaux by doing only one thing at a time.

She stood back and opened the door wider. 'Thank you,' she said to Daniel. 'Go to the kitchen. I don't know what there'll be to eat, but I'm sure there'll be something.'

'I am to wait for a reply,' he said, almost apologetically.

She gripped the letter fiercely, wishing she could tear it up unopened. 'Go and eat.' She kept her voice as even as she could.

When she was alone, she broke the seal. As she'd expected, the tone was angry and impatient. She skimmed over the angular black sentences, coming to the heart of the matter. Her father ordered her to wait upon him in Versailles as soon as she arrived in Paris.

Her stomach churned with frustration and temper as she balled the letter between her hands. She'd only been in Paris a day, and already her father was trying to take control. She was so sick of being ruled by men—used by men—to achieve their own ends. In a sudden rush of fury she threw the letter at the wall. She would never let anyone rule her again.

Chapter Two

Afternoon, Wednesday, 8 July 1789

Pierce stood impassively as the lawyer read the letter he'd just delivered from Mélusine, and his references.

'Your testimonials appear to be in order,' Barrière said at length. He sat back and looked at Pierce. 'The Comtesse's late husband entrusted me with her affairs. Be assured you would be ill-advised to take advantage of your situation in any way.'

Pierce studied the lawyer with equal interest, but less openly. He gained the impression Barrière was a shrewd and intelligent man. He'd have expected no less of anyone Bertier had chosen to deal with his affairs. But was the lawyer also involved in the blackmail scheme? The blackmail letter had been written in Latin and delivered by a man who'd been recognised as the Comtesse the Gilocourt's footman. During Pierce's interview Mélusine had refused to talk about her previous footman, but Pierce knew very well his predecessor in the role had been seen in London acting as the blackmailer's messenger. Pierce speculated the blackmail letter might have been written in Latin to keep its contents secret from the footman delivering it. Was the lawyer the one who'd composed the letter for Mélusine?

'Why did the Comtesse's last footman leave?' Pierce asked.

Barrière frowned. 'Madame the Gilocourt was widowed last November,' he said. 'Now she has returned to Paris she needs staff for her new establishment. That is all I can say.'

Establishment was rather a grand term for an unfurnished, first-floor apartment, but Pierce didn't comment.

'So you've only been working for the Comtesse since her husband died,' he said, earning another frown from the lawyer. 'I just want to be sure my wages will be paid,' Pierce added, since it was now obvious Barrière couldn't be drawn into gossiping about his noble client.

'Madame de Gilocourt has instructed that you be given the first week's wages in advance,' Barrière said coldly. 'If you betray her generosity I will see you are severely punished. Call Ladoux in from the outer chamber.'

Ladoux was more amenable to gossip than his master, and Pierce discovered Monsieur Barrière had only met Mélusine on two occasions. The first time had been when he visited her immediately after her husband's death, just before she left Paris to go back

to Bordeaux. The second time had been a couple of
days ago when she'd returned to Paris. Anything was
possible, but Pierce thought it was unlikely they'd
formed a criminal partnership on such a slight acquaintanceship.

After the arrangements for his new livery were
complete, Pierce headed to the Palais Royal. Before
he'd come to France he'd known the country was in the
midst of a political and financial crisis, but until he'd
arrived in Paris he hadn't realised how volatile the
mood of the people was. The Palais Royal, even though
it was owned by the Duc d'Orléans, a relative of the
King, was the focal point for vehement opposition to
the government. Pierce's priority was hunting the
blackmailer, not following the intricacies of French
politics, but he didn't like to be taken by surprise by
events, so he went to read the latest pamphlets and hear
the latest oratory.

It seemed as though half of the population of Paris
thronged the garden and arcades of the Palais Royal.
There were booksellers here, cafés, *modistes*, even a
waxwork museum. Pierce strolled through the crowds,
keeping an alert eye for pickpockets.

'Pinks, *monsieur*. Buy my beautiful pinks?'

Pierce looked at the bunch of draggled flowers under
his nose and then up into the eyes of the girl offering it
to him. He had no use for the flowers, but the girl was
thin and her eyes a little desperate. Bread was scarce and
the price high. He thought she was probably hungry.

He looked into her basket and said, 'Hmm, let me see. I do not think one bunch will be sufficient to express my feelings for my sweetheart. I will have one…two… three…four seem to fit comfortably in my hand. No, four seems an unlucky number. I will have five.'

She gave a little gasp. *'Monsieur!'*

'I must lay them down for a moment to count out the money,' he said, putting the bunches back in the basket to do so. 'Here you are.' He was mildly amused that the first thing he'd bought with his footman's wages was a handful of pinks.

He reclaimed his purchase and turned away.

'Monsieur,' she called after him. 'You have left four bunches behind.'

'On second thoughts, I was afraid she might think me overeager if I gave her five bunches,' he explained ruefully. 'Keep the others. I will claim them from you another time. It won't be today.' He smiled at her, and saw she understood he'd never ask for them. She was free to sell them again.

'Thank you, *monsieur,*' she whispered, her eyes suddenly shimmering. 'Good fortune be with you.'

'And with you.' He moved on through the crowds, wondering what he was going to do with the one bunch of pinks he'd kept.

A pamphlet seller thrust the latest vicious attack on the Queen into his free hand. On his arrival in Paris, Pierce had been amazed at the lurid obscenity in the images of Marie Antoinette sold openly in the streets.

English cartoonists lampooned prominent members of society, and sometimes the cartoons could be cruel, but Pierce had never seen any pamphlets in London which so blatantly portrayed their victim as irredeemably depraved. Even though Marie Antoinette had spent more than half her life in France, married to Louis XVI, the people still called her *l'Autrichienne*—the Austrian woman—and much worse besides.

But the hostility to the Queen was only one contributing element to the volatile mood in Paris. France was in crisis. The previous winter had been severe and the harvest poor, which was why the price of bread was now so high that many could not afford it. Earlier in the year the King had been forced to summon the Estates-General—the general assembly of the three orders of French society—for the first time in nearly two centuries.

Even before the Estates-General had first met there had been controversy over the voting—if each estate had one vote, the first two estates could always outvote the third estate. The opening procession and ceremony, when the first two estates, the clergy and the nobility, had worn their grandest robes, while the third estate, the people of France, had been confined to sombre black, had provoked more ill feeling and resentment. Since then there had been continual disputes, with the third estate in constant conflict with the other two estates. The conflict had come to a head when the third estate had found itself locked out of its meeting hall. The representatives had gone en masse to a nearby tennis court and taken an oath that they would never separate until an acceptable constitution had been established.

All these events had been reported in England, but it was one thing to read about dramatic happenings in newsprint and another to find oneself at the very heart of the events being reported. Pierce was fascinated by all he saw and heard.

The Tennis Court Oath had been taken on June 20. It was now July 8th and tensions had continued to rise. The Estates-General was taking place in Versailles and news of events there was constantly reported and debated in the Palais Royal. The King had responded by sending troops around and into the city, which only increased the suspicions and resentment of the people. Pierce paused for a while to listen to a man who jumped on a table to harangue the crowds with the need to support the third estate. Many of the people gathered around him shouted back. It seemed to Pierce that everyone in Paris had turned politician and had an opinion. By temperament his sympathies were with the third estate, but he was in France hunting a blackmailer and he couldn't afford to let himself be distracted for too long.

He left the Palais Royal and headed to the rue Saint-Honoré. His destination was the shop of the *marchande des modes*, Clothilde Moreau. Clothilde's shop was one of the most fashionable in a very fashionable street. It sold all kinds of gorgeous accessories to suit the taste and requirements of the most elegant ladies.

Pierce had been slightly overwhelmed by the range of ribbons, flowers, feathers, gauze and lace in which Clothilde traded. In between speaking to her during his first visit he had listened to her advise and cajole several customers into trying new styles or experimenting with a different accessory.

She was also Pierce's means of contact with England. She didn't know his real name and she had no idea who was in overall command of the chain of people who communicated via her shop but, as she'd cheerfully told Pierce, she was a practical businesswoman who enjoyed making a profit. All kinds of profit. And she was paid well for her clandestine activities. Pierce suspected she also enjoyed the intrigue, but he hadn't said so.

'Ah, *monsieur*, you are back.' She came over to him as he entered the shop. 'Was your purchase successful? Did the lady like what you offered? Ah, you have bought her flowers?' She glanced at the pinks he still carried. Compared to the opulent finery in her shop, they made a very poor display. Pierce wasn't surprised she looked askance at them.

'I believe she was charmed with the gift,' he replied, smiling. 'Your advice was most helpful. Please accept this small—very small—token of my gratitude.' He presented the pinks to her with a handsome flourish.

'Thank you, *monsieur*! I am pleased I was of assistance. Is there any other way I may be of service? Some ribbons, perhaps—or an aigrette for her hair?'

'It is certainly along those lines I'm thinking,' he replied, glancing at a stand displaying a magnificently feather-plumed hat.

'You want to buy her a hat?' Clothilde asked, following the direction of his gaze.

'No, *mam'zelle*, I want to learn how to do her hair,' he replied.

Midday, Thursday, 9 July 1789

'Thank you, Suzanne, there is no need for you to remain while Pierre dresses my hair,' Mélusine said to her maid.

Since her new servants had been chosen for her by Monsieur Barrière, she didn't know any of them very well. So far Suzanne had barely said a word. Mélusine hadn't sensed any overt ill-will from her, but she'd been acutely aware of how the maid surreptitiously watched her whenever they were together and she didn't want to be under such close observation while Pierre dressed her hair for the first time.

She sat very still as Pierre approached, her fingers locked tightly together beneath the folds of her muslin peignoir. Despite her best efforts to appear composed, she tensed even more as he untied the ribbon she'd threaded through her curls first thing that morning. He pulled it slowly free and dropped it on to the dressing table. Then he put his hands under the weight of her hair and she felt the first shock of contact as his fingers grazed the back of her neck. She couldn't control her quick intake of breath. It was the first time a man had touched her hair since Jean-Baptiste. The first time a man had touched her in *any* way since Bertier's death.

She couldn't take a deep breath to steady herself because he was so close to her that he would immediately guess she was disturbed. She kept her gaze slightly lowered, fixed on the folds of the cloth covering the dressing table. She could see him in the mirror from the corner of her eyes, but there was no risk of meeting his gaze.

She'd always had difficulty tolerating the two hours or more it could take to create a suitably fashionable style. Some married ladies gathered a group of admirers they'd entertain in their boudoir as they completed the final stages of their *toilette*. To Mélusine's relief, few gentlemen had ever shown any interest in calling upon her in such circumstances, and those who had, had never returned. Her inability to hide her embarrassment had been uncomfortable for all concerned but, try as she might, she simply could not feel at ease entertaining when she considered herself half-dressed. Not that Bertier would have objected. He'd been as fashionable as any other Frenchman in that respect.

Pierre bounced his hands gently under the mass of her hair. She suppressed a slight shiver at a sensation which was unexpectedly pleasurable. She lifted her gaze slightly, just enough that she could see him more easily in the mirror. He was looking down at her hair, his expression very focused. She imagined her hair must be falling over his wrists in a cascade of deep auburn. She couldn't remember Jean-Baptiste ever doing such a thing, or looking so absorbed in his task.

To her huge relief there was no carefully concealed disdain in Pierre's expression as there had so often been in Jean-Baptiste's face. He stepped around her to pick up a comb from the dressing table and began to pull it gently through her hair. He was wearing a black waistcoat over a white shirt, and a white powdered wig. Unlike Jean-Baptiste, who'd never removed any part of his livery in her presence, Pierre had taken off his coat and laid it aside. After her first moment of shock she'd realised it was a very practical action. It would be easier for him to work in his shirt sleeves. Now he was wearing well-fitted clothes, she could see that she'd been right in thinking he had a strong, compact body. She wondered what he looked like without his shirt. The thought was intriguing and a little exciting, but of course she couldn't do anything about finding out until she was completely confident he would not misinterpret her request.

She had spent the morning sewing silver lace to his coat. Everyone else in the household had had more pressing duties, but Mélusine couldn't attend her first dinner since returning to Paris without a liveried footman in attendance, and she wanted him to look impressive.

'You will not tell anyone I sewed your braid,' she said.

He glanced at her briefly in the mirror.

'No, *madame*,' he said. Something in his tone that suddenly made her feel once again like the inexperienced, provincial girl who'd been thrust by marriage into the upper ranks of Parisian society.

Pierre had served a Duchesse, most likely been the Duchesse's lover, though he'd refused to confirm that. He must consider it a step down in the world to serve her. She had haughtily told him she would give him a trial for a week, but was he already looking around for a more stylish, distinguished mistress?

He was looking at her hair, so she felt safe to look directly at him in the mirror. At first glance he was indistinguishable from many other menservants she'd seen. Neatly dressed, unobtrusive in his movements… professionally expressionless.

Except in her experience, that was the ideal—not the reality. Her father might have missed the twitch of bad temper when he'd ordered a footman out into the rain, but she'd always seen it. Just as she'd seen and inwardly cringed from the disdain she'd sensed in Jean-Baptiste. He'd never said anything out of place. Never *done* anything out of place except for the occasional sideways glance or dismissive flick of his fingers, yet she'd known he considered her an object of contempt.

Whereas today, apart from his cool response to her anxiety about the silver braid, Pierre was the perfect servant. And even then, she'd only had an indefinable sense that he considered such gossip beneath him.

Perhaps his tone had not meant that at all. She watched his blank expression as he combed her hair and decided she had seen fairground automatons revealing more individual personality, but she knew he had one.

She'd remembered their first meeting many times, and anticipated this moment with a combination of illicit excitement and terror that she'd made a dreadful mistake. Yet since he'd entered her boudoir, he'd not said or done anything challenging. He had not, in fact, said anything at all. Apart from his brief 'yes, *madame*', all his attention had been fixed on her hair.

She watched him more closely, and saw what she had missed when she'd been tensed for him to make some teasing, inappropriate remark, and half-afraid he might touch her improperly. He was concentrating *very hard* on her hair, and on what he was doing with it. By this time, Jean-Baptiste would have finished combing it out and would be sculpting it into some fashionable coiffure with deft, unfeeling hands. It had been the complexity of the styles which had taken the time, not lack of skill. And Jean-Baptiste had not been over-concerned if he occasionally pulled.

Pierre's hands were larger than Jean-Baptiste's, but she could see—and feel—he was taking care not to pull. His grey eyes were intensely focused, and when he drew the length of one heavy wavy lock of hair through his fingers she was suddenly, inexplicably convinced he'd done so because he enjoyed the sensation.

Pierre laid the comb aside and ran the fingers of both

hands through the heavy mass. Then he started to massage her scalp. She hadn't expected that. Her heart beat a little faster and she only just suppressed a gasp. She became very aware he was standing only a few inches behind her. His body wasn't touching hers, but she could easily imagine that if he moved closer it would. Her hair fell over her eyes and now she was conscious only of the sensation of his fingertips on her scalp, the silky, raspy sound of her hair sliding through his fingers.

Her head was tilted forward; she was blinded by a curtain of auburn curls, and more vulnerable than she'd ever wanted to feel again, yet for a few moments the sensation was so enjoyable she couldn't bring herself to move away. Then she remembered her suspicion that he was taking his time because he wasn't a very experienced hairdresser. He had sounded slightly surprised during his interview when she'd said she expected him to dress her hair. Her brief acquaintance with him led her to believe he wasn't the man to reveal areas in which he was less competent. But perhaps he might be *quieter* than usual when trying to carry out an unfamiliar task? And perhaps he was trying to use his skills as a lover to seduce her attention away from his lack of competence?

'Do you know what you're doing, *monsieur*?' she demanded in a slightly muffled voice.

'Yes.'

'Be more specific.' It was difficult to sound authorita-

tive with her head bent forward and her hair over her
eyes, but she tried to inject a note of command into her
voice.

'I am stimulating your hair to grow even more
luxuriantly.'

'By rubbing my head? You don't know how to do my
hair, do you?' She lifted her head and pushed her hair
out of her eyes. 'You're just trying to distract me from
noticing. The Duchesse hired you because of
your...because...in short, it wasn't for your hairdressing skills.'

'*Madame*, that is a very strange conclusion for you
to draw,' said Pierre coldly.

'I don't see why. Jean-Baptiste would have been
jamming pins in me ages ago—and it only took him
two hours to do it. At the rate you're going, we'll still
be here at midnight.'

'Jamming pins?' Pierre repeated. 'Sacrilege...'

'Oh, for Heaven's sake.' Mélusine reached up and
seized the comb. 'If you can't do my hair, you can't. It
doesn't matter as long as you can open doors and hand
me into my carriage and *look* the part of a footman. You
can pour wine and serve vegetables without spilling
them, can't you?'

'Even in bed,' said Pierre drily. 'However, *madame*,
in defence of the Duchesse's reputation, if not my own,
I must reiterate that she was not, *ever*, my lover.'

'I suppose technically, since she employed you,
you were *her*—'

'I have *never* been paid—' Pierre took a deep breath and muttered something too low for Mélusine to hear. 'Sit quietly and let me work,' he barked.

She jumped and instinctively straightened her spine at the command. Then she remembered she wasn't going to take orders from anyone any more.

'You are not naturally suited to a subordinate role, are you?' she said. 'I noticed that when I was interviewing you. Domestic service does not seem your forte. I can much more easily imagine you as a schoolmaster, perhaps, or…you can read, can't you?'

'*Yes*, Madame de Gilocourt.'

'There is no need to be offended. Many people can't, and it would explain why you haven't risen higher in the world. I could teach you if you like.'

'I don't…' He paused. 'I can read and write French, of course,' he said, 'and speak a little English, though I can't write it. It might be useful to learn more English. Can you teach me that—or any other languages?'

'I can't speak English.' Mélusine sighed. 'Bertier promised to teach me when we were married, but he never did. I have a little Latin, though. That would be useful for a schoolmaster.'

'Yes,' said Pierre. His tone had changed, though Mélusine had no idea why he suddenly sounded so remote when he was accepting her offer. 'I would like you to teach me Latin. Who taught you?'

'The nuns,' she said. 'I was educated in a convent. You don't have to be a schoolmaster if you don't want to.'

He didn't say anything for a while. She watched in the mirror and wondered why there was an underlying grimness in his expression she hadn't seen before. He reached for the curling tongs and she had a sudden, horrible vision of her hair burned off at the scalp.

'Stop!' she shouted. Pierre jumped and then swore under his breath.

'*Madame*, if you do not cease interrupting we really will be here till midnight. Kindly sit still and do *not* shriek when I have hot tongs in my hand.'

Mélusine swallowed, slightly daunted by his tone and reluctant to offend him any more, but very concerned about the future of her hair. 'You are absolutely sure you know what you're doing, aren't you?' she said.

'Yes, *madame.*'

Short of commanding him to stop completely, there was nothing more she could say. She took a deep breath and closed her eyes.

He startled her by laughing. 'Anyone would think you were going to your execution, not having your hair done.'

She opened her eyes and glared at him, even as she recognised there had been nothing unkind in his laughter. 'That's your fault for introducing doubts about your skill into my mind.'

'*Touché, madame.*' He smiled. 'Have no fear. Your hair is so naturally curly the tongs need be applied only lightly.'

To her relief, he was as good as his word.

'I must wear powder today,' she said.

He glanced up, nodded and began to smooth the lemon-scented pomade through her hair, which would fix the powder he later applied. Then he shaped and pinned up her hair in the wide curls that were currently so fashionable. She'd been so sure he didn't know what he was doing that she was quite surprised as the style began to form beneath his hands.

'You have not worn powder before,' he remarked.

'Today I will be among those who will judge me for any lack of…any lack…' Her voice petered away.

He glanced at her in the mirror. 'Do you care?'

'I will learn not to.'

'If you do not expect to enjoy this dinner party, why are you going?' he asked.

'My friend invited me,' said Mélusine. 'She was married while I was in Bordeaux. I wrote to her when I knew I was returning to Paris and her invitation was waiting for me when I arrived. It is not Amalie, it is her guests—' She broke off, annoyed with herself for revealing her nervousness at re-entering French society. 'I'm sorry,' she said.

'Sorry?'

'For doubting your skill as a hairdresser.'

His brief smile didn't reach his eyes. 'I have dressed hair before,' he said. 'Just not recently.'

Mélusine couldn't bear the silence that fell between them. Despite Pierre's brief amusement earlier, even her apology hadn't lightened his mood. She was sure when he'd first started doing her hair he'd been silent simply because he was concentrating on his task, but now she was convinced they were somehow at odds, yet she had no idea why.

'Tell me more about your mother and sister,' she said, remembering how his expression had softened when he'd spoken of them before.

He looked up sharply; for a moment she almost thought he was suspicious of her question, but that made no sense. 'Why?' he asked.

'You came back from America for them,' she said. 'You are doing this for them. I think it is admirable. Not all sons and brothers are so considerate. Not that I have either.' She sighed.

'Would you have liked a brother?' he asked.

'Oh, *yes*,' she said fervently.

'To look after you when your husband died?'

'No. If I'd had a brother, I'd never have needed a husband.'

'You think he would have supported you more generously?'

'No. But it would have been his problem to give my father the noble grandson and heir that obsesses him.' As she met Pierre's shrewdly appraising gaze in the mirror and realised how much she'd just revealed, her stomach cramped with sudden anxiety. 'You must never repeat that to anyone,' she ordered.

'No, *madame*,' he said.

Chapter Three

Dinner was served at the fashionable hour of three, but even before the guests sat down to eat Mélusine felt on edge. Five months ago Amalie had married the Comte de La Fontaine. Mélusine had only a distant acquaintanceship with La Fontaine, but what she'd known of him she hadn't liked. She hoped marriage had improved him but, from the satirical glint in his eyes as he greeted her, she feared it hadn't. When she glanced around and realised all the other guests were the Comte's friends, not Amalie's, she wished she'd visited privately with Amalie before venturing into society in such potentially unfriendly surroundings.

'The Marquis de Sade's been moved from the Bastille,' said La Fontaine.

'Good God! I thought he'd be there for the rest of his mortal life,' the Marquis de Chaumont exclaimed.

'He was shouting licentious slogans at the people below his tower,' La Fontaine explained, which provoked general laughter around the table.

'His wife used to visit him once a week,' said Amalie.

'More fool her—I wouldn't have bothered,' said Sabine de Foix, with a sideways glance at her hostess. Amalie flushed and looked down at her plate.

'Now Saint-André is the most illustrious guest in that Hôtel,' said La Fontaine.

Mélusine froze, hardly believing she'd heard correctly.

'Nicodème de Saint-André in the Bastille!' Chaumont exclaimed. 'For God's sake, why? I hadn't heard that? Are you sure?'

'I heard it from a friend who's a distant cousin of the governor's.'

'No wonder he disappeared so suddenly. I thought he'd gone on a foreign tour.'

'No, he's a prisoner. No idea who's behind that. He's such a paragon of virtue I can't imagine he's committed any sins. Someone must have taken offence at his radical opinions.'

Mélusine gripped her knife so tightly her knuckles turned white. From the moment she'd decided to return to Paris she'd been sick with apprehension whenever she contemplated her first encounter with the Marquis de Saint-André, but she'd never suspected it would be impossible for such a meeting to take place. Why on earth was the man who'd been her husband's closest friend a prisoner in the Bastille?

She realised Chaumont had just asked her a question and with an effort brought her attention back to the conversation.

'I've been back in Paris a couple of days, *monsieur*,' she said.

* * *

Pierce stood behind Mélusine. She was an easy mistress to wait upon at dinner. She did no more than occasionally touch her wine glass to her lips or nibble at her food, and he was able to give most of his attention to the conversation. He'd seen Mélusine's fingers tremble slightly before she gripped her knife, and once she'd gripped it so tightly her knuckles had whitened, so he knew she was aware she was under scrutiny. He'd already discovered she was a very observant woman. He'd assumed the role of servant several times over the years, and few of his temporary employers had ever displayed any curiosity about him, or looked below the surface of what he chose to let them see.

Mélusine watched him all the time. Even while he'd been doing her hair he'd had the sensation she was mentally removing his shirt. Yesterday, when she'd stared at his legs, he'd assumed there was an erotic motive for her behaviour, but now he was less certain.

Her body had been rigid with tension when he'd first touched her hair. She'd tried to conceal her apprehension behind a bored expression, but her demeanour was very far from that of a woman planning to seduce a new lover. She was undoubtedly curious about his supposed affair with the Duchesse, but it was the curiosity of an observer, not someone who intended to participate in similar activity. And when the conversation turned in that direction, her eyes became as wary as a doe in the presence of a hunting hound.

None of that meant she wasn't the blackmailer. Until Pierce had conclusive proof one way or the other, she was still his most important suspect. Despite that, he didn't like putting his hands on a woman who was manifestly nervous of his touch. What he'd really wanted to do was rub the tension out of her shoulders, but as her hairdresser he had no reason to touch anything but her head, so he'd rubbed her scalp instead.

She'd enjoyed it. Even though he'd been able to feel nothing but the hard planes of her skull beneath his fingertips, and the silky fall of her hair over the backs of his hands, he'd sensed the rest of her body becoming more fluid as she relaxed beneath his ministrations. Her skittishness had become part of the challenge. Pierce could imagine no pleasure in bedding a frightened woman. But there would be great reward and satisfaction in coaxing Mélusine from rigid apprehension to back-arching ecstasy.

Underlying that thought was another, darker, one. Who had taught her to be afraid? Her late husband— or another man?

Pierce knew she'd decided to employ him at least partly because she supposed him to be kind to his mother and sister. In fact, he had two sisters and two brothers, but it was safer not to reveal too many precise details about his family. In any case, only one of his sisters was getting married in September, and she was the one he'd been thinking of when he'd answered Mélusine's question. If the evidence in the blackmailer's possession ever became public knowledge, there would be no wedding for Anastasia. But Pierce would not let anything happen that could destroy his sister's happiness.

If, as he suspected, Mélusine was the blackmailer, it was because she needed money. She would gain nothing by revealing that one of London's most prominent and respected bankers had founded his early fortune on the profits of smuggling, because then her income from the blackmail would cease. Pierce would have time to find and destroy the evidence, and there would be no need to take any harsh measures against her. Once she no longer had proof that Henry de La Motte and Bertier de Gilocourt had been partners in a smuggling business, any accusations she made would be easily brushed aside. But if she wasn't the blackmailer, or the evidence she'd found fell into the hands of one of La Motte's enemies, the danger would immediately increase. Pierce found himself torn between the practical hope that she was the blackmailer, because that would be easiest to deal with—and the fugitive desire that she wasn't because, despite himself, he liked her.

So far the conversation at the table had revolved around society scandal, but now it veered to the events unfolding at the Estates-General in Versailles. Even though it brought him no closer to the blackmailer, Pierce listened with interest.

'The opening procession was a mistake,' said the

Marquis de Chaumont. 'I knew from the minute I saw it there would be trouble.'

'It was a glorious sight,' Sabine de Foix protested.

'It was wantonly provocative,' Chaumont replied. 'To have the clergy and the nobility parade in all their pomp and finery while the third estate was constrained to wear drab black. I ask you, *madame*, would you be well disposed to your fellow guests if you'd been obliged to attend this dinner in plain calico while everyone else wore silk and jewels?'

'I am not a commoner,' said Sabine. 'The noble origins of my family can be traced back three centuries.' Her gaze slid to Mélusine as she spoke.

Pierce sensed, rather than saw, Mélusine draw in upon herself. In his opinion, whatever her pedigree, she looked every inch an elegant noblewoman. Since she had now entered the second six months of mourning for Bertier, she was wearing a black silk gown with white trimmings on the sleeves. There was an ebony necklace at her throat, which drew attention to the purity of her pale skin. She also wore black ribbon, ebony beads and a few, well-placed, small black feathers in her heavily powdered hair. Pierce was mildly worried the feathers might come adrift if she moved her head too violently but, all in all, he was impressed with his first attempt at producing a formal hairstyle. Of course, the six hours he'd spent last night, losing sleep while Clothilde taught him a few basic tricks, had played a significant part in his success.

'I have not said how pleased I am to see you back in Paris, Comtesse,' said Sabine.

'I am glad to be back, *madame*,' Mélusine replied quietly.

'I am surprised you decided to return during such restless times,' said Chaumont. 'You would surely have been more comfortable remaining with your family in…Bordeaux, I think?'

'Yes, Bordeaux,' said Mélusine.

'Now your first period of mourning is over, I knew you could not stay away from Paris much longer, Comtesse,' Sabine said vivaciously. 'Have you seen him yet?'

'Seen who, *madame*?' Mélusine asked, sounding confused.

'Ah, you are a tease!' Sabine exclaimed. 'You have more talent for the game than I thought. I'm talking about your lover, of course.'

Sabine's words rang out clearly, and all other conversation suddenly stopped, as everyone turned to see Mélusine's reaction. From his position behind her, Pierce couldn't see her face, but he saw her breasts rise and fall as she drew in a deep breath. Once again her grip on her knife tightened, but when she spoke her voice was steady.

'Why do you say I have a lover?' she asked.

'That is no secret,' said Sabine. 'It's his identity only that remains a mystery, dear *madame*.'

'You'll forgive me,' said Mélusine, 'having been

away from Paris for so long, I had no idea my affairs were of such interest to others.'

'Great interest,' Sabine assured her. 'If not for the tiresome business at Versailles that has distracted so much attention, I'm sure your paramour's name would have been discovered by now. Bertier was a hero to many.'

'Bertier? *Madame*, are you suggesting I was unfaithful to my husband?' Mélusine's voice was hard and brittle. 'That is a lie. I have never had a lover. I did not betray my marriage vows!'

'You still cling to your virtuous image. But your husband was killed by a single sword thrust. All Paris knows it. And who but a nobleman would have the skill to kill Bertier so cleanly? It was a duel in all but name—and what other cause can they have fought for, except your favours?'

'Bertier wasn't killed in a duel!' Mélusine exclaimed. 'He was waylaid and robbed in the Bois de Boulogne. His body was brought home by an inspector of the police. You have been the victim of baseless rumours, *madame*.'

'Do you say so?' Sabine's eyes glittered. 'Or perhaps it is the rumours that have foundation and the story of the street thieves that is…less accurate.'

Despite his continuing suspicions that Mélusine was blackmailing La Motte, Pierce instinctively tensed to defend her from the insults she was receiving. It offended all his principles to hear a lady being treated so discourteously. But he was here to investigate her, not protect her.

A quick glance around him showed him that Amalie,

the hostess, looked distressed at what was happening at her table, but clearly lacked the strength of personality to intervene. Her husband looked raptly interested. The Marquis de Chaumont looked disapproving, but seemed as interested as the Comte de La Fontaine. No one had any intention of intervening.

It took more effort than usual, but Pierce kept his face impassive and his stance relaxed. He was determined to do nothing to draw attention to himself, not least because a footman leaping to his mistress's defence in such a situation was more likely to fan the flames of gossip than douse them.

'My father spoke to the police inspector,' said Mélusine.

Pierce was startled and not entirely comfortable to discover he was proud of her cool, controlled tones. He could not afford to let his attraction to her cloud his thinking.

'Your *wealthy* father,' said Sabine meaningfully. The implication that Mélusine's father had bribed the police was unmistakable. 'You saw Bertier's body. Clean and unmarked. No sign of the injury that killed him hidden beneath his clothes. If he'd been beaten and abused by brigands, his body would have been cut and bruised, his face marked. No, he died from one, single sword thrust. I salute you, Madame la Comtesse. I had no idea you had the capacity to attract a lover of such skill and vigour. And ruthlessness.'

For several seconds Mélusine did not respond. Then she laid her napkin down beside her plate and picked up her gloves. The whole table watched in complete silence as she drew them slowly on to her hands. The gesture was as eloquent as any words she could have uttered.

Pierce was ready to pull her chair back as she stood.

'Forgive me, *madame, monsieur,*' she said, ignoring everyone else present as she addressed her hosts. 'I regret I must leave now.'

Mélusine was trembling so much she had difficulty stepping into the carriage. Pierre's hand at her elbow steadied her.

'Oh, get in!' she exclaimed, as she saw he was about to take his position outside.

'Madame?'

'What does it matter? Paris thinks I had my lover murder my husband! Who's going to care if I take you in my coach?'

'Anyone who places more value on etiquette than morality?' Pierre said mildly, but he did as she'd ordered.

'Oh, my God!' Despite the fact she'd only just put them on, Mélusine stripped off her gloves. She lifted her hands to touch her hair, felt the mixture of chalk and starch beneath her fingers, moved her hands away and spread them wide. As she remembered everything Sabine had said, she began to open and close them convulsively.

'I didn't kill him!' The horror of that accusation still resonated through her.

'She didn't say—'

'She said my lover.' Mélusine started up from the seat

and her head collided with the top of the carriage. *'Ow!'* She recoiled and started to topple sideways.

Pierre grabbed her and pushed her firmly back on to the seat. 'Sit still!' he said.

She took a deep breath and tried to calm down. She didn't remember him taking her hand, but now she had something to hold on to, she squeezed it tightly.

'Why don't I ever know what to say?' she whispered after a while.

'What do you mean?'

'You'd have known. If you'd been in that situation, you wouldn't have been struck dumb and stumbled out of the room.'

'You made a dignified and courteous departure,' said Pierre. 'It was only after you got in the coach that you started to have the vapours.'

Mélusine detected the mild, slightly dry humour in his voice and straightened her spine. 'It is not an amusing situation.'

'But sometimes finding the humour in a difficult situation can make it more manageable.'

'So you're claiming to be laughing with me, not at me,' she said.

'I don't think you have any difficulty knowing what to say in most circumstances,' said Pierre. 'I have never noticed any lack in your conversations with me.'

'Everything she said was a lie,' said Mélusine. 'I did not have a lover. I do not have a lover. So he *couldn't* have murdered Bertier.'

'She didn't say he was murdered,' Pierre corrected her. 'She said he was killed by a single sword thrust. Because only noblemen are supposed to have the privilege of wearing a sword, she thinks that means he must have been killed by a nobleman. Perhaps it hasn't occurred to her that a pedigree isn't the only qualification for wielding a sword effectively.'

'Looking for the humour in the situation,' said Mélusine, 'at least she is crediting me with attracting a noble lover, rather than some upstart bourgeois from Bordeaux.' Her voice wavered slightly.

'Her whole argument rests on the condition of your husband's body,' said Pierre gently. *'Madame…?'*

'I didn't see it,' she whispered. She closed her eyes and leant her head back as she remembered the horror of that morning. 'I didn't even talk to the police inspector. I only know what my father told me.'

'You didn't wish to see…?'

'No!'

'Did he mistreat you, *madame*?'

Mélusine stared straight ahead, but she was remembering one of the last things she'd heard Bertier say, two nights before his death.

'No,' she whispered. 'He did not know I'd heard.'

'Heard what?' Pierre's voice sharpened.

Mélusine suddenly remembered who she was talking to. If she hadn't been so shaken, she wouldn't have revealed even as much as she had to a man who was both a near stranger and a servant.

'It's not—' She broke off as something hit the side of coach. 'What's that?' She looked around, belatedly becoming aware of voices in the street outside.

'Bread! We want bread!'

Pierre swore under his breath. 'Sit back from the window!' he ordered.

'I have no bread.' Mélusine was so shocked she took the shouted demands literally. 'I haven't even any money,' she added, as she began to think more clearly. 'I didn't take any to dinner.'

'Hush, Georges is speaking to them.'

The carriage was still moving slowly forward. Mélusine's heart hammered in her chest as she waited for the next rock to strike the coach or even for the door to be wrenched open by an angry mob.

Until Sabine's revelations at the dinner party, she'd believed Bertier had been killed in an encounter that might have begun in a similar fashion to this. He'd died during a winter in which there'd been many night attacks on coaches by hungry brigands. But now it was late afternoon at the height of summer. She was on the way home from a dinner party! It was shocking, terrifying and completely unbelievable that her carriage had attracted such attention.

She tried to make herself as small as possible, aware of Pierre beside her, poised to act, his expression intent as he listened to the shouted exchanges between her coachman and the crowd.

Georges had lived in Paris all his life. He sounded irritated, but not frightened or intimidated by the situation. He kept talking and, most importantly, he kept the carriage moving. Gradually the shouts became more distant until Mélusine could hear nothing but the normal sounds and street cries of Paris.

'I could hear only five or six separate voices,' said Pierre.

Mélusine sensed the release of tension in his body and discovered her own legs were trembling.

'It was not a large mob,' he continued. 'From what I could tell, they were bored and overexcited youths. Georges handled it well.'

Mélusine drew in a shaky breath. 'I must give him a good reward,' she said. 'You must find out what he wants.'

'I?' Pierre glanced at her.

'What he really wants.' She wished her legs would stop shaking. 'I do not know him well enough to be sure.' She became aware that she was still clinging to Pierre's hand.

She was glad he'd been inside with her when the coach was waylaid. She'd have been even more frightened by the shouts and thrown stones if he hadn't been beside her. But it was totally inappropriate to hold his hand, even if he hadn't been her footman. She tried to pull away. For a moment he didn't relax his grasp, but then he allowed her to withdraw.

At that moment, the carriage entered the small courtyard of her house. She was so glad to be home she barely waited for Pierre to assist her out of the coach. Paul opened the door for her and she hurried past him and up the stairs towards the sanctuary of her own apartments on the second floor. She'd interviewed the candidates for the footman's post in the first-floor apartment, but she didn't live there.

She was aware of Paul calling something after her, but she wasn't calm enough to stop and talk to him. She needed to compose herself after the shocking accusations at the dinner party and then the frightening interruption to her journey home.

She reached the top of the stairs and gasped as a man emerged from her apartment. Even before the light fell on his face she knew who it was. Her step faltered, then she continued upwards. She would not allow him to look down on her any more than the difference in their heights made inevitable.

Raoul Fournier looked over her shoulder at Pierre, just long enough to establish the footman's status in her household and dismiss him from consideration, then gave his full attention to her.

'Good evening, Father.' She walked past him into the blue salon. It was the only room in her apartment which was furnished adequately to receive guests.

'Don't be impertinent.'

'Impertinent?' She turned on her heel to face him. 'I wished you good evening.'

'I ordered you to attend me at Versailles as soon as you arrived in Paris.' Her father was red-faced with anger.

'I beg your pardon, I had already received the invitation from Madame de La Fontaine. It would have been discourteous to have cried off.'

'Disobedient. Ungrateful. Get out of here!' he roared at Pierre.

To her secret comfort, Pierre ignored her father. He looked at her, waiting quietly for his next order.

'Thank you,' she said. 'You may leave us now.'

He bowed, at his most expressionless, and walked out of the room. He closed the door behind him, but Mélusine noticed he left it very slightly ajar. Her father had his back half-turned to it and hadn't noticed. Mélusine wasn't sure whether she felt reassured or mortified by the certainty that Pierre was within earshot.

'How dare you leave Bordeaux?' her father said furiously.

'It's not my home.' Mélusine lifted her chin.

'It's the best place for you until I've arranged another marriage for you.'

'No! I won't marry again.'

'You need a husband to control you. And after all I have invested in you, you owe me a grandson.'

'That is for the good Lord to decide, not you.' Mélusine gripped the back of a chair. She had not invited her father to sit, nor had she offered him refreshments. She just wanted him to leave as soon as possible.

'Not if you bear a bastard before I've found you another husband.'

'What?'

'As a widow you cannot afford the indulgence of a lover.'

'I don't have a lover!' Mélusine was appalled that her father could accuse her of such a thing. 'You cannot believe that.'

'The whole of Paris believes it. You lived here for two years before Bertier's death. There was more than enough time—'

'But I didn't...I don't...' Mélusine faltered as she suddenly grasped the implications of what her father had said. 'You mean you would have looked the other way if I broke my marriage vows—but now there is no one to betray you are concerned about my virtue?'

'Any child you bore would have been Bertier's heir. Now it will be a bastard.'

The room spun round Mélusine. She gripped the chair back even harder. She could not bear to hear this. Could not bear to hear herself described only as a vessel for producing heirs. To know that she had no other value to her father.

'Will...?' Her voice croaked. She swallowed and tried to force the same tone of absolute inflexibility into it which came so easily to her father. 'There is no "will." There is no child, there can be no child. I do not have a lover. I have never had a lover.'

Her father ignored her. 'You must return to Bordeaux immediately,' he said. 'If I'd known what you planned, I would have forbidden it. I am already negotiating another marriage for you, but it will be impossible if your reputation becomes tarnished beyond repair.'

'Why? You sold me once—I'm sure you can find someone sufficiently desperate to buy me again,' Mélusine said bitterly.

'The *right* man,' said her father. 'I will send Daniel Blanc to take you back to Bordeaux. This house must be rented again. It is a loss of income for it to stand empty. It is a gross inconvenience.'

'No,' said Mélusine. 'This is my house. I own it. You have no control over what I do with my house, or over me. I will do as I choose.'

Her father's cheeks grew mottled with outraged indignation. 'Everything you have and everything you are you owe to me.'

'Including my libertine nature?' Mélusine was light-headed with anger. 'Why didn't you tell me how Bertier died?'

'What?'

'Haven't you heard the rumours—or do you pick and choose the ones you believe? This afternoon I heard Bertier had been killed by a single sword thrust from a nobleman. You told me he'd been attacked by brigands.'

Her father stared at her. 'So I believed. So I was told.'

'You didn't look at his body either?'

'He was no use to me dead,' her father said brusquely. 'Precious little good alive, in the end. I believed him when he told me his first wife was barren. I should have investigated that more closely.'

'Perhaps insist he impregnate one of the maids first, so you could be sure he was capable of servicing your daughter,' Mélusine said bitterly.

'Do not be crude,' her father said impatiently.

'So you don't know how he died?'

'Only what the inspector told me. I had no reason to doubt it. I considered it more important to take you to Bordeaux.'

'And arrange my next marriage.'

'He'll be younger this time,' said her father, a slightly more conciliatory note in his voice.

'With two or three bastards to his credit?'

'A legitimate daughter by his first wife, perhaps.'

'My God.' Mélusine lifted her hands and then dropped them back on to the chair.

'Go back to Bordeaux,' said her father. 'I will soon find you a new husband. One who can give you the sons I need—'

'*You* need,' Mélusine said. 'I only want to live in peace and quiet. That's all I've ever wanted.'

'Until you're safely married and a mother, you'll have neither.' Raoul walked out of the room without a backward glance. 'I will send Daniel to take you back to Bordeaux,' he said from the doorway.

Chapter Four

Pierce followed Mélusine's father downstairs at a discreet distance to make sure he was really leaving. He was furious at what he'd just overheard. It had taken all his self-discipline not to intervene and unceremoniously throw Raoul Fournier out of the house. No man should speak so abusively to his daughter. It was cruel and dishonourable. Pierce couldn't condone blackmail, but he better understood the desperate need that might have compelled Mélusine to do such a thing. Money couldn't solve all problems, but it would help her to break free of her father's control.

He went back up to the salon, two steps at a time, but he was only just in time to see Mélusine fly out of the room and up the stairs. He went after her without any hesitation.

She rushed into a room at the top of the house he'd never seen before. The windows were uncovered and the room was illuminated by warm evening sunlight. In his first, swift glance around he noticed two solid work-benches, a couple of artist's easels and a number of barrels.

Mélusine wrenched open one barrel, seized what appeared to be a large lump of clay and slammed it down on one of the workbenches.

Pierce watched, slightly bemused, as she began to beat and pound it on to the solid surface. 'What are you doing?' he said at last.

'It cannot be fired with air bubbles. It will explode inside the kiln.' She snatched up a piece of wire with two wooden handles and used it to slice through the lump of clay. She slammed one piece down into the other and began to knead, ramming the heels of her hand into the clay in fierce, jerky movements.

Pierce stared at her. He'd expected her to cry or take refuge in her bedroom, not express her anger and frustration in such a directly physical way. He'd never suspected she was capable of such a passionate outburst. He took a few minutes to get his own temper under control—and wondered if she was capable of equal passion with a lover. Already the white trimmings on her sleeves were matted with drying clay, there were splats of clay all over her black silk gown and her hair was falling around her shoulders in total disarray. One black feather drifted downwards, was caught briefly in the rush of air around her flailing arms, and then crushed into the surface of the clay. She brushed her hair out of her eyes with the back of a clay-coated hand.

'I—have—no—lover,' she said through gritted teeth. With each word she thrust down on the clay.

'No, *madame*.' But her fury was so extreme Pierce wondered whether she had had a lover who'd betrayed her. Perhaps he'd promised to help her escape her loveless marriage, only to abandon her to impoverished widowhood.

'I have *never* had a lover! How can he think so little of me? My virtue—my honour! Nothing. Less than nothing. He didn't even *care*—only lest I bred a bastard! How *could* he think so little of me?' She snatched up a beaker and hurled it across the room. It clattered against the wall a few feet to Pierce's right and rolled into the shadows.

She stalked across the room to stand immediately in front of him. 'Men are callous, hypocritical beasts! Well, say something! Aren't you going to say something?' She shoved his shoulder with the flat of her hand.

'Not all men,' he said quietly.

'Oh, no. You are here because you have to provide for your mother and sister. Have you got a husband all lined up for your sister? Someone to take her off your hands so you can return to your lover with a clear conscience?'

Pierce gripped her wrist in his hand. '*Madame*, the Duchesse was not my lover. Tell me why I should believe you don't have a lover when you persist in believing that I do, despite the fact I tell you it is not so?'

She caught her breath and then bowed her head. Her hair tumbled in disorder around her shoulders. He could see pins sticking out at odd angles. He released her wrist and began to gently untangle the pins, beads and remaining feathers from her hair.

She jerked her head up and gave a small squeak of pain when her hair pulled. 'What are you doing?'

'You're moulting,' said Pierce.

'Oh.' She lowered her head again and let him continue his ministrations. Once or twice she seemed to sway slightly towards him, almost as if she wanted to lean on him, but the movement was so subtle he couldn't be sure his senses—or his own impulses— were not deceiving him.

'Here.' He gave her the pins and small hair ornaments as he removed them. She held them cupped in her hands before her.

'*Madame*, did you ever have a lover who betrayed you?' he asked quietly. 'One perhaps you trusted who did not fulfil his promise to you?'

Pierre's gentle touch in her hair had soothed Mélusine to such an extent that she was slow to grasp his question.

She threw her head up, ignoring the discomfort when his tangled fingers pulled her hair. 'I have said over and over…'

'I know. Stand still or I'll hurt you.'

'Your accusation hurts.' It did, far more than the comment of a servant and virtual stranger should have done. 'I don't care about my hair.' She tried to step away, but he gripped her shoulder with his free hand.

She froze. The neckline of her dress meant his palm was pressed against her bare skin. He was touching her.

She suddenly realised they were not only alone in the room but well beyond earshot of anyone else. Earlier her heart had been pounding with anger. She'd calmed since then, but now her pulse began to increase with uncertainty and apprehension. Since her first meeting with Pierre, the topic of lovers had frequently entered the conversation. He'd originally thought she was hiring a lover—did he now think—?

'Stand away!' she ordered, her voice cracking slightly with nervousness.

'Are you afraid of me?'

'Of course not.' She wanted to pull away from his grasp, but she was too proud to do so. Besides, she'd seen cats chasing mice often enough to know that running only incited a hunter's instincts. 'I'm not a mindless mouse.'

'No.' He untangled his fingers from her hair, but then, instead of moving away, he put that hand on her other shoulder.

She clenched her own hands, felt the bite of pins and beads against her palms and dropped everything she was holding so she could fend him off.

'*Madame*, if you really think I'm about to assault you, a hand on my chest isn't an effective defence,' he said. 'I might even misconstrue it as a sign of affection.'

She snatched her hands away and saw him smile. Frustrated and confused, she took the risk of looking straight into his eyes.

Behind his smile his gaze was watchful. She had the unfamiliar sensation that, for once in her life, a man was looking at her, trying to fathom what she was thinking.

'I have never forced a woman,' he said. 'Why would I, when half my pleasure derives from her pleasure? When she sighs and arches against me, grips me between her thighs and…'

Shocked, fascinated, hideously embarrassed, Mélusine ducked her head and covered her ears with her hands. Then she realised it was his mouth she needed to stop, so instead she covered that.

She felt his lips move against her palm and the tingle of unexpected sensation rippled through her whole body.

'Stop talking!' she commanded, her voice mortifyingly husky.

She felt his soundless laughter and whirled away from him.

'I did not accuse you of having a lover,' he said. 'I *asked* if you'd ever had one.'

She'd forgotten his earlier question. After what had just happened between them she felt vulnerable and exposed and now she felt unreasonably betrayed by his continued lack of trust.

'How many times must I say it?' Her voice rose as she turned to confront him. 'Why do men think all women are liars when it is they—?'

'You are so vehement in your denials,' he said. 'Ever since our first meeting you have persisted in believing the Duchesse was my lover, even though I have told you it is not true, but I do not fly into rages at the false accusation.'

'Because it is a matter of pride for a man to boast of his conquests! Even moments ago you were doing so!'

'I did not!'

'You were boasting of your…your *skills* in that—'

'I was reassuring you I would not hurt you.'

'You were talking of the pleasure you give your…' Mélusine faltered slightly with embarrassment. 'Which really means you were boasting about *yourself* and your ability to please.'

'I suppose that is one interpretation.'

'What other can there be? And how could you learn such skills without seducing and discarding—?'

'My wife.'

'What?' Mélusine stared at him, totally disorientated as thoughts and images of both Bertier and Pierre whirled through her mind.

'Don't you think a man might perfect such skills in the marriage bed?' he asked.

'Are you married?' she whispered. The possibility had never occurred to her before, and was unaccountably disturbing.

He hesitated; then shrugged in what seemed to be a fatalistic acceptance of her question. 'I was,' he said.

'What happened?'

'She died of smallpox,' he said, his lips tight.

'Oh.' Mélusine looked into his face. 'I think you were sorry.'

'Yes.'

She turned her head away. Ashamed because she

could not say she was sorry that Bertier was dead. Oddly bereft because she believed Pierre had grieved for his wife and perhaps still grieved for her.

'That is all for tonight,' said Mélusine at last. 'Tomorrow you may accompany me to the Hôtel de Gilocourt.'

'Your old home?' His voice sharpened. 'Why?'

'It was Bertier's house,' Mélusine corrected. 'Now it is his brother's. I lived there during my marriage. I must speak to Thérèse Petit—'

'Who?'

'The housekeeper. She will still be there, I'm sure. She has served the Gilocourts since Séraphin was a baby.'

'Don't you think she would have told you at the time if she'd noticed anything odd about your husband's body?'

'I don't know.' Mélusine turned away. 'Thérèse considers herself part of the family. I was only Bertier's wife—' She broke off. 'I must find out the truth. I did not see his wounds. I cannot say whether he was beaten to death or killed by a sword. I cannot counter the rumours until I know the truth. He did not fight a duel for my favours, I know that much.' Her lips twisted bitterly. 'But I cannot clear my reputation until I know who did kill him and why.'

'And for that you are willing to perhaps stir up even more unpleasant scandal?'

'My virtue, my honour, my reputation—they belong to me now,' said Mélusine. 'I am not a chattel to be passed from hand to hand, valued only for my dowry and the heirs I can breed. And I will defend my reputation.'

Dawn, Friday, 10 July 1789

The studio was lit by cool, pre-dawn light when Pierce opened the door. Mélusine was still in bed. Even the few servants were not yet up and about their chores.

He stood in the middle of the room, revolving slowly as he studied his surroundings more carefully than he'd been able to when he was with Mélusine. He'd seen yesterday that this was where she'd run in her greatest distress. Unlike most of the rest of the house, which still echoed from lack of furnishings, this room was almost overcrowded with various artistic equipment. As well as two workbenches—one of which was still caked with dried clay—there was a potter's wheel. There were also several easels, canvases leaning against the wall, and large containers along one wall, one of which he knew contained clay. There was a large, scarred desk, the only piece of furniture he'd seen anywhere in the house that might have locked or secret drawers.

He started his search there. Only one drawer was locked. He opened all the others, quickly glancing through the contents and feeling underneath, before turning his attention to the locked one. He'd known people who locked away their possessions, but kept the key conveniently nearby, or even locked away in-

nocuous items and left their most prized possessions in
the open. It took only a few minutes to reveal that
Mélusine hadn't made either of those mistakes. It was
a while since he'd picked a lock, but he still remembered what he'd been taught.

The drawer was wide but shallow. The sides stuck
slightly as he eased it out, but at last he had it half-open.
All he could see was a large sheet of paper, which
seemed to be sitting on top of a pile of other papers.

He sat completely still for a few seconds, listening
intently to the sounds coming from the rest of the
house, then lifted the papers on to the desk and moved
the blank sheet aside.

He stared downwards, so startled by what he saw he
completely forgot to listen out for potential discovery.

The image of Mélusine gazed back at him. She was
totally naked. For several seconds he was transfixed by
what he saw. In the sketch she was standing, her unclothed body slightly twisted away from the viewer,
although she was looking straight out of the picture.
There was no mistaking her features. The artist had
captured her intent, assessing expression with an
accuracy that suggested the rest of the picture was
likewise a true depiction of her form. Pierce already
knew her arms were shapely; now he could see her legs
were equally comely. The artist had depicted the curve
of her breasts and hips and obviously didn't have any
patience with the ideal of classical purity because he'd
included her pubic hair as well.

Pierce's mouth was dry. He spread the thick papers over the desktop and saw they were all of Mélusine, and in nearly all of them she was effectively naked. Sometimes she had a sheet draped across parts of her anatomy, sometimes her long hair provided a hint of modesty, and sometimes only part of her body was completely sketched. In many pictures her face was only briefly suggested.

Pierce stared at the pictures, his heart thumping with a disturbing mixture of desire, anger and unaccountable jealousy. He'd still suspected Mélusine of blackmail, but until a few moments ago he'd been sure she was telling the truth when she said she'd been faithful to her husband. These pictures gave the lie to that. He knew Bertier couldn't have drawn them, which left only a lover. No lady would pose in such a way for anyone but a lover.

He clenched his fists on the desk beside the pictures, furious with himself for having fallen for her pretty face and air of innocence and even more disgusted with the stab of jealousy he felt. Who was the man Mélusine had allowed to see her like this when she'd frozen with apprehension whenever Pierce touched her?

He glared down at her image. It took several moments before he realised she was more or less glaring back at him. After the shock of the first sketch he'd been more interested in the various poses than the details of her expression. Now he studied her face more closely in those pictures where it had been most fully rendered. In each one she wore the same, focused, sometimes slightly frowning expression. It was not at all the look of a woman gazing at her lover, nor were the poses designed to be particularly alluring. Sometimes they seemed rather tortuous, but not noticeably erotic.

Pierce frowned. The clue came in one picture where she was holding two pencils in her hand, which was braced on her upraised knee. He glanced around and saw a large, full-length mirror he hadn't noticed the night before. It was something he'd expect to see in a lady's dressing room, but the sketches suggested Mélusine had another use for it.

The realisation that Mélusine must have been sitting or standing in front of the mirror as she drew naked self-portraits of herself startled a disbelieving laugh from him. He wondered what it would take for her to pose naked for him. One thing was certain. If she ever did so, she would very quickly lose that focused, alert expression.

He slipped all the sketches back into the drawer, taking one last look at Mélusine standing naked before somewhat reluctantly covering it with the blank paper and relocking the drawer. His body was aching with unsatisfied lust, and it took all his self-control to complete his search of the studio. By the time he'd finished he was content there was no evidence to be found in the room that Mélusine was a blackmailer, and very discontented with her powerful impact upon him. If he didn't stop thinking about the pictures he'd just seen and imagining how he could enjoy the real Mélusine in an equally unclothed state, he was in danger of sabotaging his purpose.

He thought instead about his family. His mother would be planning his sister's wedding. He wondered if she knew disaster threatened them all. Pierce had never confided every detail of his life to Rosalie. Even though he'd met her because he'd been in Guernsey to facilitate La Motte's dealings with the merchants who sold brandy to the English smugglers, and he'd spent the few months of their marriage living on the island with her, he'd never revealed the full extent of his involvement with the illicit trade. He'd gained the impression that La Motte confided considerably more in Justine, but it was not something any of them had discussed.

La Motte's banking affairs had become increasingly legitimate over the years, and just as profitable. But if the secrets of his past ever unravelled in public, they would all be facing catastrophe. And if La Motte was tried and found guilty, his execution was a real possibility. There were many powerful people who owed him favours, but there were others who resented his success and would be eager to witness his destruction.

La Motte's only option in those circumstances would be to escape England before he could be caught, taking his family into exile. Pierce set his jaw. He would not permit any of that to happen. The blackmailer and any accomplices must be found and their silence assured. Only then could he indulge his personal impulses.

* * *

It was the first time Mélusine had returned to the Hôtel de Gilocourt since she'd left within days of Bertier's death. Her heart began to thump as the carriage drove through the great archway into the courtyard at the front of the grand house. It had been designed by Bertier's forebears to be a residence worthy of a distinguished noble family, to display their status, wealth and power. Even in these restless times, when it might seem like wanton provocation, the entrance was still guarded by gorgeously liveried lackeys holding halberds.

Mélusine had been mistress here for the two years of her marriage, but she'd never felt truly at home. She'd known very well she was Bertier's much younger, bourgeois second wife. He'd married her because he'd needed heirs. She hadn't given them to him and, though he'd treated her with rather formal courtesy, she'd had little status in the eyes of his household.

Mélusine sometimes wondered if Bertier himself had been fully at home here. He'd been estranged from his father for most of his adult life, and had only returned to this house after his father's death. He'd inherited many of the servants from his father, but most of them had been strangers to him when he'd moved in. Now Séraphin owned the house and, in his turn, had inherited many of the household staff.

The carriage stopped and a few moments later the

door was opened for her. Mélusine felt an unexpected flicker of relief at seeing Pierre waiting to assist her down the steps. After her outburst the previous night she'd felt awkward when she'd first seen him that morning, and he'd been at his most reserved while he'd dressed her hair for this visit. She'd worried that she'd fallen in his estimation and if she hadn't felt so apprehensive about her return to her old home, she would have tried to talk him into a better mood.

Despite her conviction Pierre was sitting in judgement of her, and had somehow found her wanting, she was still glad he was with her. There was something reassuringly direct about him. Even though she was afraid he disapproved of her, he'd never sneered at her, or treated her with subtle disdain.

'*Madame*, we are honoured that you have visited us again.' The *maître d'hôtel*, who had once been Mélusine's *maître d'hôtel*, bowed before her. 'I regret, the Comte is not here. He is a representative at the Estates-General in Versailles.'

'I thought he might be absent,' said Mélusine. 'I am pleased to see you again, François. I hope you are in good health.'

'Thank you, *madame*. I am very well.' He bowed again. 'I will inform the Comte you have called.'

'Please do. Now, I wish to speak to Thérèse Petit,' said Mélusine briskly. Her heart was in her throat and she felt slightly sick, but she hoped her manner didn't reveal her discomfort. The housekeeper's silent determination to remain mistress in fact, if not in name, of the house, had often made Mélusine's life difficult.

To her surprise, François seemed disconcerted and then ill at ease at her question.

'Alas, again I regret, *madame*, she is not here,' he said.

'Not here? Where is she?'

'Her sister has been taken ill. The Comte generously gave her leave to visit.'

'When will she be back?'

'Alas, *madame*...' François spread the fingers of both hands '...I do not know.'

Mélusine was nonplussed. Thérèse had prepared Bertier's body. She had insisted she perform the task alone as befitted her position as devoted, lifelong servant to the Gilocourt family. Mélusine had no idea whether the housekeeper had actually done everything herself, or whether, as with so many posts in public life, she had claimed the privileges of her position, while deputising someone else to carry out the actual work.

In the circumstances, it was possible Pierre might have more success in discovering what had happened than she.

'I would like to meditate in the family chapel for a few minutes,' she said. 'I'm sure my footman would appreciate some refreshment while he's waiting.'

She glanced at Pierre, wondering if he understood what she wanted of him. His expression gave nothing away, but he nodded very slightly.

* * *

Talking to the servants suited Pierce's purposes very well. Since Mélusine would want to know, he first made sure that Thérèse Petit really wasn't in the house, and then he lingered to sip the watered wine he'd been offered and charm a couple of the maids.

'You've not worked for *madame* long?' said one, who'd identified herself as Laurette.

'A few days only,' said Pierce. 'Since she returned to Paris. Is she a good mistress?'

'Oh, yes.' Laurette smiled. 'She is kind and polite.' Then her eyes narrowed and she rapped her knuckles against Pierce's upper arm. 'Take care you serve her well.'

'Hey!' Pierce rubbed his arm and frowned in mock-indignation. 'If you're so quick to champion her, why aren't you still working for her?'

'If she'd asked, I would have been,' said Laurette. 'But her father whisked her away so fast. The poor lady was so distressed I doubt she knew what she was doing.'

'Did she take any of the other servants with her?' Pierce asked. 'What of the footman who did her hair—Jean-Baptiste, I think I've heard her call him?'

'Jean-Baptiste?' Laurette wrinkled her nose. 'He stayed here with the rest of us. She wouldn't have wanted *him* to go with her, I'm sure—even if she'd had the chance to take any of us.'

'Why not?' Pierce asked. 'Did he do something to offend her? Now I'm serving her in his place, I'd not want to repeat his mistakes. What can you tell me, *chérie*?'

'I don't know he did anything in particular to the Comtesse,' Laurette said. 'He thought he was better than the rest of us. He was a foundling, brought up by the monks, but he was convinced his father was a *duc*. He had ideas above his station. But he wouldn't have been like that with *madame*. I think she knew he wasn't nice, though. She used to talk to me a lot—just everyday things. But she never said anything to Jean-Baptiste unless she had to.'

'Why did she keep him, then?' Pierce asked.

'The Comte hired Jean-Baptiste for *madame* as a wedding present,' Laurette explained.

'So she had to put up with him or risk offending her husband?' said Pierce.

'I think so. At least one good thing came out of that dreadful time—she's got you instead of Jean-Baptiste to do her hair now. Mind you look after her properly. You'll never have a better, kinder mistress.'

'I will do my best,' said Pierce, with a slight bow. 'Is Jean-Baptiste still serving the current Comte?'

'I don't know,' said Laurette.

'Why not?' The question emerged more sharply than Pierce had intended and Laurette momentarily looked confused. 'I'm sorry, *mignonne*,' he said easily. 'I was just surprised you don't know.'

'He was here for months after the old Comte's death,' said Laurette. 'Then a couple of months ago he disap-peared, but most of his clothes were still here. It was the talk of the household for days. He'd never said he was leaving and no one had heard the Comte dismiss him. The Comte asked if anyone had seen him, but no one had. I think he must have been attacked, like the poor old Comte was—but maybe they stole his clothes and the police didn't know where to bring his body.'

'It must have been a terrible shock, the day the old Comte's body was brought home,' said Pierce tactfully. 'It's hardly the kind of thing you expect to happen— the master being killed by common brigands.'

'*That* didn't surprise me so much,' said Laurette. 'I didn't expect it, mind you, but he would insist on going out at night, walking alone—quite unbecoming to his position.'

'I heard his body was brought back to the house by a police inspector,' Pierce said.

'It was a scandalous thing,' said Laurette. 'Madame Petit was appalled by the indignity of it all.'

'*She* doesn't sound as if she's easy to work for,' said Pierce.

Laurette grimaced. 'As far as she's concerned the world revolves around the Gilocourts,' she said. 'And she's the only one capable of serving them. After the Comte died, she wouldn't even let me—' She broke off as François appeared. He gave Laurette a narrow-eyed, disapproving glance before addressing Pierce.

'Your mistress is ready to leave,' he said haughtily. 'Don't keep her waiting.'

Pierce stood up with deliberate slowness, but resisted the urge to make a sharp retort. He'd never been a guest of Bertier's in Paris, and the chances of being recognised by any of the Gilocourt servants was remote, but there was no point in drawing more attention to himself than was necessary.

The return to her former home had unsettled Mélusine. Meditating in the chapel was the first excuse she'd been able to think of to delay her departure so Pierre could talk to the other servants. But once she was there, she sat with her hands clasped and her head bowed, remembering her years in the house.

In the beginning it had been particularly awkward and embarrassing. She'd only met Bertier twice before the wedding, and it had been hard to begin married life with a stranger. But she did have some happy memories. Bertier had been quite happy to let her have a studio for her artistic activities and a few months after the wedding they'd been visited by one of his old friends from England.

Mélusine hadn't always been comfortable with Bertier's friends. She'd felt at ease with the Marquis de Saint-André until her opinion of him had changed in one horrific moment, but most of Bertier's friends had been twenty years older than her, and she'd found it hard to talk to them. Sir Henry and his wife had been very different. Mélusine had enjoyed their visit and been sad when they'd left. Though Sir Henry was English, he was the descendent of French Huguenots who'd fled to England at the end of the previous century when the French government had started to persecute Huguenots for their Protestant faith.

Mélusine had been raised a Catholic, but it did not seem right to her that anyone should suffer for their religion unless they had done deliberate harm to others. In any case, she'd liked Sir Henry, who spoke very good French. His wife *was* French, so there had been no impediment to easy communication. They'd been straightforward and kind, and she'd not once sensed they considered themselves innately her superiors as she so often did when she was talking to Bertier's French noble friends.

Perhaps it was because Sir Henry wasn't a noble himself. Mélusine didn't fully understand English noble ranks, but apparently Sir Henry been given his knighthood because of his services to banking, and it wouldn't be inherited by his young son.

'They'd have to make me a baronet for that,' he'd said, 'but Felix can earn his own knighthood if he's of a mind to.'

Mélusine had smiled politely, more charmed by the sturdy, five-year-old boy than interested in the intricacies of English inheritance.

'He is a handsome boy,' she said, amazingly gratified when he was willing to sit on her lap. At that time she'd still assumed she would soon have a baby, and she'd hoped the child would be as friendly and affectionate as Felix.

'He has been very much spoiled by his older brothers

and sisters,' said Lady de La Motte, 'but it does not seem to have done him any harm.'

That was when Mélusine had discovered that, though Sir Henry was not a nobleman, his wife's first husband had been the son of a...*vicomte*? Mélusine hadn't been entirely sure, but she thought that's what Lady de La Motte had said. In any event, a few months earlier, Lady de La Motte's oldest son had inherited his grandfather's title. Mélusine couldn't remember the boy's name, but she vividly recalled his mother's pride in him.

She felt a pang of sadness. The one thing she'd wanted from her marriage had been children, and they had been denied to her.

She looked up, startled to realise she'd been sitting in the chapel for over half an hour. That was surely long enough for Pierre to learn anything interesting from the servants. She stood up and walked sedately out.

She was deep in thought, trying to decide what to do next about her total failure to discover any more about Bertier's death, when her carriage entered the courtyard of her own house.

Pierre opened the door, let down the steps and stood ready to assist her. She steadied herself with a hand on his arm, momentarily distracted by the lean muscles she could feel beneath his sleeve.

Then she saw the other carriage in the small courtyard. The sight shocked her so much she missed the last step and nearly fell on to the cobblestones. The next second Pierre caught her, with one hand on either side of her waist. He lifted her right off her feet, swinging her round to put her down gently well clear of the carriage steps.

'Father,' she whispered, staring past Pierre at the other coach. 'He's come to send me back to Bordeaux.' She looked at Pierre, reaching out unconsciously to grip his arm. 'I won't go!' she said in a fierce under-voice. 'I *won't*!'

Chapter Five

'It is your choice, *madame*,' Pierre said.

'He thinks it's his.' She took a deep breath, trying to control the wild beating of her heart. 'But it is mine.' She tightened her grip on Pierre's arm. 'You are *my* servant,' she said fiercely. 'I pay you. You obey me. Remember that. Ignore any order he gives you.'

'Yes, *madame*,' said Pierre. His tone was so dry that it cut through Mélusine's near-panic. She looked at him. His expression was as bland as ever, but the gleam in his grey eyes was so self-confident it verged on arrogance.

'You won't let him take me?' she said. It was a question, not a plea. She was wondering exactly what his cryptic response signified.

'If you don't want to go to Bordeaux, you won't,' he said, as if the issue was in no doubt.

'Men are always sure they can do everything—until it turns out they can't,' she said, a little acidly.

'I can certainly prevent you from being taken to Bordeaux against your wishes,' he said.

'Really?' she said. 'Your reply would carry more weight if you conceded there are areas in which you do doubt your ability.'

'Every man has weaknesses,' said Pierre. 'Or perhaps I should say a lack of aptitude for certain activities.'

'You do admit you don't excel in all areas,' Mélusine said. Despite, or perhaps because of the confrontation she knew awaited her, she was intrigued by Pierre's response. Given his aura of self-confidence, she'd been sure his reply would be an unqualified affirmation of his abilities.

He raised one eyebrow. 'Yes, *madame*. But you need have no concern. In the matter of dealing with unwelcome visitors, I have an unsullied record. Though I dare say it would not be politic to knock a representative of the Estates-General down two flights of stairs, so I hope the conversation with Monsieur Fournier will end peacefully.'

'So do I!' said Mélusine, slightly shocked at the image of her father being sent sprawling. 'You must not resort to violence. Father's servants will defend him, and then you'd be outnumbered. Oh dear, I wish he'd just go away,' she muttered under her breath. 'Well, let us go in,' she said more loudly.

Her porter, Paul, opened the door to them. He looked slightly haunted and, when Mélusine saw Daniel Blanc standing silently in the entrance hall, she understood why. Though she'd never been nervous of him, Daniel's silent presence often had an intimidating effect on others.

'Where is Father?' Mélusine demanded edgily.

'Versailles,' said Daniel.

Mélusine gave a sigh of relief. 'Come upstairs,' she said.

'He sent me to escort you to Bordeaux, *madame*,' Daniel said, as they reached the first landing.

She stopped and turned to look at him. 'I'm not going,' she said flatly.

'*Madame*...' Daniel hesitated. 'It will be safer, more comfortable for you, in Bordeaux,' he said. 'Paris is so unsettled now. And it is not seemly for you to be living here alone.'

Mélusine flinched, afraid she heard more than one meaning in Daniel's words.

She stared at him, trying to decipher his thoughts. She'd known him all of her life. He was a steady man who carried out his duties efficiently. He'd never been talkative, but when she was a child he'd been an indulgent listener. He'd taken her to and from the convent or elsewhere, and she'd often filled the journey with her childish observations. Daniel had rarely said more than a few words in response, but she'd been aware of his patient goodwill towards her. She'd never dared speak so freely in her father's presence.

'Have you heard the rumours?' she asked abruptly, her voice harsh with sudden anxiety that she might have lost Daniel's good opinion.

He pressed his lips together, as if he disapproved of her raising the question. Then he gave a brief, almost imperceptible nod.

'Do you believe them?' She laced her gloved fingers together, gripping tightly as she waited for his answer.

His eyes narrowed. The silence lengthened until Mélusine thought it would suffocate her.

'I do not believe you had a lover,' he said at last.

For a moment Mélusine remained tensely poised, then she closed her eyes and swayed slightly as relief flooded through her.

'Thank you,' she whispered.

'*Madame*, you should sit down,' said Daniel.

'Yes.' She opened her eyes. 'We will go up to the salon. It's all right, Pierre. You won't have to knock Daniel down the stairs,' she added as an afterthought, as she started upwards. 'I'm sure he's not going to force me to do anything I don't want to.'

Pierce paused beside Daniel on the landing as Mélusine continued to climb the stairs. He was well aware of the older man's intense appraisal.

'Who are you?' Daniel asked.

'Pierre Dumont. Footman-hairdresser to Madame de Gilocourt,' he replied.

'For how long?'

'Since Wednesday.'

'Why—?'

'What are you talking about?' Mélusine called from the top of the next flight of stairs. 'If you're not coming up I will come down.'

Pierce gestured silently for Daniel to precede him. After another sharp glance, the older man did so.

* * *

'Sit down. Sit down,' Mélusine ordered impatiently, as soon as all three of them were in the blue salon.

'Madame!' Daniel protested.

'I hate having people stand over me!' she said, with unexpected vehemence. 'If you want me to sit down, you have to sit too!' She looked at Daniel. 'If you don't believe the rumours about me—do you believe the one about Bertier's death?'

'No,' he said, after a brief hesitation.

'Then why were you so precise in your answer before?' Pierce asked. 'You could simply have said you didn't believe the rumours.'

Daniel glanced from Mélusine to Pierce and back again. Pierce gained the impression his main concern was protecting Mélusine's sensibilities.

'I know *madame* would not have behaved so—'

'Father did not have such faith in me,' Mélusine interrupted, then pressed a hand to her mouth and looked away.

'I do not have any opinion on how the Comte de Gilocourt died,' said Daniel 'I have no reason to doubt what I was told at the time. I have no particular reason to believe it, either.'

Pierce smiled slightly. 'Like Doubting Thomas, you want to see the evidence with your own eyes, before you commit yourself,' he said.

'Not always,' said Daniel. 'I needed no proof to have

faith in *madame*. But as far as the Comte's death is concerned...' He shrugged.

'I must find out the truth,' said Mélusine.

'Why?' said Daniel. 'He's dead. Why waste any more of your life on him?'

Pierce saw Mélusine's startled expression and wondered if Daniel had ever spoken so bluntly to her before. Daniel must have seen her reaction too.

'You asked me to sit down,' he said. 'This is a time of change, *madame*. If you did not want my honest opinion, you should not have asked for it.'

'I did,' she said. 'I do. I just never suspected you had such a low opinion of the Comte.'

'As a man, I had no opinion of him at all. As a suitable husband for you—'

'I'm not going back to Bordeaux,' said Mélusine.

'It would be safer for you,' said Daniel. '*Madame*, may I speak with you alone?'

Pierce waited for Mélusine's nod before he stood up. Since she'd been so determined he wouldn't obey her father's orders, it seemed tactful not to respond instantly to the request of her father's servant.

He left the room, but he stayed close to the door. He didn't think Daniel was going to take advantage of his absence to carry Mélusine out of the house, but he'd promised he wouldn't let her be taken away against her will, and he wasn't about to let his guard down because Daniel appeared well disposed towards her.

Especially as he was now almost certain Mélusine

wasn't behind the attempt to blackmail La Motte. According to Laurette, Jean-Baptiste had remained at the Hôtel de Gilocourt for months after Mélusine had left, and the maid had no reason to lie. Moreover, Laurette's belief that Mélusine hadn't liked her previous footman-hairdresser was consistent with Mélusine's reluctance to talk about him—and even her tension the first time Pierce had dressed her hair. Pierce knew it was possible for people who disliked or even feared each other to conspire together, but that didn't fit with what he'd seen of Mélusine's personality.

She wasn't the blackmailer. He shouldn't have felt so relieved, because his task had just become much harder, but he was foolishly glad Mélusine wasn't his quarry. Séraphin de Gilocourt, who'd become Jean-Baptiste's new master after Bertier's death, had just become his most likely suspect. He stood close to the salon door, listening for any sound that might indicate Mélusine was in distress, while he calculated what his next move should be in the hunt for La Motte's blackmailer.

'*Madame*, go back to Bordeaux,' Daniel said, when he was alone with Mélusine. 'Go while your father is preoccupied with the Estates-General. Find a young man to marry. One of your own choice.'

'I don't want another husband—'

'You'll not be free of your father's interference until you're married again. Find a man strong enough to stand up to him.'

'With a noble pedigree two centuries long?' Mélusine couldn't believe what she was hearing.

'No.' A flick of Daniel's hand dismissed her suggestion. 'A prosperous man, but young, with a good future ahead of him. One who'll give you a comfortable life.'

'A comfortable life,' Mélusine repeated. 'I know you want the best for me—'

'Always, *madame*,' he said, startling and touching her with his unequivocal agreement.

'I can't leave yet,' she said. 'I want to know the truth, Daniel. And how can I present myself as a suitable wife for a prosperous, respectable man if everyone believes I had an adulterous affair during my first marriage?'

He frowned. 'I do not like the idea of you living alone in Paris.'

'No one will pay any attention to me,' she said. 'Even before I heard the rumours I never intended to go out in society. And a new scandal always comes along to overshadow previous gossip.'

'What do you know of Dumont?' Daniel demanded. 'Be wary of him. He may intend to take advantage of you.'

'How?'

'A wealthy widow, in need of protection? An ambitious young fellow with ideas above his station might easily plan to seduce his way to a better position in life.'

'You don't believe I had a lover before. Why would you think I'd take one now?' Mélusine exclaimed.

'You're not tied by your marriage vows now,' he replied. 'And he's young, strong, and ready-witted. And you're…'

'What?' she demanded tensely, already offended in anticipation of being told that, after marriage to a man old enough to be her father, she was ripe for a young man's seduction.

'Lonely,' said Daniel, with one word deflating her indignation and replacing it with a much more painful emotion. Did he really think she was so desperate for love and attention she'd succumb to any show of false kindness?

'Be wise in your choice of friends, *madame*,' he said, and stood up.

Mélusine wanted to cry out that of course she'd be wise, but Daniel's lack of confidence hurt her even more than her father's abuse. For a few moments, it was an effort to force any words past her cold lips.

'What are you going to tell Father?' she asked at last.

'I will delay a while before I return,' said Daniel. 'I'll tell him you had noble visitors. He would not expect me to force you to leave under such circumstances. And when you've had more time to think things over, I hope you'll decide returning to Bordeaux is the best thing for you to do.'

Mélusine sat very still for several minutes after Daniel left. She was still sitting with her hands locked together in her lap when Pierre came into the room. She stared at him for a few seconds, then jumped to her feet.

'Come with me,' she ordered.

Pierce followed Mélusine, not surprised when they ended up in her studio.

'Stand there,' she ordered. She pointed to a spot in the direct light from the window, then stripped off her gloves and removed her hat.

He did as he was bid, watching as she settled herself on a stool before a drawing board on which she'd placed several sheets of paper.

'Now,' she said. 'You must stand in one position for a few minutes, then move to a new position. For the first few times I will tell you when to move. But if I forget, you must move anyway.'

'Why?' he asked, amused and oddly touched by her brusque manner. She'd been furious after her father's visit, but Daniel's visit had left her with a hurt, lost expression in her eyes. Pierce was reasonably confident Daniel did have Mélusine's best interests at heart, but whatever he'd said to her in private had wounded her and perhaps even shaken her confidence. Now Pierce thought she was demonstrating to herself and to him that she was back in control in her own home.

'It is good discipline for me,' she said. 'I must learn to draw quickly and accurately. Start now. Look out of the window.'

Pierce gazed at the rooftops on the opposite side of the square, considering the implications of Mélusine using him a model. Even though he no longer believed she was the blackmailer, he didn't want to leave recognisable pictures of him in her possession. As her servant, he had no reasonable grounds to object to her order. When he left, he'd have to find and destroy any sketches of himself.

'Move,' she said abruptly.

He turned towards her, taking up a pose which allowed him to watch her work. Her brows were drawn together in intense concentration, but her expression was increasingly dissatisfied. Either she wasn't pleased with her efforts, or he was proving to be an unrewarding model.

'This is no good.' She slammed her hand down on the drawing board. 'Take off your coat.'

'My coat?'

'And your shirt.' She narrowed her eyes. 'And your wig.'

'*Madame!*' he exclaimed. Then he remembered the naked pictures he'd found of her and was less surprised. 'Is there anything else you'd like me to remove?' he asked drily.

'No.' She glared at him. 'Hurry up.'

He removed his neckcloth, laid his coat carefully to one side and began to unfasten his shirt, his eyes on her face. He suspected her show of curt impatience was a cover for her embarrassment, and when she flushed beneath his steady gaze and briefly averted her eyes, he was sure of it.

A second later she looked straight at him, determinedly lifting her chin.

'I must study the details of anatomy if I am to improve,' she said. 'Do you know that Monsieur David first sketches the people in his paintings without clothes to ensure he positions them correctly?'

'I didn't know,' said Pierce. 'Does he ask his noble patrons to sit for their portraits naked?'

'I don't—' She looked startled. 'No, he cannot do. It would be unseemly. But he will have had many other opportunities to study anatomy.'

'And I am your opportunity,' said Pierce. 'Did you ask your last footman to pose for you? Jean-Baptiste?'

'Never!' Angry revulsion blazed in Mélusine's eyes as she swayed backwards. Then she took a deep breath and, with a creditable attempt to appear offhand, said, 'He wouldn't have been suitable.'

'Why not?' Until his conversation with Laurette, Pierce had been more interested in Jean-Baptiste's actions than his personality. Now he was becoming more curious about the man.

'He wasn't the right shape,' Mélusine said, her tone indicating the subject was closed.

'And I am?'

'I think you…could be,' she said, her gaze locked on his chest as he pulled off his shirt.

He saw her take a couple of quick breaths and suck her lip between her teeth. Her gaze lowered to his flat stomach, then lifted to scan the breadth of his shoulders as he pushed his shirt back.

Pierce felt his own heart rate quicken as he watched her watch him. She liked looking at him. He'd already known it, seen the way her eyes followed his movements in the mirror when he dressed her hair. But now he could see her eyes darken as he undressed. He was ten feet away from her, but he was very conscious of every breath she took and every subtle movement of her body as she watched him. He held the shirt in one hand for a moment before tossing it on top of his coat. Her eyes followed the movement of his arm. Her fascination and approval were unmistakable.

Pierce had never experienced anything like it. He'd undressed for women before, and received his share of feminine compliments, but he was sure Mélusine didn't intend this to be a prelude to making love. He was also confident she was aware of him in a way that had nothing to do with her desire to improve as an artist. He suspected that, if she realised it, she would be surprised and perhaps even dismayed by her reaction.

The devil in him wanted to put his theory to the test. What would she do if he took a few steps towards her? Perhaps even pulled her up into his arms?

He put his hands on his hips, standing relaxed but poised. 'You may touch me, if it would help your anatomical studies,' he said.

Her fingers flexed at his suggestion, then she blinked and seemed to return to herself.

'Oh, well,' she said, looking flustered. 'No. That will not be necessary. No. Thank you. Take off your wig.'

'Is that really necessary?' he asked, hesitating for the first time. The footman's wig was the last part of his limited disguise left. It would make little difference to anyone who knew him well, but it was a small barrier to recognition by anyone less familiar with him.

'Why do you mind?' she asked, intrigue lighting her eyes. 'Are you bald?'

'No!' Unreasonably offended, he threw the wig on top of his shirt and ran his fingers through his own hair. He saw the interest in her eyes intensify.

'I knew you didn't have brown hair,' she said, with satisfaction. 'Black hair, black brows, grey eyes. You look much more commanding without your clothes. Turn round slowly.'

'I feel like a horse in a sale yard,' he said as he obeyed. The situation could have been humiliating, even demeaning, but he was amused by rather than resentful of her commands. If he were genuinely dependent on Mélusine's good will for his continued employment, perhaps he would be less tolerant of catering to her whims. He also felt tenderly protective of her sensibilities. Her father and even Daniel had undermined her with their lack of respect for her wishes. It cost Pierce nothing to allow her authority over him in the sanctuary of her studio.

Mélusine stared at Pierre, completely entranced by his male beauty. He was standing in full daylight, and she could see every plane and angle of his upper body. Just as she'd suspected, his shoulders were pleasingly wide in proportion to his hips and his muscles lean and well defined. His natural grace was even more apparent without his clothes. She could see every bunch and flex of his muscles as he tossed aside his shirt and wig.

His skin was perfectly smooth apart from a thin scar across one shoulder, and the dark curls on his chest. His stance was relaxed, yet inherently self-confident. Without the camouflage of the footman's livery, his commanding presence seemed to fill the studio. The sight of him left her a little breathless and over-whelmed.

Her fingers flexed of their own volition as she wondered what his firm flesh felt like. He'd invited her to touch him. By now she knew it amused him to tease her, but he hadn't come any closer to her—which would be very disconcerting in his current state of undress—and he hadn't unkindly mocked her artistic ambitions.

As she continued to look at him, she felt the tension in the studio begin to rise and the silence to thicken. A rapid pulse began to beat in her throat. She was still staring at his chest. She wanted to look away com-pletely, but that would be cowardly. Nervous excite-ment filled her as she lifted her gaze to his face. He was watching her. His gaze had darkened into an intense ex-pression she couldn't read, but which she found pro-foundly unsettling.

Her mouth was dry. She swallowed. Drew her lower lip between her teeth and saw him focus on her mouth. She imagined him kissing her. Wondered what it would be like. Her body swayed slightly towards him.

The piece of charcoal broke between her tense

fingers. The snap seemed very loud in the silence. She looked down, startled, and became aware of her surroundings once more.

She took a deep breath, willing herself to regain her composure. She'd seen and felt a man's chest before. Even though he'd been in his forties, Bertier had still been in good physical condition. She'd only seen her husband without his shirt a couple of times, and she would never have asked him to model for her, but he'd been a strong man, though his stomach had acquired a small paunch. His chest hair had been grey. She'd been startled the first time she'd seen it, because he'd favoured a dark wig and he'd had the vigorous demeanour of a younger man.

She stared at the paper on the drawing board, trying to erase the image of Bertier from her mind. Soon she would have to think about him, their marriage and the manner of his death, but not for an hour or two. And it would be much better for her peace of mind if she only thought of Pierre as a means to improve her artistic understanding of anatomy.

She glanced around the studio for inspiration. 'Pick up that broom and hold it like a trident,' she said.

'A trident?'

'Or a spear. It doesn't matter. I'm going to sketch you in many different positions.' Her hands were still trembling from her reaction to seeing Pierre without his shirt, but she hoped, once she began to draw, that she'd feel more composed and like herself.

* * *

Pierce found his first half-hour as an artist's model moderately intriguing as Mélusine ordered him into frequent changes of position. After that the novelty of pretending his broom was everything from a medieval knight's lance to the pole of a regimental standard began to pall.

'I propose I lie down and pretend to be asleep,' he said testily, as Mélusine opened her mouth to command him into a new pose.

'You can't possibly be tired,' she protested.

'Did I say I was tired? This is confoundedly boring, *madame*!'

'Well, I am sorry you are bored, but I could have asked you to do something much more distasteful. Be glad you're not cleaning out the stables.'

'Hmm.' He put down the broom and sprang up to sit on one of the solid work benches a couple of feet away from her.

There was a smudge of charcoal on one of her cheeks and the auburn hair he had carefully pinned up before their visit to the Hôtel de Gilocourt was tumbling around her shoulders. He was afraid that was a reflection of his limited skills. Without the aid of pomade and powder to help fix them in place, he'd had a devil of a job to get her wayward curls to do what he wanted.

'I'm not over-fond of mucking out, but at least there is something to show for one's time,' he said.

'I didn't tell you to move,' said Mélusine.

He arched an eyebrow at her and stayed exactly where he was on the bench. He wondered what she'd do next. He was much closer to her now than he had been earlier and, because she was still sitting on the stool, she had to look up to meet his eyes. He already knew that wasn't a position she was likely to tolerate for long.

'Did you behave so impudently with the Duchesse?' Mélusine asked.

'She never told me to take my shirt off,' he replied. 'You must concede, *madame*, asking a man to take his shirt off does encourage him to take other liberties.'

Mélusine stood up so suddenly the stool fell over.

He laughed, and the next moment found she was hitting him with her discarded straw hat.

'Stop it!' she shouted between blows. 'Don't laugh at me! You have no *right* to laugh at me!'

Her attack took him completely by surprise. The straw hat was far too flimsy to injure him. Considering the number of makeshift weapons available in the studio, including the broom he'd cast aside, he doubted she really wanted to hurt him.

He ignored the flailing hat and caught her arms, pulling her up against the bench in front of him, and closing his knees on either side of her hips to keep her in place.

He heard her gasp, and she went absolutely still. She stared at him, her green eyes wide in her suddenly pale face. He saw the flash of fear and knew that in another second she would either scream or start to fight in earnest.

'Hush, don't look at me like that, sweetheart,' he murmured, shaken. 'What do you think I'm going to do to you, hmm?' He cupped her cheek briefly with his palm, then began to unwrap the hat ribbon from where it had become tangled around her wrists.

Mélusine looked down, breathing quickly, but holding her arms still as she watched Pierre unravel the ribbon. He was still holding her between his thighs. The pressure against her hips was light enough that she could step away if she wanted to, but for a few moments she didn't move. She was full of conflicting emotions and sensations. Even though she was nervous of his strength, it also excited her. She wanted to reach out and trace the outline of his biceps and explore the texture of the black curls on his chest. Of course she did no such thing—besides, her wrists were caught in the ribbons. It shook her even more as she realised that by becoming entangled she'd put herself at a greater disadvantage with him. But he was freeing her, and his gentleness was as enticing as his strength.

He pulled the ribbon clear and tossed her hat aside, but he put one hand under her elbow to keep her close and she was still standing between his legs.

She looked up into his eyes. Her heart was beating so fast she was afraid he'd hear it in her voice when she spoke. She was torn between a desire to escape and an equally compelling desire to press closer to him. She remained exactly where she was.

'I did not invite you to take liberties!' she said. 'If a male student wants to study anatomy or draw from life, no one laughs at him or thinks he's encouraging unseemly familiarity.'

Pierre smiled. '*Madame*, don't you know how many artists' models have combined the role of muse and lover?' he said. 'Do you think a man with a naked woman stretched out before him thinks only of pigment and perspective?'

Mélusine swallowed. She knew very well her first thoughts on seeing his bare chest had had very little to do with her artistic ambitions. Considering how distracted she'd been by his masculine beauty, she was amazed at the quality of the sketches she'd produced. But she had taken great pleasure in drawing him, and trying to capture on paper all that virile strength and energy.

'You said you didn't know anything about art,' she said.

'I don't know much. I'm speaking as a man.'

'Not all men paint women,' she pointed out, quite proud she was thinking clearly enough to come up with such a rejoinder.

'Not all men lust after women.'

'Oh.' Mélusine's thought processes hit a dead end.

Pierre stroked the side of his thumb against her lower lip. His grey eyes had darkened. All she could think was that *he* lusted after women, and right now he was lusting after *her*. No one ever had before. Bertier had fulfilled his marital obligations, but she'd never sensed the performance of his duty with her had given him any great pleasure.

Pierre was still cupping one of her elbows. Without thinking she lowered her other hand to rest on his thigh. When she felt his muscles flex beneath her palm she nearly snatched her hand away, but his grip on her hips tightened, and that did not seem a rejection, so she left her hand where it was.

The moment extended. Every fibre of her body was taut with expectation. She could not move, even a fraction of an inch. She waited for him to move…

And he did not.

Her thought processes began to grind slowly forwards again. Her position between his legs was completely inappropriate. Scandalous. Her whole body flushed with embarrassment. Just before she ducked her head in mortification, she saw the expression in his eyes change. It was not exactly rueful, but she knew he'd gone further than he'd intended. He touched her lip again, but this time it was not a prelude to seduction, it was…what…an apology? She didn't know for sure, but it helped her step away from him with a reasonable display of composure.

He was not laughing at her or mocking her, which meant their friendship was not irrevocably damaged by what had just happened.

'You may put on your shirt and coat now,' she said, proud her voice sounded so matter of fact. 'I will practise sketching you again tomorrow,' she added, partly from bravado and partly to reinforce the idea she had only an academic interest in his body. 'I wish to make a series of studies of your…shoulders…the full range of movements, I mean.'

'When you've finished studying my shoulders, will you study my legs next?' he asked, pushing off the bench and turning away from her to reach for his clothes.

'What?'

'I understand your interest in them at my interview now,' he said. 'I was wondering when you want to study that part of my anatomy more closely.'

'Never. I don't need to.' She took another couple of hasty steps away from him. On the day of his interview she'd thought perhaps she would sketch his legs one day, but now she knew what a potent effect his semi-nakedness had upon her, it would be completely unwise…outrageous…*terrifying* to let him remove any more clothes in her presence.

Fascinating. Intriguing. She could still remember the tantalisingly brief feel of his thigh beneath her hand. But it wouldn't be seemly to ask him to take off anything more than his shirt when he was modelling for her. She'd found it difficult enough to keep her mind on technique while she was drawing his torso. It might prove impossible if he wasn't wearing any breeches!

'You don't need to?' He was still standing half-turned away from her, but he paused, one arm in his waistcoat, to glance sideways at her. *'Madame*, it is very difficult

for a man to throw a spear, hold a lance or wrestle a
bear without the use of his legs.'

'Yes, but…' She hesitated. Explaining why she didn't
need to look at his legs meant revealing a secret
ambition she'd never shared with anyone else.

But so far, although he sometimes teased her, he'd
never made fun of her—and she wanted him to understand that her interest in his body was quite legitimate.

Even after she'd decided to show him, it took a little
while before she could, because she had to unwrap all
the layers that both protected it from damage and prevented the clay from drying out. She'd made it in the
Hôtel de Gilocourt, then carried it all the way to
Bordeaux and back again to Paris. She was afraid it
might have been hurt by so much transportation. She
thought perhaps now she could do better—or perhaps
she'd never make anything so fine again.

By the time she removed the final layer from the
piece of work which was closest to her heart, she was
churning with anxieties and hopes. Even though she
meant to show it to him, she couldn't help standing protectively between Pierre and the object she was about
to reveal. At last she took a deep breath and stepped
aside.

'She's not finished,' she said, speaking so fast her
words fell over each other. 'And I may try again with
another pose. I am still learning. I'm keeping her damp
so I can continue to work on her, although I don't think
the journey to Bordeaux was good for her. Not that I

mean to blame her flaws on anything but my limited skills…but I *am* still learning…'

She ran out of words and breath and stopped speaking. Her heart was beating so fast she felt sick and she twisted her fingers into knots as she waited for Pierre to say something.

Chapter Six

Pierce was still trying to control the urgent instinct to pull Mélusine back into his arms. He wanted to kiss her—he wanted to do a lot more than that with her. When she'd put her hand on his thigh, it had taken all his self-discipline to remain unmoving. He wanted to touch her and he wanted her hands on him—and not just on his leg. He wondered if she'd noticed his state of arousal when she'd stepped out of his reach. He'd turned away as he'd dressed to protect them both from his unruly passion, but the devil in him had compelled him to ask when she wanted to sketch his legs. Even though it was hardly the action of a gentleman, he had a strong desire to be naked in her presence—and for her to be equally naked. There were many precedents for the artist's model to be nude. He wondered how many artists had worked in the nude.

He knew Mélusine had, because he'd seen her self-portraits. Just the thought of it caused his body to harden more demandingly. He'd touched her. He'd very nearly kissed her and, though she didn't know it, he knew the charms concealed beneath her modest gowns.

He slammed the door shut on the mental image before he did something that would shock Mélusine and be to his dishonour. It had been one thing to contemplate seducing her when he'd thought she was a blackmailer who chose her lovers from among her servants. But now he'd seen how highly she prized her virtue and how deeply offended she was by the accusation she'd had a lover, an affair was out of the question. His mind knew that, even though his body rebelled.

Because he was struggling to control his own turbulent emotions, it took him a little while to notice Mélusine's agitation as she waited for his reaction to her work. Her cheeks were flushed. She was biting her lip, and she was twisting her fingers together so much he was afraid she'd hurt them if he didn't soon say something to lessen her anxiety.

He stepped forward and squatted down by the table so he could study the clay figurine she'd revealed. He'd meant to say something politely complimentary, but when he took a closer look he forgot his charitable intentions in genuine delight.

'She's a mermaid!' he exclaimed. 'She's beautiful.' The mermaid was sitting on a rock, her elegant tail curling gracefully down so one fin just dipped under the surface of the water. One small breast was modestly covered by her flowing hair, but the other was bare. Her hands rested together on what would have been her lap if she had had legs, but she was leaning forward, and her chin was raised. He had the impression she was looking far out to the horizon and that any moment she would slip back into the ocean and swim away.

'I'm still learning,' said Mélusine.

He glanced up and saw she'd stopped contorting her hands, though she was still holding them clasped together in front of her.

'I see many things I must improve upon,' she continued. 'Bertier allowed me to have my own studio at Hôtel de Gilocourt. He was generous in that respect— he was generous in many respects,' she added a little sadly. 'I was going to learn about kilns and firing techniques, but then he died and I went back to Bordeaux. It was not so easy there.'

'She's beautiful,' Pierce said again, not sure how to put into words the emotions the mermaid conjured in him.

'Do you mean it?' Mélusine's voice caught. 'I have not shown her to anyone else. I don't know if she is good or not. But I wanted you to see why I don't need to know about your legs.'

Pierce gazed at the figurine for a few more moments. He could tell that the overall proportions were slightly awkward, the angle of one arm not quite natural, but the little mermaid had a personality that emerged even through the clay and brought her to life. Whether Mélusine knew it or not, she had put a great deal of herself into the figure. He guessed she'd tried to disguise the facial features, but he had a good memory of the sketches she'd drawn of herself. The line of the shoulders, the curve of the breast and the indentation of the waist were all Mélusine's. A few minutes ago he'd been trying to forget those sketches—now they'd been given form before his eyes. There was something both stimulating and disorientating in gazing upon the naked image of a woman he desired, when the clothed, living original was standing at his shoulder, breathlessly awaiting his verdict.

He took a moment to remind himself that Mélusine wanted reassurance about her artistic skills, not her feminine allure. It would surely embarrass her if she guessed he'd recognised her in her creation. He stood up and glanced at Mélusine's flushed cheeks. 'You have a gift. You should develop it,' he said.

She searched his face, then smiled at him with such misty happiness she took his breath away. 'Yes, I should,' she whispered. 'I should. And I'm going to!'

'I see why you didn't need to know about legs for your mermaid,' he said. 'But if you make a man, he will need them.'

'Not man,' she said. 'I'm going to make a merman. He'll be the perfect companion for her. They'll be the perfect pair.'

Pierce looked down at the figurine, then up at Mélusine's wistful expression. He delicately touched the little mermaid's tail with one finger, just where her knees would be if she'd had any.

'But they'll never be able to experience the ultimate

union,' he said gently. 'Not if they've nothing but fish tails from their waists down.'

Mélusine reddened, then she pushed his hand away from the mermaid, and curved her own hands protectively around the clay figure.

'They will sing and make music and talk. They'll talk about the songs of the sea and all the new things they discover as they swim from place to place. I expect they'll go to England and America and the South Seas…'

Whether she knew it or not, she'd just told him a great deal about her experience of marriage. It would embarrass her to comment on it—and he wasn't in a position to teach her that there could be great pleasure in physical union. So he smiled and said, 'If they were ever spotted, Mer people in New York harbour would cause a stir. I wish I'd seen them. Do they ever come up the Seine to visit Paris, do you suppose?'

Mélusine didn't say anything for a moment, and he wondered if she thought he was laughing at her. She stunned him by suddenly flinging her arms around him and hugging him tight before just as quickly stepping back and well out of his reach.

'Your sister is lucky to have such a brother,' she said in a small, gruff voice.

'That has not always been her opinion,' he replied, startled into honesty by her unexpected behaviour. He'd frequently transgressed the bounds of behaviour between servant and mistress, but he hadn't thought Mélusine would act so spontaneously towards him. He could still feel the pressure of her hands on his back through his waistcoat. If she hadn't taken him so completely by surprise, he wouldn't have been able to resist catching hold of her, and perhaps even kissing her.

'I'm sure you tease her unmercifully when you've a mind to,' Mélusine said, still bright red, and obviously trying to pretend she hadn't behaved so impulsively. 'But you have a kind heart. I must wrap her up again. I do not want her to dry out before she is finished.'

'Why a mermaid?' Pierce asked, watching how tenderly she packed the figurine away. 'Because you grew up in Bordeaux, so close to the Atlantic?'

'Partly. But it is also my name. Of course, Mélusine was not exactly a mermaid, but still…'

'Of course.' Because his mother was French, Pierce spoke the language like a native. But he'd grown up in England and he'd not immediately remembered the French legend of Mélusine, the fairy who turned into a serpent from the waist down every Saturday. The legendary Mélusine had made her mortal husband promise never to visit her on that day. Eventually his curiosity had become too strong and he'd seen her in a serpent form, condemning her to an existence as a wandering spirit.

Now he'd remembered it, Pierce thought the story could stand as a useful warning of the hazards of marriage. Ask for too much and you risk losing everything. And if one partner has a secret they cannot share with the other, disaster will surely follow for both of them.

He thought of La Motte's secrets which, if ever discovered, threatened to destroy the lives of so many people. And even his own secrets, though of far lesser magnitude than La Motte's, made him a far-from-desirable match. In his heart he knew he'd not been a good husband to Rosalie, though he'd never been unfaithful to her. He prayed she'd never sensed his gradual loss of enthusiasm for their marriage.

'It's how I got my name,' said Mélusine, recalling Pierce's attention to the present.

'I don't understand.'

'The fairy Mélusine gave a terrible cry of despair when her husband saw her tail,' she said. 'The *"cri de Mélusine"*. Father gave just such a cry of despair when he heard I'd been born a daughter. That's what I was told. So that's what I was called.'

She turned her back on Pierce and went to put the carefully wrapped figurine away.

By his side, Pierce's hand clenched slowly into a fist. He already despised Raoul Fournier, and now Mélusine had given him another reason to loathe the man. Before he could say anything he heard footsteps running up the stairs and then Suzanne burst through the door.

'Madame," the maid gasped, 'the Comte de Gilocourt is here to see you.'

'Séraphin?' Mélusine spun round. 'He was in Versailles this morning.'

'He's in the blue salon now, large as life,' said

Suzanne, startled out of her usual taciturnity by the un-expected visitor. She glanced curiously at Pierce, still in his shirt sleeves.

He said nothing, but made a mental note to be prepared for questions when he encountered Suzanne later in the servants' quarters.

'Offer the Comte refreshment and say I will be with him shortly,' said Mélusine. 'You must stand outside the door and listen,' she said to Pierce after the maid had gone, as she washed her hands in a basin of water. 'I will leave the door slightly ajar when I go in. I'm going to ask him about Bertier's death.' She started towards the door, then hesitated. 'How does my hair look?' she asked. 'Do I have any smudges on my face?'

'There's some charcoal on your left cheek. Allow me.' He rubbed the mark gently with a spotless hand-kerchief, and tweaked a few curls into different posi-tions. Then he stood back and gave her an appraising look. 'Fashionably dishevelled,' he announced. 'Some women pay their hairdressers a fortune to achieve that look. You make the task easy for me, *madame*. Does he know of your interest in art?'

'He has never seen my work, but he knew Bertier let me have a studio,' said Mélusine.

'Then you have no need to worry about the odd smear of dust on your skirts,' said Pierce. 'If he is rude enough to comment, you may give him the impression you were seeking solace for your grief in your art, and no further explanation will be required.'

Mélusine frowned. 'If it hadn't been for Daniel, I would not have worn black silk in here,' she said. 'If I'm not more careful, I will soon have nothing fit to wear when I go out. But it is convenient now. And I don't suppose Séraphin ever considers wearing anything less than finest silk whatever his activity.'

'He's a fop?' said Pierce, putting on his coat and replacing his footman's wig over his own hair.

'No...o...o,' said Mélusine slowly, beginning to descend the stairs. 'He wears lace, silk and scent—but underneath I think he is like you. He is taller than you. But he moves—not in exactly the same way, but he has the same arrogant certainty his body will not fail him. Not all men have that. Bertier did, even though he was so much older. The King doesn't. He shambles—' She broke off as they reached the bottom of the flight of stairs. 'You must tell me your opinion later,' she said softly. She closed her eyes and drew in a slow breath. Pierce could see her gathering herself for the coming meeting. Then she opened her eyes and noticed him watching her.

'Séraphin is so graceful and elegant I always feel clumsy in his company,' she said ruefully. 'Ah, well, there's nothing I can do about that, so I won't think of it.'

'If he distresses you, tell him to leave,' said Pierce. 'I will make sure he does.' Even if he hadn't already suspected Séraphin of being the blackmailer, he wouldn't have felt charitable to Mélusine's brother-in-law. He didn't appreciate being told he was like another man, especially when that man's defining characteristic was apparently a preference for wearing scent and lace.

Séraphin was standing with his back to the empty hearth when Mélusine entered the blue salon. It was the most elegantly furnished reception room in the house, but it was a long way from the grandeur of the Hôtel de Gilocourt and hardly did justice to Séraphin's sartorial splendour.

His appearance hadn't changed since the last time Mélusine had seen him. As Bertier's brother and heir, he was only required to wear mourning for six months, and he was exquisitely garbed in full court attire, with a light dress sword by his side.

He turned as he heard her enter the room and immediately approached her with both hands outstretched.

'My dear sister, I am glad to see you again.'

'Thank you.' She endured the chaste kiss on her cheek and stepped away as soon as courtesy allowed. 'I'm pleased to see you also. How are you?'

'Very well. I'm sorry I missed you this morning. François told me you called.'

'I thought you were in Versailles. Please, sit down.' She gestured to the sofa, and was immediately conscious of the lack of finesse in her own movements as he gracefully responded to her invitation.

She didn't believe such elegance was innate to the

nobility—if that was the case, Louis XVI would cut a much more impressive figure than he did—but Séraphin imbued even the most mundane activities with aristocratic refinement.

'I've been returning to Paris regularly,' he said. 'It was remiss of me not to call upon you before. I had not realised you'd returned.'

'I only arrived a couple of days ago,' said Mélusine.

'If there is any service I can perform for you, please tell me at once,' he said. 'Who is managing your affairs—your inheritance from Bertier?'

'Monsieur Barrière. He was Bertier's lawyer—'

'One of them,' said Séraphin. 'I had no idea my brother's affairs were so complex until I had occasion to look into them.'

'I was surprised he left me this house and the others,' said Mélusine, wondering if Séraphin resented Bertier's generosity towards her.

'No more than you deserve, my dear,' he replied. She caught a hint of patronising indulgence in his tone and inwardly bristled. She was two years older than Séraphin. It annoyed her that he'd always treated her as if she were a child.

'Do you have confidence in Barrière?' he asked. 'Though Bertier is now lost to us, we will always be bound by ties of family and affection. I would be honoured to assume responsibility for your affairs.'

'You are very kind. Very generous,' Mélusine said, startled and horrified at the prospect of Séraphin's interference. 'I would not wish to trespass so far on your time or goodwill. Besides, Bertier chose Monsieur Barrière for me. I am sure he would not have done so if there was any doubt about his trustworthiness. So far he has been irreproachable in the way he has collected the rents and dealt with the tenants.'

'As you wish.' Séraphin shrugged elegantly. 'Did you have a particular purpose when you visited the Hôtel de Gilocourt this morning?'

'To see you, of course, and let you know I'm back in Paris,' said Mélusine, which was a polite lie. She'd been prepared to meet Séraphin but she'd hoped he wouldn't be there.

'Most gracious. Most punctilious. And?'

'And what?' The uncharacteristic sharpness in his usually suave tones disconcerted her.

'Was there another motive for your visit?'

'Oh.' Mélusine resisted the urged to smooth her skirt and instead folded her hands in her lap. 'Yes. I heard the most bizarre rumour yesterday. If it wasn't so grotesque it would be laughable. I wondered if you'd heard it.'

'Paris is full of rumours,' said Séraphin, negligently moving his long legs from one elegant position to another. 'You must tell me more before I can comment.'

'This rumour concerns Bertier's death,' said Mélusine. She took a careful breath. 'Apparently there are suspicions that he was not attacked by street robbers, but that he fought a secret duel and died from a sword thrust,' she said very evenly.

'I have heard whispers,' Séraphin said dismissively. 'There is no need to regard them.'

His offhand manner annoyed Mélusine. 'Did you see Bertier's body?' she asked.

'Naturally I paid my last respects to my brother,' he said haughtily.

'Then you saw the nature of his wounds. What were they?'

Séraphin raised his eyebrows. 'I did not wash and dress his corpse,' he said, even more haughtily. 'I have no reason to doubt what I was told by the police.'

'And the other part of the rumour?'

'Which part?' Despite his pretended ignorance, his half-closed eyes gleamed with knowledge.

'The false claim that I had a secret lover—and it was he who fought the duel with Bertier,' Mélusine said tightly.

'I have heard something to that effect, but naturally I discounted it,' said Séraphin.

'There is no truth in it,' said Mélusine.

'Knowing you, my dear sister, I am sure that is true,' he said, and something in his tone made that less than the compliment it should have been. He stood up. 'Forgive me, I'm afraid I must leave you. I have another engagement this evening.'

'What about Bertier's lover?' Mélusine asked, just as Séraphin reached the door.

'Bertier's lover?' he repeated.

'His mistress,' she said, reddening with embarrassment, but irritated by Séraphin's aloof, dismissive manner. 'Isn't it possible he fought another man over *her* favours?'

Séraphin was silent for several moments, then he smiled coolly. 'Bertier didn't have a mistress,' he said.

'He *did*!' Mélusine had known that almost from the start of her marriage. 'There is no need to protect my feelings. I always knew he had a mistress.'

'Not when he died,' said Séraphin. 'At the time of his death you were the only woman in his life, my dear.'

Pierce had listened to the conversation from beside the salon door, which Mélusine had not completely closed. Now he took a couple of steps to one side and gazed impassively into space as Séraphin passed him and languidly descended the stairs, the delicate scent of cologne wafting around him. The sight—and smell—of Mélusine's brother-in-law set Pierce's teeth on edge. He had no difficulty believing Séraphin would resort to blackmail, but after seeing him, he did resent Mélusine's suggestion he had anything in common with the French nobleman. But he'd learnt to respect her powers of observation, so he looked again, more closely.

Mélusine had claimed Séraphin moved as if he had complete confidence in his body. As Pierce watched him walk down the stairs, he saw what she meant. The artificially exaggerated grace of Séraphin's movements was an initial distraction, but closer study suggested there was some strength in the long limbs encased in satin and lace. And his conversation with Mélusine indicated he was not a fool. Pierce suspected he'd known from the beginning why Mélusine had visited the Hôtel de Gilocourt. Once Séraphin had confirmed his suppositions, and discovered Mélusine had no further information to add, he'd left.

There was another reason why Séraphin was very likely to be the blackmailer, and why Pierce had finally discounted any possibility it could be Mélusine. He's always assumed she was in desperate need of money to ensure her independence, but he'd just discovered her inheritance from Bertier was in the hands of her lawyer, not her father, and was sufficiently substantial for Séraphin to fish for control of it. Pierce still didn't know why she was living in a house with bare floorboards and empty, echoing chambers, but apparently it wasn't because she couldn't afford to furnish it.

Séraphin, on the other hand, was clearly a very expensive flower of the nobility.

'Bertier *did* have a mistress,' Mélusine said as soon as Pierre joined her in the salon. 'I know he did. I saw her.'

'He introduced you?' Pierre sounded both startled and disapproving. 'Is she a member of fashionable society?'

'No. But I saw them together once. She is very vivacious. It doesn't make sense. Why would Séraphin pretend Bertier didn't have a mistress? He must know I already knew.'

Pierre stood for a moment, then sat in the chair opposite. 'He said your husband didn't have a mistress at the time of his death,' he reminded her. 'Not that he'd never had one.'

'That's true.' Mélusine frowned as she remembered Séraphin's exact wording. 'I wonder when he lost her.'

'Lost her? Could he not have set her aside because he realised the wrong he was doing you?' Pierre demanded.

'Oh, no!' Mélusine exclaimed. 'He wouldn't have done that. She'd been his mistress long before he married me. No one ever pretended he wanted me for anything other than an heir.'

'Did he often treat you unkindly?' Pierre asked.

Something in his voice caught her attention. She'd been puzzling over the mystery of Bertier's mistress, but now she looked at Pierre. She was startled and then unaccountably warmed that he appeared to be offended on her behalf. She wasn't used to anyone else being angry on her behalf. She remembered the way he'd almost kissed her earlier and felt a strange flutter as she wondered what it all meant. She couldn't think about it now. Not when Pierre was expecting an answer and she had the mystery of Bertier's death to solve.

'At first he didn't treat me unkindly at all,' she said, wanting to be fair to Bertier. 'It wasn't comfortable, of course. We were strangers on our wedding day. The first time I ever set eyes on him was when the marriage contract was signed. He was very formal, and sometimes it was awkward, but for the first year or more he was quite amiable.'

'And then he changed?'

'He started to have terrible rages—and then he became quite morose. I tried to avoid him,' she admitted.

'Do you know why he fell into a black mood?'

'At first I thought it was because I hadn't given him an heir yet, and I felt very unhappy,' she said. 'But then I considered—he'd been married to his first wife for years without having children. Why should it be my fault?'

'Your father seems to have come to the same conclusion,' said Pierre.

'I don't know why he didn't think of it before,' said Mélusine bitterly. 'It's not as if he doesn't know it can happen.'

'*Madame?*'

'He was very ill several months before I was born,' she said. 'They didn't expect him to live, but he did. Mama told me once when she was particularly upset. Everyone has always assumed it was her fault they had no more children. But she told me that after his illness he could never father any more children—that's why he was filled with such despair when I was born a girl. I'm the only child he would ever have.'

'Then he should value you all the more as a gift of God!' Pierre said furiously.

Mélusine stared at him, wide-eyed. She could feel the anger radiating from him. 'No one's ever said that before,' she said.

'They should have done.' He sprang to his feet and walked over to the window.

Mélusine gazed at his rigid shoulders. 'Mama once said it was God's punishment for Father,' she said. 'But I cannot agree. It would be very unjust to punish Father in a way which makes him unkind to others. I think it was just…something that happened. By chance, not design.'

'That is a very sensible attitude, *madame*.' Pierre's voice was more clipped than she'd ever heard it, and he didn't turn away from the window.

Mélusine's stomach knotted. Pierre had his back to her, but he was unmistakably angry and experience had taught her to be wary—if not frightened—of an angry man. Her natural instinct was to remain silent and do nothing to draw his attention back to her—but after only a few seconds she realised she should not unthinkingly apply the lessons of the past to her dealings with Pierre. He had never treated her unkindly.

She stood up and walked over to him. He didn't look at her, and as he continued to gaze out of the window his profile was set and unyielding. She was almost ashamed at how much courage it took to touch his arm—and shocked to discover his muscles were as hard as marble beneath her fingers.

'Are you…are you angry at…*Father*?' she whispered.

'Yes, *madame*,' he said crisply, and turned to face her.

She stared at him, stunned and a little breathless he could feel such outrage on her behalf. 'Because…?' she said, and bit her lip as she waited for his reply.

'A man should protect those who depend on him,' he said. 'Not treat them unkindly for something that is no fault of theirs—or use them only to satisfy his own ambitions.'

Pierre's declaration was so unexpected, and so uncompromising in its condemnation of her father's behaviour, that Mélusine felt an uncharacteristic urge to cry. But she'd learnt long ago that tears solved nothing and only made her more vulnerable.

She waited until she was sure she could control the trembling of her lower lip and said, 'It was a... lucky...chance for me that you were looking for a new position just as I arrived in Paris.'

Pierre's smile was a little crooked, perhaps because his jaw was still rigid. He had his temper well under control now, but she could still sense his anger simmering under the surface. She stepped away from him, trying to think of something to say to break the tension. Nothing immediately presented itself and she went back to the puzzle of Bertier's mistress.

'What if Bertier's sudden bad moods were caused by the split with his mistress!' she exclaimed suddenly. 'That makes sense, doesn't it? And then...I can easily imagine he might fight a duel with the man who stole her from him.' She was excited at the possibility she might have come closer to solving the mystery of his death.

'It's possible,' Pierre conceded. 'But there are still no solid grounds to believe he wasn't attacked by street robbers, exactly as you were originally informed.'

'But I want to know for sure,' said Mélusine. 'Rumours start somewhere, no matter how twisted out of shape they finally become. I know he didn't fight my lover over me because I have no lover. But he might have fought his mistress's lover over *her*. I can believe he might do that.'

'Does it matter?' Pierce asked. 'You brother-in-law has told you he believes you were faithful to your husband. Everyone in Paris is more concerned with the latest news from the Estates-General than private scandals. In a few months' time no one will remember this particular rumour.'

'I'll remember,' she said. 'And I want to know the truth. Perhaps I owe it to Bertier to discover the truth too,' she said in a low voice.

'Does he deserve such consideration?' Pierce asked. 'He did not treat you well.'

'Not at the end,' she admitted. 'There were times I never wanted to see him again—but he left me this house and the others. And he made sure my affairs are managed by Monsieur Barrière, not my father. Without this inheritance I would have no hope of following my own wishes. I owe him for that, I think. Tomorrow we will speak to the police,' she concluded, and her tone brooked no argument.

Chapter Seven

Morning, Saturday, 11 July 1789

'What do you hope to gain from speaking to the police inspector?' Pierre asked as he combed out Mélusine's hair.

'The truth—' She broke off, biting her lip as she saw his sceptical expression in the mirror. 'You think if he was bribed to lie about the condition of Bertier's body, he will have no reason to tell the truth now,' she said.

'Exactly so, *madame*.'

'I could offer him more money—'

'Under no circumstances!' Pierre said forcefully. He put his hands on her shoulders to emphasize his point. 'Under no circumstances offer him money, *madame*.'

His touch ignited a shimmer of excitement in Mélusine. She was instantly thrown back to the moment in the studio yesterday when he'd held her between his knees. She was almost sure he'd wanted to kiss her. She'd spent much of the night reliving every second of the incident—and wondering if he ever *would* kiss her. She'd even crept out of her bedroom and up to the studio to fetch down some of her sketches of him. She'd gazed at them in the candlelight for a long time before concealing them from her maid's eyes at the bottom of a chest. She'd pressed her fingers against her mouth and wondered what his lips would feel like against hers. Of course she shouldn't be having such thoughts about a footman— but Pierre wasn't like any footman she'd previously known. He wasn't like any other man she'd known. His grip on her shoulders was firm and commanding, and undoubtedly transgressed the boundaries between mistress and servant. He was clearly accustomed to taking charge of others.

He was still looking at her in the mirror and she was assailed by an irrational fear he could read her mind. Instead of feeling cold, she flushed with such intense mortification her body seemed to be on fire. She was immediately convinced Pierre would feel the heat and embarrassment radiating through her shoulders into his hands. For a moment her throat was so tight she couldn't speak. She straightened her spine, tried to ignore her burning cheeks and managed to say, 'You're supposed to take orders, not give them.'

'A wise man—or woman—knows when to seek the counsel of those with wider experience,' he retorted, taking his hands from her shoulders. He lifted her hair over one of his hands and began to draw the comb through it with the other. His fingers brushed the nape of her neck and a tingle of awareness rippled through her. Did he know? Did he feel it too? Or was he quite indifferent to such accidental contact?

'If the police inspector did take a bribe to lie about the condition of your husband's body, he will not simply admit that to you today,' said Pierre. He sounded completely normal, as if he had nothing else on his mind except their conversation. He obviously didn't feel anything and it was vital she never let him guess how it affected her when he touched her.

'The only reason he might be persuaded to speak freely that I can think of is if he was asked to put about the tale of street robbers not to conceal a crime, but to protect your feelings,' Pierre continued. 'If that is the case, and if the inspector sees you find the uncertainty of not knowing what happened to your husband more distressing than whatever truth he is concealing, he might answer your questions.'

Because she was only half-concentrating on their conversation, it took Mélusine a moment to absorb what he'd just said. 'What could be more distressing than being told your husband was attacked by brigands?' she said, frowning in bewilderment. 'Pierre?' When he didn't immediately respond, she half-turned and caught his arm.

'It is remotely possible your husband could have died in the midst of some debauchery,' he said reluctantly.

'What—? But Séraphin said he didn't have a mistress.'

'We are under no obligation to believe everything Séraphin says,' Pierre replied drily. 'However, I think it is unlikely that's what happened. If the Inspector was bribed to conceal a crime...' He frowned as he began to pin up her hair. 'It may become necessary to offer him a counter-bribe, but you must not be part of that. If it does become necessary, I will deal with it.'

Mélusine drew in a sharp breath as the possible ramifications of her meeting with the police inspector came home to her. 'Do you have a lot of experience at bribing the police?' she asked, assuming he didn't, though he'd surprised her before.

'No. I would rather employ other methods to uncover the truth,' he said. 'I have friends in Paris. I will ask them to make discreet enquiries.'

'You have friends here?' said Mélusine.

'You sound surprised.'

'No. I know you must have friends. I just... It is a different world.' She tried to imagine what he would be like in the company of his friends. How would he behave? Would he seem like the same man or somebody different? Were his friends servants, trades-men—or even soldiers?

'Did you ever think of being a soldier?' she asked. She could easily imagine him engaged in a position that required more physical exertion than that of footman-hairdresser. And he had a natural tendency to give orders—though ordinary soldiers were supposed to obey orders, not give them.

'I spent some years at sea.'

'In a merchant ship?' She swivelled round to look up at him. 'Where did you sail from?'

He frowned at her. 'You have disarranged my work, *madame*. You must keep your head still until I've finished.'

She wasn't daunted by his severe tone. She could see the half-smile in his eyes and it filled her with a rush of pleasure. 'What kind of ship did you serve in? What other places have you been to apart from America? What did you *do* on the ship?'

'I served the captain. It was a privateer.'

'A privateer!' she exclaimed. 'Did you fight often? Is that how you got the scar on your shoulder? Did you capture many prizes?'

'Sometimes. Yes. A few,' he replied briefly.

'Goodness.' Mélusine exhaled as she adjusted her perception of Pierre. Her initial surprise quickly vanished as she realised she had no difficulty seeing him in such a role. 'I doubt if many hairdressers have your varied experiences,' she said. 'No wonder you're so confident you can throw people out of the house.' She paused, as a fragmentary thought flickered across her mind. What was it? Something she'd meant to ask Pierre.

'What aren't you good at?' she said suddenly.

'I beg your pardon?'

'You said yesterday that you lacked aptitude in certain things. What things?'

He looked at her for a few seconds, then gently turned her to face the mirror with a hand on either shoulder and continued to pin up her hair.

As the silence lengthened she began to wonder if she'd inadvertently touched on some particularly sensitive area. Perhaps even offended him, which was not at all what she'd intended.

'Does your pride forbid you to tell me?' she asked at last, her voice constricted with awkwardness.

'Marriage,' he said abruptly, without taking his eyes from what he was doing. 'I lacked aptitude for marriage, *madame.*'

It was the last thing she'd expected him to say and his words filled her with a strange and confusing mix of emotions.

'I…but…you grieved for your wife,' she said uncertainly. 'I was sure you did.'

'Of course. She was beautiful. Innocent. She died far too young—have you been vaccinated for smallpox?'

'What? Oh, yes,' she stammered slightly as his sharp change of topic took her off balance.

'Good. I should have asked Rosalie. I didn't think— and then it was too late.'

She could hear the self-censure in his voice.

'You are not responsible for her contracting smallpox,' she said, overcome by a compelling need to reassure him. 'You cannot say you were a bad husband because you never asked your wife if she'd been vaccinated for smallpox.'

'No.' He smiled faintly. 'I don't think that. Not often, at any rate.'

'Then why do you say you have no aptitude for marriage? Were you unfaithful to her?'

'No.' He sighed. 'You are very persistent.'

'Only because you are allowing me to be,' she said. She knew it was true. She'd never have questioned any other man she'd known so boldly. It was only because Pierre had become so important to her she had the courage to continue this conversation now that it had strayed into such an uncomfortable area. 'You have such a kind heart that you don't want to hurt me, even though I'm annoying you.'

'Hmm. Very well, then. The truth is I should never have married,' he said bluntly. 'I knew I'd made a mistake within months of the wedding, but it was too late. She was virtuous and desirable, and I'd been driven by a combination of lust and honourable intentions. I would have done better to suppress both.'

For a few moments Mélusine was at a loss for words.

'You...lusted...after her, but you didn't love her?' she said at last.

'Something of that nature. I *liked* her. We never had an argument in all the months we were married. Only when she tried to order me from her sickroom, because she was afraid for me.' He looked away, his lips twisting before he once more regained his familiar, composed expression. 'The fault was mine. Is mine. I am not suited to the confines of marriage. I get... restless...if I stay in one place too long.'

'You'll not marry again?' A heavy weight seemed to settle on her chest.

'No.'

'But...you'll not remain celibate for the rest of your life?' The question burst out of her before she had time to consider it.

He glanced at her. 'Very unlikely,' he agreed drily.

'So how...?' She looked down and smoothed a crease in her peignoir. She sensed he was ill at ease with the direction of their conversation and she was acutely embarrassed by it, yet she was also painfully interested in his answer.

'Not all women are looking for marriage,' he said. 'And before I take any woman to my bed in future, I will make sure she understands what I can—and what I can't—offer her. Your hair is done, *madame*.'

Mélusine stared unseeingly at her peignoir. She didn't know for sure—she was completely inexperienced in such matters—but had Pierre just told her why he hadn't kissed her the previous day? Because he believed she wasn't the kind of woman who took lovers? He had every reason to believe that. From the moment she'd heard the rumour about her non-existent lover she'd been vehement on the subject. But for the first time since Bertier's death she began to question her decision to hold herself aloof from all men. She was

not bound by marriage vows now. Her conduct was
entirely her own affair.

She became aware of Pierre watching her in the
mirror. The idea was so new she was uncomfortable
thinking about it in his presence. She could reflect on
the matter alone later. She pushed it aside to concentrate on the matter in hand.

'We will go first to the Hôtel de Police,' she said. 'I
don't know where to find the inspector I want to talk to,
so I'll speak to the Lieutenant of Police. I've met him,'
she added, hoping those few brief words she'd exchanged with Louis de Crosne would stand her in good
stead.

'At the time of your husband's death?'

'Oh.' She blinked in surprise, because she'd been
thinking of another occasion entirely. 'Yes, I believe
he did call, but I didn't see him. He spoke to
Séraphin, I think.'

'When did you see him before then?' Pierre
sounded puzzled.

'At various receptions. Bertier introduced him to me.
He's an important man. He goes to see the King every
week. There are not many people who see the King so
frequently, or even at all. The Hôtel de Police is in the
rue Neuve des Capucins. It is so close we can walk there.'

Pierce was instinctively opposed to Mélusine's visit
to the police, but he'd already learnt that once she had
set her mind on a course, she wasn't easily dissuaded

from it. She was pale with apprehension as they walked through the streets, and when they came in sight of the Hôtel de Police she lost what little colour remained in her cheeks. He was torn between admiration for her courage and frustration at the situation in which he found himself.

Mélusine wanted to find out who'd killed Bertier. Pierce wanted to find the blackmailer. It was possible they were looking for the same man, although Pierce still thought Séraphin was the most likely candidate to be the blackmailer. The first blackmail letter hadn't been delivered until months after Bertier's death, which suggested Séraphin had discovered the evidence of La Motte's smuggling partnership with Bertier by chance after he'd gained possession of his brother's papers.

If Bertier had been deliberately murdered, Pierce didn't want Mélusine anywhere near the killer. And if Bertier's death and the blackmail *were* linked, he didn't want the police to re-investigate and perhaps stumble across the evidence that was being used to blackmail La Motte. Pierce had great respect for the Parisian police—although until now he'd been more interested in the activities of the section that dealt with smuggling than that which investigated homicide.

Above all, he had a fierce urge to protect Mélusine. That wasn't a novel experience for him. He was aware of his tendencies in that direction—and sometimes they caused him a certain wry amusement. But his feelings for Mélusine were much more complex than a combination of desire and gallantry. He wanted to protect her, but he also had deep respect for her courage and determination.

He enjoyed talking to her, and he was fascinated by the pictures she'd drawn and the clay figurine of the mermaid. His sleep had been disturbed by erotic dreams in which Mélusine had been completely naked—but her lower half hadn't been encased in a virginal mermaid's tail. In his dream her legs had been wrapped around his hips. It took all his self-discipline to push those images out of his mind. When he'd believed Mélusine was the blackmailer, he'd have had no qualms about becoming her lover. Now an affair was out of the question. If he allowed himself to imagine her in his bed too often, he'd end up in a state of extremely dissatisfied frustration.

Mélusine stopped suddenly, just outside the Hôtel de Police. She lifted her gloved hand to her lips and he saw her throat move convulsively.

'*Madame?*' He touched her arm in concern.

After a moment she gave him a tight smile. 'My mouth was too dry to swallow,' she said hoarsely. 'It is reasonable, I think, that I should want to know whether they have found those responsible for my husband's death.'

'Very reasonable,' he agreed.

'That is how I will begin. I won't mention anything about the rumours at first. Perhaps I won't have to mention them at all. I will say that now I have returned to Paris I am able to speak to the police myself. As Bertier's widow I have a right to know the full details of his death.'

'Certainly, *madame*.'

'Even though you don't approve of this visit at all?'

'I do not wish you to be distressed by it. Perhaps you could ask Monsieur Barrière to enquire on your behalf?' he suggested, even though on a practical level it was better for him if Mélusine asked the questions because then he'd be confident he had the true answers. He was within a heartbeat of saying he'd make the enquiries himself. But the Parisian police were notoriously keen on identifying and recording the details of all visitors to their city, and in the circumstances he didn't want to risk drawing their interest.

'I could ask Monsieur Barrière. But then he might hear the rumours and…and…I just don't want him to if he doesn't have to.' Mélusine took a deep breath. 'You will stay with me at all times,' she instructed. 'Don't say anything. At least, not after you've announced my wish to speak to the lieutenant. But stay with me and listen in case I miss something. Also…' she glanced at his fine livery '…you make me look more important. They will have to pay attention to me, I am the Comtesse de Gilocourt.'

She sounded almost surprised as she claimed the title.

'It is you who give grace to the title, *madame*,' said Pierce, with complete sincerity.

Mélusine blinked, then a brief but warm smile lit up her face. 'Thank you. That's kind of you to say. Well...' Her smile faded and she took another deep breath. 'Let us proceed.'

It took some time after Pierce presented her card and explained her wish to see the lieutenant before they were finally ushered into the police chief's presence.

'Comtesse, it is a pleasure to see you again.' Lieutenant de Crosne bowed over her hand. Unobtrusively watching, Pierce judged him to be in his early fifties.

'Monseigneur, I trust you are in good health,' Mélusine replied. Her slight breathlessness was the only indication she wasn't entirely at ease. Pierce was proud of her composure.

'I am very well, thank you,' said Crosne. 'Please, sit down. How may I serve you?'

'I have come about my husband's death,' Mélusine said.

'I was sorry not to be able to give you my condolences in person.' Beneath the lieutenant's formal courtesy, there was a hint of impatience, as if he felt he had more important things to do than talk to a grieving widow, no matter how noble her late husband had been.

Pierce wasn't surprised. Among other things Crosne was responsible for keeping order in Paris. The Palais Royal was outside the lieutenant's jurisdiction because it was owned by a member of the royal family, but Crosne could not fail to be aware that a significant part of the population was in a state of simmering readiness to riot.

'Thank you,' said Mélusine. 'Your condolences were passed on to me. I'm sorry I was too distressed to speak to you then. At the time I left Paris, it wasn't known who was responsible for his death,' she continued, speaking much more quickly. Pierce thought she'd probably noticed the lieutenant's ill-disguised impatience to end the conversation. 'Has any more information come to light since then?'

'I am not aware of any.' Crosne tilted his head and glanced at the door.

'I would like to speak to the inspector who brought the Comte's body home,' Mélusine said. 'I don't know where to find him.'

Crosne frowned briefly at the question. 'I will have one of my secretaries speak to you,' he said. 'I regret, *madame*, I must ask you to wait in another chamber now.'

'Inspector Trouard is dead.'

'Dead?' Mélusine stared at the lieutenant's first secretary in obvious disbelief. 'How did he die, *monsieur*? When?'

'He was killed in the disturbances a couple of weeks ago,' said the secretary. He looked even more harassed than the lieutenant.

'You don't know who killed him?'

'*Madame*, there have been outbreaks of violence in

many parts of the city,' said the secretary. 'Inspector
Trouard's body was found in an alley, close to where
a customs barrier had been attacked. I cannot tell you
the name of the individual responsible.'

'Have many police been killed in the riots?' Pierce
asked. It was the first time he'd spoken and both the
secretary and Mélusine looked at him in surprise.

'No.'

'Thank you for your help.' Mélusine stood up. 'I will
not trespass any further on your time.'

Pierce followed her out of the Hôtel de Police. He'd
never expected to learn much from Lieutenant de
Crosne, but the news of the inspector's death put a new
slant on the situation.

'How can he be dead?' Mélusine said, when they were
back on the street. '*Two weeks* ago? If I'd been back in
Paris two weeks ago, I could have spoken to him.'

'Yes,' said Pierce.

She walked a few more paces, then stopped abruptly.
'Do you think someone wanted to make sure he
couldn't talk about Bertier's death?'

'Or talk any more,' said Pierce, still considering all
the possible angles. 'It's possible.'

'What do you mean?'

'It was my impression that not everyone at the dinner
party had previously heard the gossip Madame de Foix
recounted,' he said. 'Perhaps the rumours are of recent
origin and haven't spread very far.'

'I hope not,' said Mélusine fervently.

'Someone had to start the rumours,' said Pierce. 'You wanted to find the inspector to prove them wrong—but perhaps he was the source of them.'

Mélusine stared at him for a few seconds. Then her eyes widened in shocked understanding. 'In which case the part about Bertier's death must be true!' she exclaimed.

A cart was bearing down on them, but she was so distracted she hadn't noticed. Pierce caught her elbow and pulled her out of the way. Despite the fact it was midsummer, a river of mud ran down the centre of the road. As the cart wheels jolted over the hidden cobblestones, mud splashed on to her skirts. Not far away a hawker was shouting, 'Good ink! Good ink!' A woman with a basket of brooms on her back was striding towards them. Mélusine seemed oblivious to her surroundings.

'*Madame*, the street is not the place for this conversation,' Pierce said gently.

'No.' She turned and headed back to the place Vendôme without another word.

She walked quickly. Her head bent forward as if she was deep in thought. A few yards further on she stopped so abruptly Pierce bumped into her. He caught her shoulders to prevent both of them overbalancing. She didn't seem to notice. She turned to face him, her eyes huge and dark.

'We have to go to the Bastille,' she said.

'*What?* Why the *devil*—?' He broke off. '*Madame*, keep walking home, if you please.'

'Yes. We'll have to take the carriage. Arrange it as soon as we arrive.' She started to walk so fast she was almost running.

'We will talk upstairs,' said Pierce, as soon as they reached the house.

'Paul, tell Georges to ready the carriage,' Mélusine said to the porter.

Pierce put his hand under her elbow and urged her forwards. 'Upstairs, *madame*.'

Her face was as white as a sheet but at his tone he saw sparks of temper flare in her eyes.

She opened her mouth, caught sight of the porter's interested expression, picked up her skirts and ran upstairs. Pierce followed less precipitously as she burst into the first-floor apartment. The salon was still empty and their footsteps rang on the floor.

'I am not taking you to the Bastille,' he said, as she whirled to face him.

'I *knew* you were going to give me orders. I knew it! You have no business telling me what I can or can't do! It's my decision—not yours.'

'Tell me why,' he demanded. Over the past few days he'd learnt Mélusine always had a reason for doing things. There must be some explanation for her sudden, outrageous decision to visit the most notorious prison in Paris.

'You don't have to know why. You just have to do what I tell you.' She was breathing so fast she was almost panting.

'I'm a servant, not a slave,' he said quietly. 'I have a right to know why you want me to accompany you to such a hazardous area of the city.'

She stared at him, a shocked, bereft expression gradually replacing the sparking temper. Her mouth worked for a few seconds, then she lifted her chin. 'If you're too scared to come with me, I will go without you,' she said, and started to walk past him.

'No, by God, you won't!' He caught her arm, his own temper rising.

'Let me go!'

'You are not going to the Bastille alone.'

'Georges will be with me. I'm sure he won't make such a fuss over a little drive.'

'You know perfectly well I'm not scared for my own safety,' Pierce said impatiently.

'You said it was a hazardous area.'

'It is. Why have you suddenly decided to go to the Bastille? I'm sure you had no such plans earlier.'

Mélusine stared at him, biting her lip. She looked away abruptly. 'There is no one else to talk to,' she said. 'I cannot talk to Thérèse Petit. The police inspector is dead. Now it seems as if *some* of the rumours about Bertier's death might be true. I don't know who else to talk to.'

'But *who*?'

'The Marquis de Saint-André.'

Pierce recalled a fragment of conversation from the dinner party. Saint-André's imprisonment had been discussed briefly by the guests. He knew Saint-André had been one of Bertier's acquaintances, but his incarceration in the Bastille had made him an unlikely candidate to be the blackmailer, so Pierce hadn't wasted any further consideration on him.

'He was Bertier's closest friend,' Mélusine said through tight lips. 'Don't you think it suspicious that Bertier is dead, the police inspector who brought his body home is dead, and his best friend is a prisoner in the Bastille?'

Pierce went still. Put in those terms, Mélusine's determination to talk to Saint-André made a lot more sense. What didn't make sense was that this was the first time she'd mentioned him.

'Was he not your friend as well?' Pierce said slowly.

'I thought he was.' She turned away and walked to the window.

Pierce stared at her in dawning suspicion and anger. 'Did he hurt you?' he demanded harshly.

'I don't want to talk about him!'

'But you want to go and see him in the Bastille?'

'I have to. There's no one else left to talk to. Tell Georges to hurry.' Mélusine turned back towards him, bright spots of colour burning in her pale cheeks.

Pierce struggled to control his own turbulent emotions. He was torn between his anger and frustration at Mélusine's refusal to answer his questions, another emotion that felt uncomfortably like jealousy—and his need to protect and comfort her. He hated to see that haunted, scared expression in her eyes.

'If it is essential you communicate with him, I will act as your messenger,' he said.

'No. You can't.' She instantly rejected his offer.

'Is it so personal, then?' he asked sharply.

'Yes. No. If I could send you, I would. I don't know what to say to him. I must see what's in his eyes. You don't know him...so you won't know what signs might be significant.'

'Was he your lover?' Pierce demanded.

'No!' She reared away from him.

'Did he want to be?'

'I don't know. It wasn't his idea. No, I don't think it was.'

'What?'

'Don't shout at me. I must think.' She put her hands over her ears in obvious distress.

Pierce took a deep breath. He seldom lost control of himself or his emotions. He was shaken to realise just how deeply affected he was at discovering Mélusine had secrets about another man she refused to share with him. It took a few moments before his head cleared enough to recall she'd said she would send him if she could.

'You can tell me what I must watch for when I speak to Saint-André, and then I will visit him on your behalf,' he said.

Mélusine hesitated. At last she sighed. 'I wish you could,' she said. 'But they are more likely to let the Comtesse de Gilocourt see him than her servant. It will be a shock for him to see me, I expect. Perhaps it will startle him into an indiscretion.'

'*Madame*—'

'I have to do this,' she said. She laid one hand over Pierce's. 'You see, I am not hysterical now I've made my decision. I am calm and resolved. We will go to the Bastille. I will talk to Saint-André—'

'You're not talking to him alone,' Pierce said categorically.

Mélusine stared at him for a moment, then ducked her head in acquiescence. 'Very well,' she said. 'But you must not say anything during the interview. Just listen and observe.'

Pierce didn't reply. He would not agree to anything that would limit his actions, but Mélusine didn't seem to notice he hadn't accepted her terms.

'Then we can go home and I will make some more sketches of you,' she said, with rather forced brightness. 'You can pretend to be asleep if you wish.'

He smiled faintly. 'That is very generous of you, *madame*. Before we go we must both change our clothes.'

'Why?' She looked startled. She glanced down at herself and gave an exclamation of annoyance. 'I'm covered in mud!'

'A small splash. But Saint-Antoine is a poor area and the people there have already shown their willingness to riot. You will be less likely to attract their abuse if you don't flaunt your nobility,' he said grimly, and waited to see if his words would have the desired effect.

She stared at him, uncertainty and apprehension clouding her eyes. Then he saw the renewed resolve in her expression.

'Thank you,' she said. 'I appreciate your foresight. We must hurry. Send Suzanne to me.'

Chapter Eight

They didn't have to cross the Seine to get to the Bastille. Pierce sat on the box beside the coachman as they made their way slowly down the rue Saint-Antoine. The closer they came to the Bastille the more imposing the eight-towered fortress became. Since his arrival in Paris this time he'd discovered there'd been serious rioting in Saint-Antoine three months earlier in which scores of people had been injured or killed. From the demeanour of the people they passed, he didn't think it would take much to spark another riot.

He didn't like taking Mélusine into such a volatile area, but once she'd understood his point, she'd been completely amenable to wearing her least expensive gown and hat. So much else had happened on the day of the dinner party he thought she'd almost forgotten the youths who'd thrown things at her carriage on the way home. When he'd reminded her, he'd seen apprehension flare in her eyes, but she hadn't changed her mind about visiting the Bastille.

'There are two courtyards,' said Georges. 'This gate takes you into the first one. It's a dogleg round the walls of the prison. There's barracks for the soldiers on the left and shops on the right. At the end there's another gate with a drawbridge and a moat and beyond that the inner courtyard with the governor's lodgings and garden. Grows good cabbages.'

'You've visited the governor's garden!' Pierce said in disbelief.

Georges shrugged. 'Not recently. My brother lives a few streets away. He knows the gatekeeper. In quieter times we used to stroll up for a chat and a smoke.' He squinted up at the nearest tower and his expression became dour. 'They shouldn't be turning the cannon on their own people like that. Looks like it's true. They are getting ready to turn Paris into rubble.'

Pierce followed the direction of the coachman's gaze. It was clear preparations had been made to withstand an assault. Some of the windows in the towers and walls had been blocked up and the mouths of the cannon were all pointed downwards at the surrounding streets. It was a chilling sight. He couldn't blame the local people for being on edge and suspicious.

He jumped down and went to open the door for Mélusine. She climbed out, holding very tightly to his hand as she looked up at the forbidding walls. She gasped as she saw the cannon.

'Are they going to fire them?'

'You could ask the governor—if the opportunity arises,' said Pierce. 'Are you still determined to go in?'

She lowered her eyes to his face and nodded. 'I will be glad when it's over,' she whispered, as they walked into the first courtyard.

'So will I.' They walked unchallenged along the narrow passageway to where the courtyard turned the corner and broadened out.

Mélusine moved closer to him, slipping her hand through his arm. That wasn't appropriate behaviour for a lady and her footman, but since Pierce wasn't wearing his livery, he didn't comment. He was disconcerted to discover how much he liked the feel of her hand on his arm. But the fact that she was unconsciously treating him as her escort rather than her servant would make it easier if he decided to take charge of the situation.

Just as Georges had said, there was another gate with a drawbridge at the end of the first courtyard. Pierce spoke to the gatekeeper, and they passed into the inner courtyard.

'That was a perfume shop!' Mélusine hissed at him as they waited for the governor to respond to their request to see him. 'There's a perfume shop right next to the gate of the Bastille!'

Pierce glanced at her. Her cheeks were pale, her eyes round with a mixture of nervousness and amazement. She was clutching his arm so tightly he thought she'd most likely leave bruises, but he was oddly relieved that she was sharing her reactions to her surroundings with him. She'd not told him everything about Saint-André, but it didn't seem as if she was holding him at a greater distance in any other way.

'Madame de Gilocourt, I regret I've not previously had the pleasure of meeting you. Allow me to introduce myself—Bernard-René de Launay, at your service,' said the Governor. 'And you, *monsieur?*' he added courteously.

'Pierre Dumont,' Pierce replied, before Mélusine could speak. 'The Comtesse honoured me with the request to escort her on her current errand.'

'As to that, I am a little puzzled, *madame.* How may I assist you?' Launay asked.

'You may know my husband died last November,' Mélusine began.

'My deepest sympathy, *madame.*'

'Thank you. I believe—that is, I have heard—that the Marquis de Saint-André is…here,' said Mélusine.

The governor hesitated. 'That is correct,' he said at last.

'He was my husband's greatest friend.' She paused and visibly swallowed. 'My husband died suddenly and unexpectedly. The Marquis was one of the last people who spoke to him. For Bertier's sake—for my sake—I would be most grateful…very appreciative…if I could speak to the Marquis.'

Launay thought for a minute. 'You will have to go to his cell,' he said. 'I cannot permit him to be brought out.'

'I understand,' said Mélusine. 'I'm willing to do that.'

'Very well.' Launay nodded solemnly. 'I will take you to him myself.'

The entrance to the Bastille itself was on the opposite side of the courtyard to the governor's lodgings. Pierce and Mélusine crossed it in the company of Launay and waited for the drawbridge to be lowered. Mélusine clutched Pierce's arm even more tightly than before as they finally entered the infamous prison. Pierce covered her hand with his as he made a quick assessment of his surroundings, noting the cannon positioned to fire through the gate they'd just entered.

'You seem to be preparing for a siege, *monsieur*,' he said.

'As to that…the people are in a turbulent state,' said Launay.

'Are you planning to quell them into obedience?'

'Indeed not!' Launay said. 'The preparations are in case the Bastille is attacked. The cannon aren't loaded.'

They reached the entrance to one of the towers and Pierce didn't make the obvious reply that the cannon *could* be loaded, if the governor gave the order.

A circular stone staircase led up from the doorway. They followed the warder's lantern round and round the coiling steps until they reached a passage leading off from the stairwell. At the end of the passage, the flickering lantern light revealed a door.

It was early afternoon outside, but here, inside the thick walls of the tower, it was cold, silent and dark.

Mélusine was standing so close to Pierce he could feel her trembling. He put his hand on her waist, confident no one would notice in the shadows—or question why she needed reassurance in such circumstances if they did notice.

The warder unlocked the door and swung it open to reveal an octagonal cell. By comparison with the darkness of the stairwell it was unexpectedly light, though in fact the illumination provided by the window set into the thick wall was not very bright.

Over Mélusine's shoulder, Pierce saw the occupant of the cell stand up and turn to face the visitors. As he did so the light fell full across his bearded face.

Only years of self-discipline prevented Pierce from exclaiming in startled recognition. Even though the man had been clean-shaven last time Pierce had seen him, he recognised him at once. Mélusine might know the prisoner as the Marquis de Saint-André, but the last time Pierce had met him he'd been calling himself Nicolas Gerard—and he'd been smuggling censored philosophical literature into France in the name of liberty, and brandy out of it in pursuit of profit.

Saint-André had learnt self-control in a similar school to Pierce. His eyes went first to Mélusine. Total disbelief flickered only briefly on his face before he assumed an expression of courteous interest. His expression didn't change when he saw Pierce, though Pierce saw both the quickly masked recognition in his eyes and the way his gaze flicked quickly to Mélusine and back to Pierce before focusing once more on the lady.

'You have a visitor,' said the governor.

For several desperate seconds after the door opened Mélusine couldn't force herself to move, much less to speak. She knew she had to do both. She'd come to question Saint-André—but all she could think of was the last time she'd heard his voice. Her stomach clenched with remembered horror. But he didn't look exactly the same as he had last time she'd seen him. He had a beard, and she stared at it in amazement.

The Marquis had never been a fop, but he'd always been punctilious in all matters of etiquette and good manners. Whenever he'd been in her presence he'd always been perfectly clean-shaven and his attire had been faultless. He was a couple of inches over six feet, with broad shoulders. His size gave him the potential to be a formidable presence in any company, yet he normally adopted an unobtrusive manner. On a couple of occasions she'd seen him exert himself sufficiently to dominate the room, but usually he was softly spoken and gentle in his manner. Which only made what had happened all the more shocking...

He bowed to her with familiar grace. As he did so he moved into the narrow beam of sunlight from the window and a few strands of his light brown hair gleamed gold.

'I am honoured, Comtesse,' he said. 'May I offer my

belated, but most sincere, condolences on the sad loss of your husband.'

It was Saint-André's voice, but she'd never expected it to issue from a mouth surrounded by a beard. Her mental picture of him had never encompassed such an unlikely alteration to his appearance. But it was her surprise over his beard that helped her overcome the much more shocking fact that she was face to face with him.

She took a step forward, into the cell. 'Thank you,' she said unsteadily, taking refuge in the same courtesy Saint-André had displayed. 'I hope you are well.'

'My existence is very restful,' said Saint-André. 'I have taken the opportunity to refresh my knowledge of Greek literature.' He waved towards several books laid out on the desk at which he'd been sitting.

Mélusine felt as if she was suffocating. There were questions she had to ask about Bertier's death. There were questions she wanted to ask about how Saint-André was enduring his imprisonment—and there were other questions she'd never be able to ask, but for which she desperately needed the answers. She'd trusted Saint-André's friendship for most of her married life. She really wanted that trust to have been justified.

Saint-André said quietly, 'I'm sorry my quarters are so spartan, but this chair is quite comfortable.' He placed it for her as he spoke, and then stepped back.

Mélusine took a few slightly jerky steps and sat down. Although she didn't turn to look at him, she sensed Pierre instantly move to stand behind her. Even though she was embarrassed at what he might hear, she was comforted by his presence. She suddenly wished with all her heart she was back in her studio, sketching Pierre, not here in a cell in the Bastille. Saint-André glanced between them, but made no comment. He sat down in the remaining chair and smiled at Mélusine.

Hurried footsteps sounded outside and the governor stepped away to take part in an urgent conversation.

Saint-André looked towards the door and his eyes narrowed. 'Comtesse, I am honoured by your visit, but I confess I'd be much happier if I knew you were safely at home,' he said.

'What do you know of Bertier's death?' Mélusine burst out.

Saint-André's gaze sharpened. 'I was told he was attacked in the Bois de Boulogne by robbers.'

'Is that all you know?' she said.

'I'd already taken up residence here when I was told of his death,' said Saint-André.

'Why are you here?' she demanded.

He looked at her for a moment, then he shrugged and gave a fatalistic laugh. 'Comtesse, I have no idea.'

'You must have!' she exclaimed.

'No. I was eating breakfast, considering whether I should buy Chaumont's chestnut gelding—and a company of guards arrived at the door with a *lettre de cachet* to have me brought here. And here I have been ever since. The governor has been most hospitable, but I'd be more than happy to relieve him of my presence.'

'That makes no sense,' Mélusine said. She could not allow herself to imagine how Saint-André must feel about the horrific thing that had been done to him. 'Why would anyone want you incarcerated here?'

His eyes narrowed briefly, then he said gravely: 'Thank you, I have always valued your good opinion of me. Rest assured, *madame*, I would never do anything to harm you or cause you to think less well of me.'

Mélusine sat very still for several moments, wondering exactly what he was trying to tell her. Then she said in a rush, 'There is a rumour that Bertier was not killed by brigands, but died in a secret duel. They say it was with my lover, but that is a lie, I had no lover,' she said harshly.

'Of course not,' said Saint-André immediately.

'The police inspector who brought his body to the house is dead too. He was killed two weeks ago. I never saw Bertier's body, so I don't know what his wounds were.'

Saint-André stood up. In the confined space he was an imposing figure. 'Go home, Comtesse,' said the Marquis. 'You trust your man here?' He looked at Pierre.

'Pierre Dumont,' said Mélusine. It was a very brief introduction, and by Saint-André's standards of exquisite courtesy, an inadequate one, but she didn't know what else to say.

'Indeed?' said Saint-André, a dry note in his voice. 'Dumont.' He inclined his head in acknowledgement. 'You should not be here,' he continued to Mélusine. 'Trouble is brewing. I can feel it, even through the walls. Where do you live now?'

'The place Vendôme'

'Go home,' he repeated. 'I will think about what you've told me, and I'm sure Dumont will contrive a way to speak to me again.'

Mélusine thought it was an unsatisfactory end to the visit, yet she had no idea what more they could say. Saint-André hadn't known about Bertier's death until after he was in the Bastille and he had—or said he had—no idea who was behind his imprisonment.

'I am sorry to see you in such circumstances,' she said.

'I am sorry you've been exposed to such uncongenial surroundings,' he replied. He paused, then added quietly, 'I confess I am not sorry that you visited. I hope you will think kindly of me in future, Comtesse.'

Pierce travelled on the outside of the coach again on the return journey. He watched the people in the street and considered the meeting with Saint-André. It was easy to surmise that the Marquis had filled a similar role in Bertier's life to the one that Pierce filled for La Motte. Even though he'd never met him as Saint-André, Pierce had already known the Marquis's name. He was even aware of some of the Marquis's public denunciations of various aspects of French legal and political practice. What he hadn't known was that the Marquis de Saint-André was also Nicolas Gerard, smuggler.

All he'd known of Gerard was that he was fearless, intelligent and that he'd fought in the War of American Independence. It had mildly amused both men to know they'd been on opposite sides a few years earlier.

Pierce wondered if Saint-André really was ignorant of who was behind his incarceration. The *lettres de cachet* were one of the most notorious abuses of liberty in France. They were letters which were signed by the King, countersigned by a minister and stamped with the royal seal, by which a man could be imprisoned without any trial or the chance to defend himself. Despite the use of royal authority, the King often knew nothing of those who were imprisoned by such means. All that was required to obtain a *lettre de cachet* was influence with a minister. They were used for political reasons, but they were also used by private individuals for entirely personal reasons, as part of a feud with an enemy, or by families to punish unruly or scandalous sons. One man had his son imprisoned by *lettre de cachet* as punishment for his huge gambling debt.

It seemed unlikely that Saint-André had no idea who was responsible for his imprisonment. But was that the information he was trying to conceal from Mélusine—or was he more concerned Pierce might reveal he was also a smuggler?

* * *

When they arrived at Mélusine's house, Pierce followed her upstairs, half-expecting her to head straight for her studio. Instead she went into the blue salon.

'I don't like this room,' she said, glancing around as she stripped off her gloves. 'I think I'm going to have all the furniture thrown out and start again.'

'Then you won't have anywhere suitable to receive guests,' Pierce said mildly.

'I'll make all the bad memories first,' she said. 'Then I'll throw out the furniture, and the bad memories can go with it. It's a good plan, I think.'

It was the plan of a woman who was either completely heedless of money—or confident she could afford it. She wasn't extravagant. They had not been on one shopping trip since he'd begun as her footman. Spending money on frivolities didn't seem to be among her vices.

'It shows foresight,' Pierce agreed.

She looked sideways at him. 'Now you want to know why we went to the Bastille,' she said.

He gave a silent nod of assent, watching her carefully.

She stood quietly for a moment, as if she was gathering her thoughts, then she said, 'You may sit down.' She waited until he'd chosen a chair, then moved another one until it was quite close to his. He started to rise to help her, but she waved him back into his seat. 'It's not heavy. It's just that I do not wish to shout. What I must say is confidential.'

He felt a surge of satisfaction she was finally going to confide in him, but he also tensed in anticipation of what he might hear. He was annoyed with himself for that betraying thread of tension, but he couldn't control it.

She took a little time arranging her skirts, and he waited impatiently for her to begin.

'Did it seem to you that Saint-André was conscious there might be a little awkwardness between us—him and me?' she said at last.

'Yes, *madame*.'

'I think he might have guessed I know. It wasn't as mortifying speaking to him as I'd feared. But I was glad when the meeting was over.'

Pierce watched as she fanned the fingers of both hands and laid them palm to palm in front of her. She pulled her hands slowly back and forward across each other, her eyes unfocused as she apparently searched for the words she needed. He wanted to take her hands between his. He'd done so in the carriage on the way home from the dinner party without a second thought, but now such a gesture would have much more significance. To him at least it would hint at a commitment he could not make.

'Saint-André was Bertier's friend,' she said abruptly. 'Well, you know that, but I never knew how good until…' Her voice faltered. She drew her hands apart and involuntarily clenched them into fists. She suddenly seemed to notice what she'd done and lowered them to rest on her lap.

She took a breath and started again. 'Perhaps you will think I made too much of it.' She gave a small, awkward laugh. 'It was the night before Bertier died,' she continued rapidly. 'Not the night that ended with the police bringing his body home in the morning—the night before that.'

'I understand,' said Pierre.

'I heard him talking to Saint-André. I didn't deliberately eavesdrop. It was quite by chance.'

'Their conversation distressed you?' Pierce was relieved at the implication that she'd only *heard* something which upset her.

'Yes. Bertier…they were talking about me. He said…in short, Bertier told Saint-André to seduce me and—I cannot say the words Bertier used—but he wanted Saint-André to do it again and again until I was with child.'

It took a few seconds for Pierce to comprehend what Mélusine had said, to take her convoluted sentence and convert it into the short, crude words Bertier must have used, which she could not bring herself to repeat. A flame of anger began to burn inside him, getting steadily stronger with every moment that passed.

'Your husband wanted Saint-André to bed you and make you pregnant,' he said in a very controlled voice.

Mélusine had been staring down at her hands, but she looked up and nodded jerkily. 'Saint-André said—what if it's a girl? Bertier said he'd have to do it again until it was a boy. Again and again. Bertier sounded so cruel.

Jeering. I think he'd been drinking. I'd never heard him be so crude.'

Pierce rose from the chair, his movements as controlled as his voice had been. As he had done once before, he walked over to the window and stood with his back to her. He'd been angry when he'd heard about her father's mistreatment of her, but now the mist of rage in front of his eyes was so great he couldn't see the square below.

Mélusine said something, but he was too angry to comprehend her words. A few moments later she spoke again and this time her voice did penetrate his fury.

'Are you angry with me?'

Her question jolted him back to the present. His heart was still pounding with the effort of preventing his temper from boiling out of control, but the need to reassure her was suddenly even greater. He spun on his heel to face her. 'No! Good God! *Madame*, how can you ask me that?'

She smiled tremulously. 'You don't think I've made too much of the incident? I'm sure my father would—'

Pierce bit back an oath and returned swiftly to sit beside her, even though his body demanded the release of forceful movement. 'Did they know you overheard them?'

'I don't think so. When I realised they were talking about me, when I heard what Bertier said—at first I couldn't move. I should have confronted him there and then. Walked in on them and denounced his sordid scheming. I've regretted ever since that I did not have the courage,' she whispered. 'No one is going to use me again. No one.'

'It wasn't lack of courage,' said Pierce. 'You were too shocked to think clearly. In any case, walking in on two men plotting your seduction wouldn't have been sensible. Especially if they were in their cups. You were wise not to draw attention to yourself.'

Mélusine stared at him, and then pressed both hands over her mouth. 'You think they would have…started… then, if I'd gone in?' she choked.

He cursed himself for putting that look of horror in her eyes. He should be reassuring her, not increasing her distress, but it was hard to comfort her when he was still trying to deal with his own reaction.

'Don't.' He caught her wrists and drew her hands gently away from her face. 'I'm sorry. I did not mean to distress you more. I only wanted you to know I don't blame you for not confronting them that night.'

She took a couple of quick breaths, her eyes locked on his face, and then nodded. 'Do you think Saint-André knows I overheard?' she asked.

'That would be one way of interpreting his comments,' said Pierce. He released her wrists and put his hands on his knees. He needed to balance his thoughts and his emotions, but it was much harder and taking him much longer than usual.

'Saint-André said today he would never do anything

to harm me or to cause me to think less well of him. Of course, he might believe I'd enjoy being seduced by him and think better of him as a result,' she said bitterly.

'Possibly,' said Pierre. Her acid tone lessened some of his tension. He remembered she was telling him about things that had happened eight months ago, not yesterday. She had not suddenly become more fragile than the woman he'd spent the past few days with. 'Did you suspect him of being your husband's secret assailant?'

'No.' Mélusine looked startled by the suggestion. 'Saint-André was Bertier's closest friend. I thought he might know if Bertier had had an argument with someone *else*. Saint-André would know about Bertier's mistress, don't you suppose? If he was willing to talk about me to his friend—he would have talked about other women, wouldn't he?' she said uncertainly. 'Or are men more circumspect in what they say about their mistresses?'

'That would depend on the man,' said Pierce. 'Tell me the rest of what happened that night and the next day, and then we won't need to speak of it again.'

'There isn't much else to say,' said Mélusine. 'I was scared they'd discover me and I tried to creep away. I was trembling so much and so clumsy I fell over the little table in the alcove. I tried to pick it up, but one of the legs was wedged. I was sure they'd hear me. I decided to leave it. I jumped back and knocked over Jean-Baptiste—'

'You...*what*? Knocked over *Jean-Baptiste*? Where did he come from?'

'I don't know. It's all a confusion in my mind. It was awful. I just wanted to get away. I was so upset. I jumped back and banged into something. Then Jean-Baptiste was sprawling on the floor in front of me. I must have knocked him over, somehow. I jumped over him. I think I trod on him. I nearly overbalanced again. Then I ran and shut myself in my bedroom.' She was speaking faster and faster until Pierce could only just understand her, but he didn't ask her to slow down. 'I kept thinking Bertier would come, but he didn't. I didn't know what to do, so in the morning I told the maid to say I was ill and staying in my rooms for the day. I did feel ill. I don't know what Bertier did that day. He went out in the evening, and next morning the police inspector brought his body back to the house.'

She stopped abruptly and dragged in a couple of deep breaths. After the speed at which she'd been speaking, Pierce wasn't surprised she needed them. He was only glad he'd finally heard the whole story.

'I don't know how it can have anything to do with Bertier's death. And yet it seems so…coincidental…if it doesn't.'

'It does, doesn't it?' said Pierce. He needed to think about it. Preferably after he'd had time to work off the tension still cramping his muscles.

'Have you got any ideas?' Mélusine asked hopefully.

He looked at her and saw the haunted, anxious expression had gone from her eyes. She wasn't quite back to normal, but she was almost ready to resume her quest for the truth about Bertier's death. It dawned on him he was partly responsible for that. He hadn't blamed her and—somehow—he'd managed to avoid frightening her with his scalding fury. He felt a rush of pleasure that he could affect her moods so profoundly, even though he'd never meant to become so deeply entangled in her life. It was going to be difficult to extricate himself without hurting her—and he wasn't even sure if he wanted to. But he couldn't lose sight of the fact he was in Paris to find the blackmailer.

'Has it occurred to you that Jean-Baptiste might also have heard what your husband said to Saint-André?' he asked.

She nodded. 'I felt besmirched by it. It was bad enough knowing he looked down his nose at me as mere bourgeois. I couldn't bear the notion of him smirking over what Bertier planned for me. I was so glad he didn't come to Bordeaux with me. What are we going to do now?'

'I'm going out,' said Pierce. He needed to walk off the anger still tightening his muscles. 'With your permission, of course,' he added politely.

'Where?' It was a very blunt question, and a moment later she flushed, but Pierce didn't comment.

'To speak to some friends of mine,' he said. 'I may see if I can speak to Laurette again. We were interrupted by your pompous François last time.'

'He's not *my* François,' Mélusine protested. 'He wasn't quite as bad as Thérèse Petit, but there wasn't much in it. Anyone would have thought they were the Comte and Comtesse de Gilocourt and *we* were the interlopers.'

'Did it never occur to your husband he should pension off his father's servants and start anew?' Pierce said with exasperation.

Mélusine bit her lip. 'I mentioned it once, but Bertier took it very ill. I think it might have been a point of pride. I never mentioned it again. I think Saint-André wants to talk to us again. Perhaps he knows something he did not feel able to reveal in front of the warder.'

'Most likely,' Pierce said drily. 'I'll speak to him again in due course. He's not going anywhere.'

Chapter Nine

Afternoon, Sunday, 12 July 1789

Mélusine had too much to think about to concentrate on fine detail, so she prepared some clay for the wheel, methodically kneading it into shape as her thoughts raced back and forth. She'd never expected to tell anyone what she'd overheard Bertier say. Even now she couldn't quite believe she'd done so. But it had been easier to tell Pierre than she'd anticipated. She still felt a little vulnerable and jittery—but the shame she'd felt for the past eight months had gone. She had done nothing wrong. She hadn't deliberately set out to eavesdrop. And Pierre had reassured her she hadn't been a coward for not immediately confronting Bertier and Saint-André. She separated the clay into equally sized portions, and began to work on each one in turn.

She'd spent most of the night thinking about Pierre, Bertier and Saint-André, but she'd thought about Pierre far more than she thought about the other two. When she did sleep, she'd woken from unfamiliar, erotic dreams to discover her body tingling with unfulfilled yearning. She had to decide what she was going to do about her feelings for Pierre. He had told her quite plainly he would never marry again and that he wouldn't have an affair with a virtuous woman. She was undeniably a virtuous—and inexperienced—woman. He would consider it dishonourable to make love to her, and it might be equally dishonourable of *her* to seduce him into abandoning his principles.

She jammed the heel of her hand rather viciously into the clay, then frowned at the misshapen lump. Letting him seduce her would be easy, but she knew instinctively he wouldn't do so. His decision not to take advantage of another virtuous woman had the force of a deathbed promise, even though she was sure he'd never uttered a word of it to his dying wife. It would take courage for her to act in a way she'd hitherto considered brazenly immodest. But it seemed to her she would also have to take responsibility for tempting Pierre to act against the dictates of his conscience. Was it fair of her to do that?

She collected one of the prepared balls of clay and a beaker of water and sat down at the potter's wheel, still pondering the moral dilemma. She was angry with Bertier because he'd had so little regard for her honour he'd ordered Saint-André to seduce her. Would she be guilty of the same thing if she tried to tease Pierre into kissing her—and perhaps more?

She positioned the clay on the wheel and sprinkled it liberally with water. Then she started the wheel spinning with her foot on the treadle and centred the clay between her hands. She wanted to talk to Pierre, but he'd left the house in the morning and hadn't yet returned. After all the dramatic revelations of the past few days, she needed to talk to him quietly about everyday things.

Most importantly, she had to talk to Pierre about Saint-André. The Marquis was condemned to indefinite imprisonment in the Bastille without trial or possibility of appeal. Seeing him there had brought into sharp focus the injustice of what had been done to him. She didn't know for sure he wouldn't have seduced her as Bertier wanted, but she believed he'd been obliquely trying to reassure her on that subject the previous day. Even if he had agreed to Bertier's demands, she was certain he would have done so as kindly and considerately as possible. After his initial exclamation at Bertier's demands, she hadn't heard him say another word. At the time she'd been too upset to consider the implications of his silence, but now she thought it was likely he'd been as shocked as she by Bertier's proposal.

Someone with connections and influence had had him consigned to the Bastille. She needed to find someone with sufficient influence to help her get him out. Someone who was part of the network of patronage at Versailles. But powerful men expected a return for any favours they performed. She'd never been part of that world and she had nothing to offer that would be of any value to such a man. It was going to be a lot harder to get Saint-André out of the Bastille than to solve the mystery of Bertier's death, she thought grimly.

She was so preoccupied with Saint-André's problem, and so familiar with the noise of Paris that at first she didn't notice the change in tone and volume, but eventually the sounds rising from the square below penetrated her concentration. She picked up a cloth to wipe her hands and went to the window to see what was happening. The place Vendôme was formed of continuous rows of houses on all four sides, with only one street that allowed entrance or exit. Because it wasn't a main thoroughfare, it was usually relatively peaceful, but now it was full of angry people.

Mélusine stared down at the mob, the cloth forgotten in her hands. Even from this height she could feel the rage and potential violence. Some of the crowd had weapons, most of them were shouting.

'*Vive la Nation!*'

'*Long live the Third Estate.*'

She watched, horrified, as cavalry began to force their way into the square. The mob's fury increased. The cavalry had their sabres drawn. She caught her breath, appalled at the prospect of watching them hack their way through the crowd, then she realised they were trying to use the flats of their swords. But the press of the people was so great the horses could not move. The crowd began to throw things at the trapped cavalry.

Quick footsteps sounded outside the door. As it burst open, Mélusine spun round, heart bounding. She half-expected to see the mob breaking into her studio and gave a gasp of relief that it was Pierre.

'Come away from the window!' He crossed the room in a few strides, and lifted her to one side.

'What? What's happening?' She gripped his upper arms, feeling the taut muscles beneath his sleeves. Instead of his footman's livery and wig, he was dressed in the same ill-fitting coat he'd worn the first day she met him and his own black hair was uncovered. Despite the coat, he looked lean and alert, with not a trace of the wooden-faced servant's expression he'd worn at their first meeting. She gazed at him, still shocked by what she'd just seen in the square and captivated by the undisguised masculine energy radiating from him.

He searched her face as if to assure himself she was all right, then went to look out of the window. She followed him immediately, only to have him sweep her back with one peremptory arm.

'Why have you got leaves in your coat?' she asked, noticing them for the first time.

'Because I wanted to get home without being assaulted by the mob,' he said tersely.

'Let me see!' She tried to push past him to the

window. 'I don't understand. Why did chestnut leaves stop you being assaulted?'

'Just because you aren't involved in the skirmish, doesn't mean you can't be hit by a bullet,' he said, keeping her away.

'We're so high—'

'A musket knocked out of alignment as it fires—'

'I didn't see many muskets.'

'There will be,' he said grimly. 'Gunsmiths' shops are already being looted—the cavalry are retreating.' He let her see out of the window, but kept his hands firmly on her upper arms, as if he might fling her to one side at the slightest hint of danger.

She looked down. The cavalry were indeed retreating towards the place Louis XV, with the crowd following them. A few moments later she heard musket fire coming from that direction.

'Paris is at war with itself,' she whispered, appalled.

'Hmm.' He put his arms around her from behind, holding her so tightly she was aware of the rapid pounding of his heart. She'd wanted him to hold her, but she'd never expected it to be under these circumstances. She could feel the tension in his body. She suddenly remembered what he'd said about avoiding the anger of the mob, and tried to twist round to look at him.

'Did they hurt you?'

'No. I was afraid the mob might try to break into the house before I got back.' His arms momentarily tightened even more, then he released her.

Mélusine went cold at his words. 'Did they try?' Until that moment the possibility hadn't even occurred to her.

'Paul says no. The doors are barred now, but it's unlikely the crowd will try to break in here. They want guns, ammunition and powder. They'll go where they think they can find it.'

'But what has happened? Why are they suddenly so angry?'

'The King dismissed Necker last night,' said Pierre, drawing Mélusine to a chair well away from the window. 'The news reached the Palais Royal today, while I was there, and since then the turmoil has been growing. The people had faith the Finance Minster would solve the crisis. They believe he is an honest man who would have protected their interests. The price of bread is high, people are hungry, rents are due that cannot be paid. They pinned all their hopes on Necker—and now the King has exiled him.'

'Father was not exceedingly impressed by Necker,' said Mélusine. She sat down and was glad Pierre brought a stool to sit close beside her. She wished he still had his arms around her. She'd felt remarkably safe there in what suddenly seemed a very unsafe world. 'There are many things Father says or does I do not agree with, but I've never doubted his gift for business matters.'

'At this point it matters less whether Necker *can* rescue France from its financial crisis and more that the people believe he can,' said Pierre. 'Most of them are afraid this is the first step towards the King using the soldiers stationed in Paris to batter the people into submission. There are rumours the cannon in the Bastille will be fired on the city.'

'That would be madness! Why would he want to attack his own people?'

'To force them into obedience?' Pierre smiled sardonically. 'Obedience is the one virtue many men value above all others in those beneath them.'

'But I think he is a kindly man,' Mélusine protested. 'It is true I only met him occasionally and he is not at all an easy conversationalist. Nor am I, so that made it doubly difficult. But I did feel that beneath his gruffness and lack of…address…he was well disposed towards people.'

'But was it his decision—or his advisors'?' said Pierre. 'The people hate the Queen, and if they think she was behind Necker's dismissal, that will only increase their hostility to the crown.'

'Are you—we—not people too?' asked Mélusine, slightly puzzled by his tone. 'You sound as if you are somehow holding yourself apart from the people you are talking about.'

He looked at her for a moment, then smiled and shrugged. 'You are very acute, *madame*,' he said. 'I am not Parisian by birth, and I've spent so much time away from France recently I do feel more detached than might otherwise be the case. Besides that, some men are motivated by abstract ideals—Saint-André perhaps is one, and the man shouting from the tabletop in the Palais Royal an hour or so ago may be another one. He bade us all wear green as the colour of hope and in support of the Third Estate. The crowd took his suggestion to heart with such enthusiasm it wasn't wise to abstain.'

He pulled the leaves from his coat and laid them on the table. 'If you have some green ribbon, it would be less inclined to wilt,' he said. 'Other men are motivated by more concrete concerns, closer to home. Can they find work? Can they house and feed their family? The time they rebel, either individually or collectively, is when those things are threatened. Between the idealists, the practical men and opportunists, Paris has become a dangerous powder keg.'

Although the rioting moved away from place Vendôme, they continued to hear the sound of fighting from the direction of the Tuileries and place Louis XV and frequent musket or pistol fire from other directions. Mélusine would not let anyone leave the house to see what was happening. Nor could she contemplate going to bed. After she'd had supper, she went up to her studio, leaving the candles unlit so she could look out without drawing attention to herself.

In more orderly times Paris was a well-lit city at night, but tonight every house in the square was in darkness. Mélusine moved restlessly from the window to a chair to her work bench and back again.

There'd been a full moon the previous Tuesday. It was no longer as bright as it had been, but Mélusine decided it was bright enough to try turning a pot on the wheel. It would be good discipline to do it in the semi-darkness.

An hour later the door opened and Pierre appeared carrying a cup of hot chocolate and some small cakes.

'You've brought me breakfast before I've even been to bed,' she said, as she caught the familiar smell of the chocolate.

'You should be in bed,' he said. 'But since you aren't…'

'I'm not sure I could lie down, much less sleep at the moment,' she said. 'I suppose it's not the same for you. There must have been many times when you were on board the privateer when you didn't know what was going to happen next—when you might be about to sail into danger…'

'You're not sailing into danger,' said Pierre. 'I don't think there is any serious threat to any of us from what's happening on the streets tonight—not as long as we stay indoors. They want weapons and powder, and they won't look for either here.'

'Have we *got* any weapons?' Mélusine asked.

'If you're asking me whether I'm armed, the answer is yes,' said Pierre. 'So is Paul. But I've impressed upon him that he must not fire in the very, very unlikely event the crowd makes a serious attempt to break in.'

'What should he do?' Mélusine asked, wondering

what the point of having a weapon was if they weren't going to use it.

'Open the door and give them a tour of all the rooms,' said Pierre. 'Offer refreshment—food and wine, of course. And apologise profusely that, alas, though we whole heartedly support their cause, we don't have what they're looking for.'

Mélusine drew in a deep breath. 'And you think that would satisfy them? What if they expected more…hospitality… than just food and wine?'

'I would courteously draw their attention to the fact I don't share my women. And when they'd gone,' he continued, before Mélusine could say anything, 'I would courteously beg your pardon for my earlier presumption.'

A stone settled in Mélusine's stomach. She'd been right earlier, when she'd been sure that Pierre would not seek to become her lover.

'Is that on account of your principles—or lack of inclination?' she asked. And then her cheeks and her ears and every other part of her began to burn with embarrassment at having put her thoughts into words.

Intense silence followed her words. Despite the pale moonlight it was too dark to see his expression. Perhaps he hadn't understood. Her embarrassment grew until she half-expected the heat radiating from every pore of her body would be sufficient to light up the room.

'I meant…' she began.

'I know what you meant.' He didn't sound angry. She couldn't decipher his mood, but at least he didn't sound angry with her.

Her lips were so stiff it was difficult to force words past them, but now she'd started she had to continue. 'It would be helpful…less confusing…to me to know,' she said painfully.

'*Madame…*' He stopped. 'You are a very brave woman,' he continued after a moment. 'And an honest one.'

'Oh.' Her muscles were so gripped with tension it was difficult to expand her chest to draw breath. He'd paid her a compliment, she supposed, but he hadn't answered her question. The longer he delayed, the more sure she became she'd made a terrible, mortifying mistake.

'I am sorry to embarrass you,' she whispered. She wished the floor would open up and swallow her.

Then he took her hand.

Her heart skipped a beat and continued at a faster pace. For a moment he held her hand between both of his, then he lifted it and she felt his lips brush against her fingers.

He'd kissed her! He was still kissing her. His mouth caressed her hand and she thought—her breath caught in her throat—she could even feel the brief, illicit stroke of his tongue against the backs of her fingers.

She closed her eyes, sensation flooding her body. It was as if she could feel that small caress in every part of her being. Her breathing quickened. Sweet fire coursed through her veins. An ache began to grow between her legs. The same ache she'd felt when she'd woken from dreaming of him the previous night.

'*Madame,*' he said, his voice so low that it too became a caress, 'you know it is a matter of principles. And of honour. Yours and mine.' He kissed her hand one more time and laid it gently back in her lap. 'Let us not talk about this now,' he said.

'Does that mean we're going to talk about it at some other time?' Mélusine asked boldly.

He laughed slightly. '*Madame*, in the short time I have known you, I have never known you to deviate from your intended path. I am sure we will talk about this again.'

Mélusine stared at his shadowy outline. Perhaps he too needed time to adjust to the…friendship…growing between them. He'd foresworn marriage at the side of his first wife's death bed. He would need time to consider that perhaps he'd made a mistake. And she needed time to decide whether she still aspired to a life of unsullied virtue. Was she really willing to share the bed of a man who wasn't her husband?

'Tell me about your father,' she said, suddenly anxious to learn as much about Pierre as possible.

Pierre didn't say anything.

'When did he die?' she asked.

'When I was seventeen.'

'Then what happened?'

'I sold myself to the privateer captain to pay his debts and save my family from destitution. Is that what you wanted to know?' Pierre sounded thoroughly exasperated. She wasn't sure whether it was with her or himself. She wished she could see his expression.

'You *sold* yourself?'

'More or less. I offered my services without remuneration on condition he paid my father's debts.'

'And he *did* it?' Mélusine stared at Pierce in the darkness. 'I don't know whether to be more impressed by your...boldness...or his... What did he make you do?' she asked, suddenly suspicious. 'Was it very unpleasant and dangerous?'

'My unmitigated arrogance and impudence,' said Pierre, and she could hear the humour in his voice. 'I didn't see it that way at the time, mind you. I was so full of myself I never questioned whether anyone would think my services were worth having—let alone paying for. No, he didn't ask me to do anything exceptionally unpleasant. He was—and is—and honourable man. Looking back, he treated me better than I deserved.'

'He honoured your motive for what you'd done,' said Mélusine, smiling mistily. 'Your mother and sister must be very proud of you.'

Pierre threw up his hands. 'Enough!' he exclaimed. 'What is sauce for the gander must be sauce for the goose. Tell me—' He broke off. Even in the darkness Mélusine could sense the change in his posture.

Church bells were tolling.

At first there were only a few, but within a short space of time it seemed as if every bell in Paris was ringing, sounding the tocsin.

'Oh, my God,' Mélusine whispered.

Pierre was already by the window when she reached his side. There was very little to see in the square below. She jumped as cannon boomed, loud even amidst the clangour of the bells. She rested the palm of her hand against the window. The tolling of the bells was unrelenting, the sound so dense it seemed to have physical substance. She could feel it vibrating through the house, the window pane, her whole body. Her skin rose in goose bumps. The cannon fired intermittently, but she began to hear something else beneath the ringing bells—as unremitting as the tolling, but faster.

'Drummers are marching,' Pierre murmured, and she saw two drummers, flanked by several other men, walk slowly across the dark square below.

'Stay here,' said Pierre, and then he was gone.

'Wait…!' She stretched out a hand to call him back, but it was too late. She bit her lip, knowing she had to trust him to take care of himself, knowing he was far better equipped than she was to do so.

She didn't know whether to watch the door for his return or the window to see if he appeared in the square. Though he hadn't said so, she was certain he meant to leave the house.

She felt sick. She knew what the tocsin was. The sound of danger. Warning. Summoning. But what did it mean tonight when there had been rioting, looting and even, from the sound of things earlier, a pitched battle in the heart of Paris?

She went down to the ground floor. The entrance hall was lit with a dimmed lantern. Even in the low light Paul looked pale. 'He went out, *madame*. I couldn't stop him.'

'I don't think anyone could stop him if he took a mind to do something,' said Mélusine. She sat on the stairs, her hands gripped together on her knees as she waited for Pierre to return. The maid and the housekeeper came down to join them.

'What is happening?' Suzanne asked. 'Has the King been killed?'

'I…don't think so,' said Mélusine, taken aback. 'He's at Versailles. The trouble started this afternoon because Monsieur Necker was dismissed.'

'It's the Queen who's to blame,' said Suzanne. 'She's no better than a common harlot. Such lewd things she's done with those fancy courtiers. When I went to market yesterday, the wind blew a pamphlet into my basket. It had pictures of the Queen—and the things she was doing! I hardly knew where to look!'

'She was very young when she came here from Austria,' said Paul.

'Exactly! She's still Austrian at heart. Foreign bi—' Suzanne broke off, throwing a glance at Mélusine.

'People tell lies about other people,' said Mélusine quietly. 'Unless we have met and spoken to someone, I don't believe we can say for sure what is or isn't the truth about them. I agree that some of the things she has done have not always been wise, but I do not think we can accept, without question, that she is a harlot on the basis of what her enemies say.'

'All great ladies are harlots. Some are more discreet than others.'

Mélusine stared at the floor and wondered if it would be unfair to dismiss Suzanne because she'd been frightened by the tocsin into revealing her true feelings about those she served.

She jumped up, relief flooding her as they heard Pierre's voice at the door. Paul opened it just sufficiently to let Pierre in, though Mélusine hoped such caution wasn't truly necessary.

'There was a meeting at the Hôtel de Ville earlier tonight,' Pierre said. 'The electors have decided to summon emergency meetings at the headquarters of each district in Paris at dawn tomorrow...today,' he corrected himself. 'That's what all the noise is about. They're going to form a citizens' militia. Each area must provide eight hundred volunteers.'

'Eight hundred!' Mélusine exclaimed.

At the same time, Paul said, 'I'm not volunteering. My duty is with *madame*.'

'Whose side will they be on?' Suzanne asked suspiciously.

'An interesting question,' said Pierre. 'The *gardes françaises*, though they are supposed to be loyal to the Crown, have been joining the rioters as often as not. The King can't count on their support. But, as far as I could tell from my conversation just now, the decision to raise the militia did not come from the King. They are to be identified by blue-and-red cockades. The colours of Paris. We will have to see what the morning brings. In the meantime, I suggest everyone goes back to bed.'

Mélusine allowed Suzanne and the housekeeper to precede her up stairs. When she was sure they were out of earshot, she asked Pierre to come up to the studio. As she opened the door she saw that the first faint light of dawn was beginning to illuminate the sky. The night was nearly over.

'Is there anything you did not say downstairs?' she asked.

He shook his head, smiling faintly. 'No. How many districts are there?'

'I don't know exactly. About sixty, I think.' She was slightly surprised he didn't know, because he always seemed so well informed, but then remembered he wasn't originally from Paris and possibly hadn't spent long here in the past.

'Forty-eight thousand men,' he said. 'Eight hundred from each district. If they succeed in raising so many it will be a formidable force.'

'I cannot imagine what will happen next,' said Mélusine. 'The whole world—or at least Paris—seems to have gone mad!'

Pierre laughed. 'Go to bed, *madame*,' he said.

'It's nearly dawn.'

He shrugged. 'The best time to go to bed,' he said. 'Especially when you've spent all night on sentry duty.'

* * *

Early afternoon, Monday, 13 July 1789

Mélusine slept better than she'd expected after the alarms of the night and woke just after noon.

'Do you think I'm a harlot?' she asked Suzanne, when the maid had finished pouring water into a basin.

'N-no, *madame*,' Suzanne stammered.

'You said last night that all great ladies are harlots,' Mélusine reminded her.

'But I don't think you're—' Suzanne broke off in obvious consternation.

'A great lady,' Mélusine finished drily. 'You're right. Though my husband was a nobleman, I'm a commoner by birth.'

'No, *madame*, you are a true lady,' said Suzanne. 'You have always been very polite to me. It's not the harlotry I mind so much, anyway. I dare say we all have our moments of weakness. It's the cruelty. I don't like it when a lady has a tantrum because her lover has been unfaithful and throws her favourite perfume bottle across the room—and then blames me because it's broken.'

'Well, no,' said Mélusine after a moment. 'That seems very unjust.'

'I'm not afraid you'll do anything like that,' said Suzanne.

'I'm glad to hear it,' said Mélusine.

'You haven't got much in the way of fancy perfume bottles,' said Suzanne.

'That's true,' said Mélusine.

'You're an eccentric,' said Suzanne. 'I've never worked for an eccentric before. It's an education, seeing you draw and make your pots. That Pierre is an odd one, isn't he? Good body—but the strangest footman I ever met. Very free with his orders, but always polite and soft-spoken.'

'You've seen his body?' said Mélusine.

'Only in your pictures. Pity he didn't take his breeches off. Not that you couldn't get him to do so if you put your mind to it, I'm sure. He's not very good at doing your hair, is he? Not terrible, mind you, but I've seen a lot better. His natural *métier* seems to be telling people what to do.'

'It does, doesn't it?' said Mélusine faintly. 'I know he's not the best hairdresser in the world. But all things considered, I much prefer him to my last footman-hairdresser.'

'What was wrong with him?'

'He sneered at me behind my back,' Mélusine said.

'You should have dismissed him,' said Suzanne.

'My husband had chosen him,' said Mélusine. 'It seemed ungrateful to reject his choice.'

'Well, you don't have to worry about what a husband thinks now,' said Suzanne robustly. 'You can make up your own mind.'

'I can, can't I?' Mélusine smiled. She'd been afraid

she'd have to give Suzanne a month's wages and, as soon as she had somewhere safe to go, ask her to leave. She decided that wouldn't be necessary after all. Suzanne in full flow was even more disconcerting than Suzanne the taciturn, but she didn't appear to bear Mélusine any ill will.

By evening the army had withdrawn from the centre of Paris, but the newly formed blue-and-red-cockaded militia were bringing the rioters under control. As darkness fell the street lamps were lit and most house-holders were sufficiently confident to light their houses.

'It's still very tense,' Pierre reported when he returned from a brief trip out. 'People are attacking the tax col-lectors' wall around Paris with anything they can find. The militia want weapons, and all most of them have managed to obtain so far are ancient halberds and pikes. What they want are muskets and powder. No one is to leave the house.'

'*You* went out,' said Mélusine. 'Aren't you afraid of being drummed into this new militia?' She'd meant it as a joke but, as soon as the words were out, she felt a *frisson* of anxiety at the possibility.

He smiled. 'I can be very inconspicuous when I want to be,' he said.

'Make sure you are,' she said. 'We cannot do without you.'

A troubled expression flickered briefly across his face. It was gone so quickly she wondered if she'd imagined it, but it worried her. She was increasingly certain he had his own secrets he hadn't shared with her. Even without Suzanne's comments, she'd come to the conclusion he had limited experience as a hairdresser. So why had he been interested in becoming *her* footman-hairdresser? She was a completely obscure widow—but one with a husband who'd died in mysterious circumstances. Was Pierre here because of Bertier's death? When that matter was resolved, would he leave as suddenly as he'd arrived?

Yesterday she'd thought all she had to worry about were his honourable principles. Today she feared they might be the least of her concerns. She was bleakly aware she'd be devastated if he left now.

Chapter Ten

Morning, Tuesday, 14 July 1789

The sky was heavy with clouds as Pierce made his way towards the Hôtel de Gilocourt. Mélusine thought he was on his way to see her lawyer, to talk about Saint-André, and he would do so later. But he had pressing concerns of his own. For the past few days he'd been almost certain Séraphin was behind the attempt to blackmail La Motte. The riots had forced him to put his plans for hunting the blackmailer in abeyance, but he couldn't let the matter drift indefinitely. He needed to find the document from which the blackmailer had torn La Motte's incriminating signature, destroy it, and make sure Séraphin didn't possess any other evidence of Bertier and La Motte's illicit activities. He didn't know whether Séraphin would have taken the documents with him to Versailles or kept them safe in his Paris townhouse. It was too late to seek employment himself with Séraphin, so he needed any ally in the

Hôtel de Gilocourt. He didn't want to compromise Laurette's position, but he was hoping she might tell him of a gap in the household that could be filled by one of Clothilde's contacts.

Despite his concern about the blackmailer, Pierce remained vigilant to his surroundings. The streets were full of people, and the closer he came to the rue de Varenne, the thicker the crowds became. From the shouted slogans of the men around him, he realised they were converging on Les Invalides. They wanted weapons, and they clearly believed that's where they would find them. Within moments he was being swept along by the press of agitated, shouting people. He glanced about, estimating his chances of breaking free of the jostling throng. Someone trod on his heel. Another man elbowed him in the side.

The image of cattle, wild-eyed, frightened, herded through narrow city streets to market, filled his mind. All too often the cattle escaped their herders' control and stampeded through the streets, trampling or goring terrified pedestrians. He was glad none of his companions had horns, but if they suspected for a moment he wasn't on their side, he knew they'd be even more dangerous than maddened cattle.

He kept pace with them, alert, wary, and unwilling to do anything that might draw attention to himself. Eventually they burst on to the parade ground in front of Les Invalides, joining thousands of other men already there. The air rang with shouted demands for weapons.

Above their heads, under the leaden sky, the gold-decorated dome of the church glinted dully. Behind them more men surged into the parade ground, pushing forward those already there.

'In the cellars! In the cellars! The muskets are in the cellars!'

There was another surge. Chaotic scrambling, during which Pierce's only concern was to stay on his feet. Some of those who'd first gone into the cellars emerged, their arms full of firearms.

'Here, friend!' A musket was thrust into his hands.

'Is there shot, powder?' he asked, knowing the musket was useless without both.

He was answered by the growing roar of disgust reverberating through the mob. They'd found cannon and muskets, but no powder or cartridges.

'Nails. I've got some nails,' said a man close by. 'They might do in place of shot.'

'We still need powder,' another man objected.

'They took the powder to the Bastille.'

'The Bastille.'

'The Bastille.'

The mob, which had surged towards Les Invalides, began to surge away, taking Pierce with it. He found himself in a small group of men composed of the fellow with nails, the one who'd pointed out the need for powder, and several others.

'I'm Samuel Brissot, cobbler,' said the man with the nails as they hurried along. 'Who are you?'

'Pierre Duval, tailor,' Pierce replied, confident no one in the crowd was going to ask for a coat fitting.

'You can have some of my nails—my God, look at that!'

Several of Pierce's new companions were obviously familiar with the area around the Bastille. Instead of leading them the length of the rue Saint-Antoine, they'd approached from a side street—so the high walls of the fortress prison suddenly loomed above them.

Samuel stared up in horror at the mouths of the cannon pointing down at them from the towers and walls.

'It's true! They're going to fire on us! Bombard Paris until there's nothing left!'

'No, they won't!' another man said confidently. 'The soldiers inside won't fire on us—they're on our side.'

'There's powder in the cellar!'

'Will they give it to us?'

'We want the Bastille! Out with the troops!'

'What's happening?'

The crowd behind kept pushing forward. Pierce and the men around him were forced forward, into the first courtyard. It had seemed narrow when he'd walked through it with Mélusine and she stared in amazement at the shops on the right side. Now, with men pressing him on all sides, it was claustrophobic. The drawbridge straight ahead was raised. There was nowhere to go. Pierce had no intention of being pushed into the moat, beneath the drawbridge, so he concentrated on holding his position well clear of the gate.

He grabbed Samuel's shoulder to prevent the little cobbler being carried too far forward.

'What are you doing? We need to go on!' Samuel shouted angrily.

'There's nowhere to go except the moat!' Pierce shouted back.

A roar of fear and anger suddenly rose from the crowd.

'They're pulling in the cannon! They're loading them!'

'They've killed our delegates! Now they're going to slaughter us!'

Pierce looked up at the towers, then back the way they'd come. There was no way to retreat. More men continually pressed forward. Every second he was jostling to keep himself on his feet and prevent Samuel from being pushed too far forward. His heart pounded. He'd been in many dangerous situations, but none which was so thoroughly beyond his control. He glanced around the narrow courtyard again, seeking some escape route. He saw several men climbing on to the roof of the same perfume shop that had caught Mélusine's attention. Was that a way out?

As he watched, the men jumped from the shop roof on to the rampart wall and disappeared from view into the inner courtyard on the other side. They were clearly a lot keener than he was to get into the next bottleneck. He had a very vivid memory of the cannon inside the Bastille, lined up to point through the main entrance into the inner courtyard. So far no shots had been fired on either side. From what he could tell, at least two sets of delegates had gone inside to talk to the governor. He hoped there would be a negotiated outcome.

'The drawbridge is coming down!'

'Back! Back!'

Over the heads of the people in front, Pierce saw the drawbridge begin to swing down. It gathered speed as it fell, and shouts of anguish and groans from ahead indicated some men hadn't been able to get out of the way.

'He's dead!'

But the crowd surged forward, over the drawbridge and the body of one of their fellow besiegers, into the inner courtyard. The governor's lodgings were on the right. The main gate to the Bastille on their left, its entrance blocked by another drawbridge.

'They let us in here to massacre us!'

There was musket fire from the crowd and inside the Bastille—and then cannon roared from tower walls.

Pierce seized Samuel and dragged him to the nearest cover he could see, the buildings on the right of the main entrance. A few seconds later, he found himself in the kitchens of the prison-fortress.

It wasn't exactly a safe haven but, for the first time since he'd found himself trapped in the outer courtyard, he breathed slightly easier. Around him men were already arguing how they would breach the entrance. Some, bolder than the others, ran straight out to renew their attack, but they were driven back by heavy fire.

In the end, it was decided to pull up some carts of hay to provide a smokescreen.

It was the perfect moment—and excuse—to escape into the streets of Paris. An offer to help with the carts would get him out of the confines of the Bastille. Once in the street, now he knew what was at stake, he was confident he could disappear.

He cradled the looted musket he'd been given and thought about Saint-André, who'd spent eight months confined in a cell as a result of one man's murderous ambition. There was no reason for him to remain shut away from the world—hadn't been for months—but Pierce knew the man who'd had him incarcerated would never trouble to arrange his release. He stayed where he was.

'Is he back yet?'

'*Madame*, if he was back I would have told you! *He* would have told you,' said Paul.

'I'm sorry. I know you would. He shouldn't have gone out. He wouldn't let the rest of us go out!'

'*Madame*, Pierre is a man who knows how to take care of himself,' said Paul. 'I'm sure he—'

'It's the Bastille!' Suzanne dashed in from the back of the house. 'I was just speaking to the footman next door. The people are attacking the Bastille!' She glanced between Paul and Mélusine. 'Isn't Pierre back yet?'

'No,' said Mélusine. For a brief instant she felt hollow with shock, then fear rushed in to fill the void.

'There you are, then,' said Paul robustly. 'Pierre's much too canny to get involved in a rash undertaking like that.'

'A rash undertaking,' Mélusine repeated, remembering the cannon that had pointed so threateningly from the towers of the Bastille.

'The Bastille *should* be destroyed,' said Suzanne vehemently. 'Evil place. They keep the prisoners chained in the dungeons with only the rats for company. The warders have to face the wall when new prisoners are brought in so they don't see their faces. It's a terrible, horrible, place.'

'The prisoner I visited on Saturday had quite a nice room in one of the towers with a window, a desk, and several books,' said Mélusine. 'Tell Pierre I want to see him as soon as he arrives.'

She left Paul and Suzanne staring open-mouthed after her as she went back up the stairs she'd already run up and down at least once every half-hour since mid-morning. There was no point in running up and down any more. She knew where Pierre was. She didn't know how he'd become involved. But they'd talked about the injustice of Saint-André being locked up without explanation or trial and the difficulty of obtaining his freedom. She wondered what would happen if the Bastille fell to the attackers. Surely they'd release the prisoners? Still, Saint-André was noble, with all the identifying mannerisms of a nobleman. How would they treat him?

* * *

Pierce stood in the shadows of the kitchen and rubbed the back of his hand over his damp forehead as he watched the newly arrived cannons being aimed at the raised drawbridge. He'd just helped to move away the carts which had been dragged in front of the entrance that morning to provide a smokescreen. The carts had been heavy and two of the men hauling them away had fallen to musket shots from the Bastille. Pierce hadn't enjoyed putting himself in the line of fire, but he wanted the siege over. From all he could see, the longer it lasted, the greater the confusion and bitterness grew on both sides.

Proof of that came all too quickly. In the battlements above a drummer began to beat the retreat and two men waved white handkerchiefs, but the men below took no notice. They just kept firing their muskets and shouting, 'Down with the bridge! Down with the bridge!'

Most of them weren't soldiers. They had no military discipline and little organisation. Pierce drew a deep breath. Even soldiers under the control of officers they respected tended to run amok at the conclusion of a siege. If the drawbridge came down, was he about to witness the massacre of the defenders?

There was a shout from the men around him and he saw a piece of paper being waved through a slit in the drawbridge. But the drawbridge was on the other side of the moat, and some of the besiegers had to run to get planks of wood before they could read the note they were being offered. If the situation hadn't been so tense and potentially lethal, the sight of the men trying to balance on the wobbling plank would have been comical. The first one fell, but the second successfully snatched the note and dashed back with it.

'The governor says if we don't accept his capitulation, they'll blow up the Bastille and the whole neighbourhood! They've got twenty thousand pounds of gunpowder!'

Pierce listened to the crowd's furious reaction to the governor's ultimatum and wondered if Launay had the resolution to carry out his threat. The men around him were driven by deep-rooted hatred and fear of all the Bastille represented. He could feel something of it himself, though it was not his country or his battle.

'No capitulation! Down with the bridges!'

A man strode towards the cannon, so purposefully Pierce was sure he was going to fire them....

The drawbridge came down. Pierce tensed, expecting cannon fire from within—but all remained silent.

He exhaled. The Bastille had surrendered. How would the crowd behave now?

He followed the first rush of men through the gate, listening grimly, but without surprise, to the shouts of, 'Hang them! Hang them!' from the victorious besiegers.

Some of them were heading to the dungeons to free the prisoners, but Pierce knew that Saint-André was in a tower room. He pushed his way through the confusion to the stairwell leading to the Marquis's cell. By the time he'd risen a few turns, the sounds of the crowds outside were muted by the thick walls. In the midst of so much uproar, it was a disturbing reminder of how isolated the prisoners were in their cells.

'A key would be helpful, but needs must,' he murmured to himself as he contemplated the lock on Saint-André's door. He hoped the short blade concealed in his coat pocket would be sturdy enough for the job at hand.

Several minutes later, poised to react swiftly if necessary, he swung the door open. He wasn't surprised to discover the Marquis on his feet, alert and wary.

Saint-André's posture relaxed very slightly when he recognised Pierce. 'You look as if you've been in a battle, my friend,' he said.

'I have. The people have taken the Bastille.'

'Good.' Saint-André watched Pierce close the door. 'Are we about to have a battle of our own?'

'Would you have done what Bertier asked you to do?' Pierce asked.

'Ah—' Saint-André's eyes narrowed '—regarding his wife?'

'Yes.'

'I wondered if she knew when you visited. Did he tell her?'

'Would you have done it?' Pierce ignored the question.

'No. May I ask how you became acquainted with the lady?'

'I'm her footman,' said Pierce.

'Indeed.' Saint-André raised his eyebrows. 'You are a man of many parts, I perceive.'

'As are you, *monsieur*.'

'But what prompted you take such a position?'

'I'm looking for a blackmailer—'

'And you suspected *Madame de Gilocourt*?'

'Not after I met her,' said Pierce.

'Who's the victim? You or...' Saint-André's eyes narrowed again. 'We can talk in riddles for a while longer, of course, but I've spent too long living with un-answered riddles and I want to get out of here,' he said briskly. 'Bertier is dead, therefore he cannot be black-mailed. Anyone associated with him, however, could be at risk. The most obvious candidate would be the in-dividual with whom he first went into...business.'

'You obviously know about his business, since you were engaged upon it when we first met,' said Pierce.

'Now the question I have,' said Saint-André softly, his eyes watchful, 'is whether you know the name of his partner?'

'Do you?' asked Pierce. 'Yes,' he said, as he saw the answer in the Marquis's expression.

'Then my deductions lead me to the conclusion I may be speaking to that man's stepson—oldest stepson,' Saint-André said precisely.

Pierce sighed. 'I admire a cautious man,' he said. 'But I am tired and dirty and we still have to get out of here without anyone deciding to parade you as one of the rescued victims of the Bastille. I assume you would not enjoy that. They're searching the dungeons for chained wretches in rags.'

'From what Launay said, I don't think the dungeons are in use,' said Saint-André. He picked up one of the books from the desk. 'A souvenir of eight wasted months,' he said. 'I'll leave everything else. After you, *monsieur*.'

Night had fallen, and the clouds that had threatened Paris all day finally opened. Mélusine stood at the studio window, staring into darkness and listening to the rain beat on the glass. By turns she felt angry, helpless and afraid. Her fear was not for herself, but for Pierre. He'd been gone all day. He'd not called upon Monsieur Barrière. She knew the Bastille had been attacked. She knew men must have been killed or injured. When was it time to stop waiting and go in search of him? If she left too soon, she might miss his return and head needlessly into danger herself. If she waited too long, she might not find him before his injuries proved fatal—

The door opened.

She spun round. All day, every time the door had opened, she'd hoped it would be Pierre and been disappointed. Now, despite her hopes, she was expecting to see Suzanne or Paul. When it wasn't either, she stared in disbelief for a couple of heartbeats before flying across the room.

'Are you hurt?' She seized Pierre's shoulders.

'Where have you been?' She began to shake him. He wasn't wearing his footman's wig and his hair was wet with rain, his face streaked with soot. 'I'm so angry with you. Are you hurt? I know you were fighting. I can see. Look at you.' She stopped shaking him to touch his grimy face. 'You smell like guns. Are you hurt? You had no *business* fighting. I'm so angry I could k-kill you.' She burst into tears.

'Hush.' He put his arms around her and drew her close. 'I'm safe. I'm sorry you were frightened.'

'I'm not frightened. I'm f-furious!' she said into his shoulder, and then her emotions completely overcame her. She collapsed against him, all the anxiety, helplessness and fear of the past day finding release in her tears.

He stroked her back and her hair, murmuring soothing words she was too overwrought to understand. He was back with her. He was safe. And she felt a crazy determination never to let him out of her sight again.

When he first picked her up, she was still so overwhelmed by her feelings she barely noticed. It was only as he started to carry her across the room that she lifted her head from his shoulder.

'What…?'

'I'm tired, sweetheart,' he said, a note of slightly wry amusement in his voice. 'So…I'll sit down and rest my legs and you can cry as long as you want.'

'You are hurt.' She wiped her sleeve across her

cheeks and gazed intently into his face. 'What happened? Where are you hurt?'

'I'm not hurt. I'm a little weary,' he admitted, almost as if the acknowledgement embarrassed him. 'I've done a harder day's labour many times—but there's something about a siege that is a trifle...tiring.'

'You *were* at the Bastille. How did you get involved? You were supposed to go to Monsieur Barrière's. That's not even in the right direction! You promised you wouldn't get drawn into any fighting. You said you were inconspicuous. You *promised* no one would notice you—'

'Shush!' With a half-laugh he laid his fingers over her lips. 'I *was* inconspicuous and nobody did notice me.'

'Then how—?'

'I was swept along by the crowds—'

'Oh, you wouldn't be unless you wanted to,' she scoffed.

'You flatter me.' He smiled. Then he brushed his fingers gently over her tearstained cheek and his smile faded.

'I've never seen you cry before,' he said.

'I do cry.' She looked away, embarrassed.

'Not after the dinner party or your father's visit, or even Daniel's.'

'You don't know that for sure.'

'Did you?'

'No.'

He turned her face towards him. In the candlelight

she could see the flecks of darker grey around his pupils. Then he slipped his hand behind her head and slowly drew her closer and closer until their lips finally met.

She closed her eyes. His tongue stroked her mouth, pressing gently, and she instinctively parted her lips. She could taste the salt of her tears, but it was the seductive pressure of his mouth and tongue on hers that filled her awareness. He stroked and teased and probed until she was dazed with pleasure, and oblivious to everything but him. She was conscious of the hard muscles of his thighs beneath her legs, his arm supporting her back as he held her in just the right position to ravage her mouth with his. She lifted her hand to touch his face. Her fingers fluttered into his hair.

At last, when her body was singing with pleasure, he raised his lips from hers. She sighed and rested her head against his shoulder. After all the anxiety of the day she was completely beguiled by the comforting strength of his embrace.

'Kisses are supposed to make the princess wake up—not put her to sleep,' he said, after a while.

'I'm not asleep,' she said, opening her eyes. 'And I'm not a princess.'

'If it comes to that, I'm not a prince.'

'You are to me.' She was too relaxed to guard her words.

He didn't say anything. Nothing in the way he was holding her changed, but in his silence she gradually became aware of his rejection of her claim.

She stayed as she was a moment or two longer, then she lifted her head. She gave no other indication of how she'd interpreted his behaviour, and she didn't get off his lap. He'd put her there, and she liked being in his arms.

'Tell me what happened,' she ordered. 'Since you did *not* do as I told you to, and you've denied me your services all day, you owe me a full account of your deeds.'

'You're an exacting mistress.' He smiled faintly. 'Very well, then.'

'I was going to the Hôtel de Gilocourt when I was swept along in the crowds going to Les Invalides,' he began.

As he talked he caught her hand in his free hand and started to play gently with her fingers. He was so focused on his story, she was sure he wasn't aware of what he was doing. Even though she really wanted to know what had happened to him, she couldn't help wondering what it meant that he was playing so naturally and unthinkingly with her hand while she sat on his lap.

'I didn't like being trapped in the courtyard,' he confessed. 'Until then there'd been no risk and I was curious to know what would happen. I prefer more elbow room if I'm called upon to fight.'

'But you did fight?' She could see he had. There were small cuts on his hands, a long scratch across one of them and, though he'd washed them, she could still see the powder stains. Even though he was safe now, she was horrified anew at the thought he could have been hurt or even killed.

'Not much. I put my best efforts towards staying out of firing range in the kitchens and, when the need arose, impersonating an indignant citizen.'

'Then why did you stay? I'm sure you could have found an excuse to leave at some point during all those hours. Even if it was only that you'd suddenly remembered a secret supply of powder and you were going to hurry and get it.'

'That did occur to me,' he admitted. 'But Saint-André was inside, and—'

'Where is he now?' In her first concern over Pierre, she'd forgotten the Marquis. '*He* isn't hurt, is he? You would have told me if he was hurt.'

'He's downstairs.'

'*Downstairs!*' She jolted completely upright.

'You wanted to talk to him again, so I brought him back with me,' said Pierre reasonably.

'But…has anyone offered him anything to eat… drink? Have you just abandoned him in the blue salon? You did put him in the blue salon, didn't you? It's the only room fit for visitors to see—'

'Any room in this house would be an improvement on his quarters for the past eight months,' said Pierre.

'But at least he had a bed in his cell,' said Mélusine. 'He can't go out again tonight, it's not safe. Oh dear, I'll have to give him my bed—'

'No!'

"There's a spare truckle bed in the servants' quarters. You can put that in one of the empty rooms for me tonight. No, you're weary, I'll ask Paul to help me.... What?'

'Is it his noble blood that has you in such a hostessly twitter? Or the fact he was your husband's friend? Or...something else?' Pierre asked.

She stared at him, distracted from her instinctive hospitality by his questions. It was the last that intrigued her most. 'You cannot be jealous,' she said slowly. 'You have made it plain that you are not...that we are not...'

'Which is why you are sitting on my lap. Did I say I was jealous?' He tightened his grip as she moved.

'You put me here.' She abandoned her half-hearted attempt to get up.

'I did, didn't I? That's because of the fatigue we both felt after such a demanding day. It won't happen again tomorrow.'

'Then we have to make the most of it now,' she said daringly.

'I suppose so.'

He looked at her. She looked at him.

She touched his mouth with her fingertip, gently exploring the shape of his firm lips. 'I would like to sculpt you.'

Beneath her fingers his mouth curved into a smile. 'I wonder how many artists have seduced their models with those words?' he murmured. He caught her hand in his and held it so that he could draw one of her fingers into his mouth. He stroked it with his tongue, and then sucked gently.

She felt his caress in every part of her body. She melted against him, languid with pleasure. 'That is very decadent,' she managed, with an almost creditable attempt at nonchalance.

'Decadence is the fashion, so I understand.' He changed his hold on her slightly so she was positioned just right, and kissed her again.

She put both arms around his neck. She wanted to hold him and touch him while they kissed. That's what lovers did. She'd never had a lover, and if Pierre was determined to be honourable, maybe she never would. But now she'd experienced his kisses, the possibility dismayed her in a way it never had before.

'You learn fast, *madame*,' he said some time later, his voice a little breathless.

'What do you mean?' She'd never been kissed on her mouth before. Bertier had confined himself to formal salutations on her cheek. Until Pierre had kissed her, she'd no idea how wonderful it could be.

He shook his head slightly, and kissed the side of her neck. When he teased her earlobe with his tongue and lips, she became giddy with delight. He stroked the outer edge of her ear with his tongue, and then said, his mouth so close she could feel his lips move against her skin, 'Saint-André is not having your bed.'

She sat absolutely still for a moment, then sat up. 'I can't give him the pallet bed,' she protested.

'Yes, you can. You'll embarrass him if you offer him your bed—especially in the circumstances. Or perhaps he'll even misconstrue your intention.'

She gasped. Between her distraction over Pierre's kisses and her determination to be a good hostess, that possibility hadn't occurred to her.

'Did you speak to him about it? You would not have brought him back here if you thought he'd behave... improperly. Would you?'

"No. Yes.' Pierre frowned. '*Madame*, you ask so many questions I've no idea if I just agreed or disagreed with you. I don't believe Saint-André poses any threat to your peace of mind, but you should speak to him yourself.'

'Yes, I will.' Even though she wanted to stay in the studio with Pierre, she started to get off his lap. He tightened his arm around her and she subsided, hoping he was going to kiss her again, but his expression was too serious and all-too-familiar apprehension began to knot her stomach.

'Has anyone told you about the governor?' he asked.

She shook her head. 'We've heard the news the Bastille was taken. It isn't always easy to make sense of the rumours.'

'The mob killed him,' Pierre said quietly. 'It is better that you hear now so you are not taken by surprise later.' He paused and then said, 'They put his head on a pike and paraded it through the streets.'

'Oh, my God.' Mélusine pressed her hand against her

mouth. The only time she'd ever met the Marquis de Launay was when she'd visited Saint-André, but it was shocking to know that someone she'd met, even briefly, could suffer such a fate. She put her arms around Pierre and hugged him very tightly. 'You are completely foolhardy and not safe to let out alone. You are not to get involved in any more such exploits, do you understand?' she said, her voice muffled against his neck.

'My involvement this time was entirely accidental,' he protested.

'Saint-André was there,' she said, and sat up. 'Do you think I'm so stupid I don't know that's why you stayed and took part in the attack? You knew his presence there was unjust. You knew we would have terrible difficulty obtaining his release by regular means. But he is free now, and there is no call for any further heroics of that nature.'

Pierre smiled crookedly. 'As you say, *madame*,' he said.

'What will happen now?' she asked. 'Now the Bastille has fallen.'

'Calmer heads are waiting for the King's response,' said Pierre.

Fear suddenly seized Mélusine as she remembered the troops that had been camped on the Champ de Mars.

'Kiss me again,' she said urgently.

'This is the last time, *madame*.'

'Mmm,' she murmured submissively as his mouth touched hers. *Tonight*, she thought, as his tongue slipped between her lips, *the last time*, tonight.

Chapter Eleven

Despite her relief that Saint-André was free and her determination to be a good hostess, Mélusine felt extremely awkward as she entered the blue salon. Saint-André was sitting quietly in the candlelight. Although there was a book on the small table beside the chair, he wasn't reading it. He seemed to be gazing at some inner vision, but she had no time to reflect on her impression because as soon as he heard the door open he looked around and immediately stood up.

'*Madame.*' He bowed with his usual grace, but there was some discomfiture in his manner. 'I regret I must present myself to you in such a dishevelled guise—' He broke off, as his gaze moved past her to where Pierre had entered the room behind her.

Mélusine looked quickly over her shoulder. Pierre was wearing his impassive servant's face, but she sensed some silent communication had passed between the two men.

'I said that your relief at discovering he was free

would outweigh any insult you felt at being visited by a gentleman in an outmoded coat and a full beard,' Pierre remarked.

Saint-André frowned. 'It is a grave breach of etiquette to appear in a lady's salon in such a ramshackle style.'

Pierre grinned. 'I will set the lady's chair so she sits with her back to you. She may then imagine that you are dressed exactly as you ought to be—and all your problems are solved.'

Mélusine looked from one man to the other, surprised and fascinated by their exchange. Saint-André had always been courteous to servants, but she'd never before seen him talk to a footman as if they were equals. Even though the Marquis hadn't done anything as ungentlemanly as laugh, or even smile, at Pierre's comment, she sensed he'd been amused by it.

'*Monsieur*, of course I am not offended by your attire,' she said to Saint-André. 'How could I be in the circumstances? Please sit down again.' She hesitated very briefly. 'Both of you,' she said firmly, feeling her colour heighten. It had been one thing commanding two servants to sit together in her presence when Daniel had visited. It was very different asking a footman to do so in the presence of a marquis. But how could she sit on Pierre's lap and kiss him in private—then treat him as part of the furniture when she had noble company?

She'd been prepared to defend her action, but she was

relieved neither man openly questioned it—though, from the slight quirk of Pierre's eyebrow, she wondered if he'd comment later.

'*Madame*, I would like to return to the terms of easy friendship we used to enjoy,' said Saint-André. 'To do that I believe we must first talk of less pleasant things so that we can then set them aside for ever. I am more than sorry you overheard Bertier that night. I can only imagine your shock and distress.'

Despite her determination to appear composed, Mélusine couldn't bring herself to look at the Marquis. It was almost unbearably embarrassing and humiliating to remember what her husband had asked Saint-André to do to her while Saint-André himself was sitting only a few feet away, watching her.

'*Madame*, I would not have done it,' said the Marquis gently. 'Did I ever tell you about my mother?'

The apparent change of subject surprised Mélusine into looking up. 'No.'

'My father suspected her of infidelity when I was eight years old. As punishment for her offence, he had her confined in a nunnery for the rest of her life,' said Saint-André. 'He did not allow her to see her children. He did not allow her children to see her. I never forgave him for that. At the time of his death, I had not spoken to him for ten years.'

In all the time Mélusine had known Saint-André, even when she'd visited him in the Bastille, she had never heard him speak in anything but mellow, well-modulated tones. But when he spoke of his parents his voice changed. She could hear the harshness of pain that had still not healed.

'In this I had something in common with Bertier,' said Saint-André, 'though we seldom spoke of it. His father never had his mother confined, but they hated each other for most of Bertier's youth. When she died his father erased all evidence that she'd been part of his life. Bertier was captured by a privateer and held hostage when he was about twenty, did you know that?'

'No.' Mélusine was amazed and bewildered by Saint-André's revelations. 'What happened?'

'His father refused to pay the ransom. Thus Bertier was left in no doubt his father would have been happy if he'd been erased also. I seem to have drifted from my point, somewhat,' Saint-André said apologetically. 'Too much time in my own company has given me the bad habit of rambling. *Madame*, to be direct, I would not willingly, deliberately put you or any other woman at risk of suffering my mother's fate.'

Mélusine considered everything Saint-André had just told her. 'You don't have affairs with married women,' she said, for the first time realising that, in a society in which adultery was not only common but fashionable, she'd never heard any gossip about Saint-André in this respect.

'No.'

'Bertier must have known that.'

'He did, of course.'

'Then why—?'

'Why did he ask me? Why did he think I'd do it despite my usual scruples? Why did he come up the plan in the first place? Why didn't you hear me reject his request as soon as he made it?' Saint-André sighed. 'Bertier was my friend for many years. You must not think, because I understand the reasons for it, I condone the way he behaved in the months and days before his death.'

'You understand more than we do,' said Pierre, breaking his silence for the first time since they'd sat down.

'Forgive me. My mind is wandering tonight,' said Saint-André.

'I think, *monsieur*, it is not that your mind is wandering, but that you are trying not to upset me,' said Mélusine. 'For most of our marriage Bertier was not unkind to me, and he was so generous when he left me this house and the others. Perhaps if I understand why he asked you...' She paused to steady herself. 'Please tell me,' she said.

Saint-André didn't say anything for a few moments. Mélusine noticed that the glass on the table beside his book was empty. She glanced around and saw that the bottle had been left on the sideboard. It was almost full. Saint-André had been a frugal guest. She started to rise, but Pierre had seen the direction of her gaze and guessed her purpose. He stood swiftly and refilled Saint-André's empty glass.

The Marquis smiled faintly. 'I do not usually find my

courage in a bottle,' he said, 'but I appreciate your thoughtfulness.' He picked up the glass and took a few sips of wine. 'Comtesse, you will have guessed Bertier was unable to sire children.'

She nodded.

'He did not suspect until you'd been married for over a year,' said Saint-André. 'He'd believed—as did everyone—that it was his first wife's fault that there were no children from his first marriage. He'd taken lovers, of course, but until he finally inherited his title, he'd not given much consideration to the need for heirs.'

'That's why he married me,' said Mélusine.

'I would like to say his motives were more romantic,' said Saint-André, 'but I know you didn't meet him until after the contract was signed. He did arrange to observe you unseen beforehand. He found you charming.'

'I didn't know that.' Mélusine was disconcerted by the revelation. 'I know he had a mistress. I'm sure he did, even though Séraphin said he didn't.'

'Ah,' said Saint-André. 'Yes, Bertier did have a mistress. Julie Dubois—'

'I never knew her name,' said Mélusine.

'He was very fond of Julie,' said Saint-André.

'Did he love her?' Mélusine asked.

Saint-André hesitated, then he said, 'I think he loved her more than he was aware. He was devastated when he lost her.'

'How?'

'Another man seduced her away from him. She became more elusive, and then he saw them together.'

'Was that when he became so morose?' Mélusine asked.

Saint-André nodded. 'He was hurt and angry. It may seem unreasonable to you, *madame*, but he felt bitterly betrayed. In time I believe his mood would have improved, but he saw Julie again—and she was pregnant. He knew for sure then he'd never father children. That was the morning before you overheard him speaking to me.'

Mélusine sucked in a breath. She wasn't sure if she'd ever entirely forgive Bertier for what he'd planned for her, but she could better understand how the wound to his pride as well as his heart had provoked his behaviour.

'So he decided he had to have an heir by any means possible, and you were to be the means,' she said with some difficulty. 'You must have found it an…uncomfortable…conversation, *monsieur*.'

'I did not enjoy it,' he said. 'I knew there was no point arguing with him in that mood. I was going to wait until he was calm enough for rational conversation. I regret the opportunity never arose.' He sounded genuinely saddened.

'Thank you for telling me,' said Mélusine.

'Who was the man who seduced Julie away?' asked Pierre.

Saint-André glanced at him. He didn't speak, but Mélusine caught the merest flicker of warning in his eyes. She had the sudden inexplicable, but absolute, conviction that if she didn't assert herself, the two men would continue the conversation in her absence. The idea infuriated her so much she jumped to her feet without thinking. Both men immediately followed suit.

'Stop!' she exclaimed.

'*Madame*, we appreciate your delicacy,' said Pierre. 'I believe the conversation has come to a natural conclusion. I will bring the spare bed up from the servants' quarters to the first-floor apartment for the Marquis tonight. I understand while he was in the Bastille he was able to terminate the lease he'd had on his apartment. It occurred to me you might wish to consider leasing the first-floor apartment to him, *madame*.'

'Stop, stop, *stop*! Sit down again, both of you!' Mélusine pointed imperatively to the chairs they'd just vacated. When they'd obeyed, she put her hands on her hips and glared at them impartially. 'I will not have you both managing my affairs behind my back!'

'You cannot want to haul the bed up the stairs yourself!' Pierre protested.

'That's not what I'm talking about, as you know perfectly well,' Mélusine declared. 'Do you think I didn't see you ask a question the Marquis didn't want to answer? He warned you with his eyes and then you start distracting me with talk about carrying beds and leasing apartments—'

'Only one apartment,' said Pierre reasonably. 'The Marquis appears to be a well-mannered gentleman of sober habits. By his own account he has a comfortable income—which is always desirable in a tenant—and he is currently without suitable accommodation.'

'Or, indeed, any accommodation,' Saint-André murmured, picking up his wine glass and taking another sip. 'At your leisure, Dumont, I would be delighted to view the first-floor apartment.'

'*Of course* you can have the first-floor apartment, if you would like it,' said Mélusine. 'I will show it to you myself later, while Pierre brings the bed up. Now, tell me the name of the man who seduced Julie from Bertier.'

Saint-André stared into space for a few moments.

'*Monsieur*, I know you do not want to upset me,' said Mélusine. 'But I can deal more easily with the truth than with endless uncertainty. Or is it the seducer you are trying to protect rather than me?'

Saint-André's lips twisted in a wry smile. 'You are not easily deterred, *madame*. It was Séraphin. The man who seduced Julie and made her pregnant was Séraphin.'

'*Séraphin!*' The mere thought of Séraphin laying his hands or lips on her was enough to make Mélusine shudder. 'Why on earth would *any* woman…?'

'Some women—of less discriminating taste—seem to find him quite appealing,' said Saint-André. 'He had several notable conquests even before Julie.'

Mélusine rubbed her temples.

Pierre immediately stood up. 'You are tired,' he said.

'It has been a long, traumatic day for everyone. Let us—'

'Wait. No, wait.' She lifted her hands in a staying gesture. 'Yes, I am tired, but that's not it. I am trying to see my way forward—and how I can avoid the pair of you leading me in circles through the maze while you do exactly as you see fit. Séraphin is *dangerous*, do you understand? I cannot imagine why any woman would take him as a lover. But I can easily imagine him leaving the police inspector for dead by the customs barrier because he'd no further use for him. I am *not* having your bodies carried home to me the way Bertier's was.'

Pierre sat down again. In the silence following her words, the rain lashing against the window panes seemed very loud.

Mélusine's heart was beating so fast she felt sick. She took several deliberately slow breaths, trying to compose herself. She hadn't meant to say so much. If they hadn't already guessed, she might have precipitated the very disaster she was desperate to avoid.

'How long have you known?' Pierre asked at last.

'I don't know. I suspect,' she corrected him. 'Most likely I'm wrong. Of course I am wrong. Now Saint-André is free, we don't need to think of the past any more. We will all go to bed. And in the morning the Marquis can borrow your razor and buy some new clothes so he doesn't feel embarrassed to be seen in company and you can explain why you took it upon yourself to assume command of my household and choose my tenants—and we'll all discuss what the King will do about the fall of the Bastille.'

'Is that why you suddenly decided you didn't care who killed Bertier, but were fierce in your determination to free Saint-André from his imprisonment—because you'd realised who was to blame for both?' said Pierre.

'Until I'd spoken to the Marquis, I couldn't think clearly about that night at all,' said Mélusine. 'But I felt calmer after I'd spoken to you…' She looked at Saint-André.

'I'm glad of that,' he said.

'And then I thought—who would benefit from Bertier's death and you being shut away from the world? And I wondered if it was someone trying to make sure you didn't do what Bertier had asked you to do. Because Jean-Baptiste could have told someone. I was so mortified at falling over him I never stopped to wonder if he'd been there on purpose, spying. But he could have told someone. And that someone could have decided to make sure Bertier never had an heir by any means. And the only person I could think of who'd want to do that was Séraphin.'

'And you haven't said anything about your suspicions for the past three days,' said Pierre, a mixture of disbelief and indignation in his voice. 'After dragging me to the Hôtel de Police, and the Bastille, and insisting in the most vehement manner we had to clear your reputation of the slur against it—you didn't tell me you'd solved the mystery.'

'I didn't want you to do anything rash,' Mélusine said defensively. 'Besides, we still don't know for sure Bertier wasn't killed by brigands, just as the police inspector originally claimed. Everyone knows it was a bitterly hard winter. It makes perfectly good sense that Bertier was attacked by people who wanted to rob him.'

'In that case they'd have stripped him of everything they could sell—his clothes, everything,' said Pierre.

'Not if they were interrupted before they could do so,' Mélusine argued.

'Then why weren't they caught? Your lack of confidence in my ability to deal with Séraphin is insulting, *madame!*' Pierre stood up. 'I will fetch the bed for Saint-André.'

The door closed very definitely behind him. Mélusine stared after him in confusion, which quickly turned to indignation.

'Not exactly a slam,' said Saint-André, 'but close.'

'He has no business slamming about my house!' she exclaimed. 'He's my *footman*, for Heaven's sake!'

'I think he's forgotten,' Saint-André murmured, as Mélusine rushed out of the room.

'Pierre! Pierre!' Mélusine ran down the stairs after him.

He turned on the landing and caught her as she nearly overbalanced on the last two steps.

'Why are you so cross?' she demanded. 'It's not even your problem. You can be glad Saint-André is safe and we can stop worrying about it.'

'Are you going to stop worrying about it? When you next meet your brother-in-law at a reception, are you going to be able to forget he killed your husband?'

'We don't know that for sure.'

'Don't we? And don't you think Saint-André might also have guessed who is responsible for his incarceration? Do you think a man, however skilled, who has just spent eight months in a sixteen-foot cell will be *better* equipped to deal with Séraphin?'

Mélusine gasped. 'You think Saint-André will challenge Séraphin?'

Pierre picked her up and carried her into the nearest of the rooms in the first-floor apartment. He put her down and closed the door behind them. The room was suddenly very dark.

'Saint-André had eight months to work out why he was in the Bastille,' he said. 'And if he hadn't worked it out before you turned up on Saturday, he will certainly have done so since. He may be sitting there languidly sipping your wine now—but how long do you think he'll wait to take revenge for what was done to him and his friend? And do you think he'll wait to regain the strength and endurance he lost while he was caged up before he acts?'

So many thoughts, questions and arguments whirled in Mélusine's head that she didn't know what to say first.

'You must have guessed too!' she said accusingly. 'Why didn't you tell me?'

'I was considering the best way to deal with the situation.'

'We could have discussed it! You're supposed to be taking orders from me—not taking over my life!'

'I have been taking orders from you. There was no reason to cause you additional distress if my suspicions proved unfounded,' said Pierre.

'Yes, they're still only suspicions.' Mélusine seized on his comment. 'We must have absolute proof before *anyone* does anything rash. You have no business keeping secrets from me, attacking the Bastille when you're supposed to be modelling for me, and offering people the tenancy of my apartment without even discussing it with me first.'

'Not people, Saint-André,' he said reasonably.

'You think I owe him recompense for what Séraphin did to him?'

'No. You're not responsible for anything that happened. But you might as well make some profit on this empty apartment.'

'We don't know for sure Séraphin did anything. I think we must be absolutely sure of our facts before we make any decisions at all,' said Mélusine. 'I am so tired I can hardly think straight—and I wasn't involved in any siege. Your ears must still be ringing. You must promise me you won't do any more about anything until we have discussed it again.'

'I'm not inclined to do much more than fetch the bed for Saint-André,' Pierre admitted.

'And we will make him promise not to do anything rash as well,' said Mélusine.

'I don't think he's likely to do much until he's rid himself of his beard,' said Pierre. 'He's greatly embarrassed by it.'

'Perhaps you'd better hide your razor,' said Mélusine. 'And Paul's and the coachman's,' she added as an afterthought. 'The sooner we all sleep, the better we'll feel. Perhaps the world will make sense tomorrow.'

Late Morning, Wednesday, 15 July 1789

It was late morning when Mélusine had breakfast with Saint-André. Pierre served them in his footman's livery. Mélusine thought he was making a point about his unsuitability to kiss her, which annoyed her. She didn't say anything, partly because it would be embarrassing to do so in front of Saint-André, and partly because she fully intended to take advantage of his show of subservience. If he was making a big issue about being her servant then, by Heaven, he could act like a servant and do as he was told!

Somewhere between retiring for the night and appearing for breakfast, Saint-André had lost his beard. He looked far more like the elegant nobleman she remembered, but she wasn't entirely pleased by the transformation. Pierre was the one who'd warned her of the risk of the Marquis taking hasty action against Séraphin— why had he let him have a razor? Now Saint-André was clean shaven, he would be much more comfortable appearing in public. What was to stop him dashing off and issuing a challenge to Séraphin post-haste?

'I have been thinking,' she said.

'Yes, *madame*?' said Saint-André politely.

'First, I would like to remind certain people that I am mistress in this house, and I do not expect my orders to be flouted,' she said tartly.

'I am aware of no outstanding orders,' said Pierre.

She frowned at him. 'That is not all I've been thinking.'

'I didn't think it would be,' he murmured. 'May I pour you some more coffee, *madame*?' he continued blandly.

She looked at him suspiciously. 'You didn't by chance end up the captain of the privateer you served on, did you?' She saw the startled acknowledgement in his eyes before he controlled his expression and could hardly believe she'd hit the mark. 'You did! Then why are you doing my hair?'

'Very insecure profession, privateering,' said Saint-André. 'As soon as the war's over a fellow would be out of a job—pouf!' He illustrated his comment with an eloquent flick of his hand. 'Hairdressing, on the other hand, offers a talented, industrious man many more opportunities of advancement. If you continue to work hard and improve your skills,' he said to Pierre, 'you could eventually have your own salon, with a dozen assistants to help you keep up with all your fashionable customers.'

'My ultimate ambition,' said Pierre gravely.

Mélusine glanced between them. She'd half-wondered if the undercurrents of familiarity she'd sensed between them the previous night had been the result of her over-tired imagination. This morning she was increasingly sure she wasn't imagining it.

'Did you have breakfast already?' she asked Pierre.

'Yes, *madame*.'

'Sit down anyway. Have some coffee. I have to decide what we're going to do next.'

'Are you going to decide what I do—or just Dumont?' Saint-André asked as Pierre sat down and poured himself a cup of coffee.

'I don't want anyone to be hurt,' she said.

'Even Séraphin?' said Pierre.

At the same time, Saint-André said, 'Don't you think we can take care of ourselves?'

'Bertier couldn't.'

'Bertier was more than fifteen years older than both of us,' said Saint-André.

'He was a war hero. A master swordsman.'

'He was forty-six,' said Saint-André quietly.

'But he was still strong and fit. I know that. I was…I was his wife.' She blushed slightly at the reference. She'd not had much opportunity to look at Bertier's naked body, but she'd felt the strength in it when he came to her bed. She knew he'd still had the energy and poise of a much younger man.

'And so?' said Pierre.

'The rumour was of a duel,' she said. 'Over a lover.

The false rumour was that he fought my lover over me, but I have no lover.' She said that for Saint-André's benefit, though even as the words left her mouth she wondered how much longer they would be true. Her relationship with Pierre was unlike anything she had ever experienced, but it seemed to her the connection between them was compelling. She didn't know where they would end up, but her instincts told her Pierre would find it harder to keep the correct distance from her than he wanted. The thought that he would kiss her again filled her with nervous excitement and anticipation.

'But what if he did fight a duel over a woman? The mistress he'd lost to another man—Séraphin?' She saw the glance Pierre and Saint-André exchanged. 'That *is* what you think happened, isn't it!' she exclaimed.

'Oh, yes,' said Saint-André softly. 'That's exactly what happened. Séraphin stole Julie. Flaunted her pregnancy before his older half-brother. Bertier's initial reaction—his plan to obtain an heir by alternative means—may have surprised Séraphin. But when Séraphin confronted Bertier…issued the challenge—he'd have accepted it in a heartbeat.'

'Then it wasn't murder,' said Mélusine. 'It was a duel. Bertier had fought and won duels before. The police inspector's death, if Séraphin was responsible, was murder. But Bertier's death was the result of a duel.'

Saint-André glanced at Pierre, then at Mélusine.

'You know as well as I, *madame*, that Séraphin has practised his swordsmanship since he was a child. In your first distress at realising we'd also guessed how Bertier died, you said *Séraphin is dangerous*. It is because you're afraid of his swordsmanship and his willingness to kill that you don't want us to take action against him. You're afraid for our safety. Yet we're both in the prime of life. Bertier was twice Séraphin's age. You cannot argue it both ways.'

'Of course she can,' said Pierre. 'Logic is not her primary concern. She just wants to make sure we do what she tells us to. She will be as devious and inconsistent as she feels the situation requires.'

Saint-André looked slightly startled by Pierre's blunt assessment, then he smiled. 'I salute your resolution, *madame*.'

'I understand that having you consigned to the Bastille was heinous,' she said. 'It was entirely wicked. But you are at a disadvantage because you are honourable and he is not. It is not that I doubt your ability to defeat Séraphin in a duel—' although after Pierre's reminder that Saint-André's eight months in a cell would have reduced his speed and stamina, she was seriously concerned '—it is that what he did was a crime that should be punished openly *as* a crime.'

'You are not worried about the scandal if it should become known the current Comte de Gilocourt killed his brother—your late husband?' Saint-André said.

'From my point of view, it is considerably better than

the rumour, which is already circulating, that my lover and I conspired to murder my husband,' said Mélusine tartly.

'I would like to know how it started,' said Pierre. 'We assume the police inspector said more than he should, but it would be nice to be sure.'

'We need evidence to take to the Lieutenant of Police,' said Mélusine. 'If Séraphin did all we suspect him of, he must have bribed the police inspector. I should think the Lieutenant would be very upset if he knew one of his men had been first bribed and then murdered.'

'After what happened to Governor de Launay yesterday, I imagine at this moment he's much more concerned about keeping his head on his shoulders,' said Pierre drily.

Mélusine gasped.

'I beg your pardon. That was unnecessary.' Pierre reached out and briefly covered her hand with his.

'Surely it is over now,' she said unsteadily. 'The people hated the Bastille. *I* hated the Bastille. But they have secured a major victory for liberty. Surely they will not wantonly attack all signs of authority or good order.'

'We don't know the King's reaction,' said Saint-André. 'Whether he will be conciliatory or vengeful.'

'He's not prone to be vengeful.'

'*He's* not. I would not care to hazard a guess as to the Queen or his ministers' reactions. I have been out of society for so long I have no idea whose influence is in the ascendancy.'

'Then we can't do anything about Séraphin until we know what is happening in Paris,' said Mélusine.

'I believe I will take a stroll through the streets,' said Saint-André.

'I'll come with you,' said Pierre.

'Not in that livery,' said Mélusine.

'I'll change into something less conspicuous,' Pierre said gravely.

'And I'll come with you both. No, I know you don't want me to,' she said, forestalling both their protests. 'But this is the only way I can be sure you won't allow yourselves to be sucked into another siege or riot because your curiosity got the better of you. I cannot imagine either of you would allow *me* to do such a thing. And if you're keeping me safe, you'll have to keep yourselves safe as well.'

When they first left the place Vendôme, the mood on the streets was tense. Most places were closed as the people waited anxiously for news from the King. Without stopping to consider the proprieties, Mélusine took Pierre's arm. In their most ordinary clothes, she and Pierre looked like a lower bourgeois couple. Saint-André wore a selection of his own and borrowed clothes, which made him much harder to place, but certainly disguised his aristocratic pedigree. Given his usual fastidiousness about his appearance, Mélusine had been afraid he might be uncomfortable in his ragtag wardrobe, but now he'd eliminated his beard he seemed at ease.

The weather had cleared since the previous night's rain and it was a warm summer's day. Bertier's body had been brought home when the frost lay thick on the ground, and so Mélusine associated the winter with death and fighting. It was terrible to imagine the King might order his troops to attack the city on a sunny summer's day.

The echoes of cheering drifted to them from distant streets. Mélusine sighed with relief. No one cheered their own destruction. They went in the direction of the cheers and discovered that delegates had arrived from Versailles with the news that the King had ordered the dismissal of the troops from the Champs de Mars. For a while the people of Paris were in a state of relieved exhilaration.

Mélusine felt rather giddy with relief herself. But as they walked towards the Hôtel de Ville, the mood began to change. They could hear the chants from ahead.

'Bring back Necker! Bring back Necker!'

Pierre stopped. Mélusine's grip on his arm tightened. The King had withdrawn his troops but, by the sound of things, had not reinstated the people's favourite minister.

'Stay here. I'll see what's happening,' said Saint-André.

'No.' Mélusine instinctively reached out to him. 'We will all go, or all return home.'

'Don't worry.' He smiled briefly. 'I'm a phlegmatic Frenchman. I won't get into any trouble.'

'What did he mean?' said Mélusine in bewilderment, as he walked swiftly away. 'We're all French.'

'No idea,' said Pierre. 'Probably some obscure, noble joke, incomprehensible to us bourgeois.'

'I knew you weren't born a peasant!' said Mélusine. 'Not that there would have been anything wrong in being born a peasant if you had been. Your family fell on hard times at the death of your father.'

'Yes, *madame.*' Despite his nonchalant attitude, Pierre was watching the street and the people around them.

'I cannot understand why you decided to become a footman-hairdresser. It's not as if you have a natural aptitude for hairdressing.'

'I beg your pardon.' Pierre briefly stopped looking at their surroundings to look at Mélusine.

'It's not that I don't enjoy you doing my hair, but you must admit you're not that good at it,' she said. 'Suzanne said so only yesterday morning.'

'You discussed my hairdressing skills with Suzanne?' he said indignantly. 'Don't you think it would be more appropriate to tell *me* first if you aren't satisfied—rather than discussing me with your maid?'

'I didn't discuss you with her—not much. It came about after I asked her if she thought I was a harlot. It turns out she wouldn't actually mind if I was—as long as I don't blame her if I have a temper tantrum and break my perfume bottle.'

Pierre looked at her as if she'd gone mad. 'I do not have the faintest idea what you are talking about,' he said. 'But I am certain this is not the place for this discussion. If your maid is impudent you should dismiss her.'

'If I dismissed all my impudent servants I wouldn't have a footman,' said Mélusine. 'And since you've just admitted to being bourgeois, I don't understand why you *are* a footman. Surely—'

'Here comes Saint-André,' said Pierre.

'The King has ordered the withdrawal of the troops, but he hasn't reinstated Necker,' said the Marquis. 'The people are angry. Barricades and trenches are being put across the streets around the Hôtel de Ville. As I watched, armed men stopped a passerby to demand his name and business…'

'Time to beat a strategic retreat, I think,' said Pierre.

'I have missed so much,' said Saint-André, frowning, as they headed back to the place Vendôme. 'I am completely out of touch with events.'

'You must find it very disorientating,' said Mélusine sympathetically. 'I'm a little disorientated myself, and I only went to Bordeaux.'

'Now what?' said Saint-André. It was late evening, Mélusine had retired to bed, and the two men were alone in Marquis's new apartment. 'We've established that Séraphin killed Bertier,' Saint-André continued, 'and is probably blackmailing La Motte.'

'You're not convinced of that?' Pierce said sharply.

Saint-André frowned. 'Mélusine is right about Séraphin, he is dangerous. I hadn't realised her instincts are so acute. But though I can easily imagine him challenging Bertier and convincing himself it was an honourable fight, I find it harder to picture him lowering himself to common blackmail.'

'For an uncommonly large sum of money,' said Pierce drily. 'Jean-Baptiste was spying on your conversation with Bertier and carried the news straight to Séraphin. Jean-Baptiste also delivered the first blackmail letter. Who would have had a better opportunity to discover Bertier's secret papers than Bertier's heir, living in the same house?'

'There you have me,' Saint-André admitted. 'You don't want Séraphin dead until you're sure you've recovered any incriminating documents in his possession, do you?'

'Do you think he could be frightened into talking?'

Saint-André rubbed his hand across his chin. 'I'd grown strangely accustomed to my beard,' he admitted. 'But the last thing I wanted was to be paraded through the streets as one of the rescued victims of the Bastille, like that poor fellow we saw yesterday. I swear he thought he was Julius Caesar. Séraphin is too arrogant to be easily frightened. I doubt if either of us have the stomach for torture.'

'Even after your last eight months?'

'I'd like to see him sweat,' said Saint-André. 'I'd like to *make* him sweat—and know that this time he is not facing a man twice his age who suffers from night blindness. I'd like him to see the death of all his hopes on the end of my blade.'

'Phlegmatic *and* poetic,' said Pierce. 'Night blindness?'

'Bertier's eyes had started failing him in poor light,' said Saint-André grimly. 'I'd not go so far as to claim he could definitely have won if they'd fought that "duel" in full daylight—but by lantern light… I'll go to Versailles tomorrow,' he continued after a moment. 'I can do the one thing you can't do without risking everything. I can call upon him without disguise and speak to him directly.'

'How much chance is there that he'll try to have you incarcerated again?' Pierce asked. 'Mélusine won't be very happy if you end up back in prison.'

'I wouldn't be ecstatic myself!' said Saint-André. 'As long as he doesn't suspect I've guessed he was behind my imprisonment, I doubt he'll be much bothered by my escape. There's no chance now of Mélusine bearing Bertier a posthumous heir.'

'Don't challenge him,' said Pierce abruptly.

'Do you believe I'll be so overcome with fury when I see him I won't be able to control myself?' Saint-André asked quizzically.

'I can imagine I might be,' said Pierce.

'But you're only half-phlegmatic Frenchman,' said Saint-André. 'The other half is excitable Englishman. When are you going to tell Mélusine?'

'That I'm a half-excitable Englishman?'

'Why you're here. Why you'll be leaving. I note you've arranged it so I'll be here to protect her when you've left—but a husband would be a more effective and scandal-free solution to that problem.'

'She doesn't want to marry again,' said Pierce shortly.

'Really?'

'Nor do I.'

'I didn't know you'd been married before,' said Saint-André.

'She died of smallpox five months after the wedding. I hadn't inherited then.' Pierce had tensed but, to his relief, Saint-André didn't pursue the subject any further.

'Well,' said the Marquis, 'we have a lot to do before you can go back to England.'

Chapter Twelve

Morning, Thursday, 16 July 1789

'We must go to Séraphin's country house,' Mélusine announced over breakfast the next morning. 'We can go today. It might be best to ride. Georges told me they've been stopping carriages and carts from entering and leaving Paris.'

'Why are we going there?' Pierre asked mildly, but she wasn't fooled. She knew he was about to forbid the visit.

'To talk to Thérèse Petit,' she said. 'We were told she wasn't at the Hôtel de Gilocourt because she'd gone to visit her ill sister, but I don't think that's true. I think after the rumours started Séraphin sent her to the château and told the servants to tell anyone who enquired that she'd gone to her sister. She was his wet-nurse. That was long before she became the housekeeper, of course.'

'You want to ask her about the condition of Bertier's body,' said Pierre.

'Yes. We need evidence to take to the Hôtel de Police,' said Mélusine.

Saint-André glanced at Pierre, and then said: 'I hope you will excuse me from accompanying you. I will be pursuing another angle today.'

'Don't do anything foolhardy,' said Mélusine, suddenly anxious.

'I wouldn't dream of it,' Saint-André assured her.

'Can you ride?' she asked Pierre.

He grinned. 'Possibly even better than I dress hair,' he said. 'How far is it?'

'A couple of hours,' said Mélusine. 'It's a pleasant ride when the weather is good. When we were first married, Bertier often took me. We would have dinner there and return to Paris by the early evening.' She smiled a little sadly. 'I do have some happy memories of my marriage,' she said.

Mélusine wasn't surprised to discover Pierre was an expert horseman, nor was she surprised to see that he clearly considered himself in charge of their expedition. They were riding hired horses the coachman had obtained. Pierre had studied both animals carefully before he'd finally put Mélusine into the saddle and swung on to his own horse. While they were riding through Paris, he kept a close eye on her mount, but they passed through the city gate without mishap and soon they were riding along a leafy country road.

The only sounds that disturbed the peace were the

birds singing in the woods around them and the beat of their horses' hooves. It seemed a world away from the violence and fighting in Paris. Mélusine sighed with pleasure. She wasn't looking forward to her conversation with Thérèse Petit, and she was so out of the habit of riding she knew her muscles were bound to be stiff tomorrow, but right now promised to be a perfect interlude. She was going to be alone with Pierre in beautiful surroundings for nearly two hours.

She smiled and turned her head to speak to him. He was looking straight ahead, a grim set to his jaw. Foreboding began to nibble at her fragile contentment. Over the past day she'd sensed an increasing restlessness in him. It wasn't so much that his outer demeanour had altered—though she saw subtle changes even in that—but sometimes she was convinced he was concealing an impatient urgency to be somewhere else, doing something else. At first she'd thought he was just feeling the effects of becoming caught up in the violence at the Bastille, but now she wondered if it was rather that his involvement in the siege had caused him to drop his mask more often.

She'd said she'd give him a week's trial. When she'd done so, she'd thought the decision about whether he stayed or left would be hers. Now she knew it would be his. He'd told her that he'd made a mistake in his marriage, that he'd felt trapped by the commitment to his wife he believed with hindsight he should never have made. At the time she'd been sceptical, wondering if perhaps he was trying to mitigate his grief by telling himself he was glad to be free. Looking at him now, she was sadly willing to believe he really did have the roving spirit he'd claimed.

Even if she hadn't been able to sense the coiled tension in his body, his restless mood had communicated itself to his horse. The gelding was dancing as if its legs were on springs. Pierre hadn't even noticed. He rode as if he were part of the horse, one hand resting lightly on his thigh, the other holding the reins.

The week's trial had ended two days ago. In some ways she knew so much about him—and in other ways nothing at all. He wasn't a hairdresser. She'd doubted that from the first, though originally she'd thought it was because his former employer had been more interested in his skills as a lover. He'd admitted he'd been the captain of a privateer. More often than not, Saint-André treated him as an equal. That alone had roused her curiosity. The Marquis had many liberal ideas, but he'd been born and brought up in a noble family of ancient lineage. She couldn't imagine him bantering over breakfast with Paul or the coachman the way he had with Pierre.

If it hadn't seemed so unlikely, she would have suspected the two men already knew each other. But that made no sense. She could not imagine any reason why they'd want to conceal a previous meeting. It must be the circumstances of Saint-André's release from the Bastille that had accelerated their friendship, just as her own friendship with Pierre had been spurred to un-precedented intimacy after they'd both heard the ma-licious rumours about her and about Bertier's death at Amalie's dinner party.

She was sure Pierre and Saint-André had conversa-tions—and perhaps even made decisions—in her absence. She was both indignant and hurt at the likeli-hood they were excluding her from their discussions, but more than anything she was frightened. She hated it when men started making secret decisions that might end up changing her life.

'You are not to have secrets with Saint-André,' she said suddenly.

'I beg your pardon?' Pierce glanced at her, one eyebrow raised questioningly.

'Don't look so haughty,' she said impatiently. 'I don't mean you can't talk about…about…the latest fashion in waistcoats, or whatever men talk about…'

'Not waistcoats,' said Pierre. 'I can't speak for Saint-André, but the only man I ever discuss my waistcoats with is—' He broke off. He had enough self-control not to swear, but Mélusine saw it in his eyes. He looked away, as outwardly composed as ever, but the gelding danced sideways before continuing forwards once more.

'Your tailor? Your valet?' She stared at him, strug-gling to make sense of all the separate pieces of infor-mation that made no sense at all.

'*Madame*, the first time we met you were extremely disparaging of my coat,' he said. 'You cannot imagine any self-respecting tailor would send a customer away like that.'

'Stop it!' Mélusine shouted. Her own mare, which had hitherto been unfailingly placid, was startled into shying sideways. Pierre instantly leaned sideways to seize the rein.

'Let go!' she ordered tightly. 'I can manage my own horse. If you're not going to tell me the truth, don't say anything at all!'

Pierre sat upright again as the mare returned to her former placid progress. Mélusine swallowed, frightened and infuriated by the sense her life was slipping completely out of her control once more. Tears constricted her throat. When she felt the moisture on her cheek she turned her head away, determined not to let him see she was crying.

They rode in silence for several minutes. Mélusine kept her face averted and brushed a surreptitious hand across her cheek.

'Do not,' she began, when she thought she could trust her voice, 'do not have secret discussions about my affairs with Saint-André and make decisions without telling me. Do not decide what you're going to do about Séraphin without telling me.'

'*Madame*—'

'Do you have any idea what it is like to go through life never knowing what's going to happen to you until someone else tells you? You're to go to the convent tomorrow. You're to return home today. You're to marry the Comte de Gilocourt. Who is he? Don't be impertinent, girl! We're going to Court. We're going to Paris. You're to fu—' She broke off, choking on the words she'd heard Bertier say to Saint-André that night. He'd not said them directly to her, but it didn't make any difference. If he'd had his way, she'd have had no more choice in the matter than in any other important event in her life.

Both horses had stopped. Her eyes were so clouded with tears she didn't notice Pierre had dismounted until she discovered him standing at her knee.

'Come down,' he said.

Even though his voice was gentle, she was so sensitive to receiving yet another order she nearly kicked him in the ribs.

She must have given some indication of her feelings, because he put his hand lightly on her shin through her riding habit. 'Don't. Please, come down.'

She unhooked her leg from the pommel and slid down into his arms. She tried to push him away, but he kept her close.

'What are you afraid of?' he asked.

'I'm not afraid. I'm—'

'Furious. Yes, I know. But I just saw stark fear in your eyes. Tell me what you're afraid of.'

She clutched his coat. 'If you weren't such a slippery, devious, disobedient *man*, I wouldn't have to be afraid.'

He held her against his chest with one arm and stroked her back with his free hand. For a few seconds she held herself rigid, then gradually relaxed against him, listening to what he was telling her without words. Bertier had never touched her like that, and she couldn't recall her father touching her at all.

It took her a little while before she had the resolution to look up and meet Pierre's eyes. They were standing under a tree and dappled light fell across his face. His expression was quietly troubled. There were so many questions she wanted to ask him, but only one thing really mattered, even though it took more courage than anything else to say.

'Don't leave without telling me,' she whispered.

'Mélusine—' He sounded shaken.

She laid her hand across his mouth. 'I know you'll leave,' she said. 'Tell me when you go. Don't leave me wondering where you are. If you're hurt. Or if your body will be carried home. I can't bear to do that again—' Her voice caught as she remembered waiting for him on the day the Bastille fell.

'My God.' His hold on her tightened. 'Mélusine.... My God...don't cry.'

She found his visible distress at her distress comforting. She smiled tremulously through her tears. 'I will if I want to,' she said. 'It's my decision.'

'Not if I hurt you.'

'I can choose whether I let you hurt me,' she said, trying once more to extricate herself from his embrace. 'I know very well you have secrets you haven't told me. There must be a reason why you wanted to be my footman enough to learn how to dress hair. You did, didn't kou? Between the interview when you looked startled at the prospect, and the first day when you dressed it before I went to the dinner party?'

'Yes,' he admitted. 'Stop pulling away.'

'Why? You're the one who said there weren't going to be any more kisses.'

'You're the one who decided there would be.'

Mélusine stood still in sheer surpise. 'How did you kno—'

His mouth closed over hers, cutting off the rest of her question. Her hand flexed against his shoulder, then she put her arms around his neck, clinging tightly. She was instantly caught up on a tide of almost desperate passion. Dazed and breathless, she dimly sensed the desperation was as much his as hers. She understood why she was desperate; she could think of no reason for him to be.

When at last they drew apart, she continued to lean against him, waiting for her racing pulse to slow and her head to clear.

'What is it?' she whispered.

'What's what?' he asked. He'd pulled off his gloves and he was stroking her hair with his bare hand.

'The urgency inside you, driving you?'

His hand stilled. 'You are a little witch!' he exclaimed.

'I am not! Is that an insult?' She wasn't sure whether to be pleased she'd startled him or to be offended at being called a witch.

'No. It just means you're the most dangerously observant woman I've ever met,' he said.

'That sounds good to me.' She was amazingly flattered by his comment.

'Hmm.' He sounded less convinced. He cupped her face in his hands so she was compelled to look at him. 'I won't leave without telling you,' he said. 'I promise.'

Tears pricked her eyes, even as she smiled at him. In that promise he had given her the assurance she'd asked for—but he'd also confirmed her fear he would leave.

They rode in silence for several miles after they remounted.

'Did you really come back from America because your mother and sister needed you?' Mélusine asked suddenly.

He glanced at her. 'It might be more accurate to say that I came back from America *and* my mother and sister needed me,' he said at last.

'That wasn't a complete lie, then?'

'No.'

'What about the Duchesse de la Croix-Blanche? Were you ever her footman?'

Pierre exhaled a long, carefully controlled breath. 'No,' he admitted.

'Why did she give you a reference?' Mélusine stared at him. 'She didn't!' she exclaimed. 'You wrote it yourself. Do you even know the Duchesse?'

'I have spoken to her,' he said. 'Briefly.'

'This is outrageous! Impossible! It makes no sense! Why on earth did you go to all that trouble to be *my* footman?'

'It wasn't a great deal of trouble,' he corrected her. 'I assumed you weren't familiar with the lady's handwriting, so producing the testimonial was quite straightforward.'

Mélusine's mouth fell open. 'Why?' she said, when she'd found her voice. 'Why did you want to be my footman?'

Pierre's expression became infuriatingly wooden.

'If you were any closer I'd box your ears!' She lost her temper with him. 'You are the most insufferable, impossible man I've ever met.'

He smiled faintly. 'Perhaps we should continue this conversation at another time,' he suggested.

She looked ahead and saw they were approaching a village—and the villagers were standing across the road, blocking them from continuing.

'It's the Queen!' one boy shouted out, and the small crowd murmured dangerously until a woman shouted back, 'Don't be daft! That's Comte Bertier's widow', and the mood changed again.

The woman shouldered to the front of the group.

'Never thought I'd see you riding this way again, *madame*,' she said, laying her hand on the rein. The people behind her fell silent. Mélusine knew Marthe was the unofficial leader of the village and was cautiously grateful for her appearance.

'I didn't expect to be riding here again, either,' she said. 'How are you, Marthe?'

'Well enough. My eldest had her first babe two weeks ago. Child seems strong enough so far. So does she.'

'I am so pleased,' said Mélusine. 'I'm sure your care has much to do with Marie's strength and the child's. Is it a boy or a girl?'

'Girl.' Marthe's face crinkled into a smile that was as much a dour acknowledgement of the accuracy of Mélusine's memory as an indication of pleasure. 'The new Comte's not at the château.'

'I didn't think he would be,' said Mélusine. 'I've come to see someone else.'

'Is it true the Bastille is down?'

'Yes. They're already demolishing it and selling bits as souvenirs,' said Mélusine.

'Good riddance!' shouted the boy, and received answering cries of agreement.

'It was a sad day for us when Comte Bertier died,' said Marthe, under the noise of her companions. 'Séraphin has put doves back in the dovecote.'

'I'm sorry,' said Mélusine.

'No, *he'll* be sorry,' said Marthe.

Mélusine quietly drew a coin out of her purse and gave it to the woman. 'For your daughter and the new baby.'

Marthe smiled grimly. 'Go safely, *madame*,' she said, released her grip on the rein and stepped back.

'Séraphin has put doves in the dovecote?' Pierre repeated, when they were clear of the village.

'The lord's doves eat the peasants' grain in the fields, but the peasants aren't allowed to harm them,' said Mélusine. 'Apparently one of the first things Bertier did when he inherited the château was to invite a few of his sporting friends to shoot all the doves. He said it was in vengeance because one of the "foul fat lazy things" had decorated his head when he went for a walk in the garden without his wig his first evening here. But he gave the carcases to the villagers, and he didn't let the doves breed all the time we were married. Bertier's eccentricity, his friends called it. I saw him mime his rage at the bird who'd offended his head several times. But in private he said it was an extra tax on the peasants, and he didn't like dove meat anyway. He was a good man, until circumstances—and Séraphin—drove him to behave otherwise.'

'Séraphin expects his full dues as lord,' said Pierre.

'I'm sure he does,' said Mélusine.

They turned a corner in the road and the château was immediately before them. Movement to one side of the house caught her eye and she saw a group of people running towards the dovecote. Most of them were carrying a farming implement of some kind, or even just a stout stick. Her heart kicked into double time as the villagers reached their target and began to attack the cote.

'Let's not linger,' said Pierre. 'The sooner you speak to Thérèse, if she's here, the sooner we can leave.'

'I didn't expect to see rioting *here*!' said Mélusine, shaken by the viciousness of the assault on the dovecote.

'The whole of France is in a ferment,' said Pierre.

When they entered the château, they discovered the staff too were in disorder, uncertain how to deal with the peasants attacking the dovecote, many of whom were their relatives. When they saw Mélusine, their confusion increased.

'Good afternoon,' she said. 'I would like to see Thérèse Petit.' As she spoke, she wondered if she'd brought Pierre on a wild goose chase, but then she looked around and saw Thérèse standing in the doorway.

Thérèse's eyes were narrowed with hostility. 'Is that your doing?' she demanded.

'What?' Mélusine was bewildered by the question.

'The dovecote. You've come to gloat as your rabble destroys it.'

'I've only just arrived!' Mélusine exclaimed. She'd been about to say she had nothing to do with the peasants' actions, then decided not to. She had far more sympathy with them than with Thérèse or Séraphin. 'I came to talk to you,' she said.

'We've nothing to discuss,' the housekeeper said disdainfully.

'Don't turn your back on me!' Mélusine was outraged at Thérèse's undisguised insolence.

Thérèse looked over her shoulder. 'You're nothing but a jumped-up tradesman's daughter. I don't take orders from you any more.'

Though she'd taken upon herself the arrogance of the Gilocourts, Thérèse was a servant. She'd achieved her current position primarily because she'd once been Séraphin's wet-nurse. How far did her devotion to her former nursling extend?

'Did you hide the fact that Séraphin killed his brother?' Mélusine asked, as the housekeeper walked away.

Thérèse froze. Then she spun around, her expression so full of hate Mélusine took an unwary step backwards. 'How dare you insult me or the Comte with your filthy suggestion,' she snarled. 'Get out of here.'

'Bertier was a Gilocourt too.' Mélusine held her ground. 'Where was your loyalty to him?'

'I was loyal to him. I took care of his body when you, his wife, would have nothing to do with it—'

'You wouldn't let me near him! Tell me about his wounds.'

Thérèse paused, then smiled unpleasantly. 'It's too late now, isn't it? You had your chance to see and missed it. It's better this way. You couldn't give Bertier the heir he needed, and Séraphin is a worthy Comte. Tell your rabble to leave the dovecote alone.' She walked out.

'She could give the Queen lessons in stupid, self-destructive arrogance,' said Pierre.

Mélusine took a deep breath and discovered she was shaking. Pierre moved closer and rubbed his hand reassuringly up and down her arm.

'Let's get out of here,' he said. 'She's not going to tell you any more plainly than that, and I'd like to put some distance between us and the villagers' justifiable vengeance.'

Mélusine crossed her wrists, gripping her forearms in an effort to control the trembling, and let him guide her towards the door. As she did so, she caught sight of the tapestries hanging on the wall. She knew what they were, knew the legends they represented.

One tapestry depicted the monster, Bigorne. He was very fat because he ate hen-pecked husbands and legend claimed he had a never-ending supply to feast upon. The other tapestry was of the monster Chiche-fache. Chiche-fache was so thin her ribs stuck out because she only fed upon faithful wives and they were very rare.

The tapestries had been made up on the orders of Bertier's father. They were based on frescoes from the medieval château which the present house had replaced. Bertier had considered them a good joke. Mélusine had always disliked them, but Bertier had refused to have them moved. As she remembered his laughing rejection of her request, and the way he'd later deliberately planned to turn her into an adulteress, the smug masculine insult embodied in the tapestries suddenly enraged her beyond bearing.

She broke out of Pierre's grip and ran forward. She seized the first tapestry in both hands and used all her weight to haul it from the wall. She heard it tearing as she dragged it down and the sound filled her with bitter satisfaction. She jumped at the next tapestry, swinging off her feet in her blind determination to destroy it.

* * *

Pierce was dumbfounded by Mélusine's sudden, furious assault on the tapestries. He had no idea what provoked it. The scene with Thérèse Petit had been ugly, but he could see no connection between that and the wall hangings. The room was on the ground floor, with a picturesque view of the garden and surrounding countryside through glass-panelled doors. But now the view was obscured by villagers. Before Pierce could react, they broke through the doors and into the salon. He was afraid they were going to turn their rage on Mélusine, but instead they seemed take their cue from her.

She'd snatched one of the tapestries from the floor and was trying to rip it in half. A couple of the villagers surged forward and did the job for her. Others began to attack the room with their makeshift weapons. Porcelain went crashing to the floor. Feathers flew as cushions burst. A man with a scythe began to flail at the elegant furniture.

Mélusine looked up, her face stark white with shock.

Pierce dragged her behind him, poised to defend her. No one paid them any attention. A moment later the room was empty except for drifting feathers, and the sound of destruction echoing from other parts of the house.

'Come on.' He pulled her after him to the broken door, checked the way was clear, and headed swiftly to the stables.

She stumbled on the gravel. He paused long enough to lift her in his left arm, but kept his right arm free.

'I can run! Let me run!' she gasped.

'Walk,' he said, setting her on her feet again. 'Fast, but walk. Let's not call unnecessary attention to ourselves.'

To his relief, the only disturbance in the stables was the chirping of a couple of sparrows. The birds flew away as he walked in, and there wasn't a groom in sight. Either they were taking part in the destruction or they were hiding. As he'd ordered, their horses were still saddled. He checked the girths and the bridles and threw Mélusine up on to her mare.

'Can we get back without going through the village?' he asked, springing on to the gelding.

'Yes. This way.' Her hat was askew, there were feathers in her hair that weren't part of her coiffure, and her eyes were huge with shock, but she was perfectly steady as she chose a route out of the grounds of the château.

After seeing the near-frenzy with which she'd launched herself at the tapestries, Pierce was amazed at her equally sudden return to controlled practicality. He wondered again what it was about the tapestries that had so incensed her, but decided to ask no questions until they were safely home.

In the meantime, he kept a careful check on the way they'd come as well as the way they were going. By the time they'd rejoined the road, a mile below the village, there was a plume of smoke rising from the location of the château.

'Have they set it alight?' Mélusine asked in a near-whisper.

'It would seem so,' said Pierce. 'By accident or design. We won't linger.'

'No.' Mélusine urged the mare into a trot. They were nearly back to Paris before she spoke again.

'I've never started a riot before,' she said, still sounding dazed.

'You didn't start this one,' said Pierce. 'You just… caught the spirit of the moment.' He still couldn't quite believe what he'd seen. 'And that may, perhaps, have redirected their attention,' he conceded. 'But I suspect the house would have been their next target whatever you'd done.'

'Poor house,' said Mélusine. 'There was nothing wrong with it. Only that it had the wrong owner.'

'Saint-André isn't here,' said Mélusine. It was evening by the time they were safely back in the place Vendôme, and they'd checked the first-floor apartment before heading up to the blue salon. The Marquis wasn't in either location.

'He doesn't seem to be,' said Pierre.

'Where is he?' She stripped off her gloves. 'Don't prevaricate and tell me you can't speak for him, or don't know where he is this precise minute. Where was he going?'

'Versailles,' Pierre said after a moment.

'*Versailles!*' Mélusine stared at him in disbelief. 'To

see Séraphin? You're the one who warned me we
mustn't let him issue a challenge when he's still weak
from prison. And you just let him go?'

'He's not going to issue a challenge,' said Pierre. 'But
it will be interesting to see how Séraphin reacts—'

'Interesting?' Mélusine balled her gloves and hurled
them at him. 'My God! You're a pair of fools. Why
won't you believe me when I tell you he's dangerous?'

'I do believe you. But you must trust me—'

'Why should I trust you? I don't know why you're
here. I don't know when you're leaving. You keep your
face as wooden as that table, but all the time your eyes
are watching, measuring, assessing. One minute you're
happy to kiss me—the next you're desperate to get
away from me—'

'I'm not desperate to get away from you.'

His interruption jolted her into silence. 'You are not
being fair to me,' she said after a moment in an
unsteady voice.

'No.'

'You're not desperate to get away from me?' She
went back to his previous comment.

'No.'

'You act as if you are. I can feel it in you. The effort
you make to seem relaxed while inside you're impatient to move on.'

'I have…an errand I must perform,' he said slowly.
'Whatever you feel, it is my impatience to complete
that task.'

'What task?'

'Why did you pull down the tapestries?'

'You're impossible.' He wouldn't answer her questions, yet he was so insistent with his own.

'Hmm.' He sat down and stretched out his legs.

She glanced around the salon and frowned. 'Why are we in this room? I don't like this room. It's only for visitors.'

'Well,' said Pierre. 'The first thing in its favour is that we don't have to climb another two flights of stairs. The second, more important point, is that the seats are upholstered. Charming though your studio is, it's damned uncomfortable.'

'It isn't!' Mélusine gasped with indignation. 'I liked you much better when you just did as you were told.'

'The novelty wore off. Tell me about the tapestries.'

'Come to think of it, you never were particularly obedient. You *are* very stubborn.'

'There's an obvious reply to that, but I'll be a gentleman.'

'You *are* a gentleman, aren't you?' said Mélusine. 'I should order you out of the house right now.' Instead she sat down beside him. He put his arm around her and she curled into his side as if they'd sat like that a hundred times in the past. She felt soothed by the feel of his body against hers, and the way he'd welcomed her so naturally into his embrace. She sighed.

Pierre kissed the top of her head. 'Tell me about the tapestries.'

'Bigorne and Chiche-fache. Have you heard of them?' When he shook his head she told him the legends attached to them.

'Ah, I'm not surprised you were offended. Did you ever lose your temper so completely with your husband?'

'No. I've been practising. It was difficult at first— but you've made it much easier.'

'The pleasure is all mine.' She could hear the smile in his voice as he lazily stroked her shoulder.

She rested her hand on his chest, feeling the steady beat of his heart, and realised his body was completely relaxed. She lifted her head to look at him, but that gave her a crick in her neck, so she scrambled round to sit in his lap. She was slightly impressed with her own boldness, but he'd put her there himself the first time he'd kissed her, so she didn't think he'd object too strenuously. One of his hands was on her waist, the other rested lightly on the top of her thigh. She was glad to see that he didn't seem displeased with their new arrangement. It was because his touch was always welcoming to her, even though what he said was sometimes more discouraging, that she had the confidence to continue questioning him. His expression, as he met her eyes, was rueful.

'You are being deliberately evasive and obstructive,' she said.

'I have no idea what to say to you,' he said simply.

'You could tell me the truth.'

'It's not my secret.'

'Oh.' She didn't know what to say. She felt as if her world was built on quicksand. Whose secret was it? What did they mean to him? 'Is it a lady's secret?'

He shook his head, smiled slightly and stroked her cheek. Then he lowered his hand to follow the neckline of her riding habit. She was wearing a chemise beneath the jacket that ensured her modesty from her throat down, but when his fingers came to rest immediately above the cleavage of her breasts, her pulse increased. He wasn't touching her bare skin, but she wanted him to.

'Are you going to?' she asked unsteadily. She'd meant to ask him more about his privateering past and the secrets that weren't his, but she couldn't think of anything else but his hand resting on her breast and the tension coiling between them.

'Going to what?' His eyes became wary.

'Make love to me.' The words emerged so harshly they sounded more like an order than a question.

'No.'

Mélusine caught her breath. The rejection hurt, but she'd almost expected it. 'Then why are you teasing me so?' she cried, her voice full of frustration and pain.

'Don't. I'm sorry.' He pulled her to him.

She tried to resist, then collapsed against him in a storm of tears.

Chapter Thirteen

Pierce cradled Mélusine close. He felt as if a knife was twisting inside him. For once in his life he had absolutely no idea what to do. Mélusine's tears scalded him with guilt, but he told himself he wasn't the only cause of her overwrought state. It was Thursday. The previous Thursday she'd attended a dinner party and heard the rumours about Bertier's death and her supposed lover. In the intervening days she'd had little respite from further alarms and new anxieties. It wasn't surprising her emotions were getting the better of her.

He was feeling the effects of all the excitements himself. He'd come to France to hunt a blackmailer. He hadn't expected to find himself in the middle of a revolution. Nor had he anticipated he might be in danger of losing his heart to the woman he'd originally suspected of being the blackmailer. Mélusine was wrong. He wasn't desperate to leave. The restlessness she'd sensed was driven by frustration that he hadn't yet dealt with

Séraphin and his increasing fear over what might be happening in England. He'd had no news from La Motte via Clothilde, but he didn't know if that was because there was no news, or because the upheavals in France had prevented the message from getting through.

On the ride to the château he'd been astounded, disconcerted and even slightly mortified by Mélusine's perceptiveness. She'd misinterpreted the reason for his edginess, but he wasn't accustomed to other people being able to read his moods at all. It was unnerving. She might accuse him of always giving orders, but he'd never felt less in control.

He'd comforted himself with the belief his wife had never sensed his feelings of confinement. Now he wondered if he'd deceived himself, because Mélusine would certainly have suspected. But Mélusine was not Rosalie.

If Mélusine had noticed the slightest change in his mood she would have bombarded him with questions and, if that hadn't worked, started hurling the cushions at him. Exactly the kind of behaviour many husbands deplored, though so far he'd not found it troublesome. But she hadn't thrown cushions at Bertier, or wept all over him. Though she'd never explicitly said so, she'd been in awe, if not a little afraid of the husband who'd been old enough to be her father.

Her tears had subsided. She was resting quietly in his arms and he was humbled by her trust when he'd given her so much reason not to trust him. He stroked her hair. There were still a few feathers tangled in it from the burst cushions at the château. He picked them out, remembering the black feathers he'd put in her hair before the dinner party.

'Were you embarrassed to go out in the hairstyle I gave you for the dinner party?' he asked.

'Of course not.' She rubbed her hand across her cheek, and then felt around in her skirts for the opening to her pocket. She pulled out a handkerchief and blew her nose.

'Beginner's luck.' He smiled and tucked a damp strand behind her ear.

'I am looking very ugly now,' she said, and sighed. 'I don't suppose the great courtesans and seductresses of society go about their business with red, puffy eyes and a blocked-up nose.'

'Are you planning on seducing me?' he asked.

'I don't know. I thought I might. It has to be me because you're so honourable and I made such a great issue of my virtue.'

'How can you say I'm honourable when you don't know anything about me or why I'm in your house?'

'I know you are,' she said simply. 'I don't know who or what you are, but if you didn't have a gentle heart you wouldn't tell me you're not going to take advantage of me and let me cry all over you.'

'That's an interesting definition of honour.'

'It's my definition,' she said, 'and I must learn to trust my own judgement. It is not your secret. That means your honour forbids you to tell me. Would you if you could?'

He smiled crookedly. 'You already know my most discreditable secret,' he said. 'You're the only one who does.'

She put her head on one side. 'That you believe you shouldn't have married your wife?' she said.

He nodded. He had other secrets that could have far more damaging consequences if they became public knowledge, but it was only his misuse of Rosalie that tweaked his conscience.

'Are all the things you've told me true? That you sold yourself to the privateer captain when you were seventeen? And so on.'

He frowned. 'As far as I can recall,' he said cautiously. 'The man I sold myself to was no longer actively engaged in privateering. But he owned several privateer vessels.'

'Hmm.' She narrowed her eyes thoughtfully, absently rubbing her fingers up and down his coat front. 'It's to do with Bertier's death or Séraphin, I think. Or Saint-André. They're the only people you've talked about or been interested in since you arrived. And that would explain why you wanted to be my footman. Though surely it would have been better to get a position with Séraphin if you were already suspicious of him. Are you a government agent?'

'No!' he exclaimed. 'Good God! *Madame*, what a suggestion to make.'

'There is no need to be offended,' she said, stroking him soothingly. 'I have heard that one in three people in Paris are spies for the police—and they aren't all disreputable wretches in back alleys. Even the Chevalier de… Well, that's neither here nor there if you're not a government agent.' She began to play idly with his neckcloth.

'I can't help feeling you've met Saint-André before,' she said. 'But I don't see how that can be—' Her eyes suddenly lit up with excitement. 'Privateering!' she exclaimed. 'That's the connection. You were a privateer. Saint-André told us Bertier was held hostage by a privateer… No, that's no good. You aren't old enough to have held Bertier hostage.' She chewed on her lip and tugged irritably on his neckcloth as she tried to unravel the problem.

Pierce had never been interrogated by a woman who was also, as far as he could tell, simultaneously trying to undress and seduce him without him noticing. Or maybe she'd forgotten she was trying to seduce him because her gaze was currently cloudy with puzzlement, not simmering passion.

She untied his neckcloth and pulled it aside. Still frowning in deep concentration, she unfastened the top of his shirt. Her eyes cleared and she smiled with appreciation. 'You have a very nice chest,' she said, running her fingers across it. 'I only saw Bertier's chest a couple of times. He had grey hair here. How old are you?'

'Twenty-eight,' he said hoarsely. If he was as honourable as she'd claimed, he'd stop her, but she was rapidly destroying his will power.

'Twenty-eight is a good age.' She smiled at him. 'There's nothing wrong with being forty-six, of course…'

'My mother's forty-six,' he said, trying to think of something other than Mélusine's fingers, teasing his chest.

'Your mother?' Her hand stilled. He thought she was about to ask him what his mother had to do with his errand in France and tensed. She noticed at once and interest sharpened her gaze.

'Enough, *madame*,' he said, catching her wrist. 'Do you think I hadn't noticed you're trying to seduce me? Is that the act of a modest, virtuous woman?'

'I hope not,' she said. 'Being modest and virtuous never brought me any joy at all.'

'What about my virtue and modesty?'

'You were willing to take off your breeches the first time we met.'

'You know perfectly well I wouldn't have done so.'

'Yes, you would,' she said. 'When you saw you'd disturbed me you stopped at once. But I don't think you would make a threat or a promise you weren't willing to keep.'

'*Madame*, I hope you never share the details of our first encounter with anyone else,' he said with some feeling.

'Privateers,' she said. 'Is that the connection? It seemed to me that you honoured the privateer you sold yourself to when you were seventeen almost as if he were a second father. Is *he* the one who held Bertier hostage all those years ago?'

Pierce opened his mouth, then closed it again. He had no idea what to say.

'Saint-André didn't tell us what happened to Bertier when his father refused to pay the ransom,' said Mélusine. 'But the privateer obviously didn't kill him. Perhaps he felt sorry for him. Perhaps they became friends. I could easily imagine Bertier being friends with a privateer. Yes, yes!' Her eyes glowed with excitement. 'When Bertier was killed and the person who'd done it wasn't brought to justice, Bertier's friend, the old privateer, asked you, the young privateer, to come and avenge his friend's murder. That's it, isn't it?' she exclaimed triumphantly.

Pierce took a deep breath. She'd got some details completely wrong, but he was both appalled and impressed she'd made the connection between La Motte and Bertier, even though she had no idea of La Motte's name or current circumstances. He was still trying to decide what to say when she continued.

'You suspected I was involved at first, didn't you?' she said. 'I couldn't understand why one minute you were cold and distant and the next you were kind and friendly. You had to keep reminding yourself I might have cold-bloodedly plotted my husband's murder. When did you decide for sure I was innocent?'

'I never suspected you of cold-bloodedly planning anyone's murder,' said Pierce honestly.

She subsided for a moment, then a militant spark flared in her eyes. 'You suspected me of something. That's why you were willing to take your breeches off the first day. Now you know I'm inno…now you know I haven't done anything illegal—you won't take them off.'

Pierce stared at her for several moments, not quite sure how to respond. Despite an almost overwhelming desire to make love to her, he was determined not to do so until he had given her at least a chance to reconsider. Ever present in his mind was the knowledge that he couldn't stay, couldn't make her any promises, and before he could allow himself to make love to her he needed to be sure she was truly aware of that.

'It's been an exhausting day,' he said, and stood up with her still in his arms. 'You need to sleep.'

Very Early Morning, Friday 17 July 1789

Pre-dawn light was just beginning to brighten the room when Mélusine woke up. Neither the bed nor the window curtains had been drawn. When she turned her head she could see Pierre lying beside her. They were both still dressed. When he'd brought her to bed she'd guessed his honourable scruples would inhibit him from—as he would see it—taking advantage of her. But she had been filled with grateful pleasure when he'd stretched out beside her. She'd rolled over and put her hand on his arm.

'I'm not going anywhere,' he'd said, and she'd heard the humour in his voice.

He'd been true to his word. He was still sleeping quietly beside her several hours later. There was no colour in the pearly light and not much strength. She could see his profile, and the shape of his body on top of the bedclothes, but little else. She was hot and uncomfortable in her riding habit. After a few minutes of consideration she eased gingerly towards the edge of the bed, glancing back anxiously in case she disturbed him. She didn't want him to wake up yet. She wasn't ready. When she was sure he was still asleep, she stood up and tiptoed into her dressing room.

With a sigh of relief she pulled off her jacket and skirt and the trousers she wore beneath the skirt to protect her modesty and dignity while she was riding. She poured water from the jug into the basin and pressed a damp cloth against her face, trying to wipe away the marks of her earlier tears. Then she removed the rest of her clothes, shivering slightly as the morning air touched her skin. She continued hastily with her preparations, glancing over her shoulder at every slightest sound in case Pierre caught her unawares. At last she slipped on a new chemise. She smoothed her hands over her waist and hips, took a steadying breath, and crept back into the bedroom.

To her relief, Pierre was still asleep. She tiptoed back to the bed and very, very cautiously climbed on to the mattress. Too late, she remembered she'd been sleeping on top of the covers before, but perhaps it would be more subtle to pull a sheet over herself now she was so skimpily attired. She stared up at the shadows of the bed canopy and tried to decide what to do.

The mattress moved and she found herself looking up at Pierre instead. Her heart rate kicked up. Butterflies danced in her stomach. She sucked her lower lip between her teeth, wondering if she'd been too bold.

He put his hand on her waist. She could feel the warmth through the thin muslin of her chemise. She drew in a quick, excited breath.

'I wasn't sure if you were coming back,' he said.

She felt as if his low voice was reverberating through her body.

'I…thought you were asleep.' Her mouth was so dry it was hard to speak.

'I was being tactful.' His hand moved down over the top of her hip, then back up to graze the lower curve of her breast. 'I didn't want to embarrass you if you were making a discreet escape.'

'I was coming back.' She winced at the inanity of her comment. Of course he knew she was coming back—she was lying beside him.

'Yes. I hoped you would. Are you sure?'

'Yes,' she said simply.

'You know I cannot make you any promises.'

'I know. I still came back.'

He nodded. He hesitated for one second longer, then stroked his fingers up over her breast and swirled them around her erect nipple.

The sensation was so intense and unexpected she arched off the bed, inadvertently pushing her breast more firmly into his palm.

Her reaction startled both of them.

'My God!' Pierre exclaimed, pulling back.

'I'm sorry.' Mélusine was close to tears with mortification.

'No, no. God, no, don't be sorry.' He leant over her again, his hand warm on her ribs and kissed her lips and then the side of her neck.

'I didn't mean to do that.' She put her arms around his shoulders.

'Ah, sweetheart.' His lips curved against her skin. 'Did you jump from pleasure or disgust?'

'P-pleasure.' She couldn't stop trembling. 'I d-don't know why I'm shaking,' she said. 'You mustn't think it means I'm afraid or I don't w-want…'

He brushed a kiss over her mouth. 'You want me now—even though you know I'll be leaving? That there'll be no marriage at the end of this?'

'Yes.' She rubbed her hands on his shoulders. 'You have to take your clothes off. You don't have to marry me, but you have to take all your clothes off first.'

He laughed and rested his forehead lightly against hers. 'So you can see my muscles, Madame Artist?'

'No. It's too hard to explain.' But she tried. 'If my body belongs to you for this night, then yours has to belong to me. Not hidden. Not just come…take…and go.'

For a moment he neither moved nor spoke, then he pushed himself up and rolled away from her off the bed. For an instant she was afraid she'd asked too much, but almost immediately she saw he was undressing. She lay still, her heart thudding. The whole situation had spun wildly out of her control or expectations. She knew it was her behaviour and demands that had made that happen. She was thrilled and terrified at what she had set in motion.

Pierre walked around to her side of the bed, standing so the pearly light from the window fell across his naked body. Hardly aware of what she was doing, she sat up. She already knew what his torso and arms looked like, now she scanned the length of his lean, muscular legs, his narrow hips—and the jutting manhood that demanded her attention.

She'd been married. She knew what happened to a man's body when he was aroused. Knew what followed. But she'd never before seen male lust on such blatant display—a display she'd requested, though she hadn't expected this. She wasn't sure how she'd expected Pierre to respond to her request. She hadn't thought. She still couldn't think. She was scared. Excited. Fascinated.

He moved closer. She gasped, then realised he'd responded to the gesture she was only half-aware of having made. He came close enough to take one of her hands in his. She clutched convulsively at his fingers.

'Should I fetch your sketching materials?' he asked softly. 'I warn you, *madame*. You may sketch me from the waist up—or the waist down—but not all in one picture.'

She looked up into his face and saw that, despite the thrusting urgency of his body and the passion darkening his eyes, there was still kindness and humour in his expression.

She stood up and flung her arms around his neck. He held her close, stroked her back and murmured softly as he kissed her beneath her ear and along the curve of her shoulder. She could feel his erection pressing against her stomach. Anticipation began to ripple through her.

She stroked her hands over his back, down to the hard planes of his buttocks. He went still in her arms, his breath warm on her shoulder, as she began to explore every part of his body she could reach. When she finally eased back enough to look up at him, they were both trembling.

He slid her chemise up her body and pulled it off. He took her wrists and put her hands back on his shoulders. He put his own hands on her waist, then slowly raised them to touch her breasts. He began to toy with her nipples. Delicious sensation radiated from his fingers, coursing through her body, intensifying the ache between her legs. She bit back a moan and clutched at his shoulders, feeling the firm, tense muscles beneath her fingers. She couldn't stop herself edging closer to him. She lifted one foot off the ground, responding without conscious awareness to the instinct demanding she rub her leg against his. Her foot brushed his ankle…

He pulled her closer, leaning sideways to hook one hand behind her knee as he kept her balanced with his other arm around her waist. He drew up her leg almost to his hip-height, sliding her inner thigh over the outer side of his leg. As he did so, he lifted her with his other arm and lowered her slowly, their bodies pressed closely together.

She gasped as she felt his erection press intimately against her. He hadn't entered her, but as he held her in position he moved his hips back and forth, stroking the swollen, damp flesh between her legs, though he hadn't touched her there with his hands.

She trembled uncontrollably, whimpered and clung to him, pressing her face against his shoulder. His body was taut with tension, his muscles tight as whip cord. He'd swept her well out of her depth and all she could do was hang on to him as her body flooded with overwhelming sensation.

'Put your other leg round my waist,' he ordered in her ear. His voice was so husky she hardly recognised it, but she obeyed without question. He lifted her a little higher and she groaned in protest because now she couldn't feel him so intimately. 'Hold on,' he said.

The next moment she was lying on the bed and he was braced above her.

She'd relaxed her grip on his shoulders out of sheer surprise at their change of orientation. She took advantage of the opportunity to stroke his arms and chest. His skin was damp with perspiration, his muscles hard.

He aligned himself carefully and eased slowly into her. She cried out as he filled and stretched her. He paused when she fully enclosed his length and dragged in several panting breaths.

She opened her eyes and looked up at him. The room was lighter and she could see his face was flushed with passion. He met her eyes. The intense intimacy of the moment stunned her. During the good months of her marriage to Bertier, they'd enjoyed a rather formal friendship in the daytime during which they had, for the most part, ignored what took place in the bedroom at night. When Bertier had come to her at night the few words they'd spoken had been just as formal and they'd never looked into each other's eyes at the height of passion. Or at the height of Bertier's passion. Her feelings had most often been embarrassment and discomfort.

'We could have a conversation,' she gasped. 'While you're here, in-inside me…we could have a conversation.'

Pierre's eyes widened in disbelief. 'You want to talk *now*?'

'No. But we could. You're still you.'

He shook his head as if he couldn't make any sense of what she was saying.

'Later,' he said grittily. 'Unless you want me to stop—we'll talk later.'

'Don't stop.' Without conscious thought she wrapped her legs around him, flexing her hips as she drew him even deeper into her.

He groaned, then pulled almost out of her and thrust

back in. The intimate slide of his flesh against hers was exquisite. Her body took on a will of its own, arching against him as she sought more of those wonderful feelings. She kept her gaze fixed on Pierre's face, holding on to his shoulders as he thrust faster and faster. Her heart pounded, her breath came in short, shallow gasps. Even though her own vision had grown misty with arousal, she could see his eyes were dazed with passion. But he was still looking at her, knowing it was her. Intense, delicious pressure was building within her. She was hovering on the brink—desperate to crash onto the other side. She pushed her pelvis up to meet him. His movements became faster and less controlled.

Ecstasy suddenly burst upon her. Her body clenched around him as waves of shuddering delight rolled through every part of her body from her central core to her toes. She cried out and clung to him, feeling a new spasm of delight seize her body as he continued to thrust. Then his own climax began. She felt the hot release of his passion deep inside her and her legs tightened convulsively on his hips.

At last he stilled and braced himself above her, his head bowed, his chest expanding as he dragged in deep breaths. Her body felt limp. Her heart was drumming in her ears. She rested her hand on his arm, completely overwhelmed by the experience he'd just given her.

She'd thought when they were finished that he would roll away from her, but he didn't. She was too pleasantly tired to think about it at first, but then she wondered if this was what men did with their lover rather than their wife.

'Are we…going to do it again?' she asked, though she could feel he was no longer fully hard within her.

He lowered himself carefully to rest on his elbows. 'Am I crushing you?' he asked.

'No.' She liked the pressure of his firm chest against her breasts. She wiggled a bit to have the pleasure of his chest hair tickling her skin.

'Good. Now, what was it you wanted to talk about?'

She stared at him, saw the twinkle in his eye. 'You are making fun of me!'

'I'm not making fun of you. I find my current situation…very pleasing.'

'You do?' His expression reassured her. A lock of his hair had fallen forward and she brushed it back, the gesture giving her a feeling of tender familiarity with him, which was less spectacular than the sensations she'd just enjoyed but wonderfully warm and powerful.

'Mmm.' He smiled lazily.

'You could kiss me,' she said, because she loved it when he kissed her.

'I could.' He bent his head and brushed his mouth over hers.

'It tingles,' she murmured, running her tongue over her lower lip.

'You're very sensitive. Do that to me.'

'What?'

'Your tongue, my mouth.'

'Oh. All right.' She held his head between her hands and carefully stroked his lips with the tip of her tongue. She felt his murmur of approval and grew bolder with her explorations. They played gently for a while, but gradually the passion began to rise in both of them until he finally took possession of her mouth with an undisguisedly carnal kiss.

'Yes,' he said against her ear, 'we are going to do it again.'

It was late morning when Mélusine went down to the first-floor apartment to see if Saint-André had returned. Between her ride yesterday and the unfamiliar exercise she'd had with Pierre, her muscles were a little stiff and she was very conscious of a more intimate tingle and slight soreness between her legs. Pierre had gone down to his own room in the servants' quarters on the ground floor an hour ago. He'd said he would check on Saint-André on the way, but he hadn't reappeared. She didn't know if that meant Saint-André hadn't returned or whether he had and the two men were conspiring without her.

She was mildly embarrassed at meeting Saint-André so soon after making love to Pierre in case he guessed what had happened between them, but she was too anxious to wait upstairs any longer. She didn't regret making love to Pierre, but she wasn't under any illusions that she'd divined all his secrets, or that she would have much influence over what he did next. At the very least, she had a lot more questions to which she wanted answers.

She knocked on the first-floor-apartment door. When she didn't hear a reply, she pushed it open and went in. The main salon was still unfurnished. Late morning sunlight streamed through the tall, large-paned windows, casting patterns of light and shadow on the floor. Her heels echoed as she crossed to the door that connected to the inner room. She didn't expect to find Saint-André. The apartment felt empty, but she wanted to know if he'd been back.

He'd slept on the pallet bed the first night, with a small chest brought up from the servants' quarters to rest his candle and book upon. She'd been upset at offering him such poor hospitality, but he'd assured her the freedom to leave at any time he chose more than made up for the lack of luxurious furnishings.

There were two chairs in the bedroom, which increased Mélusine's suspicions that Pierre and Saint-André had been having discussions without her, but, as far as she could tell, there was no sign the Marquis had been back to the house since he'd left.

She felt a lot more worried about him as she returned to the main salon. She started for the door, determined to go down and find Pierre. She was halfway across the room when the door opened. Hope flared briefly then she juddered with shock.

Séraphin stepped over the threshold. He was scanning

the room as he did so. As soon as he saw her, his gaze locked on her and he shut the door behind him.

'The porter said you were on the second floor,' he said. 'You should employ more competent lackeys, sister.'

'What have you done to him?' Fear spiked through Mélusine.

Séraphin shrugged. 'Nothing of consequence. You burned down my house.'

'No, I didn't.' He was between Mélusine and the door to the apartment. She wondered if he was fast enough to reach her if she tried to escape back into Saint-André's bedroom. Was there a key in the lock? She tried desperately to remember.

'Oh, my dear lady, Thérèse told me all about your visit.' Séraphin strolled forward. It was the first time she'd seen him looking less than immaculate. She could still smell the vestiges of his usual cologne, but the taint of smoke clung much more strongly to him. He was wearing riding boots, and the sword at his side was intended for more than dress wear.

If she ran from Saint-André's bedroom into the next room, she could get to the servants' staircase—if she was faster than Séraphin. She knew she wasn't. If she ran, he'd hurt her when he caught her. If she screamed, Pierre and the other servants would come rushing and Séraphin would hurt them.

'What do you want?' she asked, taking a step backwards.

'Compensation.'

'For the château? You want me to sign this house over to you?'

'What?' He paused, confusion flickering briefly in his cold eyes before they filled with contempt. 'And live next to *bankers*!'

'You've got the Hôtel de Gilocourt to *live* in,' said Mélusine, trying to slide one foot unobtrusively backwards. Her legs were trembling. 'Of course you'd lease *this* house. The rents are very high.'

'This house, and the other two Bertier left you,' said Séraphin. 'Yes, that is appropriate. They should always have been mine.' He moved towards her again.

She stepped quickly aside. 'You'll need my signature on the documents,' she said breathlessly. 'If anything happens to me before that, my father will inherit the houses.'

'I'm not going to hurt you,' said Séraphin. 'I'm going to enjoy you. Give you what Bertier couldn't—'

The door opened behind him.

Pierre threw one quick glance around the salon, then walked calmly in. He was naked from the waist up. His hair was wet and slicked back. Water dripped unheeded down his chest and shoulders. He held a sheathed sword in one hand. His eyes on Séraphin, he slowly drew the sword. The deadly rasp of steel echoed through the unfurnished salon.

Séraphin moved so fast Mélusine missed the precise details. All she saw was that he now had his own sword in his hand. She backed against the wall and began to

edge around the salon. She wanted to scream at Pierre
to get out, but she daren't distract him. She'd remembered the musket he'd brought back from the Bastille.
If she could find it, she could shoot Séraphin. She
would shoot Séraphin if it was the only way to stop
him.

'What uncouth barbarian are you?' Séraphin exclaimed.

'I'm looking for your footman,' said Pierre. 'When
do you expect to see Jean-Baptiste again?'

'*Jean-Baptiste?*' Séraphin momentarily sounded as
confused as Mélusine by Pierre's question. But keeping
them both alive was far more important than unravell-
ing that puzzle, so she kept edging towards the door.

Séraphin must have caught the movement from the
corner of his eye, because he started to turn towards her,
but Pierre lunged forward and back, and Séraphin responded instantly with deadly grace. Mélusine's
stomach clenched with fear. So far their swords hadn't
crossed, but any second the duel would begin in earnest.

'How do you contact him?' Pierre asked, as they
began to circle.

'What are you babbling about, peasant? Did you take
Mélusine to the château? I'll kill you for that alone.'

'I'm younger than Bertier,' said Pierre. 'Stronger.
Faster. This time it will be your death.'

Séraphin laughed. But as he laughed he attacked.
Mélusine never knew if he laughed to distract Pierre or
for the pleasure of fighting.

The swords slithered sickeningly across each other. Mélusine stopped breathing—then they disengaged and each leapt back, watching each other like hawks. Mélusine scrambled along the wall to the door, her eyes darting between the two men. Pierre's expression revealed no emotion except the deadly determination blazing in his eyes.

'You've had some trifling tuition,' said Séraphin.

'Bertier gave me one or two lessons,' said Pierre.

'He had no discrimination in his choice of pupil,' said Séraphin.

They engaged again, a longer, more intense bout that terrified Mélusine into complete paralysis. The blades flashed too fast for her to see what was happening. Or who had the advantage. Séraphin was taller, his reach longer. To her eye Pierre seemed just as fast and skilled, and more steadily resolute—but she had no idea if that was wishful thinking.

She remembered her purpose, made it to the door and backed through it, her gaze still locked on the combatants. She banged into something solid, felt arms close around her from behind and nearly screamed from the shock. A hand closed over her mouth as she was still sucking in breath.

'Quiet!' said Saint-André in her ear. 'Don't distract him.'

She shook her head desperately and he moved his hand. 'I'm going to find the musket,' she said in a sobbing under-voice. 'I'm going to shoot Séraphin.'

'No need.'

She looked down and saw the pistol in Saint-André's other hand. 'My God!' She grabbed at his wrist, trying to lift his arm. 'Shoot him now!'

'Hush. If I have to. Stay out of the way.' He lifted her body away from the door and took up his station there.

She stared up at him, wanted to beg him to intervene, but his eyes were fixed on the duellists. She bit her lip, not noticing when it started to bleed. Bertier had taught Saint-André. Unlike her, the Marquis knew what he was looking at, knew how to judge the relative skill of the two men before him. It wasn't enough for her. A slip, a stumble, a moment's lapse in concentration and Pierre would be dead. Saint-André might avenge him with his pistol, but it would be too late for Pierre.

'We have to stop them,' she whispered desperately.

'Dumont will stop it,' he said, without looking at her.

'Do you think Jean-Baptiste will tell you about Bertier's death?' Séraphin said. His breath was slightly faster than normal, but his voice retained its usual undertone of arrogance.

'Can he?'

'You're on a fool's errand. He carried tales for me. But he didn't witness the duel.'

'He didn't watch you *murder* Bertier?'

Séraphin roared with outrage and lunged forward. Mélusine clamped her hands over her mouth to stop herself crying out. Pierre retreated only a few feet before he started to force Séraphin back. Despite

Bertier's famed prowess as a swordsman, Mélusine had only ever seen fencing in the theatre. Two men intent on killing each other looked very different from the flourishing of actors.

Both men suddenly stepped back out of range. Mélusine couldn't see the silent signal that had initiated the pause in the combat, but she nearly gave a sob of relief, though she knew it wasn't over.

Chapter Fourteen

'Bertier died an honourable death,' Séraphin declared. He was panting now. 'He challenged me.'

'Of course he did. After you flaunted his former mistress in his face,' Pierce said scornfully. 'How did much did you bribe the police inspector to lie for you?'

'Nothing. He was honoured to be my second.'

'Your *second*? Why did you kill him?'

'He boasted to his doxy who told the story to her mistress.'

'Who is?'

'Sabine de Foix.'

'Ah, I've seen the lady.' Pierce remembered her telling the story at the dinner party. 'She couldn't wait to spread the tale.'

'It hardly mattered,' said Séraphin. 'But I don't like being betrayed.'

'No one does. What about Jean-Baptiste?'

'Little rat. He ran away like the vermin he is. Even

if you find him, he can't tell you anything. But you won't find him. You'll be dead.' Séraphin lunged.

Pierce parried the attack. He'd been sure Séraphin was La Motte's blackmailer, but nothing Séraphin had said confirmed that suspicion. Unless Séraphin was being deliberately misleading, he thought Pierce was looking for Jean-Baptiste as a witness to Bertier's death.

'Where did Jean-Baptiste go?'

'The sewers, for all I care!' Séraphin pressed forward.

Pierce had no further need to question him, for which he was profoundly grateful. Despite Mélusine's fears, he'd never underestimated Séraphin. He didn't want the duel to last a second longer than necessary. His arm ached. Sweat was running into his eyes. There was no time to blink or dash it aside. A second's inattention was all Séraphin needed.

Pierce began to press hard, using every ounce of his experience and ruthless determination to survive. He'd suspected from their first brief engagement that Séraphin was technically more polished—but Bertier's half-brother had never had to fight for his life before. This was the first time he'd ever faced a man who had not only the will but the capacity to kill him.

Pierce saw the opening he was looking for and took it. His blade slid into Séraphin's side. He jerked it out and stepped back. Séraphin's eyes widened in surprised disbelief. He glanced down and covered the wound with his free hand. Blood seeped between his fingers, but he lifted his sword, intent on continuing the fight.

Pierce disarmed him with a vicious flick of his wrist, then stepped closer and knocked Séraphin unconscious with a blow of his sword hilt against his jaw. Even wounded, Séraphin would be dangerous, and Pierce wasn't inclined to take chances.

He heard Mélusine's gasping sobs and turned as she stumbled into his arms. He moved the sword swiftly away from her, before yielding it to Saint-André, putting his arms around her and holding on tight, immeasurably grateful to have her unharmed body pressed against his. He could feel how violently she was shaking.

'I'm sorry,' he said harshly. 'I should never have left you alone.'

'I was in my own house! I should be—' She broke off. 'What about Paul?'

'He was grumbling that Suzanne was making the bandage too tight when I arrived,' said Saint-André, going on one knee beside Séraphin. 'The fault is mine. I should have been here sooner,' he said. 'As I arrived at Versailles, I saw an old friend and it took me a little while to extricate myself. When I reached Séraphin's quarters I discovered he'd left in a hurry only minutes before. I thought it a golden opportunity, so I arranged a distraction for the servants and made a search. I didn't find anything, and then I started to wonder where Séraphin had gone in such a rush. I'm sorry. I was always one or two steps behind him after that.'

'You got here fast enough,' said Mélusine. 'I still

think you should have shot him, but that is my only complaint.'

'Mélusine!' Pierce exclaimed.

'I don't care if it's not honourable,' she said fiercely. 'Whatever he said, *he's* not honourable. I don't care what happens to him. I just want you to stay alive.'

Saint-André glanced up at Pierce and smiled faintly. 'You have more scruples than she does,' he said in English. 'He can survive this wound if it's properly tended.'

'Or die of infection,' said Pierce in the same language. 'He's not the blackmailer.'

'I heard,' said Saint-André. 'What are you going to do now?'

'God knows. But I imagine I'm about to start by explaining why we're speaking a language my lady can't understand,' said Pierce, ruefully aware that, despite her shock, Mélusine was looking back and forth between them.

Saint-André grinned. 'I stand in *loco parentis*. She deserves the truth after all she has endured. Take her back to her own apartment. I'll deal with Séraphin. You may tell her anything you need to about me,' he added.

'Very generous,' said Pierce drily, knowing Saint-André had deliberately forced his hand by speaking English in front of Mélusine. 'You may be sure I will tell her anything that diverts her indignation from me. Come, let's go upstairs, sweetheart,' he said to her, switching back to French.

She shook her head a little numbly. 'I have to see Paul first,' she said. 'Then we can go upstairs.'

'Very well.' He kept his arm around her as they went down to speak to the porter.

It was only after Mélusine had assured herself Paul would be all right that she let Pierce take her back to the blue salon. She curled up against his side and buried her face in his shoulder.

'Hush, it's over now.' He rubbed his hands up and down her back. He had no idea what Saint-André planned for Séraphin, but he trusted the Marquis to take care of that problem.

His own problems concerning the blackmailer had just become acute. He'd first suspected Mélusine, then Séraphin. Now he knew it wasn't either of them. He'd run out of options in Paris. Unless he received a message from La Motte via Clothilde within the next day saying the matter had been resolved in England, he had to go back to London.

It dawned on him after a few minutes that his upper body was still bare. He'd been washing when Suzanne had rushed in with the news of Séraphin's arrival. When they'd gone down to see Paul, he should have taken the opportunity to finish dressing, but he hadn't thought of it. So now he was sitting half-naked on the sofa in the early afternoon with the lady of the house. He smiled ruefully as he rubbed his cheek against her hair. She hadn't complained. He doubted if she'd even noticed,

but it was a good thing she wasn't accustomed to receiving social calls from any of her former acquaintances in Paris.

Mélusine sat up. 'Why didn't you bring the
musket? You should have brought the musket, not the
stupid sword.'

'What musket?' he said in bemusement.

'The one they gave you at Les Invalides. You should
have shot him. You just wanted to prove you were a
better swordsman. Reckless *imbécile*!'

'I...' He didn't know what to say. There was some
truth in her charge. It was also true that he'd seized the
first weapon that had come to hand. 'I needed to talk
to him. Ask him questions,' he said. 'Séraphin
wouldn't have said a word if I'd held a musket on him.
He liked boasting when he thought he was the superior
swordsman.'

'He was right in one thing—you're a barbarian.'
Mélusine rubbed the heel of her hand against his shoulder.
'All men are barbarians. Why aren't you dressed?'

'I forgot. Do you want me to go and put my livery on?'

'*Idiot*. A footman could not defeat Séraphin as you
did. Did Bertier really teach you?'

'A few sessions only. It was several years ago,' said
Pierce.

'Hmm.' She looked at him through narrowed eyes.
She was still pale, but he could see she was gradually
regaining her equilibrium. 'Saint-André is French,' she
said. 'I know he is. So it was your language he was

speaking. English. Are you English? Or an American? You came from America.'

'I'm English,' he said.

'You speak French like a Frenchman.'

'My mother's French. Even after nearly thirty years in England you can hear it when she speaks.'

'You're here for her sake, which I do not understand at all,' said Mélusine. He could see she was thinking.

'Some of what I guessed last night must have been right or you would not have decided it was better to be seduced than to talk,' she said at last.

He stroked her cheek with a gentle finger. 'I didn't let you seduce me until after you'd stopped questioning me. Until you'd left the bed and come back to it,' he reminded her. 'Distracting you wasn't my motive for succumbing.'

'You succumbed?' She was watching him uncertainly, with something in her eyes that looked very like wistful hopefulness. He felt his heart contract with tenderness for her.

'That was my perception of the situation.' He lifted her hand from his shoulder and kissed it.

'You don't regret giving in to your masculine impulses?' she asked. 'You don't feel compelled to put your honour ahead of yo—*our* happiness?'

'Mélusine.' He cupped her face in his hands. Part of him did feel guilty he'd been unable to resist the overwhelming compulsion to make love to her—but he could never regret their night together. 'You should be throwing things at me for deceiving you, not—God, I don't know what you're doing. Stop it, anyway.'

'I don't want to throw things at you. I'm sca—' She broke off and tried to look away.

He drew her back into his arms, cradling her against his chest. 'Don't be scared. I don't know what the hell we're going to do—but don't be scared.'

She was tense for a moment, but then she relaxed into him. Pierce stroked her hair and acknowledged to himself that he had no desire to leave her, or even let her out of his arms. What he wanted—with an urgency that almost overwhelmed every other consideration—was to stay. But he couldn't. He wasn't even sure he'd be able to return. By the time he reached England, he might find he was already a fugitive from the law and society.

She sat up and wiped a hand across her cheek. 'All right,' she said. 'Tell me everything. Start at the beginning.'

So he did. He began with the smuggling partnership Bertier and La Motte had formed twenty-seven years ago.

'So long ago,' she murmured. 'I haven't even lived that long.'

'Bertier was twenty,' said Pierce. 'He'd be forty-seven now if he was still alive.'

He'd expected her to be surprised by her late husband's involvement in smuggling, but it was Saint-André's involvement that provoked real astonishment in her.

'Bertier was an adventurer at heart,' she said. 'He

rushed off to take part in the American war when he was already thirty-six. But Saint-André—he has always seemed such an impeccable nobleman. With liberal views to be sure, but exquisite manners.'

'He was a perfectly polite smuggler,' said Pierce. 'Bertier was most interested in making money. Saint-André smuggled in censored literature as well. Philosophical tracts, not pornography,' he added, remembering some of the pamphlets he'd seen in the Palais Royal. 'He didn't turn up his nose at making a profit, but it was my impression he was also trying to alleviate the tax burden on his compatriots. At the time I thought he was from a respectable, but unremarkable, family which had fallen on hard times. Pretty much what you thought I was, I imagine.'

'I still don't know what you are,' said Mélusine. 'Tell me your name.'

He hesitated. He'd already decided to tell her everything except the names of La Motte and his family.

'All right,' she said after a moment. 'Your name is not only yours. That's what you said, isn't it? It's not your secret you're protecting. Carry on.'

He loved her. He couldn't do anything about it, but he loved her. Not because he desired her, though he did. But for her courage and her intelligence and her determination to be fair to him, even though he had not been fair to her. His arm tightened around her waist. He wanted to kiss her. He wanted to carry her into her bedchamber and make love to her. He wanted to shut out the rest of the world and only be with her. But he couldn't do any of that. He didn't even dare kiss her for fear she would interpret it as a promise he didn't know he'd be able to keep.

He told her everything, up to and including his decision to become her footman when he'd arrived in Paris and discovered she was looking for one.

'So you suspected me of being a blackmailer, not a murderer,' she said. 'I was not so very far out with my guesses last night, was I?'

'No.' He couldn't help himself, he caught one of her curls and began to wind it around his finger. She glanced sideways at what he was doing, but didn't comment.

'That's why you were so interested in Jean-Baptiste.' She grimaced. 'I can easily imagine him being involved in blackmail. He's a toad. What are you going to do now?'

Pierce took a breath. 'I have to go back to England,' he said.

She stared at him for a few seconds, then abruptly ducked her head. 'Tonight?'' she asked in a gruff voice, without looking up.

'Tomorrow. I need to talk to Saint-André first. Make some arrangements. Just because I haven't found the blackmailer doesn't mean he's not here. Perhaps one of the other servants at the Hôtel de Gilocourt. François, perhaps,' he said, knowing she disliked her former *maître d'hôtel*. 'Saint-André will have connections he can call upon. I think he'll help.'

'I'm not sure François would do anything that might bring shame on the Gilocourt family,' said Mélusine doubtfully. 'Apart from that, I can imagine he might be involved in blackmail. I think you are right, Saint-André has so many connections he will be able to pursue that more easily than we can—and stay in the apartment downstairs to make sure I'm safe,' she added.

'He has to live somewhere,' said Pierce, even as his heart rebelled at the situation. He didn't want it to be Saint-André who protected Mélusine, but he couldn't stay, and he couldn't ask her to come with him when his future in England was so uncertain.

'If I can come back—' he began.

She turned quickly and laid her fingers on his lips. 'Don't make that promise. Not even silently to your own conscience.'

He caught her hand in his and kissed her fingers. 'I don't deserve your generosity.'

'I am not generous—I am cross with you,' she said, her expression an odd mixture of a forced smile and a mock frown. 'I wanted to sketch you again. I think you have been deliberately avoiding that aspect of your duties.'

Pierce pressed his lips together. He wasn't going to suggest Saint-André modelled for her. 'Later today,' he said, 'when all the arrangements have been dealt with. If you would like it.'

She looked at him solemnly, then nodded and smiled. 'Thank you. You might as well tell me your name,' she added. 'I can't recall it at the moment, but I soon will, I'm sure.'

'You've never heard it,' he said, startled.

'Yes, I have. I've been thinking. Who could the English privateer who was Bertier's partner be? Someone who now has a respectable position in society. Someone with a French wife, perhaps?' She smiled into Pierce's shocked eyes. 'I think your privateer is Henry de La Motte,' she said. 'He and his wife came to stay with us soon after Bertier and I were married. But I can't remember your name.' Her smile suddenly faded and tears filled her eyes. 'Your mother was so proud of you,' she whispered, 'but I can't remember what she called you.'

'Pierce.' Completely shaken, he kissed her temple. 'Pierce Cardew.'

'Yes, I remember now.' She leant away from him. 'Pierce Cardew.' She frowned in an effort to retrieve the rest of the memory. 'Vicomte de…Basspur?'

'Viscount Blackspur,' he corrected her.

'Blackspur.' She practised the sound, then pressed her face against his shoulder and hugged him tightly.

The King came to Paris that afternoon and all carriages and carts were ordered off the streets. Neither Pierce nor Mélusine had any interest in seeing him, but Saint-André gave them a brief report of events when he returned to the house.

Louis de Crosne was no longer Lieutenant of Police,

though he'd escaped the fate of the governor of the Bastille and several other men in authority whose heads had been paraded through the streets by the victorious crowds.

'It's very unlikely now anyone would be interested in pursuing Séraphin's crime or the inspector's misconduct,' said Saint-André. 'In the circumstances, we have no other option but to deal with these matters ourselves.'

'You always meant to,' said Mélusine. 'Both of you. Tell us about the King.'

'The crowds were shouting *Vive la Nation! Vive Necker!* but I never heard anyone shout *Vive le Roi!* until the King put the cockade of blue-and-red ribbons in his hat,' said Saint-André. 'Monsieur Bailly gave it to him. He is the new Mayor. They have named Lafayette Commander-in-Chief of the National Guard.'

'I don't suppose the King liked it very much,' said Mélusine.

'He looked quite dazed and subdued,' said Saint-André. 'I dare say he can't believe what has happened to him. One doesn't, when the prison door first slams behind one. And for all the polite speeches, that is what has happened to the King.'

'I am sorry,' said Mélusine, seeing the shadows in his eyes and knowing he was thinking of his own imprisonment.

Saint-André's expression immediately cleared. 'I suffered only minor inconvenience and had an excellent opportunity to improve my scholarship,' he said lightly. 'I am glad to report I didn't feel remotely inclined to make friends with the rats, as poor Latude did, though a canary might have been pleasant company. I confess I missed music.'

Later that evening, after Pierce had spoken to Saint-André about continuing the search for the blackmailer in Paris, and they were once more alone in her apartment, Mélusine said, 'I promised you could pretend to sleep the next time I sketched you. My bedchamber would obviously be the most practical location.'

Pierce looked at her and she felt herself blushing. She was amazed at her boldness, but this might be the last night she ever had with him. She was determined not to waste any of it on modest hesitancy.

'You want me to take off my clothes for you and pretend to *sleep?*' he asked, a teasing, slightly challenging gleam in his eyes.

'Perhaps we could pile up the pillows so you can recline in a half-sitting posture,' she said, thinking how much she would enjoy just looking at him without his clothes. 'With one knee drawn up, perhaps, and your arm… I'm not sure where your arm can go until we experiment with the pose.'

'You really want to sketch me?' Pierce solved the problem of what to do with his arms by putting them around her waist.

'Yes. For a little while. At first. You have very good

legs. I haven't drawn your legs yet,' she said slightly breathlessly, as he moved his hands lower, pulling her hips against him.

'Perhaps it would be best if that's all you do,' he said. Even though she could feel he was already aroused, she could also see conflict in his eyes.

She did not want him to feel guilty for making love to her, so she put her hands on his shoulders and said, 'This is my choice, freely offered. I didn't have that before. You are not compromising me—or your honour—because I am making a free choice. I am the one taking advantage of you—selfishly asking you to compromise your principles for me.' She traced the curve of his mouth, wondering if she'd ever have a chance to model him in clay when he was there in the room with her.

'Most of my life I've had no choice in what I've had to do,' she said. 'From the smallest details of my days when I was a child at home or in the convent—or even who I married. I know what it is like to smile and acquiesce when all you want to do is shout "no!" and run away as fast as you can. I'm sad you must leave so soon, but I can bear the knowledge you're going, knowing you are happy in my presence now. I couldn't stand it if I ever thought you were lying honourably beside me when really you wanted to be somewhere else.' She smiled tremulously. 'So if you're considering my forwardness tonight a tiresome imposition…'

'No.' His arms tightened around her. 'Never that.

Your…pleasure, in my company, could never be an imposition.'

She could hear the deep conviction in his voice and it filled her with hope—though she was a little afraid that his feelings for her were being intensified by the hazardous situation in which he found himself. She'd only know whether he was still so eager to be with her after the blackmailer had been dealt with and his actions were no longer constrained by his deep need to protect his family.

'Let me get my sketching materials,' she said, 'and we'll go to my bedchamber.'

'If I pose for you now, it will be a very immodest picture,' he said against her ear, his warm breath caressing her skin, then his tongue began to tease her earlobe in such a deliciously distracting way that her knees went weak.

She clutched at his shoulder. 'Pehraps you should pose later.'

'That would be best.' He swept her up in one fluid movement and carried her to the bedchamber thrilling her with the virile urgency of his movements. He set her on her feet beside the bed and began to undress her.

'You were supposed to undress first,' she said, the picture of him modelling naked for her still vivid in her mind, but she didn't try to stop him. He had been determined not to take advantage of her for so long that she loved his undisguised eagerness for her.

'I've undressed for you before,' he said. 'You're going to pose for me now.'

'Are you going to draw me?' she said in surprise, as he untied the ribbon at the front of her chemise and pulled the neckline wide.

'I'm going to appreciate you.' He pulled the garment over her head and suddenly, apart from her stockings, she was completely naked. She had no idea how he'd undressed her so fast. Perhaps it was because being so close to him, anticipating making love to him, was confusing her senses.

He looked at her, his eyes dark with desire, and gently touched her sides. Her heart began to beat a rapid tattoo as very slowly he drew his hands up to cup her breasts. Her nipples tightened, and when he brushed his thumbs across their tips, intense, answering sensation flared deep within her core. She gasped, releasing a sigh that was very close to a moan.

Pierce made a sound in his throat. He dragged back the bedclothes and piled up the pillows. Then he picked her up and laid her gently against them, in a half-reclining position.

'Draw up your leg,' he said hoarsely.

'You really want me to pose for you?' She hadn't thought he meant it. For a moment she felt too shy and awkward to do as he requested, but the passionate appreciation in his eyes gave her confidence. He'd asked her to pose in the same position she'd suggested for him. She raised one knee and lifted her hand to brush her hair out of her eyes. As she did so she instinctively arched her back and immediately saw how the action drew his gaze to her breasts. She'd never expected to have such a powerful effect upon a man, nor realised how intoxicating she would find it. On impulse she pulled the pins from her hair and shook it down. Then she drew several long wavy locks forward and arranged them modestly over her breasts.

She smiled up at him. He responded to her teasing gesture with a quiet laugh, which was rough with arousal. His gaze never left her as he stripped off his own clothes and came to kneel beside her on the bed. He said something to her in English, but she was so distracted by the pleasure of looking at him she didn't ask him what he meant. She put her hand on his thigh, delighting in the sensation of firm muscle beneath her fingertips. She wanted to explore further, but he leant forward, his gaze on her breasts. She looked down and saw one erect nipple was peeping through her long, shimmering locks. She hadn't intended to tease him quite so provocatively, but he didn't seem to mind. He guided her hair away with a delicate touch that sent a shiver of anticipatory delight through her, and lowered his head to her breast. He kissed the soft underside of her breast, then his lips closed around her nipple and he began to caress it with his tongue. She moaned, arching her back as waves of glorious sensation flooded through her body.

At last he lifted his head, and it was only then she

noticed his hand was resting on her inner thigh. He glided his fingertips upwards to the patch of damp curls between her legs, to the place where she was swollen and throbbing with need. His gaze locked with hers, he eased his fingers a little deeper until he could stroke and tease her most sensitive spot. Her breath caught in her throat. They'd made love before, but the touch of his hand, exploring and caressing the most private part of her, as he looked into her eyes, seemed even more intimate than anything they'd previously done. She was too dazed with pleasure to protest or worry whether she was allowing him immodest liberties. Urgent, anticipatory tension coiled in her body. Her hips lifted against his hand of their own volition, striving towards the summit of pleasure.

Then she soared over the cliff top into quivering ecstasy. She closed her eyes, her legs falling open on to the mattress as her muscles went completely limp with the waves of delight rolling through her body. It was several minutes before she could think clearly enough to realise what had happened: Pierce had brought her to the peak of pleasure without taking any for himself.

She opened her eyes. He was kneeling beside her, gently stroking her body, his body still hard with arousal. She wondered if she dared…then reached out before doubt overcame her.

She took him by surprise. He jerked violently and swore under his breath. She snatched her hand away, afraid she'd trespassed too far, but he caught it and kissed her fingers.

'Yes,' he said hoarsely. 'I want you to touch me. I just wasn't expecting you to.'

'Oh. Like me yesterday, when I jumped the first time you…' She touched her breast with her free hand because she couldn't quite bring herself to say in words what he'd done.

'Yes.' He guided her other hand back to his erection. She closed her fingers around his hardness, fascinated and excited by the feel of him in her hand. She stroked him from root to tip and he tensed and flexed in response to her touch. His lean body was sheened with perspiration, his expression fierce with self-control. He let her explore him for a while, then he gently moved her hand aside and laid her flat on the bed. He braced himself over her, reached down to position himself—and thrust up to the hilt into her.

She gasped and clutched at his arms. Even though she'd expected it, the joining of his body with hers was a star-tling, wonderful invasion. She was slick and ready for him. Her hips jerked up against him. Immediately he began to thrust in and out. Her fingers dug into the muscles of his upper arms as she responded just as urgently, desperate for this moment of fulfilment with him, because she might never have another night with him. Together they spiralled up to an overwhelming climax.

Afterwards she was so spent with pleasure she could

hardly lift a hand. Pierce lay on top of her, all the tension drained from his body. She liked the feel of him pressing her into the mattress, but when she wondered if this was the last time night she'd experience it, she wanted to cry. Suddenly she had the energy to put her arms around him, though she forced herself not to cling too tightly lest he sense her distress. There would be time enough to grieve and worry when he'd gone. She would not waste a second on fear or sadness while he was still with her.

He smiled so tenderly she wanted to cry. 'Shall I fetch your sketching materials now?' he asked.

She shook her head and settled down against his side so he couldn't see her expression. 'Let us just rest comfortably,' she said, when she could trust her voice.

Chapter Fifteen

It took a long time for the door to open, and when it did, Daniel Blanc found himself gazing into the mouth of a musket.

He looked up into the frightened, resolute eyes of the maid levelling the weapon at him and went still. He glanced quickly around the entrance hall and noted the bandage around the head of the porter who'd opened the door. The porter seemed more nervous and less resolute than the maid.

'Is she hurt?' Daniel demanded harshly. 'Madame de Gilocourt? Is she hurt?'

'N-no,' the porter stammered.

'Pierre stuck a sword in him,' said the maid with grim satisfaction.

Daniel exhaled as the sudden fear knotting his gut slowly eased. He had no idea who Pierre had stuck a sword in, but from the moment he'd seen the musket and the bandage he'd known there'd been a recent threat to the household. Apparently Mélusine's new footman had dealt with it.

'Who did Pierre fight?' he asked. 'Why?'

'The Comte de Gilocourt,' said the porter. 'He hit my head! *Madame* burned his house down by accident and he was angry with her, but Pierre fought him and there's a bloodstain on the salon floor—'

'Be quiet, Paul!' the maid snapped. 'I know you,' she said to Daniel, still pointing the musket at him. 'I gave you some cake the first time you were here.'

'Yes, you did,' he said calmly, still not moving.

'You work for *madame's* father?' said the maid.

'Yes.'

'Where is he?'

'Versailles,' said Daniel.

The musket lowered by half an inch. 'Is that the truth?' the maid said suspiciously.

'Yes.'

'Pierre told us we must not allow Monsieur Fournier to take us by surprise,' said the maid. 'We're not letting you take *madame* away.'

'I must speak to her,' said Daniel.

The maid frowned, indecision in her eyes.

'Suzanne, *madame* spoke to him the other day,' said Paul. 'She took him upstairs herself.'

'She'll be upset if you shoot me,' said Daniel. He looked past Suzanne to the man who'd come silently down the stairs while they were talking. The Marquis de Saint-André stopped a few steps before he reached the bottom. At first glance he seemed the epitome of elegant poise. His left hand rested lightly on the bannister, his right arm was by his side—but he was holding a pistol close to his thigh. After one glance into the Marquis's cool blue eyes, Daniel knew he would not be allowed to pass unless Saint-André was sure he posed no threat to Mélusine.

'Forgive us the inhospitable reception,' said the Marquis. 'What with one thing and another, we're erring on the side of caution today.'

'You are certain Madame de Gilocourt is not hurt?' said Daniel.

'Quite certain,' said Saint-André. 'I regret the need for such discourteous bluntness but—are you here to take the Comtesse away?'

'I have to talk to her,' said Daniel.

Saint-André considered him for a few moments. 'Come up to my apartment,' he said at last.

'Is she there?'

'No. She's in her own apartment. Suzanne will tell her you're here.'

Suzanne reluctantly lowered the musket. 'Don't turn your back on him,' she advised Saint-André, as she passed him on the stairs.

'With that in mind—after you, *monsieur*,' the Marquis said politely to Daniel.

'How long have you been here?' Daniel asked.

'The Comtesse kindly agreed to lease me the first-floor apartment a couple of days ago,' said Saint-André.

'I have not yet had an opportunity to furnish it,' he added, as he opened the door and stepped aside to allow Daniel to enter the main salon.

Daniel walked over to look at the dark stain on the floor. 'Was the footman hurt in the fight?' he asked.

'No. He was more than a match for the Comte.'

Daniel nodded and turned as Suzanne came into the salon.

'*Madame* says you're both to go up to the blue salon,' she said.

Mélusine had woken at dawn from a dream about canaries and sunlight, and with Pierce's arm around her. The mood induced by the dream, and her determination not to cry in his presence, had given her the fortitude to remain calm while they'd parted. He'd tried once more to promise he'd return if he could, but again she'd not let him. She didn't want him to come back because of a promise he'd made in such fraught circumstances. She wanted him to come back because he truly wanted to in his heart.

But half an hour after he'd gone, as the realisation she might have seen him for the last time struck home, she'd clutched a pillow and wept. It had taken a little while for the storm of emotion to pass, but eventually she'd got up from the bed, bathed her eyes in cold water and dressed. Whatever happened in the future, in the past few days Pierce had given her most of the happiest memories of her life. She comforted herself with the belief that, if he really did want to be with her, whatever happened he'd find a way to return to her.

She meant to work in her studio later, but she was sitting in the blue salon, remembering everything Pierce had said and done from the moment she'd first met him, when Suzanne announced Daniel's arrival. She straightened her skirts and tried to look serene as Daniel and Saint-André entered the salon.

'Good morning, *madame*,' said Daniel, unemotional as ever, but she knew he'd noticed her reddened eyes because his lips tightened into a thin line.

She forced herself to smile. 'Please sit down, both of you,' she said. 'Suzanne said Father is still at Versailles.'

'He is,' said Daniel.

'I'm not going to Bordeaux with you.' Mélusine lifted her chin stubbornly.

Daniel glanced from her to Saint-André. 'Where's Dumont?' he asked.

'He has an urgent errand to fulfil,' said Saint-André. 'In his absence I am charged with the task of protecting the Comtesse. A duty I am honoured to undertake.'

'The footman charged *you*?' said Daniel. 'The world is certainly changing.'

Mélusine bit her lip, deciding it was wiser not to respond to Daniel's comment. 'You have come to take me to Bordeaux, haven't you?' she said.

He hesitated, looking once more at Saint-André. 'You have to go *somewhere*, *madame*,' he said at last.

'If you don't want to go to Bordeaux, I'll take you somewhere else.'

'I don't—' She stopped and stared at him. 'Somewhere else?' she said uncertainly. 'You mean…you'll take me somewhere else without telling Father where I am?'

'I have only once failed in what Raoul Fournier has asked me to do,' said Daniel. 'That was when I did not take you to Bordeaux when I came for you last time. If I fail this time, I will not be the one he sends next time. That would be bad for you. So…' he shrugged '…if you won't go to Bordeaux, we must go somewhere else. You used to say you wanted to see the statues in Florence and Rome. We can go there, if you like.'

Mélusine stared at Daniel. 'If you betray him, he'll be your enemy,' she whispered.

Daniel gave a brief nod and another small shrug, as if he was indifferent to that outcome.

'But you've served him loyally for twenty-seven years,' she said.

'No, *madame*, I've remained in his service for twenty-seven years,' said Daniel.

'There are other ways to deal with Fournier that wouldn't force the Comtesse to leave her home,' said Saint-André, as Mélusine considered what Daniel had just revealed.

'No, there aren't,' said Daniel bluntly. 'Not if you mean a legal challenge. He becomes vengeful if he is crossed or beaten. It is best for *madame* to be safely beyond his grasp before any action is taken against him.'

'You wanted to take me to Bordeaux so I'd marry a young man of my own choosing a few days ago,' said Mélusine, still assimilating the implications of Daniel's startling offer.

'You were adamant you would not do so,' said Daniel. 'That's why I will take you to Florence instead. You cannot say you don't want to go there, because I know you do.'

Mélusine shook her head in confusion and instinctive denial. She'd suspected for years that behind his impassive face Daniel had little respect for his master. She doubted her father had noticed, because he was too arrogant to look below the surface of those around him, but she'd never quite understood why Daniel remained in his service.

'I have always known you could do anything asked of you,' she said, 'but I never thought I'd hear you make such a...radical suggestion.'

An odd expression flickered in Daniel's eyes, but all he said was, 'I've been listening to the debates in the Third Estate.'

'Your rebellion against your master is inspired by the people's rebellion against the King?' said Saint-André.

'You may say so,' said Daniel, and Mélusine knew immediately there was more to his actions than that. But she suddenly remembered her canary and all her other thoughts scattered as despair overwhelmed her.

She understood better than Saint-André that Daniel was right about her father. If she was going to persist in flouting his wishes, putting herself beyond his reach would be the wisest option. But if she hid from her father, she would also be hidden from Pierce. How would he ever find her if she wasn't in the house in place Vendôme, when he returned to Paris?

If he returned to Paris. She desperately wanted to believe he would. And she had to be where he could find her.

'I can't leave,' she whispered. She pressed the heels of her hands against her temples. 'I have to stay here.'

'You can't stay,' said Daniel.

'Comtesse, I will do everything in my power to protect you,' said Saint-André. 'But it may be safer for you to leave Paris, and even France, for reasons that have nothing to do with the threat your father poses to your comfort.'

Mélusine barely heard what the Marquis said. She was gazing at an inner vision of Pierce arriving to find her absent and the house deserted. She pictured Pierce walking through the empty rooms with no idea where she'd gone. Would he be worried about her? Or would he take it as a sign she had no further interest in any aspect of the time she'd spent in the house, including him?

She couldn't leave Paris. All her hopes and dreams for the future were founded on being where Pierce could find her when he'd resolved the crisis with the blackmailer. For the first time since he'd left, her faith that they had a future together nearly died completely.

'Madame? Madame?'

She returned to a sense of her surroundings to see that both Daniel and Saint-André were watching her with worried expressions. A dim memory of the last thing Saint-André had said flittered through her mind.

'Why would I be safer away from Paris?' she said, though she hardly cared. 'Because of the recent uproar? But the King has made his peace with Paris.'

'One of his brothers and many members of court have already gone into exile rather than tolerate his submission,' said Saint-André. 'Paris—and France—is more likely to be moving towards civil war than a time of peace.'

'Civil war?' She was momentarily distracted from her own problems. 'Is that what you really think is going to happen?'

'I do not say it is certain—only that it is very probable.' Saint-André looked troubled. 'Not all the King's allies will abandon him or concede to their opponents. Some will fight.'

Mélusine thought of the fighting she'd seen, the blood that had already been shed, and her agonising wait to see if Pierce would return safely from the attack on the Bastille. The idea of that violence increasing to become a full-blown war was a horrifying prospect. At least Pierce wouldn't be at risk because it would be a civil war between Frenchmen and, despite his ease with the language, he was English.

She pressed her hands against her cheeks as the tiny

seed of an idea popped into her mind. When Daniel started to speak, she shushed him. She had to think of all the possible ramifications of her idea. As it grew into a full-blown plan, her heart hammered against her ribs with a mixture of excitement, the rebirth of hope, and anxiety at venturing so far into the unknown.

'Very well,' she said at last, lowering her hands to her lap. 'If I must leave Paris, I must. Daniel, you may take me to London.'

While the two men were still staring at her, she jumped up and ran down to order a message to be sent summoning Monsieur Barrière immediately to the house. Now she'd made up her mind, she didn't want to waste an instant before putting her plan into action.

Mélusine rushed them through the preparations for leaving Paris and they set off for Boulogne that very afternoon. After his initial surprise, Daniel was quite pragmatic about their destination. 'London is nearer than Florence, and we'll not have to cross the Alps,' he said, and thereafter went about making arrangements with his customary efficiency.

They had to travel a hundred and fifty miles to reach Boulogne and Mélusine knew they would be losing ground on Pierce all the way. Although she didn't want to be too far behind him, she wasn't trying to catch him, so they rested for two, admittedly short, nights along the route. Daniel and Saint-André occasionally made enquiries about Pierce, but they only gleaned snippets of information on a couple of occasions. The second time was when a groom remembered Pierce at an inn where they changed horses thirty miles from the coast. At that point Pierce was well over twenty-four hours ahead of them, but when they arrived at Boulogne they discovered the gap had reduced to less than twelve because bad weather had delayed the departure of his packet boat. The enforced wait must have increased his frustration and anxiety, but Mélusine couldn't help being glad he was once more less than a day ahead of her.

They sailed at night and Mélusine was on deck before dawn the following morning to see the south coast of England come into view. Saint-André stood beside her, easily adjusting to the movement of the packet boat.

She'd wanted him to remain in Paris, to fulfil his promise to Pierce to look there for the blackmailer. But Saint-André had been equally adamant he had to accompany her to England.

'I've already set in motion the initial enquiries,' he'd said, 'and once you're settled in London I can be back in France within a day or two. It may be useful to have the latest news from London before I return.'

'Yes.' Mélusine could see the sense of that, but hearing the latest news from London meant seeing and speaking to Pierce. Of course she wanted to do both, but she wasn't quite sure how she was going to manage their reunion. When he'd left Paris she'd been determined not to seem as if she was desperately clinging on to him—chasing after him to England within hours of his own departure might give him the wrong impression, make him feel trapped and burdened by her demands upon him, when she wanted him to feel free and unfettered.

The sky was still pearly grey. A cold sea breeze blew her hair into her face. She could taste the salt on her lips. She glanced at Saint-André. In his time as a smuggler he must have known many dawns like this. She pondered the question of why she hadn't suspected he had such an unconventionally adventurous side to his character when she'd first known him.

'I always knew Séraphin was dangerous,' she said. 'And I guessed from the moment I met Pierce that there was more to him than he wanted me to see, but I never suspected you could be...' she glanced around and lowered her voice '...a smuggler.'

'I'm glad to hear it.' He smiled.

'It is very interesting,' she said, trying to understand the puzzle of Saint-André, because every time she thought about her next meeting with Pierce, the butterflies in her stomach became so energetic she felt sick with a mixture of apprehension and hope. If the worst had happened, he might already have gone into exile with his family. And if, as she devoutly hoped, they were all safely in London, he might be angry with her for following him.

'Perhaps it is because they were pretending to be something they're not,' she mused. 'Séraphin wished to appear suave and sophisticated, but underneath he is not remotely civilised. Pierce tried to be a wooden-faced, unmemorable servant, but in reality he is nothing of the kind. He couldn't even be appropriately polite and submissive at his interview...'

'Whereas I am politely unmemorable in all my guises,' said Saint-André.

'No!' Mélusine was horrified he'd interpreted her words in such a fashion, then relieved to see the humour in his eyes. 'But you are a quiet, polite man with the habit of thought. I expect you are still a quiet, polite man with the habit of thought when you are in the middle of a daring adventure. It is very clever, because you are hiding in full view.'

'Hmm,' said Saint-André. 'I am glad to know you think so highly of my manners.'

'They are true good manners, because they spring from your consideration for others, rather than a wish to call attention to yourself,' said Mélusine earnestly. She didn't want him to think she was making fun of him. 'I never felt at ease with most of the people I met while I was married. But you always set me at my ease. That is the sign of true good manners—and great kindness.'

'Thank you,' he said.

She glanced at him, then looked away at the seagulls wheeling above them. *'Monsieur*, I must ask you...' she began, and then lost the courage to voice her question. 'Never mind, it's not important.'

'You want to know if there were any circumstances under which I might have agreed to Bertier's request?' he asked gently.

Even the breeze against her cheeks couldn't cool her embarrassment, but she did want to know. 'You were his closest friend. And…you must have known Séraphin is evil. You cannot have wanted him to be Bertier's heir.'

'I didn't,' said Saint-André. 'We must all have been in a state of distress the day after my conversation with Bertier. I left his presence as soon as I could because I was so furious at what he'd asked. I didn't want to quarrel with him when he was in such an excitable state—but I was insulted he had so little regard for my honour—' He broke off and smiled ruefully. 'I will confess my initial thoughts on the matter were entirely selfish. I didn't realise you'd overheard, and I didn't think he meant to tell you—so at first it was the insult to me I was most offended by. But by the evening I was over my temper and thinking more calmly.' He looked at her sharply. 'Do you believe I might have done it, *madame*?'

'I think…I think you would have remembered if Bertier had lived out his natural life it would have been too late for me to have children with a second husband,' she said, speaking with some difficulty. 'And I know you didn't like Séraphin. I think…I think… I don't know what I think.'

'I would not have seduced you,' he said gravely. 'I give you my word of honour. I thought very long and hard and it seemed to me the matter was not as simple as I'd first thought it. If Bertier had calmed down—if instead of being motivated by rage and slighted manhood he had considered your feelings and what would be best for the people who depended on him, his tenants, the villagers…'

'Séraphin was not a good lord,' said Mélusine, remembering the fury of the villagers towards him only eight months after he'd inherited the château.

'No, he wasn't. *Madame*, as much as I loved and respected Bertier, he was at his best and happiest before he inherited his father's title. It was not right that you were compelled into a marriage not of your choosing with a man twice your age who could not give you children. If you'd been young together and that had been the outcome, then so be it—'

'Bertier didn't know when he married me,' she protested.

'He didn't know for sure, perhaps. But he wasn't faithful to his first wife. By the time he married you, I believe he suspected—even if he was hoping a miracle would occur with his young bride. No, he did not treat you fairly. So…in the end I decided the decision would have to be yours. You would have to know why—and what was at stake. And I would have needed guarantees from Bertier that he would never mistreat you in any way as a result. At the time it seemed a…rational…solution.'

'My decision,' she whispered, slightly dazed by the Marquis's revelations. 'You are a true, noble gentleman, *monsieur*.'

'I'm not sure everyone would see it so,' said Saint-André wryly. 'Do not, in any way, feel offended if I say I am glad the matter was never put to the test.'

'So am I,' said Mélusine. 'You must not feel offended either,' she added hastily. 'I know you would have been the epitome of consideration, compassion, tact…'

His eyes flickered in an almost imperceptible wince. 'I was very arrogant in my benevolence,' he said. 'It was only after I'd been sitting in the Bastille for several months it occurred to me that sometimes good intentions truly can be as destructive as deliberate cruelty.'

'Oh, no,' said Mélusine, but she thought he was probably right. Though Saint-André had always been kind and considerate, he had never shown the slightest spark of attraction for her, and she didn't believe that was because she'd always belonged to another man when she'd known him. It would have been the ultimate humiliation to have an affair with a man who was only making love to her from charitable motives.

'I much prefer that we can be friends,' she said.

He smiled. 'I hope we always will be,' he said. 'The white cliffs of Dover,' he added, with an elegant gesture towards them, and she turned for her first sight of England.

It was eighty miles from Dover to London, but they'd arrived so early in the morning and they made such good time on the road, that they reached London in the early afternoon. The closer they approached their des-

tination, the more anxious Mélusine became. The only
light distraction during the journey was when she heard
Daniel speaking to an ostler at one of the coaching
inns.

'You always told me you couldn't speak English!'
She glared at him.

'I don't,' he said, even though as far as she could tell
he'd just been having a conversation with the
Englishman in which they'd both understood the other
perfectly well.

'I just heard you!'

'Sailor's English,' he said dismissively. 'Not suitable
for you to use. I didn't tell you because you'd never
have ceased nagging me for lessons if you'd known.
You must learn to speak English like a lady.'

'He can speak English and he didn't tell me!' she
fumed, as she climbed back into the chaise with Saint-
André.

'He can make himself understood in English,' Saint-
André replied. 'Though he is quite effective at making
his wishes known even when he doesn't speak.'

'He can be very dour, but I've never been scared of
him,' said Mélusine. 'He should have taught me!'

'Hmm.' Amusement gleamed briefly in the
Marquis's eyes. 'There is a certain saltiness to his word
use which might raise a few eyebrows if you repeated
them in the drawing room.'

'I have to learn English,' said Mélusine. 'Teach me
some English.'

He tried, but between her curiosity at her new surroundings and her anxiety about meeting Pierce she was too distracted to pay proper attention.

'I must find a house to lease,' she said, 'but tonight I must stay in a respectable inn. I am here to start a new independent life—just as I intended when I went to Paris. I will have a house and practise my art—only I will be living in London. But I mustn't buy anything yet, because if it turns out he can't stay in England I'll have to be a widow living in a house and practising my art in…New York, or somewhere. Where do you think they'll go if they have to leave England?' She twisted briefly to look at Saint-André, before returning to her scrutiny of the passing scenery.

'I don't know,' he said. 'Given your determination to be a woman of independent means, and the fact that I may be returning immediately to France, I think we'd better begin by going to the bank and setting your finances in order.'

'Monsieur Barrière is going to sell two of my houses and have the profits deposited in the Bank of England,' said Mélusine. 'At the moment the draft I have brought with me is only for quite a modest amount.'

'I know,' said Saint-André. 'I will have additional funds transferred from my account into the one we will have created for you—'

'Oh, *monsieur*,' she began in protest, but he held up a hand to stop her.

'You will be able to repay me when you receive the

profits from the sale of your houses,' he said. 'And in the meantime, you will be doing me the favour of relieving my mind of some anxiety about your future security.'

'Thank you,' said Mélusine, touched by his concern for her. 'It never occurred to me you might have an account in an English bank.'

'I'm not the only Frenchman who has. England isn't bankrupt,' he said rather drily.

Mélusine nodded, but her thoughts had already returned to Pierce. 'I hope he's not angry with me for coming,' she muttered, as much to herself as to Saint-André. 'I hope he and his family are safe. I hope he's pleased to see me. I hope the blackmailer has already been dealt with. Oh dear, I think you will have to leave me at an inn and go to see him alone first, just so it doesn't look as if I'm chasing him—but what if something has happened to him? I need to know.'

'I will take you to the bank,' said Saint-André, calmly breaking into her agitated stream of thought. 'Then we will hire rooms at an inn so you may change your dress and compose yourself, before I take you to see Sir Henry and Lady de La Motte. Since they were your guests in Paris, it is only courteous for you to return their visit on arriving in London. And it will be perfectly reasonable for you to ask Sir Henry's advice on leasing or buying a house in London.'

Mélusine gazed at him for a few moments. Then she nodded jerkily. 'Yes, we'll make it clear I want his— Sir Henry's—business advice. Not that I'm…anything else. Unless anything bad has happened to them. We won't ask for advice about my house if they are in the middle of a crisis.'

'Mélusine, he will be pleased to see you,' said Saint-André gently.

She took a deep breath and managed to smile at the Marquis. 'I'm sorry,' she said, feeling awkward that in her agitation she had revealed so much. 'I did not mean to witter on so.'

'I'm flattered you have such confidence in my friendship,' he said simply. 'But you need have no fears over how Blackspur will greet you.'

'I hope not. Blackspur,' she muttered. 'I must remember to call him Blackspur. Not Vicomte. What did he say?'

'Viscount. Just call him Lord Blackspur in company,' said the Marquis. 'In private you may continue as before.'

She nodded. Then, because she was unsettled by how unguarded she'd been, and wanted some time to compose herself, she turned back to look out of the carriage window. Saint-André had told her they were going to the part of London called the City, the ancient business heart of London. That was where business premises of London merchants who traded all around the world could be found—and the banks.

'Now Sir Henry is part of fashionable society, his house is further west,' said Saint-André.

Mélusine was slightly daunted at the prospect of having to learn all the same social nuances she'd encountered when she'd first moved to Paris. At least she'd been able to speak French. But perhaps, because she couldn't speak their language, the English would make allowances for her *faux pas*.

She sat on the very edge of the seat, one hand clinging to the bottom of the open window as she stared at the buildings and people they passed. The carriage was moving very slowly and sometimes stopped completely because there was so much traffic crowding the streets. That was like Paris. But unlike Paris, there was a separate walkway along the side of the street for pedestrians. In Paris, anyone on foot often had to jump behind one of the bollards that lined the streets to escape from oncoming traffic. In London, it seemed you could walk in relative confidence along the side of the street, concerned only about colliding with another pedestrian.

Mélusine was fascinated by the people. Of course the street cries were different. But she hadn't expected the people would even dress so differently. There was no doubt she was in a foreign country.

She watched one man walking towards her. He was dressed in drab clothes that made him look like a clerk, and he had a slight paunch to his belly. He looked neither to right nor left, but down at the ground a few paces ahead, as if he'd been worn down by the demands of life and the tedious pressures of his job. She'd seen many men like him in Bordeaux and Paris. As he passed close to the coach she saw his full eyebrows were streaked with grey and his mouth was drawn down slightly at the corners, as if that was his habitual expression. She guessed him to be in his mid-forties, but something about him piqued her curiosity and she kept watching as he walked away from her.

Something about him wasn't right. She frowned in puzzlement. Something—

There was a sudden commotion as a barking dog chased a cat straight across the street, right under the nose of the horse pulling the cart behind Mélusine's carriage. The horse shied and the clerk sprang to one side in alarm. When he continued walking, his posture had changed. Mélusine stared at him in disbelieving recognition. When he turned sideways as he disappeared into the entrance of an inn yard, she was sure.

'Jean-Baptiste!' She fumbled with the door catch, almost falling out of the chaise on to the street, in her determination not to let him escape her sight.

Chapter Sixteen

'Now you're here we can—' La Motte broke off as the butler came into the study with a message. He picked it up and split the seal, but waited until the butler had left before he read it. 'Dammit!' he exclaimed. 'There was a second withdrawal from the blackmailer's account this morning. But Robson wasn't in time to identify and follow him.'

'At least that adds weight to our suspicion he is treating you as a source of income,' said Pierce. Ever since he'd realised Séraphin wasn't the blackmailer, he'd been haunted by the fear that he might return to England to find the evidence of La Motte's involvement in smuggling had fallen into the hands of his enemies. A blackmailer motivated by greed would be much easier to deal with than someone who wanted to use the evidence of La Motte's illegal activities to destroy him.

'I never thought I'd be glad to find myself milked by a blackmailer, but you're right,' said La Motte. 'The first withdrawal was two weeks after the original letter was delivered. This one is six weeks later. He demanded monthly payments, so I'd expected the withdrawals to follow the same pattern.'

'Either he's trying to avoid discovery or he had to alter his plans,' said Pierce. 'Perhaps he was taken ill. The only description you have of him is that he's a greying, middle-aged man.'

'I want him fit and healthy until we've recovered the evidence,' said La Motte. 'After that he can go to the devil—what is it?'

Pierce had heard muffled voices in the hall. He thought he recognised one, and then he heard another he was particularly sensitive to. He sprang up and strode halfway to the door before it occurred to him he was the victim of his own wishful thinking. He only thought he'd heard Mélusine's voice because he *wanted* to hear it. She couldn't possibly be in London. He felt a little foolish, but since he was already nearly at the door he continued and opened it.

Mélusine was clinging to Saint-André's arm, looking up at him as she said urgently, 'You must tell him to tell Pierce…' She didn't know the butler spoke perfectly serviceable French, but that wasn't Pierce's first thought. His first reaction was one of sheer, disbelieving joy at seeing her. His second was that he would have preferred it if she hadn't been holding quite so tightly to Saint-André's arm. Finally, he registered her words.

'What do you want to tell me?' he said.

At the sound of his voice, her head whipped around. When she saw him standing in the doorway, her face lit up. She released her grip on Saint-André and ran to him.

'I saw him! I saw him!' she gasped, catching urgently at the front of Pierce's coat. 'Daniel's watching him now.'

'Who?' He put his arms round her.

'Jean-Baptiste!'

'What?'

'On Ludgate Hill,' said Saint-André.

'Good God!' Pierce tightened his arms enough to lift Mélusine off her feet and carry her inside the study. Saint-André followed.

'I will arrange refreshments for your guests,' said the butler austerely.

'Do that,' said Pierce, without looking up. He was torn between kissing Mélusine and finding out about Jean-Baptiste.

'What did he say?' said Mélusine.

'He's going to get you something to eat and drink. Speak French in front of our guests, Higgins,' he added to the butler.

'As you wish, my lord,' the butler smoothly switched languages.

'He does understand me.' Relief appeared in Mélusine's eyes. 'I was afraid I was going to have to rely on Saint-André to translate everything for me.

Daniel only speaks sailor's English. It's all right for talking to grooms, but no good for the drawing room. François would have hated it. I don't suppose your *maître d'hôtel* would like it either.'

'He's a butler,' said Pierce. Then he kissed her.

Mélusine gave a little squeak and kissed him back, but with less than her customary fervour. After a moment she drew her head back and patted his chest in agitation. 'This isn't proper. I have to greet Sir Henry,' she said in an undertone that was both scandalised and embarrassed.

'Tell us about Jean-Baptiste—then greet Harry,' said Pierce, partly because that was what both he and La Motte needed to know—and partly to give himself time to regain his equilibrium. Mélusine was in London, in his arms, and he wanted to grin with idiotic happiness.

'''Arry?' She looked confused. 'Oh, Henry. Good afternoon, *monsieur*.' She eased out of Pierce's embrace and made La Motte a very creditable curtsy, though her cheeks burned with colour. 'We were going to the bank, and I was looking out of the carriage window and I saw Jean-Baptiste. So I jumped out of the carriage and followed him—'

'What?' Pierce exclaimed. 'Are you crazy? You could have been hurt!'

'It was standing still,' she said impatiently. 'The road was so busy nothing could move. Only my skirts are dirty. Anyway, I had to follow Jean-Baptiste because you need him.'

'Yes, we do,' said La Motte. 'Please continue, *madame*.'

'I followed him into the yard of an inn,' said Mélusine. 'Saint-André and Daniel came too. At first they didn't understand what was happening. I told Saint-André we must not let Jean-Baptiste see either of us, because he would recognise us—but he only saw Daniel briefly a couple of times while I was married, so I thought it would all right if Daniel followed him more closely. Daniel came back and told us Jean-Baptiste has bought a ticket for the mail coach to Chippenham, leaving London at seven-thirty this evening.' She stopped to take a breath and smile with satisfaction at her revelations—then her face fell. 'You probably knew all this already,' she said.

'No, we didn't,' said La Motte. 'No one's seen Jean-Baptiste since I spotted him the day he delivered the original letter in Latin.'

'He doesn't look like himself,' said Mélusine, her confidence returning. 'I didn't recognise him at first, even though he walked right past the carriage—but I knew something was odd about him and I kept watching. And then he was startled by the horse and jumped aside and when he carried on walking I knew him at once.'

'What does he look like now?' said La Motte.

'He was pretending to be a middle-aged clerk,' said Mélusine. 'He had grey eyebrows and a false paunch, and he's changed the shape of his face and pulled the corners of his mouth down like this.' She demonstrated. 'I only realised the eyebrows and the paunch were false when I saw him jump. At least, I suppose he could have got fatter since I last saw him, but I'm sure he'd never let his real eyebrows look so ungroomed. They are a disguise.'

'If his appearance is so different, how can you be sure it's Jean-Baptiste?' Pierce asked.

'That's what Saint-André said, but I saw him move,' said Mélusine. 'I spent two years watching him move in my mirror and about the house. Of course there must be a small element of doubt until I've had another opportunity to watch him for longer, but I am almost certain it was him.'

'Certain enough to terrify Daniel and me by leaping out of the carriage and following him,' said Saint-André.

'The withdrawal from the account was made by a greying, middle-aged man,' said La Motte. 'Jean-Baptiste is in his twenties.'

'But he's a hairdresser,' said Mélusine. 'And for all he hated his lowly status, he is a very *good* hairdresser.'

'Unlike me,' Pierce murmured.

'You were not that bad,' she said. 'And you didn't make my skin creep.'

'A definite asset in a hairdresser,' Saint-André observed.

'It is when you have to spend two hours in his company every day,' said Mélusine with feeling. 'I'm never putting up with that again.'

'You won't have to,' said Pierce. 'Sit down.'

'What?' She looked startled.

'So we can.'

'Oh. I'm sorry. Thank you.' She looked around for the nearest chair and sat in it.

La Motte gave a brief bark of laughter. 'English hospitality at its sophisticated best,' he said. 'My apologies, *madame*, I have been a poor host, especially since you have brought us such welcome information.'

Pierce's cravat suddenly felt uncomfortably tight. He wanted to talk to Mélusine. He didn't want to do so in front of Saint-André and La Motte, and first he had to deal with Jean-Baptiste.

'Jean-Baptiste has never seen me,' he said. 'I'll take the same mail coach to Chippenham this evening, and perhaps we'll finally find out who he is working with.'

La Motte nodded. 'I'll arrange it,' he said, and left the room.

'We'll come too,' said Mélusine. 'Not in the mail coach, of course. We will follow in a private carriage. Perhaps I may be useful in recognising the person Jean-Baptiste meets,' she added, as Pierce opened his mouth to protest.

'Much as I am loath to subject the Comtesse to any discomfort,' said Saint-André, 'I believe she has a valid argument. Her instincts in these matters have proved excellent. She was explaining to me on the packet boat how she knew you were more than you seemed at your first meeting.'

'Did she explain *how* she knew?' Pierce asked warily.

'I said you were not sufficiently submissive,' said Mélusine.

'By all accounts, nor was Jean-Baptiste.'

'But he pretended to be,' said Mélusine. 'You just walked in and started telling us all what to do. That is not the normal conduct for a footman. I beg your pardon, *monsieur*,' she said to La Motte in obvious confusion, as she saw he'd come back into the study.

'No need to apologise,' said Sir Henry. He was watching his guests with interest and amusement. Pierce knew that as soon as he was alone with his stepfather he was going to receive a genial but shrewd interrogation over his conduct with Mélusine.

'I am very grateful to you, Comtesse,' said La Motte. 'Until your arrival today, we were at an impasse. In any case, I am glad to have this opportunity to renew our friendship.'

'Yes. Thank you.' Mélusine gripped her hands in her lap. '*Monsieur*, did you believe I was blackmailing you?' she asked directly. 'Is that why you sent Pierce to me first, before Séraphin?'

Pierce started to speak, but La Motte stopped him with a slight shake of his head.

'I did not believe the woman you were two years ago would have resorted to blackmailing me,' said La Motte steadily. 'But a great deal can happen in two years. People change. It was your footman who delivered the letter, and I did not know Bertier had left you so well provided for.' La Motte paused, and he seemed to be picking his words with care. 'That was a kindness he did not advertise.'

Mélusine stared at the carpet for a few moments then, to Pierce's surprise, she looked neither at him nor La Motte, but at Saint-André. 'What does he mean?' she asked.

Saint-André hesitated, reluctance in his eyes. Pierce unconsciously clenched his hand into a fist as he realised that whatever the Marquis knew had the potential to hurt Mélusine.

'Until she betrayed him with Séraphin, Bertier had left two of the Paris houses to Julie Dubois,' said Saint-André.

'His mistress. Yes, I see.' Mélusine looked up at the ceiling for a few seconds, and when she lowered her gaze her eyes were bright, but she was perfectly composed as she smiled gravely at Saint-André. 'Thank you, *monsieur*. I value your honesty.'

Pierce wanted to go to her and comfort her, but he sensed it would have been an affront to her dignity to do so in the company of others.

La Motte rose and came to stand before her. '*Madame*, I apologise without reservation for my suspicions,' he said. 'You have responded with more generosity and compassion than I, at least, deserve. Please believe me when I say I am entirely at your service. If there is anything I can do for you—'

'Oh, yes, thank you,' said Mélusine, and smiled at him. 'I would be most grateful for advice on buying a house in London. The Marquis is of the opinion you would be the best person to ask.'

The London to Bath mail coach left on time, with Pierce and the unsuspecting Jean-Baptiste as two of the four inside passengers. La Motte's man, Robson, was travelling as an outside passenger, sitting beside the driver. It was still daylight when the coach left London, and though Daniel had made sure Pierce knew which man Mélusine had identified as her former hairdresser-footman, Pierce harboured more than a few doubts that she was right. At first glance the fellow looked like a downtrodden, middle-aged clerk. And at second glance he *still* looked like a downtrodden, middle-aged clerk. In the confines of the coach Pierce couldn't stare at him too intently without drawing attention to himself and either alarming or offending the fellow. All he could do was wait and see what transpired on the journey or when they arrived at Chippenham.

His own appearance was suitably nondescript and unmemorable, and he'd introduced himself as William Frost to the only one of the other passengers who seemed inclined to talk. By the time they changed horses at Slough it was after eleven o'clock, and what little conversation there'd been had dried up completely.

The night was illuminated only by a new moon and the stars, and inside the coach it was very dark. Pierce had no intention of trying to sleep, so there was nothing to do but keep an unobtrusive eye on the clerk in the opposite corner—and think.

Mélusine, Saint-André and Daniel were on the road somewhere behind him, travelling in one of La Motte's well-appointed carriages. It had been decided they would stop at the same staging posts as the mail coach, so Pierce would be able to leave a message for them if anything happened on the journey to change their plans. Even though Pierce was glad she was close by, he hated the idea of her embarking on another uncomfortable journey within hours of her arrival in London. She'd arrived so close behind him, he knew her journey to Boulogne must have been made at a gruelling speed.

And why had she come to London at all in such precipitate haste? He'd had no opportunity for a private conversation with her, and when he'd tried to draw her discreetly aside to ask she'd simply said, 'Daniel wanted to take me to Florence to look at the statues, but I preferred to come to London', and gone back to questioning La Motte about the characters of the different areas of London. Anyone would think she'd suddenly developed a burning interest in property and investments.

But they were in the same country once more, and her mere presence close by assuaged some of the dissatisfied, unsettled feelings he'd had ever since he'd left the place Vendôme four mornings ago. She'd been so cool, almost offhand about his departure. She wouldn't even let him promise to return to her once he'd dealt with the blackmailer. It was that, more than anything else, which aggravated him, because it implied she considered him fickle. He'd become more and more frustrated and disgruntled with her and the situation on the way to Boulogne. And when he'd arrived and discovered the packet boat was delayed by bad weather, he'd had to go for a long walk to work off his ill temper.

But now it turned out she'd left Paris on the same day he had, and come to London instead of going to Florence. And though she'd spent most of the remaining time before they'd set off for Chippenham talking about buying a house, she'd been equally determined to join in the pursuit of Jean-Baptiste. If it was Jean-Baptiste. Even though he respected Mélusine's powers of observation, he had serious doubts whether she was right on this occasion, but he would never admit them to anyone. And if they reached Chippenham and the middle-aged clerk proved to be exactly what he appeared, Pierce was determined not to let Mélusine feel embarrassed by her mistake. Though perhaps she deserved to feel a little embarrassed after the way she'd disturbed his peace of mind for the past four days.

It was a long, tedious night. The clerk didn't do anything exciting. None of the horses went lame. The hours and the miles rolled by with the same unrelenting monotony. Pierce was very glad when the mail coach arrived at Chippenham just after eight o'clock in the morning. All the passengers got out. Two of them were continuing to Bath and only wanted to stretch their legs and snatch some quick refreshments, but Pierce and the middle-aged clerk had reached their destination. Robson climbed down from the outside seat, taking care not to let the possible Jean-Baptiste see him. It would be easier for Robson to follow Jean-Baptiste if Jean-Baptiste remained unfamiliar with his appearance.

The inn yard was full of activity as the horses were changed on the mail coach. Pierce kept his eyes on the clerk and took advantage of the bustle around him to remain out of the clerk's direct line of sight should he chance to look around. The clerk's only luggage was a small carpet bag, which he'd held on his lap all the way from London. If he was Jean-Baptiste, the carpet bag might well contain the money he'd withdrawn from the blackmailer's account. The clerk walked quietly out of the inn yard into Chippenham without saying a word to anyone around him.

Pierce and Robson followed, taking opposite sides of the street. Pierce watched him, trying to see him the way Mélusine might. Was he walking like a middle-aged man—or like a young man pretending to be middle-aged? Of course, spending more than twelve hours in a coach was enough to take the spring out of the step of most people.

The clerk went into another inn. He lingered in the yard for a few minutes, apparently waiting for someone. A manservant approached him, they exchanged a few words and a small object passed between them, and then they separated. There was a gallery on the first floor along one side of the yard. The clerk went up the stairs and walked along the gallery to one of the doors that opened on to it. He unlocked the door and went inside.

Robson went up the same stairs the clerk had used. Pierce glanced around and saw there was another set of stairs at the other end of the gallery. He crossed the yard so he could keep both the door and the stairs in view.

Robson strolled along the gallery, but paused opposite the door the clerk had entered while he filled his pipe with tobacco. He took his time, only continuing along the gallery at the same unhurried pace when the pipe was lit and drawing to his satisfaction.

'I could hear movement, but no voices,' he said to Pierce. 'I'd say he's alone in there.'

'Most likely, if the servant gave him the key. See if there's another door to the room from inside the inn,' said Pierce. 'We don't want to lose him now.'

Robson nodded.

Alone again, Pierce leant against the wall, one eye on the door, but keeping a general watch on his surroundings. A busy inn yard was a perfect place to loiter. A maid was hurrying across the cobblestones with a basket of bread. A man with a shovel was going into the stables. Horses were being harnessed to a private carriage…

He considered the carriage for a moment, then caught the attention of the servant and paid to hire two riding horses, to be saddled immediately.

* * *

The horses had been standing on one side of the yard for five minutes, flicking their tails against the summer flies, when the door on the gallery opened. Pierce watched over the withers of one of the horses as a man emerged. At first glance Pierce thought Robson had been wrong, and there must have been another man in the room waiting for the clerk, because this man was undeniably young. He was fashionably dressed, and light on his feet. But he was carrying the familiar carpet bag, and he was the same height and build as the clerk. He stopped to speak to the same inn servant the clerk had exchanged words with. Pierce saw several coins and, presumably, the room key change hands.

The fashionable young man said something and the servant laughed. They separated and the fashionable young man walked towards the private coach waiting in the yard. Pierce moved to one side so his face was deeper in the shadows. The tulip of fashion spoke to the postilion. He was close enough for Pierce to hear both his accent and his destination. His English was reasonable, but his accent was unmistakably French.

The servant returned from the room the Frenchman had just vacated with another bag which he put into the coach. Robson had appeared at Pierce's shoulder a minute or two earlier. Neither of them said anything until the Frenchman had climbed into the carriage and it rumbled out of the innyard.

'That's your quarry,' said Pierce. 'He's going to Bath. Don't lose him.'

He waited until Robson had left on one of the hired horses, and went to indulge in some gossip with the inn servants.

'That's the Count of Ferrydoo,' said an elderly groom. 'Making a lengthy stay in Bath. Pretty, ain't he? But the ladies seem to like him. Even the married ones, by all accounts.'

'Married ladies?' said Pierce, with an encouraging grin.

'So Jem said. One in London, at any rate, with a very jealous husband. He has to go to all sorts of trouble to avoid rousing her husband's suspicions. Don't seem like any woman would be worth such effort. Molly heard he's got his eye on an heiress in Bath. Don't suppose it will do much for his chances with her if *she* finds out about his shenanigans with a married woman.' The groom shrugged and went back into the stables.

Pierce considered what he'd discovered. Jean-Baptiste had delivered the original blackmail letter. The letter had been written in Latin, which had misdirected them into thinking the use of the ancient language might be a crude attempt to hide to contents from the messenger delivering it. But Laurette had told him that Jean-Baptiste was a foundling who'd been educated by monks. Mélusine knew Latin because she'd been educated in a convent. It seemed reasonable to suppose

Jean-Baptiste might have acquired Latin in a similar fashion.

The blackmail money had been collected by a greying middle-aged man—that must have been Jean-Baptiste himself in his guise as a downtrodden clerk. But he was posing as a French count in Bath, and apparently dangling after an heiress there. All the evidence was pointing to the fact that Jean-Baptiste had never been working for anybody but himself. He'd always been both the messenger and the blackmailer, and very likely enjoyed the intrigue of playing both roles.

For the first time since La Motte had told him about the blackmail letter, Pierce felt as if a resolution to the problem was finally within his grasp. He returned the spare saddle horse and went to wait for Mélusine and her companions at the other inn.

It was another half an hour before Pierce saw La Motte's carriage pull into the inn yard. Even though he hadn't expected them to encounter trouble on the road, he was relieved by its safe arrival. He moved so swiftly to open the door and let down the steps he was there before any of the servants.

He'd performed the service for Mélusine often enough in Paris to expect her to emerge immediately, but she didn't. Worried, he leant into the carriage in sudden anxiety. Even though he knew she must be exhausted, she was sitting upright, taking in deep, slightly jerky breaths, her face white as a sheet, her hands locked together in her lap.

When she saw him a mixture of relief and anxiety filled her eyes. 'Is it Jean-Baptiste?' she said in a tight voice.

'Yes. What's wrong?'

'Nothing,' Mélusine said.

At the same time, Saint-André said, '*Madame* is a little unwell from the coach. I am sure she will be better in a very few minutes once she can rest comfortably.'

Frustration flared in Mélusine's eyes, even as she pressed her lips together and swallowed. 'I *never* get sick from travelling,' she said after a moment.

'This is the first time you've travelled almost continuously for more than three days with hardly any sleep,' said Saint-André reasonably.

She frowned, but took a few more deep breaths before she replied, 'You and Pierce have travelled just as far.'

'Practice,' said Pierce, hugely relieved her indisposition was nothing more serious. 'Come.' He offered her his hand.

She took it and climbed carefully out of the chaise. She was trembling a little, and not quite steady on her feet. He'd already hired a private parlour, so he tucked her hand through his arm and led her there.

He guided her to a chair. 'Would you like some tea?' he asked.

She thought about it. 'I will try,' she said after a

moment, but she continued to stare rather fixedly at the floor.

Pierce glanced at Saint-André and saw that, though the Marquis wasn't trembling like Mélusine, he was almost as pale and clearly exhausted. It wasn't much more than a week since Saint-André been released from the Bastille, and for eight months before that his opportunity for physical activity had been severely circumscribed. Pierce thought it was a testament to Saint-André's fundamental stamina—and his self-discipline—that he was moving with his usual fluid grace after several days, which must have tried his endurance as greatly as Mélusine's.

'Tell us about Jean-Baptiste,' said Saint-André. 'Where is he now?'

'On his way to Bath with Robson following him,' said Pierce. He described what he'd seen and what he'd subsequently discovered from the groom.

'I *knew* it was Jean-Baptiste!' Mélusine looked up and Pierce was pleased to see there was a little more colour in her cheeks. 'But in the middle of the night, I did start to have doubts,' she admitted. 'So we're going to Bath. How far away is that?'

'Another hour and a half in the coach at least,' said Pierce, and saw her flinch. 'But there's no need for you to continue immediately. I'll take rooms here for you and Saint-André and when you've rested you can finish the journey. Later today—or perhaps tomorrow.'

'I don't want to be left behind,' Mélusine protested, as Daniel entered the parlour.

'Nor I,' said Saint-André. 'You will not be rid of us so easily, my friend.'

'I don't want to be rid of either of you,' said Pierce. 'Apart from the pleasure of your company, you have both been extremely valuable in this enterprise, but I...'

Saint-André smiled slightly. 'Elegantly expressed,' he said. 'You can't delay making further arrangements in Bath. I understand. But Jean-Baptiste has travelled all night, just as we have. I don't imagine he is planning to do anything very energetic today. Sir Henry started his banking career in this part of England, and I'm sure he still has an agent in Bath. If you are planning to use the agent to set up your plans, give me your message for him and I will deliver it while you remain here with the Comtesse. I don't believe she'll stay behind if you go on.'

Mélusine glared at Saint-André. 'Don't make it sound as if I'm chasing him,' she said. 'I just want to make sure Jean-Baptiste doesn't escape again,' she assured Pierce.

Pierce noted her comment about chasing him, but decided to pursue it later, when they were alone. He was keen not to be too far behind Jean-Baptiste, because only he, Mélusine and Saint-André knew the truth about the blackmail attempt. Robson and Daniel simply knew it was important to follow Jean-Baptiste. Even though he trusted Robson, Pierce didn't want the evidence of La Motte's smuggling background to inadvertently fall into Robson's possession. If Pierce himself didn't continue straight to Bath, he would feel more comfortable if Saint-André was there to act on his behalf. His only real qualm was the Marquis's exhaustion. He glanced at Daniel and saw that, unlike the others, he didn't seem unduly weary.

Dour humour flickered in Daniel's eyes as he noticed Pierce's measuring look. He nodded. 'I'll carry your message. Or if you prefer it to be in drawing-room English, I'll deliver the Marquis and he can present your message.'

Pierce didn't ask Mélusine what she preferred, he simply took a room at the inn for himself and his wife. That was the only way he could remain in the same bedchamber with her without causing a scandal. She didn't make any comment on his arrangements. She didn't comment on anything until she saw her reflection in the dressing-table mirror.

'Oh, my hair!' she gasped, lifting both hands to her head.

'Let it be. I'll help you with it after we've slept,' said Pierce, helping her undress.

'I'm glad it *was* Jean-Baptiste,' she said, yawning. 'If he's living in Bath as the Comte de Ferradou, I'm sure he's only motivated by greed. There shouldn't be any need for you to leave England. But I expect it will be best if you deal with him promptly.'

'I intend to.' When she was wearing nothing but her chemise, he pulled back the covers and she immediately climbed into bed.

He took off his own clothes and joined her, drawing her close so her head was resting on his shoulder. She sighed, and he felt the residual tension in her muscles begin to relax.

'I still feel as if I'm jolting in the coach,' she murmured.

'You'll feel better when you wake up,' he said.

'Of course. I'm looking forward to seeing Bath. Will you show me around when we've dealt with Jean-Baptiste?'

'Yes.'

'Good. I didn't have much chance to look at London.' Her words were slurred with weariness.

'Why wouldn't you let me promise to return to you if I could?' he asked softly, finally voicing the question that had plagued him ever since he'd left her in Paris.

'No promises.' She sighed again and nestled closer. 'You have to be free to fly back if you want to.' Her voice was so hazy with sleep Pierce wondered if he'd heard her correctly.

'What?' He dipped his head closer to hers.

'Like my canary.' Her breathing changed and he knew she was asleep. He stared at the ceiling, stroking her hair—and wondered what the devil she was talking about.

Chapter Seventeen

Pierce woke halfway through the afternoon. He rose carefully to avoid disturbing Mélusine, and went into the adjoining private parlour. He found Daniel sitting quietly by the window.

'You must be made of oak!' he exclaimed in surprise.

'Hardly,' said Daniel. 'But I've learnt to take my rest whenever the opportunity arises.' He paused. 'And it makes a difference,' he said, in a low voice. 'Being free.'

Pierce took the chair opposite Daniel's. 'Did Fournier have a hold—some power—over you?' he asked curiously.

'No,' said Daniel. 'None that he was aware of, at any rate.'

'Then why?' Pierce had his suspicions but, if they were correct, he didn't understand why Daniel had remained with Fournier after Mélusine's marriage.

'Habit,' said Daniel. 'At first there are reasons for the things you do. Then you forget what the reasons are, and you go on doing the same things, even when the reasons no longer exist. The Marquis spoke to Sir Henry's agent,' he continued straight on to business as if he was uncomfortable with the little he'd revealed. 'The agent has taken a temporary lease for you on a house in Queen Square. The Marquis and I looked in the visitor's book in the Pump Room and discovered Jean-Baptiste's entry with his false name and the address of his lodgings. The Marquis has already taken up residence in the Queen Square house as your guest. I went to Jean-Baptiste's lodgings and found Robson outside. He said Jean-Baptiste hadn't come out since he went inside. I told Robson where the Marquis was and then I told the Marquis what Robson had said. It is possible to watch the lodgings without being in full view of the windows, so the Marquis said he'd relieve Robson as soon as he'd eaten. Then I came here. I've not been here very long.'

'I'm not surprised!' said Pierce. 'Thank you.' Since he was now the only man who'd had any decent sleep in over thirty hours, he knew he had to get to Bath as soon as possible. There didn't seem much chance Jean-Baptiste was suddenly going to vanish, but after hunting the blackmailer for so long, Pierce wasn't going to take anything for granted at this late stage.

'Mélusine's still asleep,' he said, aware there was no point in trying to conceal the fact he'd shared a room with her. Daniel had heard him tell the innkeeper she was his wife. 'I'll tell her you're here, so she won't be alarmed when she wakes and finds me gone.'

Daniel nodded. 'Are you going to marry her?'

'If she'll let me,' said Pierce, briefly allowing his exasperation to get the better of him. 'At the moment, for some reason, she seems to be confusing me with a canary, and wanting me to fly somewhere.'

'Is she?' For a moment Daniel looked thoughtful, and then Pierce was thoroughly irritated to see a rare grin appear on the other man's face. 'I remember the canary. You'd best tell her I'll be here for when she's ready to leave—and then you can fly off to Bath.'

Pierce bit back all of the many sharp comments that hovered on his tongue and went to wake Mélusine to tell her what was happening.

Mélusine travelled to Bath with Daniel later in the evening.

'It's just as it was when you used to take me back and forth to the convent,' she said. 'You know, it only occurred to me when we were on the way to Boulogne—you're younger than Bertier.'

'By three years only,' he said, so quickly she knew he'd already considered the matter. 'You should not have married him. I should not have let it happen.'

'It was Father's choice,' she said, amazed at the self-recrimination she heard in Daniel's voice.

'It was a bad choice—but I thought his age and status

would mean there was more chance the Comte would be able to stand up to your father.'

'He did,' said Mélusine. 'Father tried to interfere once, but Bertier would not tolerate it. When he chose, he could be freezingly...aristocratically...polite.'

'But he was unkind to you,' said Daniel.

'Sometimes,' said Mélusine. She'd never told Daniel what she'd heard Bertier ask Saint-André to do, and she never would. 'It was no worse than many marriages.'

'But it should never have happened,' said Daniel.

'There was nothing to be done once Father had made up his mind,' said Mélusine.

'I could have taken you away then, before the marriage,' said Daniel.

Mélusine stared at him in astonishment. 'But...I, we, would have had no money,' she said. 'No means to live. Father would never have allowed me any access to my inheritance under those circumstances.'

'I have money,' said Daniel. 'Not as much as Gilocourt or Blackspur, but it would have been enough for you to live comfortably until you found a husband you favoured.'

Mélusine was so surprised she didn't know what to say first. 'What money?' she said, though that wasn't her only, or even her most important, thought.

'Do you think I lived all those years with your father without learning a something about business?' Daniel asked. 'Not that he knows. By the time you were of an age to marry, there was enough to support you. But you would not have met Blackspur—and it may be he is the man for you. So perhaps, in the end, it was better you were where he could meet you.'

'Yes, he is the man for me. If he wants me,' said Mélusine. She put her hand through Daniel's arm and leant her head on his shoulder, as she had done when she was a child travelling with him. 'We're all in the right place now, and we just have to make sure Jean-Baptiste doesn't cause any more trouble. And then I hope we can all be happy.'

Pierce wasn't at the house in Queen Square when they arrived, but Saint-André greeted them and showed Mélusine the principal rooms.

'According to his most recent message, Blackspur intends to take action against Jean-Baptiste tomorrow,' he said. 'Nothing will happen tonight, so we'll all be advised to rest while we can.'

Mélusine nodded. But when she went to bed, she wondered briefly if she would spend more than one night in it. She hoped so, because she couldn't begin to put her own plans into action until she could stay in one place for more than a few hours at a time.

Prudence kept Mélusine confined to the house the next morning. Jean-Baptiste had spent two years dressing her hair, so she was the one person they were absolutely certain he would recognise if he inadvertently caught sight of her.

To pass the time while they waited, Saint-André gave Mélusine another English lesson.

'I'm a good student normally,' she said apologetically, after making yet another mistake. 'I'm just finding it difficult to concentrate this morning.'

He smiled. 'I quite understand—'

The door opened, and Mélusine jumped to her feet as Pierce came in. 'What's happening?' she demanded.

'He's in the Pump Room, entertaining Miss Amberley and her chaperon with charmingly droll anecdotes,' said Pierce.

'Miss Amberley?'

'Letchworth's granddaughter. It looks as if he has indeed set his sights on marriage to an heiress,' said Pierce.

'I never found him charming or droll,' said Mélusine. 'But I suppose he felt no need to impress me.'

'And his exotic French accent wouldn't have cut any ice with you either,' said Pierce.

'You don't have an English accent,' said Mélusine.

'I do when I speak English,' he retorted. 'From what I've learnt, Jean-Baptiste has been living in Bath as the Comte de Ferradou for the past five weeks, apart from his brief trip to London a couple of days ago. He is considered to have exquisite manners and is generally well thought of—although there does seem to be a little jealousy in some quarters over his rapid social success.'

'He must be so happy,' said Mélusine.

'He certainly appeared to be enjoying himself in the

Pump Room,' said Pierce. 'I dare say he'll find his interview with me this afternoon somewhat less pleasant.'

'What are you going to do?' Mélusine asked.

'Daniel and I will escort him here—and then I'll talk to him,' said Pierce. 'He knows Harry's name, so there is no point in trying to conceal mine, or my relationship with him. You may wish to be present?' He glanced at Saint-André.

'Oh, yes,' said the Marquis. 'Assuredly.'

'What about me?' said Mélusine. 'I want to hear what he says too.'

'No,' said Pierce. 'I don't want you anywhere near him.'

'He's not dangerous,' she protested. 'Well, he might be if you cornered him, like a rat. But he's not like Séraphin. He'll run rather than fight.'

'He will be cornered,' said Pierce. 'And you said he made your flesh creep.'

'He did. But it wasn't because I was afraid he was going to stab me with his scissors. He's just…slimy.'

'I'm still not allowing you in the same room as a slimy rat,' said Pierce.

She frowned, because she was determined to hear the conversation with Jean-Baptiste. Then she had an idea. Two of the rooms in the house were divided by double doors, which could be opened to create one large room.

'What if we leave one of the doors slightly ajar, so I can sit behind it and hear what is said, but Jean-Baptiste won't know I'm there?' she suggested. 'That would work. That would be the perfect solution. Jean-Baptiste spied on me. It is only fair I should have the opportunity to spy on him,' she added, as she saw Pierce hesitate.

'Very well,' he said. 'But you must promise to stay behind the door, and not let Jean-Baptiste know you are there, no matter what he says. Or what I or Saint-André say.'

'I know you will have to frighten him,' she said, guessing that might be one of the reasons for Pierce's reluctance to let her hear the conversation. 'I will not be shocked. He has caused us all a great deal of trouble.'

She was positioned behind the doors in good time when Pierce and Daniel brought Jean-Baptiste into the house that afternoon. She could hear him protesting at their mistreatment, still presumably in the character of a French nobleman, but they were all speaking English, so she couldn't be sure.

Her heart was already pounding with tension and anxiety, and a sudden spike of fear that they might conduct the whole conversation in English contributed to her agitation. She should have reminded them she wouldn't understand if they did that.

Jean-Baptiste suddenly caught sight of Saint-André, and his tone changed in mid-sentence from indignation to terror. All it took was that one, half-strangulated scream, for Mélusine to be fairly sure it wouldn't take much to frighten her former hairdresser-footman into confessing everything.

She heard Daniel's voice, realised he was still in the room, and caught her breath in distress because she hadn't warned Pierce that Daniel didn't know what Bertier had said to Saint-André that night. She could only hope it wouldn't be mentioned in this conversation. This was about blackmail, not murder, after all.

When Pierce mentioned La Motte's name and identified himself as La Motte's stepson, Jean-Baptiste gasped with horror, and began to gabble his excuses.

'I had to do it.' He was already half-crying. 'I had to do it. I had to get away from him.'

'Who?'

'Comte Séraphin.'

'What had he done?' asked Saint-André. He had a more personal interest in Séraphin's crimes than Pierce.

'He killed Comte Bertier. He had you p-put in the Bastille. If he could do that to you, I knew he c-could snap his fingers and I'd be dead. Tread on me like an ant in his path. He didn't need me any more.'

'What did he need you for before?' said Daniel.

Mélusine closed her eyes and prayed.

'To spy for him on Comte Bertier and the Comtesse,' said Jean-Baptiste eagerly.

'The Comtesse?'

'Yes. I did her hair. I was to tell him if she ever did anything interesting—took a lover—but she never did.' Despite his precarious circumstances, a disparaging note still crept into Jean-Baptiste's voice. From the sound of things, he hadn't recognised Daniel as her father's servant. Perhaps he didn't pay any more attention to other servants than his social superiors.

'Then what?' said Daniel.

'I heard Comte Bertier tell the Marquis to make the Comtesse pregnant,' said Jean-Baptiste.

'What?' Daniel's voice had gone very quiet. Mélusine thought he must have changed his position, because he didn't sound as clear as before.

'I said no,' said Saint-André calmly and very clearly. 'The Comtesse and I discussed the matter later and I gave her my assurances. She has accepted them.'

Mélusine clenched her fists so tightly her nails dug into her palms as she waited for Daniel's reaction. He hadn't reacted badly to her affair with Pierce because, in his taciturn way, he both liked and respected Pierce. But he hadn't liked or respected Bertier, and Saint-André had been Bertier's friend.

'I see,' said Daniel after several tense moments of silence. Mélusine relaxed slightly. Daniel was far from stupid, and it would only have taken a minute for him to reflect that she wouldn't have leased an apartment to Saint-André, nor travelled in his company, if she hadn't trusted him to behave honourably.

'I didn't hear you say no,' said Jean-Baptiste. 'I told Comte Séraphin you'd do it…'

'You told Séraphin?' said Daniel.

'That's what he was paying me to do—'

There was a crash. Something heavy fell against the door, slamming the few open inches shut. Several other wild thuds hit the lower door panel.

Mélusine jolted back in alarm, her heart hammering. Almost sick with shock, she reached for the doorhandle and started to open the door.

'Don't kill him yet, Daniel,' Pierce said calmly, and she froze. 'There are other things we need him to tell us.'

There was another heavy thud and the sound of retreating footsteps. Then someone who could only be Jean-Baptiste began to cough and retch and Mélusine dropped a shaking hand into her lap.

It took a little while before the former footman-hairdresser was calm enough to talk. It took even longer for Mélusine's heart to stop pounding, but she was too worried about what might happen next to stop listening.

'What did Séraphin do after you told him?' said Saint-André.

'He killed Comte Bertier and had you put in the Bastille,' said Jean-Baptiste. 'But I didn't know that at the time.'

'Did you see him kill Bertier?'

'No, but he came to the house early in the morning, before anyone else was about. I saw him go into Thérèse Petit's quarters, so I crept closer to listen. He told her Comte Bertier had forced a duel on him, and cried and begged her to help him protect the family honour. Then he left, and later the police inspector brought Comte Bertier's body back and Thérèse insisted on washing and preparing it herself.'

'What did you do then?' asked Pierce.

'Nothing. I was too frightened. I never thought he would kill anyone.' Jean-Baptiste began to cry.

'But you stayed at the Hôtel de Gilocourt with Séraphin as your master?'

'I didn't have anywhere else to go. He didn't pay any attention to me when I was quiet and obedient, but I knew he wouldn't let me leave. I had to find a way to escape—go far away where he wouldn't find me.'

'So you thought of blackmail?'

'No, not at first. But I knew Comte Bertier had had secrets of his own, I just didn't know what they were.' Jean-Baptiste sounded momentarily aggrieved by that. 'I thought he might have some secret treasure I could find that Séraphin didn't know about. He wouldn't have known if I'd stolen and sold it. Then I'd have been able to escape. But I found the documents instead. And I remembered Sir Henry from his visit to Paris. I thought England would be a much better place to hide from Séraphin.'

'Why didn't you disguise your appearance when you delivered the first blackmail letter?' Pierce asked.

'I didn't think anyone would pay any attention to the messenger,' said Jean-Baptiste. 'But Sir Henry saw me, and I was afraid he might remember me—so I was more careful after that.'

'But not careful or clever enough,' said Pierce. 'Unfortunately for you, Sir Henry and I are much harder to hide from than Séraphin. One way or another, Jean-Baptiste, you have offended against every man in this room. How do you rate your chances now?'

That was effectively the end of the conversation. Once Pierce was sure that Jean-Baptiste hadn't been working with anyone else, all he was interested in was retrieving the evidence. Without it, the word of a footman who'd been masquerading as a French nobleman and trying to lure an English heiress into marriage would have no weight.

As Saint-André pointed out, *he* did have acquaintances in Bath who would remember him from previous visits to England. A few words from him would be sufficient to destroy the would-be Comte de Ferradou's credibility in Bath.

The hint that he might be allowed to escape with nothing more than the loss of his new life was enough to have Jean-Baptiste begging to take them back to his lodgings and hand over all the evidence in his possession he'd used to blackmail La Motte.

Daniel and Saint-André went ahead with Jean-Baptiste. 'I will follow you shortly,' said Pierce.

Mélusine stayed where she was, still trembling from the stress of listening to such a disturbing conversation. She heard the outer door of the other room close, but for a moment nothing happened. Then Pierce pulled open the doors in front of her, caught her hands and drew her up into his arms.

She went eagerly and leant against him. She could feel the rapid beat of his heart beneath her palm, and knew it had been a difficult incident for him too.

'I'm sorry,' he said against her hair. 'If I'd had any idea that would happen—I just meant to *say* something frightening…'

'Did Daniel try to strangle him?'

'Yes. I wasn't sure if he was going to stop when I asked him to. But getting into a fight over Jean-Baptiste was the last thing I wanted.'

'I think he's feeling guilty because he didn't try to stop my marriage to Bertier,' said Mélusine. 'It had never occurred to me that he could—or should.'

'From something he said to me, I don't think it had fully occurred to him until quite recently,' said Pierce. 'That may be why he's angry with himself and reacted so fiercely to what Jean-Baptiste said. Are you all right?'

'Yes.' She tried to smile, even though she was still feeling shaken. 'It's nearly over, isn't it?'

'Yes. I have to go after them. I trust Saint-André, but I still have to make sure I've retrieved all the evidence. But once I've done that, Harry's future—and mine— are in our own hands again. Thanks in large part to your sharp eyes and quick wit.'

He cupped her face between his hands and kissed her. 'This time you really can relax while you're waiting for me.'

* * *

Pierce didn't return to the house until late that afternoon. Despite his assurance before he left, Mélusine couldn't relax until he was safely back with her. She hadn't entirely forgotten how he'd gone to visit her lawyer and ended up storming the Bastille.

'Where's Jean-Baptiste?' she demanded.

'Already in flight.'

'I said he'd run away,' she said with satisfaction.

'His dream of elevating himself is in ashes,' said Pierce. 'At least in England. And nearly having the life choked out of him gave him a taste of what the hangman's noose would feel like. Blackmail is a vicious crime, even though we couldn't bring him before the courts.'

'Is that the blackmail evidence?' Mélusine looked at the large bag Pierce had laid on the table.

'Yes. He gave it to us immediately. But Saint-André and I both scoured his lodgings for further papers. There weren't any. I'm confident we've got everything.'

'What are you going to do with them now?'

'Burn them. I'll tell Harry what's here, but there's no point in tempting fate by trying to take any of this back to London.'

Mélusine sat and watched as he took each document out, read it, and then burned it in the hearth. The threat of blackmail had been hanging over Pierce for the whole time she'd known him. And once she'd known about it, it had become a Damocles sword above her head as well. It took a little while for her to fully absorb the fact that the crisis was over.

But by the time he was reading the last couple of pages, plans were already forming in her head, unfettered by fears they might be cut short by disaster.

'May we see the sights of Bath before we go back to London?' she asked, as the last pages crumbled to ashes in the hearth. 'I think I might buy a house here.'

'What?' Pierce's head shot up and he glared at her. 'I thought you wanted to buy a house in London.'

'I might buy one in both towns,' she said. 'Saint-André told me many people visit Bath to take the waters and need lodgings—just like us, though we haven't taken the waters. So if I had a house here, people could live in it and pay me rent.'

'Why are you suddenly so obsessed with buying houses?' Pierce stood up with his back to the fireplace.

'I'm not,' she said. 'But I must have an income. And how else can I have one if not from rents?'

'If you married me, you wouldn't have to worry about your rents.'

Mélusine stared at him. She wanted to marry him. That was the whole purpose of her plans. But she hadn't expected him to ask her in such a belligerent tone. Did that mean he *already* felt compelled to marry her, even though she'd done her best to make sure he wouldn't feel trapped?

'You said you would never get married again.'

'I changed my mind.'

'Oh.' Her stomach was tying itself in knots of anxiety and hope, but even if he didn't feel honourably bound to marry her, she was afraid his offer might be motivated by relief now the blackmail threat had been dealt with. 'Thank you,' she said jerkily. 'That is very kind of you. But I think it would be better if I buy a little house and—'

'For God's sake, stop talking about houses! Will you marry me once I've emulated your canary?' he demanded angrily.

'What?' She blinked at him in confusion.

'The canary I must imitate before you'll even be prepared to let me promise to *try* to return to you,' he said grittily.

'How do you know about that?' She was dumbfounded.

'You told me.'

'I did not.'

'In Chippenham, just before you fell asleep, you said I must fly back to you first, before you'd let me promise to return to you,' he said. 'Where am I supposed to *go*?'

'You're not supposed to go anywhere.' She bit her lip and eyed him warily. 'Are you...cross?' she asked.

'Yes, *madame*, I am.' He put his hands on his hips and glared at her. 'You reject my heartfelt commitment to you, refuse to marry me—and then I find you're measuring my behaviour by that of some damn *canary*!'

'I never refused to marry you before,' Mélusine exclaimed unguardedly. 'You never asked me before. You didn't ask me now! You just said if I married you I wouldn't have to worry about my rents. What do you mean—heartfelt?'

'What I said. *Why* wouldn't you let me make you any promises before I left Paris? You knew perfectly well I wasn't promising anything beyond my power to fulfil. It would have been dishonourable. *If I could*, I said. And you wouldn't accept even that.'

'I didn't want you to feel trapped,' said Mélusine weakly, seeing the hurt in his eyes, and realising she had unintentionally wounded him with her reluctance to let him commit himself to even the most qualified of promises.

His eyes narrowed. 'Tell me about the canary.'

'I had it when I was at the convent,' she said.

'What did it do?'

'His cage was in the garden. The cage got knocked over and the door came open and he flew away,' she said.

Pierce stopped glaring at her. 'You really want me to leave,' he said, in a very quiet, controlled voice.

'No.' Tears filled her eyes. She stood and went to stand in front of him. 'I thought I'd lost him for ever, but the next morning when I got up he was sitting on top of the cage and I opened the door and he hopped back in.'

Pierce took a breath. Then he put his arms around her. 'You want to leave the cage door open, so if I'm sitting on your perch you'll know it's because I want to be there, not because I can't escape.'

She nodded.

He rested his forehead against hers. 'Don't you think you deserve better of me than that?'

'I know what it's like to be forced into doing what you don't want to do,' she whispered unsteadily. 'That's how I've lived most of my life. I couldn't bear it if you were only staying with me because you'd given me your promise.'

'Hmm.' He pulled her close and rubbed his cheek against hers. 'How many times are you going to toss me out of the cage and see if I fly back before you let me stay for good?'

'I don't know.' She clutched the front of his coat. 'Not many. It's too hard.'

He put his hand under her chin and tilted her head up so he could see her eyes. 'I did something similar when I would not make love to you until you'd left the bed and returned to it, that first night in Paris,' he said quietly. 'But we are past that now. I learn from my mistakes. You must believe that. I married Rosalie for the wrong reasons, but I knew in Paris marrying you was the right thing—for me. I love you, Mélusine. Perhaps I am not the right husband for you—'

'You are!' she said.

'Yes?' He searched her face. 'Is that what your heart tells you?'

'My heart tells me I love you. I just want you to be sure—'

'I *am* sure.' He paused, and tenderly traced her lips

with the tip of his finger. 'I love you whole-heartedly,' he said. 'Knowing that if I don't tell you everything, you'll nag me and throw things at me until I have no secrets left from you—'

'I don't nag you!' she exclaimed indignantly. 'I have thrown things at you,' she admitted after a moment. 'But you know I wasn't trying to hit you.'

'I know. Will you marry me?'

She smiled unsteadily. 'Yes.'

For a second he didn't move, then he drew in a deep breath and exhaled slowly. At the same time the tension eased from the rest of his body. 'I promise I will do my utmost to ensure you never regret our marriage,' he said in a deep voice, which seemed to reverberate all through her body.

'So will I.' She was starting to feel light-headed with joy. 'And you'll have to model for me,' she reminded him. 'With no clothes on.'

'With pleasure. As long as you're naked too while you're sketching me.'

'I couldn't do that!' she said instinctively. 'Not while I was actually drawing you, I mean.'

'Why not? You've sketched in the nude before.'

'I've—' She broke off and looked at him suspiciously. 'How do you know?'

'I saw your pictures.'

'You saw them? How? They were locked away.' She'd brought them to England with her, terrified in case someone else accidentally saw them, but unable to bring herself to destroy them, because of the lessons she'd learnt in creating them.

Pierce grinned. 'I have a way with locks.'

'You mean you picked it?'

He nodded. 'The morning after the dinner party.'

'No wonder you thought I might have had a lover,' she said. 'I'm surprised you believed my denials after seeing them.'

'I knew they were self-portraits,' he replied.

'How?'

'Your expression. In all the pictures where you'd completed your face, you were frowning with concentration. You wouldn't have looked like that if you'd been posing for a lover.' He paused. 'You don't look like that when you're in my arms,' he said provocatively.

'I lose all power of rational thought when I'm in your arms,' she said.

'So you should.' He smiled briefly before his eyes filled with profound emotion. 'Don't ever worry that I'm wishing I could leave you because I won't be. I wasn't in Paris or at any time since, and I won't in the future. For all my honourable intentions, I'm not sure I'd have had the strength to leave you behind if I'd had to go into exile. Would you have come with me?'

She nodded. 'You know I would,' she whispered. 'I followed you to England, didn't I?

'I thought you came to buy a house,' he said.

She opened her mouth, saw he was teasing her, and changed her mind about what she was going to say. 'I did.'

'And furniture,' said Pierce. 'You forgot most of the furniture in your last house. I do insist on comfortable furniture'

Mélusine looked at him suspiciously. 'Haven't you already got furniture?'

He grinned. 'And two houses to put it in. But you can throw it all out and start again if you want. I inherited the houses with the title and I've no particular fondness for them. Perhaps we should choose a house we both like. One that will be a true home for both of us.'

Mélusine gazed at him, remembering the Hôtel de Gilocourt that had never come close to feeling like home, even after nearly two years of marriage.

'Thank you,' she said, 'I would like that.'

'So would I.' He bent his head to kiss her, and soon houses of any description were the last thing on her mind.

THE VANISHING VISCOUNTESS
Diane Gaston

The prisoner stood with an expression of defiance, leather shackles on her wrists. Adam Vickery, Marquess of Tannerton, was drawn to this woman, so dignified in her plight. He didn't recognise her as the once innocent débutante he had danced with long ago. Marlena Parronley, the notorious Vanishing Viscountess, was a fugitive, and seeing the dashing man of her dreams just reminded her she couldn't risk letting anyone get caught up in her escape…

A WICKED LIAISON
Christine Merrill

Anthony de Portnay Smythe is a mysterious figure. Gentleman by day, he steals secrets for the government by night. When Constance Townley, Duchess of Wellford, finds a man in her bedroom late one night, her first instinct is to call for help. But the thief apologises and gracefully takes his leave…with a kiss for good measure. And Constance knows it won't be the last she sees of this intriguing rogue…

VIRGIN SLAVE, BARBARIAN KING
Louise Allen

Julia Livia Rufa is horrified when barbarians invade Rome and steal everything in sight. But she doesn't expect to be among the taken! As Wulfric's woman, she's ordered to keep house for the uncivilised marauders. It would be all too easy to succumb to Wulfric's quiet strength, and Julia wants him more than she's ever wanted anything. But what future can there be for two people from such different worlds?

MILLS & BOON®
Pure reading pleasure

HIST0508 LP

HISTORICAL

LARGE PRINT

A COMPROMISED LADY
Elizabeth Rolls

As a girl she was full of mischief. As a woman she seemed
lost in the shadow. But Richard Blakehurst couldn't miss the
flash of connection between them when his hand touched
hers. Seeing Richard again brought back the taunting memory
of a dance they had once shared. But Thea *must* tame her
wayward thoughts; because she doubted even her
considerable fortune could buy Richard's good opinion
of her if he ever learnt the truth…

RUNAWAY MISS
Mary Nichols

Alexander, Viscount Malvers, is sure the beautiful girl on the
public coach is not who she says she is. Her shabby clothing
and claim of being a companion cannot hide the fact that she is
Quality. He's intrigued. This captivating miss is definitely
running away, but from what – or whom? Lady Emma Lindsay
knows she must keep up the pretence no matter how strong
her feelings grow…so Miss Fanny Draper she must remain!

MY LADY INNOCENT
Annie Burrows

As the nobility jostles for the new King's favour, Maddy is
all alone. Landless and friendless, she accepts a bridegroom
she has never met, intending to find peace at home. But
peace is in short supply when Maddy marries Sir Geraint,
a powerful protector and passionate man. Fiercely loyal to
the King, Geraint cannot trust his Yorkist bride – but
neither can he resist her!

MILLS & BOON®
Pure reading pleasure

HIST0608 LP

HISTORICAL

LARGE PRINT

THE DANGEROUS MR RYDER
Louise Allen

Jack Ryder, spy and adventurer, knows that escorting the haughty Grand Duchess of Maubourg to England will not be an easy task, but he believes he is more than capable of managing Her Serene Highness. However, he's not prepared for her beauty, her youth, or the way her sensual warmth shines through her cold façade…

AN IMPROPER ARISTOCRAT
Deb Marlowe

The Earl of Treyford, scandalous son of a disgraced mother, has no time for the pretty niceties of the *Ton*. He has come back to England to aid an ageing spinster facing an undefined danger – but Miss Latimer's thick eyelashes and long ebony hair, her mix of knowledge and innocence, arouse far more than his protective instincts…

THE NOVICE BRIDE
Carol Townend

As she is a novice, Lady Cecily of Fulford's knowledge of men is non-existent. But when tragic news bids her home immediately, her only means of escape from the convent is to offer herself to the enemy as a bride! With her fate now in the hands of her husband, Sir Adam Wymark, she battles to protect her family…

⊚™ MILLS & BOON®
Pure reading pleasure

HIST0708 LP

LADY GWENDOLEN INVESTIGATES

Anne Ashley

Prying into other people's lives isn't for Lady Gwendolen Warrender – until murder and mayhem come to Marsden Wood. Every good sleuth needs a partner – and who better than dashing master of the manor Jocelyn Northbridge? He'll make the perfect accomplice! But soon the renowned bachelor has more than solving murder in mind…

THE UNKNOWN HEIR

Anne Herries

Miss Hester Sheldon believes the American heir to her grandfather's estate is a rogue and a rebel. And she has been instructed to teach him the ways of English society and find him a suitable wife! But Jared Clinton turns out to be powerful, wealthy – and extremely handsome. And Hester is shocked by her building desire…

FORBIDDEN LORD

Helen Dickson

Life at her vicious stepfather's house is more than Eleanor Collingwood can bear. With celebrations underway for her stepsister's wedding, she believes no one will see her flee – until William, Lord Marston stops the party in an instant. He's the man who betrayed her father – the man she thought banished to the Americas. But he can offer her freedom…at a cost…

MILLS & BOON
Pure reading pleasure

HIST0808 LP